T

CARSISS

JASON HUBBARD

American Literary Press
Five Star Special Edition
Baltimore, Maryland

THE SANDS OF CARSISS

Library of Congress
Cataloging-in-Publication Data
ISBN-13: 978-1-56167-975-1

Library of Congress Card Catalog Number:
2007901453

Published by

American Literary Press
Five Star Special Edition
8019 Belair Road, Suite 10
Baltimore, Maryland 21236

Manufactured in the United States of America

CHAPTER 1
DEALING WITH A HECKLER

IT WAS BACKBREAKING LABOR and not at all fun, but he couldn't tell that to the four hecklers at his back who were getting sore throats from making catcalls.

"Hey, little man!" one of them shouted. "Why not pitch the coal for our fireplace? At least there isn't any horse dung around there!"

"I'm sure the horses just love you!" shouted another. "I'll sell you some flowers so you can give them a bouquet!"

Will turned his head at that, but then snickered and continued pitching hay. He couldn't very well stop what he was doing—that would only make things worse, and it was probably what they wanted him to do, anyway.

"I'm sure you work so hard for your money," said the heckler up front—the blonde-haired one who had started it all. "And yet all the work *I* do is *spend* all my money!"

"He could spend yours if you want him to!" called out one of his friends. "Or you could have *me* do it. I'd gladly take it off your hands!"

Will shook his head, amazed at the hecklers' sheer idiocy. Couldn't they see they were making asses of themselves in front of everyone? Didn't they know that pitching hay was hard work? Sure, hay was pretty light, but to lift it up over and over again and then transport it was no easy duty.

But he couldn't tell them that. Not only was it common sense, but again, talking back was probably what the hecklers wanted him to do. They wanted to aggravate him and have him turn aggressive, no matter how unwise that was.

"Hey, little man!" called the blonde-haired one. "Is all that hay for the horses or for yourself? Is your family going to have fresh hay tonight?"

Will's partner, Tony, threw down his pitchfork and turned around, glaring at the hecklers with malice in his eyes. Will turned to him, keeping his back to the hecklers. "Tony, let it go. It's not worth it, trust me. Just ignore him."

Tony continued to look at the hecklers, who laughed and pointed.

"Ignore him," Will reiterated, then went back to his work. After a short moment, Tony followed suit.

Will certainly understood what Tony was feeling; he had a few choice words for them himself. But getting in the face of the hecklers would only make things worse—and not just for one day. The blonde-haired man, who was all of sixteen years old, was Adam Berryworth, the son of James Berryworth, a local nobleman. Apparently Adam's sick idea of entertainment was making commoners like Will and Tony raise their fists at him and then making Daddy file a lawsuit and throw them in jail. Not quite a day at the circus, but merry nonetheless.

Will figured the best thing to do was to wait it out, make them grow bored and then leave on their own. He wasn't going to risk his good standing and peace of mind over that pathetic rich kid in his fancy purple clothes, topped with a floppy hat with a quill feather tucked in its ribbon. He could go on and make an ass of himself like those creatures in the barn who showed their buckteeth whenever they spat.

"Ooo, I think I made him angry!" Adam Berryworth cried. "I think I hit a little too close to home with that one! His favorite meal isn't steak—it's a hay sandwich!"

"Yeah, a hay sandwich," said one of the others. "A haywich, get it!? A haywich!"

Will shook his head again, thinking, *What a twit. Doesn't he know that boldness and brilliance don't always go together?*

"You know what *I* think?" Adam said, holding his hands out to quiet his friends' tittering. "I think those two must spend a little too much time with those horses. Who knows what they do to those creatures ... late at night ... in the moonlight ... just them and the horses together ..."

While hardly knowing what he was doing, Will released his pitchfork and let it drop. He turned around with a subtle expression, one with more curiosity than malice. He had suddenly decided he couldn't let Adam continue that notion—that sickening inference of bestiality. He just couldn't let him get away with that, couldn't take that lying down. He had to do something, because—as he had wondered in the back of his mind—there might've been a chance that Adam and his friends would return tomorrow and continue their derision. There could be no peace there that day; he had to teach that officious prick a lesson.

But not with his fists. It couldn't come to that. He'd have to think of some other means.

He calmly headed for the hecklers, despite Tony's whispered protests. Many others turned their heads towards the scene—the stable boys, the merchants, the pedestrians on their way to the market. Most of them had probably been waiting for that moment just as much as the hecklers did ... although if they expected a storm of fists and curses, they were going to be disappointed.

Adam kept a smug face as Will approached him, cocksure that if trouble started, his friends would back him up. As he drew near, Will put on a confident smile of his own, hoping to throw his foulmouthed oppressor off guard. "Good afternoon to you, sir," he said.

"Good day to you," Adam said in a condescending tone. Will thought to himself that if he could throw a punch and break off a tooth or two, he would be happy. At least for a little while.

"I understand you like horses," Will said.

Adam turned his head to his friends, as if making sure they had his back. "Well, if I do, then that's news to me. They are filthy, stupid creatures who are little more than varmints."

"Varmints? That's a curious word."

"Nothing curious about it. They stink and shit everywhere and make too much noise. And the way they swing their tails everywhere—well, what's with that, my friend? Tell me, what's with that?"

Will squinted a little, curious as to what would make a well-to-do nobleman's son say such things. Horses were a boon of civilization, as important to the upper class as they were to the middle and lower classes. "They do it to keep flies away," he said simply.

"Well, whenever I see those hairy tails go up and about, it reminds me of an excited woman," Adam said and then laughed in his usual juvenile fashion. "If you know what I mean!"

Will raised his eyebrows. "And that's disgusting to you, I'm sure."

"Oh, yes, surely! Why would an animal remind me of a woman? It's ludicrous!"

Will had a few choice words to say to that, but decided to keep them to himself. Instead he asked, "Are you saying you're afraid of them?"

Adam looked flustered. "Afraid? No, I wouldn't say *afraid,* of course not ..."

"Then you wouldn't mind riding one?"

"Um well, no, I wouldn't mind, I suppose ..."

"Have you taken lessons?"

"Well ... now see here," Adam said, pointing at Will. "Do you know who I am?"

"Adam Berryworth," Will replied.

"Yes, Lord Adam Berryworth, a scion of people more worthy than *your* forebears, certainly. I've taken a thousand lessons, not the least of which is horseback riding, so before you ask another stupid question, consider it before asking, understand?"

"So you wouldn't be adverse to a little race then, would you, my lord?"

"A *little* race? Don't be stupid. I don't *do* little races, my pitifully poor peasant. If I ever do a race, it'll be at the Mayweather estate, where there's a track big enough for my skill and stature. The Mayweathers are good friends of my father and mother, I'll have you know."

"Then how about we race there, you and I? You could make the arrangements for renting out the grounds, and we can supply our own steeds. People will call it 'a race for the ages.' What do you say, Lord Berryworth?"

Adam looked at Will with his mouth open a moment, then turned slightly to look at his friends. His friends merely shrugged as to say, *Can't help you with this one, mate.* Apparently Adam hadn't see the challenge coming, and if so then he was dumber than Will had first taken him for. "Me?" he asked lamely. "Are ... are you *daft?* No one challenges *me*—especially not some filthy stable boy who's got nothing better to do than hang around filthy creatures and toss hay all day! Why should I accept your challenge? Tell me why."

Will shrugged. "Because when people decide to accuse me of performing unnatural acts, I suppose they're accusing me of not being a man ... and any self-respecting man would not let that stand, so rather than lose my temper, I'd rather disprove your claim in a more self-serving manner. So what do you say, my young lord? Shall we race?"

Adam took a long, awkward time to think of an answer. He finally said, "No dirty commoner challenges *me*. I shouldn't have to race you."

Will nodded. "A pity, but so be it. Good day to you, sir." He turned and headed back to where he'd been. As he retrieved his pitchfork and continued his work, he smiled at the sounds of the hecklers behind him. No more were they bothering him; rather, Adam's friends were chiding him for declining Will's challenge.

After some time, Adam called out, "Hey, stable boy." Will turned to him as he approached and stuck out his chest. "Yes, all right, I'll take your challenge, dammit. But I make the time and date, and if you can't make it, the race is off, understand?"

"Yes, my lord," Will replied, keeping his pitchfork up as a subtle threat.

"And furthermore, no matter what the outcome, there will be no more challenges between us. The outcome of this one is final, understand?"

"Yes, of course."

"If I win, you'll have to be a servant of my household for as long as I want you. Is that clear?"

Will's heart fluttered, but it soon calmed down as he realized he had nothing to worry about. "I'm afraid that's impossible. My service is already dedicated to Sir Timothy Blackstone."

"Sir Blackstone? Never heard of him."

"Both I and Tony here are in his service."

"Then I'll buy you off him."

"There is no *buy;* we are not servants, but esquires."

"Then he'll have to lose an esquire, won't he?"

"It's not that simple. The court in Santa Cirus sent me in his charge, though I'm ashamed to say why."

Adam hesitated. Nobleman's son that he was, he couldn't overturn a court's decision. "Okay, then how about I take your horse?"

"I don't own a horse, my lord. I'll have to ride my master's."

Adam rolled his eyes. "Okay, I'll take ... I believe I'll take that fancy jewel you have on there. What is that?"

Will touched a pocket of his tunic. Fastened to it was a small gold symbol adorned with a ruby. It was attached to a chain inside the pocket, with the symbol pinned on the outside. "It's Saint Helena's Star," he said.

"Saint Helena?" Adam asked mockingly. "Well, how sweet. I'll have to relieve you of it when I win. But let's say that *you* win—what would you have me do?"

"Never talk to me or anyone around me ever again," Will said.

"That's it?"

"That is all I need from you."

Adam snickered. "You stupid twit. All right then, have it that way." He started to head away, but then turned back and asked, "What's your name, anyway?"

"Will Fontaine, my Lord Berryworth."

"Will Fontaine ..." Adam said with a small nod. "I'll see you soon. Will you be around here?"

"Just send word to my master's estate. He is Sir Timothy Blackstone."

"Blackstone, yeah ..." Adam turned and swaggered away with his friends, trying to act as if he had had everything under control the whole time.

Will lowered his pitchfork and continued pitching hay. Tony merely gave him an incredulous look, then smiled and clapped. "Congratulations!" he said at length. "I don't know what the master will think of this, but I think it's brilliant! Good job!"

"Don't," Will said, pausing in his work. "Don't congratulate me. If I could take it back, I would."

Sir Blackstone was not entirely pleased.

"A race with a noble?" he asked. "Do you really think you're ready?"

Will nodded. "Yes, sir."

"This is the biggest challenge you've yet made. I'm not sure I approve, though my approval will matter as much as a breath in the wind."

Sir Blackstone took a sip of his beer, sitting forward in his chair as if he didn't want to relax—not after Will's troubling news. He was a formidable man in his own right, the hairs on his scalp and chin as black as the night sky, though a few had turned bright white in his middle years. His eyes had a naturally stern look, much like those of a long-lost nobleman who haunted Will's dreams still. But he was a man capable of great patience and understanding without even a hint of sarcasm, though he also had a tongue as sharp as a housewife's whose drunken husband had come home too late. He was dressed in his favorite home outfit of trousers and a green tunic, much as Will was. A small fire gave ample heat in the house's study, which also served as a living quarters. Above the chimneyplace were the heads of an antelope and a gazelle, and not that of a lion or the tusks of an elephant as he had long dreamed of owning.

Will drank across from him, thinking of the long, arduous training he'd surely undergo before the race. "It was either a race or a bloody nose, sir," he said thoughtfully. "I thought I picked the better of the two."

"Oh, you probably have," Sir Blackstone said. "But tell me, was it really worth it? Just what did he say to you?"

Will recalled what Adam said.

"'Alone with the horses?'" Sir Blackstone asked with a raised eyebrow. "I don't understand. What did he mean by that?"

Will explained what Adam meant.

"What? Are you sure? No mistake? Did you hear correctly?"

Will nodded. "Yes, sir."

"What a pig!" Sir Blackstone exclaimed, sitting up straight. "He probably should be stuck like one. He must have been snorting while he said that." He sighed. "Well, I suppose it doesn't call for a bloody nose—that's mostly for insults against women. Well, what if you win?"

"He never speaks to me again."

"Oh, you should have asked for more than that."

Will shrugged. "It didn't feel right to ask for more."

"You're too modest sometimes. Well, what if *he* wins?"

"He gets my jewel," Will said, fingering his St. Helena's Star.

"And that's all?"

"No, not at first."

"What did he first ask for?"

"My servitude."

"Hmm, of course he would. And what did you say?"

"I told him of the court order, and he let it go."

"Anything else?"

"My horse. Of course, I told him it was your horse I'd have to use, then he let it go."

"Thank God. He *could* have my horse, if he really wanted it. It'd mean more paperwork, but there's no law against it." He sighed and took another sip. "You've got to be careful who you challenge. You're no knight yet, so a challenge could very well end up in servitude. Of course you have your court order to protect you, but only as long as you're in my service. Once you're out of it, you must choose your challenges very carefully. Do you know how many would-be knights I know who've gone into servitude instead?"

"No, how many, sir?"

"Only one, and that's enough. I don't want to know a second one, or a third."

Will nodded. He knew who the master meant by "third": Tony,

his second esquire. "But I could get out of it using the Indentured Service Act of 1794."

"Yes, but only after five years of it. I don't know about you, but that's much too long. Better to be polishing armor than marble floors, right? So anyway, when and where is this taking place?"

"At the track of the Mayweather estate. The date is not yet determined. We'll have to await word for what arrangements Lord Berryworth can make."

"Let's hope it's not the Wednesday of next week," Sir Blackstone said ominously. "You know what that is."

Will groaned in worriment. "Yes, I do, sir."

"It'd be an infernal shame to work so hard for the one day you'll have to miss."

"I'll pray to God it doesn't come to that."

"Damn right you will, and all the angels and saints while you're at it."

Will drank deeply, nearly emptying his stein.

"Will?"

Will wiped his chin with his sleeve. "Yes, sir?"

"Are you going to win?"

"Yes, sir."

"Will you rub it in his face?"

"I don't know. Should I, sir?"

"No, but if you do, I won't hold it against you. 'Alone with the horses ...'" And with that, Sir Blackstone leaned back and downed the rest of his beer.

CHAPTER 2
A LIFETIME OF TOIL

THE LIFE OF WILL FONTAINE wasn't all work and no play, especially since he could find ways to put both together. But it wouldn't be an understatement to say he had been working since the day he could walk straight.

When he was but a newborn, a mysterious stranger left him at an orphanage in Georgetown, a hamlet only days away from the kingdom's capital. There the residing nuns nursed him on the milk of a local new mother and raised him under their strict tutelage. He was soon sent to work at the local plantations, for it was up to all the house's children to earn their keep and have the plantation owners continue their funding. He did mostly farm work—milking the cows, feeding the chickens, gathering eggs, and helping with repairs to the various barns. He hoped to one day start work in the fields, culling hay and wheat, which was higher-paying work than that in the barns. In doing that, he would settle down and live a rather quiet, simple life.

That plan was soon shattered one day when his life took a sharp turn. In the foundation of an old house, he found the ghost of a young girl named Marie. Although she had died several years ago when she was seven, she still looked how she had been then, as if time had stopped for her. She even spoke like a seven-year-old, but Will could sense wisdom in her words, as if she had matured even after her untimely death.

Marie told him some startling news: There were people who were lying to the King, and he had to somehow stop them. She then gave him what she called "the seeing glass"—a wonderful instrument that looked like a simple monocle, but which did a great deal more than just make a fashion statement at the opera. When looked through it, it displayed brilliant colors on people's eyes and upper lips. The colors had a certain code that told you two things: how often people lied and what their innermost desires were. Will found it to be quite useful though flawed, for it could never tell him the full story of someone's intentions. In other words, it took more than just the seeing glass to accurately judge a person.

Despite some misgivings, he left the orphanage (where he always had good friends, football games, hot food, and a warm bed) and went out alone to Augustine, the capital city of the kingdom of Thayland. After a rather long stay in the lakeside town of Santa Mona, he found himself an honored guest in the King's Palace (due to a rather spectacular string of sharp thinking, strong guts, and good fortune). He had the chance to meet the King not once but twice, and soon helped to uncover a plot to overthrow the royal family and turn the kingdom down a dark and misguided path. By the time he had finally returned home to St. Helena's Orphanage for Boys, he had gained some rough experiences and influential new friends.

He also gained a court summons to Santa Cirus, Santa Mona's sister city. There he was charged with breaking-and-entering, house theft, and being an accomplice to a notorious thief. It was not one of his finer moments, to be sure.

When he had arrived in Santa Mona, he was hungry, desperate, and poor, and he needed to somehow get back on his feet so he could make it to Augustine. By happenchance, he came upon a thief by the name of James Rogers. Rogers gave him an offer: If he helped him and two of his mates slip into a mansion in the town's wealthy district, he'd have access to enough riches to last him awhile.

Going against his better judgment, Will participated in the break-in. It went smoothly at first, but they were soon spotted by the house's guards. Rogers was killed, one of his mates escaped, and Will and the other accomplice were arrested. A kindly stranger bailed Will out, but it came at a price: He had to attend a court session and await sentencing.

His negotiator cried for leniency, arguing that Will had not known Rogers for very long before the break-in. Also in Will's favor was one of his aforementioned influential friends, who claimed that Will was no hardened criminal. That seemed to appease the judge but not by much. In the end, Will had a choice: He could either be sentenced to prison for three years, do public service for four years, or do indentured service under a nobleman for three years. For Will, the choice was clear.

And so he started his service under the roof of Sir Timothy Blackstone, where he had spent those first three years mopping floors, dusting furniture, culling wheat, pitching hay, tending to guests, and many other things in and around the master's estate in inner Augustine. In those years, Sir Blackstone found Will to be an honest and hard worker, as well as a spirited lad. He offered him to continue service under his roof as an esquire, who could eventually be named in a recommendation for knighthood to the King. Although Will still longed for home in St. Helena's, he thought he was too old to go back (he was fourteen years old; orphans were let go at the age of seventeen), and a knight's sponsorship would be a better opportunity than any Georgetown could give.

And so he continued serving Sir Blackstone and had rarely looked back. He still paid visits to the orphanage from time to time, whose convent eventually gave him his St. Helena's Star for exceptional service outside the house, despite how a court order had made him do it.

However, from time to time, he thought back to that spectacular journey of his, from Georgetown to Augustine, with a special fondness. True, he had been terrified along the way, being only eleven years old, having little idea of what to do, and being chased by a mad nobleman who had a few skeletons in his closet—but that journey had been the start of something good and important. He had met various strange and wonderful people, had seen many wondrous places, and that "seeing glass" he had was like nothing he had ever seen before. There were days when he was close to bursting with self-importance and longed to tell the story to anyone who'd listen.

But of course, the tale sounded too good to be true, and upon thinking it over, he doubted even he would accept it as true if it came from another's lips. No, it was better to just keep it to himself, close to heart, and work on something new instead. He was going to be a knight one day, and to do that he'd have to work on making challenges and winning them without hardly breaking a sweat, like that race of his ...

CHAPTER 3
AN UNLUCKY COINCIDENCE

THE DATE AND TIME OF the race was delivered to him by courier. Upon reading the parchment the first time, he couldn't help but cry out "shit" and "dammit" over and over again. He'd never known Sir Blackstone to be a psychic, but at that moment he seemed like one to Will. Sir Blackstone's hope that the race wouldn't occur on the Wednesday of next week had seemed silly, for it seemed very unlikely. But there it was: The race was scheduled to occur that Wednesday, April 14—the very day which he'd been working several years for. All that work, going down the drain ...

But then he looked at the time again and felt a faint glimmer of hope. The race would start promptly at twelve o' clock. If he remembered correctly, his other appointment that day was scheduled for one o' clock ...

He showed the parchment to Sir Blackstone, who sighed and shrugged. "Well that's it, no race for you ..."

"I can't back down," Will said, controlling his frustration and excitement admirably. "It'll be impossible; it'd leave a mark I can never wash off."

"But then all those lessons of yours will be for naught. Do you want that to happen?"

"No sir, of course not."

"Right, and I refuse to let that happen myself. I'll see you at Parkinson's Temple without fail—and *on time."*

"I'll be there; it's only an hour's difference between that and the race. This says the *race,* not the preparations, will begin right at noon. There's plenty of time."

Will thought the master would further argue, but Sir Blackstone nodded thoughtfully. "We'll see," he said. "We'll work it out. It may yet be possible, but only if we play our cards right."

Two days before the race, Will had what was possibly his last class with his teacher, Professor Roth. He was too afraid of telling him about the coincidence, so he said nothing of it.

"Now repeat after me," the professor said. "'I will pay thirty-three rupees for this goat's cheese.'"

"'Anoon eau reddick par anooni harpa-tin rupees ala junta

sin caropa,'" Will said.

"Good, now this: 'The cow herd is coming this way.'"

"San roona delreka pon dooshini eau donray.'"

"Good, now, for the millionth time ... count from one to twenty."

Will sighed, partly out of exasperation and partly out of relief over it being the last time. *"Ek, do, tin, chan, panch, chhe, saat ..."*

It had been eight years since Will first stepped in that classroom at Hendricks University. Back then he wasn't sure if he was doing the right thing, learning the Carsian language—the language of a nation across the southern sea. Since then it had been hard going, and there had been times when he nearly gave up (for the Carsian language was so unlike his native tongue that he just couldn't seem to get the hang of it). But he kept at it, up to that present day when he could speak Carsian like a natural.

"'Our neighbor has just given birth to a healthy baby boy,'" Professor Roth said.

"'Dasalan en rikourtur ekh dhalarmor coni kekaichhe asimilad.'"

"No, no, *kekaichhe* is the plural form of 'rats.' You just said she gave birth to a bunch of rats."

"Maybe she's an Untouchable," Will said with a grin.

"Very funny. Now come on, you know what's 'baby boy.'"

"I think it's *kekechhe."*

"That's right. *Kekechhe*. 'Baby girl' is *kekachhe,* not to be confused with *kekaithi,* which means 'erupting geyser.'"

"Why would the Carsians name something so near and dear to them a name that sounds like 'rat' and 'erupting geyser?' That's kind of crude, wouldn't you think?"

"Well, why would 'bear' and 'bare' sound the same? There's 'bear' as in the animal, and 'bare' as in 'naked.' I think any Carsian would think that very strange."

"Yes, I suppose a shaved, naked bear would seem strange to anyone."

The professor smiled and nodded in irony.

"So do you think I'm ready for the evaluation?" Will asked.

"Yes, I do. There's nothing more I can teach you—but life in Carsiss can teach you plenty more, I assure you."

"Looking forward to it," Will said as he got up from his seat. "Maybe I'll tell you as many stories as you've told me."

"No doubt about it. Carsiss is full of history and mystery. You'll do well. Class dismissed, young man."

Will said a hasty farewell and made to leave the classroom.

"Oh, did I hear correctly that you'll be in a race?" Professor Roth asked suddenly.

Will had made it to the hall when he quickly turned around. "Oh yeah, I'm in a race for some trivial reason. I expect to get it done with in time for breakfast."

"When is it going to be?"

"Oh, sometime soon, I think. Date's not been set yet."

"Hope it's not held too late. You don't want to miss the celebration party, do you?"

"No, sir, I'll be there rain or shine." Will ran down the hallway, hoping the lie didn't show in his eyes.

He left the college grounds to find Leaping Star, Sir Blackstone's second-best horse, waiting for him along with the sir himself, his first esquire Tony Beckins, and two other steeds.

"Ready, Will?" Sir Blackstone asked.

"Absolutely, sir."

"The Temple's not far, so we'll start from here. Let's go."

Will mounted Leaping Star, and the three of them rushed off, first across a cobblestone avenue and then down a dirt path through a forest. The path was made for merchants, but every now and again reckless teenagers whose parents had just handed them the reins used it for races. Many merchants tried to look for alternate routes (for there was nothing scarier than seeing three or four horses charging straight at their carriages at breakneck speed), but it still remained the preferred route between the college and the city district of Psalmsville. Will and his companions, however, trotted along at an even pace, merely concerned with getting from one point to another.

They eventually went off the path and into rougher territory, letting their horses slow down among the thick undergrowth and unstable ground. Soon after, they reached level grassland that led to a gentle slope. They halted atop the slope and gazed at the racetrack of the Mayweather estate, which was a quarter league in length from start to finish. It was made of well beaten dirt with a whitewashed perimeter fence; within the inner circle was an obstacle course for more brazen horse-riding. Three riders were currently on the track; Will tried looking for Adam among them but couldn't make him out from afar (his shock of blonde hair would have been hidden by his helmet, anyway).

"You're lucky it's so close," Sir Blackstone said. "How many laps will there be?"

"Two, sir," Will replied.

"That's no so bad. Tony, how long do you think we took?"

"Forty minutes, sir. It might be thirty if we really pushed ourselves."

"It shouldn't take you any more than ten minutes down there," Sir Blackstone told Will, squinting at the track below. "That should leave plenty of time for you to reach the Temple ... unless, of course, our young Lord Berryworth changes the rules."

"Change the rules?" Will asked in consternation. "He can't; I don't believe so ..."

"If this Berryworth is as much the bastard as you say, he may try. He may change it to three laps, or four, or even change the starting time. It all rests with the judge—he's the ultimate authority. Let's just hope the judge isn't in Berryworth's pocket."

Will groaned as he usually did at such unsettling news (and only if politeness could be thrown out the window). "A bloody nose seems more and more the better option."

"If so, forfeit," Sir Blackstone said firmly, looking at Will square in the eye. "Your business at the Temple will fare far better in the King's eyes than this silly race."

"I believe so, too, sir ... but as you've always said, if I can get myself into trouble, I can get myself out and still be home for tea."

CHAPTER 4
THE RACE

THE NEXT DAY, THEY DID WHAT they had done every day since Will informed his master of his challenge: They practiced horseback riding.

Madame Blackstone was away in Santa Mona on business, so the master was able to join in instead of errand-running. Will was thankful for it, because his companion Tony wasn't nearly as hard-driving as the master was. Sir Blackstone could be the most personable, understanding, kindhearted man one could know, but when there was a job or training to be done, he was a virtual slave driver, quick with the criticisms and slow with the compliments. He brought out the best in Will and Tony, making them go beyond what they thought they could achieve on their own. He had sometimes told them the story of a man who thought his horse-riding days were over once he lost a leg below the knee, but under Blackstone's thumb he went on to be a contender at an annual championship race. On occasion, when his two esquires became self-doubtful, he reminded him of that man who had conquered his own fears.

Blackstone's estate wasn't quite big enough to hold a racetrack, but the backyard made for an ample training ground. It was all grassland bordered by steel fencing which separated other estates (most of them belonged to noblemen, though it wasn't rare to see a wealthy commoner setting up his own stake in the neighborhood).

For horseback training, there were several hurdles and bars set up, as well as jousting targets and an obstacle course. But for that day, their main concern was speed. The sport of racing wasn't without its tricks, including maneuvering around competitors and knowing when to push your steed and when not to. They had rudimentary start and finish lines marked with bannered poles, and for four hours and not a minute less, they ran back and forth between them, keeping in mind that they shouldn't push their horses too hard. They rarely all raced at once, often leaving one horse out to rest. Although their horses loved to ride, the men could sense they were tired of their constant running-and-stopping routine. They were both good breeds, big and strong, but Sir Blackstone was often left pondering whether it should be Leaping

Star or his own steed, Swift Blade, that Will should take to the race. Will had full confidence in Leaping Star's abilities, but Swift Blade was a bit bigger and had more endurance, more likely to win by a nose.

After training they bathed in the river running through their estate, put on their best clothes, and hired a coach to the Mayweather estate, as per the instructions on the courier's parchment. They were dropped off at the front gates and were sent through after showing the gateman the waxen seal on the parchment. They were warmly greeted at the mansion's front door by an elderly servant who showed them to the meeting room. There the lord of the manor, Frank Mayweather, greeted them like royalty, shaking each of their hands and offering their choice of wine or brandy.

The first thing Will noticed was Mayweather's daughter, who looked about as old as he was. She first appeared as a silhouette sitting within a window's blinding light, looking outside past a white curtain; she then stood up to address the new company, fruitlessly smoothing out the wrinkles on her expansive yellow skirt. She wasn't gorgeous, but she was fair with her small, watchful dark eyes and dark hair set in long loopy curls like vines around a pillar. Although Will would have liked to make her smile, he knew she was off-limits to ones such as he. Noblemen's daughters were expected to socialize only with those of their own class, which didn't include esquires in the charges of esteemed knights. There was no law against it (such laws were repealed long ago), but it was considered taboo for such young ladies to frolic with lesser folk, for fear their flowers would be taken by those considered deficient in proper manners and chivalry.

The second thing Will noticed was Adam Berryworth, who was dressed in an overly-dressy purple outfit that shone like a polished piece of pyrite. He got up from his comfortable armchair and gave Will a reserved and snide look, puffing his lips out slightly as if he was going to give someone a sloppy kiss. He clasped his hands in front of him as if expecting a handshake, which Will knew was unfortunately inevitable.

There was another man whom Will took to be Adam's father, but he introduced himself as the race's judge instead, allowing his hand to be the first for Will to shake. "I am Judge Joseph Farimer. You have quite a day ahead of you, young man—I understand this will be your first challenge under a great audience."

"Yes, Your Honor," Will replied, trying to keep his eyes on the judge and not on Adam, whom he feared had a trick up his sleeve to humiliate him with. He had known people of Adam's type before.

"Well this won't be the last time for you, I'm sure," Judge Farimer said with a smile. "I wish you luck, son."

The judge went to shake Tony and Sir Blackstone's hands. Then Lord Mayweather loudly said, "Lord Berryworth tells me he and Mr. William here got into a little scuffle last week." He looked at Will questioningly.

"I am Will Fontaine, begging your pardon, sir ... and as for that, I believe it was not merely a 'scuffle' but a wrongdoing."

"What sort of wrongdoing?"

"Just some clumsy words that felt right at the time, I'm sure. Begging your pardon again, but what all did Lord Berryworth say about our first meeting?"

"He said there was an argument over how to handle the horses down at the Frampton estate. Does that sound correct?"

Will thought about it, then said, "You *could* call it that, but that's not the whole truth. I daresay, I'm not surprised that a young man of Lord Berryworth's standing would be inclined to butter up the details."

Lord Mayweather laughed jovially as if Will confirmed what he had thought all along.

Adam sneered and stamped his foot. "How *dare* you accuse me of such a thing! I have been truthful in every regard. Of course, I should have expected you to forget your manners in a company of your betters!"

Will was tempted to say, My *manners? What about* your *manners? You accused me and Tony of bestiality!* But he knew he should say no such thing; he had rattled Adam's nerves far enough, and it wouldn't do to anger him by laying the truth wide open. Instead he said, "Indeed, manners are what this race is all about, my lord. I hope this race teaches at least one of us a lesson in humility, and that while common courtesy is always the rule in estates like this one, it is not always the exception outside."

Adam appeared to fume inside. Lord Mayweather said, "Here, here, well said," and raised his wine glass in a toast, to which Will followed suit.

After a little small talk, they discussed the conditions of the challenge, which was laid out in a contract. First off it came to light that Adam had changed the number of laps there would be: Instead of two, there would be three. "Two laps is too feeble," Adam explained. "At least three quarters of a league will be quite sporting, and it will give the crowd more entertainment. Wouldn't you agree, Mr. Fontaine?"

Will begrudgingly agreed.

The second change was the condition of Will's victory. Adam had the judge say on the contract that should Will win, Lord Adam Berryworth would never speak to him again "except on the fifth of any month."

"That makes about as much sense as dipping dill pickles in peanut butter," Will said. "How about changing it to, 'Unless in the case of a life-threatening emergency'?"

Judge Farimer agreed and made the adjustment. "And in the event of Lord Berryworth's victory, Mr. Fontaine is to offer his Star of Saint Helena and an apology for his actions on the day of the conflict."

Will was hotly against offering an apology, but he was slow in requesting a change. Sir Blackstone, however, made the request for him: "No ... under no circumstance should Will make an apology."

Both Adam and the judge looked at him in concern. "And why ever not?" Adam asked.

"Due to the nature of the offense on that day last week," Sir Blackstone said slowly and carefully. "I'll have everyone know that Will was wrongly accused of something that warrants no apology from him. I want the apology to be stricken from the conditions."

"And just what was it that Lord Berryworth accused him of?" Lord Mayweather asked.

"I do not wish to say, for fear of shaming the young lord more than what is proper. Suffice to say that this challenge was made to put all to rights."

Adam appeared to be thinking of an argument to make, but then the judge said, "Upon a strong recommendation from a knight of Thayland, I shall have it stricken from the conditions."

Adam frowned and sighed through his nostrils as Judge Farimer crossed out the apology from the contract. "Well, that is all," he said. "I am afraid I must be off. Everyone, thank you for coming ..." He went to Lord Mayweather's daughter and kissed her gloved hand. "Lady Mayweather, it was pleasant to see you again." He then made a final farewell to Lord Mayweather and Judge Farimer and started marching out of the room.

"Lord Berryworth," Will called out. "Excuse my asking, but

would you have happened to know a certain Lord Taffin? Lord Gregory Taffin?"

"No," Lord Berryworth replied with a snide smile.

"Is that so? You're not related to him in some way?"

Adam raised his eyebrows. "I said no."

"I'm sorry, my lord, it's just that you're the spitting image of him, in more ways than one. It's uncanny."

What Will declined to say was that Lord Taffin had been dead nine years past, killed in a botched attempt on Will's life. But Adam curiously seemed to know more than he let on and left the room in a huff.

Will had looked away from Adam kissing the lady's hand, but upon Adam's departure he stole a glance at her. She appeared flushed and heated, and when she met Will's gaze she turned her eyes away.

"So," Lord Mayweather said, rubbing his palms together, "who's up for a friendly wager?"

Sir Blackstone and Lord Mayweather began to talk about different bets to make. Will received permission to wander the grounds, so he left for the racetrack, wanting to get a feel for it up close. He found the groundskeeper and asked him some questions about the track conditions. The answers were favorable as they seemed to present no problems to ruin a good race. The only thing he had to worry about was the weather, although rain seemed unlikely that next day if the clear and still sky held up.

He made for the meeting room again and found Lady Mayweather on his way in an adjacent hall. "Mr. Fontaine," she called out and jogged over to him. Will bowed as she neared and tried not to look astonished. "Mr. Fontaine," she repeated with a more personal tone, "I know not of your conflict with Lord Berryworth, but I can make a good guess. He is a tasteless and ill-reputed brat, and I should like little more than to see him properly dealt with. I wish you all my luck, and I wish to see you after the race."

Will grew hot in the ears, unable to believe what she had just said—especially the last part. He was about to say something along the lines that the lady was being too gracious and kind ... but then she drew closer to him, flattening the front of her skirt against his legs, placing a hand on his chest and the other around him, and tilting her face up directly into his. Will drew in a breath and widened his concerned eyes. Her own eyes were absolutely wanting, her breasts firm and flattened against him, relaying the beating of her excited heart.

"I want to know you better," she said. "Your hopes, your dreams, all of them, all of you ... We could keep it secret; I know my father better than anyone, and he wouldn't dare think we would be ..."

Will mustered as much willpower as he could to resist, although it was hard going. A secret affair with such a forbidden yet nubile young woman? It was as tempting as Eve's apple but dangerous, too: Everyone knew you shouldn't underestimate the goodwill of nobles, Lord Mayweather being no exception. And yet if it went on for just a little while, there might be no repercussions. He could even just steal a kiss from her right then and there ...

Despite the many layers of petticoats under her skirt, she managed to lift her right leg up between both of his.

"No," he forced his tongue and lips to say, then wrestled from her grip and half-ran down the hall, never daring a look back.

He found Sir Blackstone and Tony just outside the meeting room. Tony was arguing that their master had just made an outrageous bet. "You can't afford that and you know it ..." He stopped upon sighting Will. "What's wrong? You're shaking."

Will only then realized he was, and shrugged.

"Don't worry about the race, you'll do fine," Tony said.

Sir Blackstone, though, had a mischievous look of knowing. "Oh, it's not about the race, I'm sure. I just hope Will didn't start anything else to worry about."

"What? Another challenge?"

"No," Sir Blackstone said with a sigh and a shake of the head, already heading for the front entrance. "Let's just go before Mrs. Blackstone returns, shall we?"

Will's race wasn't the only one scheduled that Wednesday: Lord Mayweather set up a multitude of races, run by those who could afford the rental fee for his racetrack. Several of them were challenges like that of Will and Adam's, made by nobles and commoners alike; others were for small tournaments whose riders competed for trophies.

Will arrived a good two hours before his own race, first leaving his mount, Leaping Star, at the stables, then heading up to the manor for the prerace gatherings inside, unmindful of how he was still in his riding clothes. A servant brought him to Lord Mayweather, who showed him around and introduced him to many of his noble guests, most of whom were completely new to Will. Will was a little flustered by the attention, thinking his race was surely of little magnitude compared to the others that day.

Lord Mayweather could tell he was. "Listen, William," he said, "out of all the other races, I'm looking forward to yours the most. I've known Adam Berryworth since he was in soil cloths. His father always gave him whatever he wanted, as if every day was Christmas. He got spoiled rotten this way, so I hope a friendly little competition will snap him out of it."

Will nodded, though he didn't share that hope. A sport that involved team cooperation would have been better for Adam than a horserace.

Half an hour before the race, Will tended to Leaping Star, making sure all the fastenings of the bridles, saddle, and stirrups were secure. The stable hands had given him a good grooming, but Will didn't care how perfectly straight the mane was—as long as Leaping Star made it to the finish line before Adam, that was all that mattered. That was just his way, his line of thinking—function before vanity.

Ten minutes before the race started, he was ordered by a stable hand to mount up, then was brought to the starting line next to Adam Berryworth, who had the inside of the track. Being so close to him, small talk was inevitable, but he postponed it as long as he could. He gazed at the crowds instead, growing a little intimidated by the sheer size of them: All of the stands appeared full, carrying at least four hundred people throughout. It was impossible to hear what any one person was saying; his ears rang only with the white noise of human speech.

Just above and beside the starting line were the box seats, where Lord Mayweather and several other nobles looked on. Beside the lord was his daughter, whom Will had mercifully not seen in the manor earlier. She looked icy and forlorn, and he looked away before she could meet his gaze.

"Getting the jitters, farm boy?" Adam taunted. "Want to call it off?"

"Not on your life," Will said. "Tell me, have you been training?"

"And what if I have?"

"It's a simple question ... my *lord.*"

"Yes, my father made me," Adam said, and at that Will nearly laughed. He wasn't racing a fierce nobleman—he was racing a man-child.

"Have you gained a newfound respect for horses, my lord?"

"I suppose ... and I'll have all the more once I win."

"Just be careful you don't like them too much, my lord. You don't want to be with them in the moonlight ... all alone ..."

"Shut your mouth!" Adam cried. "You can't take a joke, that's what your problem is! I'll have you—"

Adam stopped there, for he was interrupted by the announcer who shouted out to the immediate crowd the nature and participants of the upcoming race. Adam stayed silent while Will gazed at the racetrack, keeping half his attention on Adam in case he wanted to pull anything funny, such as nick a bridle with a knife (a common trick of a cheating scalawag).

When the announcer was nearly finished, going into vague details over the cause of their dispute, Will felt for the St. Helena's Star on his breast ... which was no longer there. He had forgotten he had given it to Judge Farimer for safekeeping, in case he should actually lose.

Once the announcer was finished and was preparing to start the countdown, Adam had one more thing to say: "I don't care whether you apologize or not, as long as you lose face before all of Thayland. That's all I care about!"

You should care about better things, Will thought ... then the announcer counted down to one and shouted, "Go!"

Will and Adam kicked their spurs into their horse's sides, and they were off while a man atop the announcement stand waved a green flag. Will could sense that he had a brief head start. He whipped his riding crop into Leaping Star's backside as if he was beating a carpet, steadily passed by Adam, and neared the inside of the track, where he intended to stay.

He kept a tight hold on the reins, leaned forward only as far as he dared, and used the riding crop only if he felt Leaping Star starting to slack. Beyond that and a little steering, there wasn't much else he could do. Well, there was one thing, which was to pray that Adam's horse didn't prove to be stronger and faster than his. Since their race was only made on a challenge and not a real competition, there was no weighing of the horses nor the riders. It was merely catch as catch can, all thoughts of handicaps thrown out the window.

Will heard Adam closing in as he rounded the southern curve

and soon saw him in the corner of his eye. Adam was whipping his horse senseless as if he was pounding a nail, yelling at it as though the devil was right behind him and gaining: *"Go, go, you bloody damn thing! Are you a pure breed or a son of a bitch? Go, damn you, go!"*

His ungainly method seemed to be working, for he steadily gained on Will inch by precious inch. Soon Will could sense a smile filtering out those vile words and knew he'd be overcome if things let up ... but only if he kept his current speed of course. Will once again hammered away with his own riding crop, and Leaping Star picked up the pace, leaving the spoiled nobleman's son in his wake.

Things progressed smoothly, and Will grew more proud of Leaping Star and glad that his confidence in the steed wasn't for naught. Adam, of course, grew more frustrated by the minute, whipping his horse perhaps too much as was needed and proper. Will wondered what it was about Adam's horse that was giving him so much trouble. Was it his treatment of it? Or was it a slightly lazy personality that shunned exercise? Whatever it was, it would surely get it cussed out by Adam—perhaps even get it sent to the glue factories.

Once Leaping Star darted past the finish line for the second time, Will felt his victory was inevitable. Adam just couldn't keep up and couldn't get Will any farther away from the track's inside. The crowd was madly cheering and applauding, and man did it ever feel so good to know it was all for him. He imagined he'd get some medal or cup from Lord Mayweather, or perhaps from the judge if Mayweather didn't want to rub Will's victory in Adam's face.

But all that dreaming and hoping came crashing down due to some small things that made a big difference: four white doves.

Will didn't see them in the previous two laps, for they were well hidden. They were settled in a bush right next to the inside fencing, and when Leaping Star was four or five meters away, they flew up into the air, directly across the horse's path.

Leaping Star immediately slowed and bucked his forelegs high into the air, suddenly losing all discipline and control. With a yell, Will quickly grasped the handle on the pommel and shifted his center of gravity on it. He locked his legs tightly around Leaping Star's flanks, not concerned with harming the animal but only with not falling off and risking serious injury.

Leaping Star took a few steps forward on his hind legs, keeping himself up as long as he could, then stepped backward as his forelegs landed. Will bounced painfully in his saddle and immediately put all his attention on the horse, rubbing and patting his neck and speaking in a reassuring tone. He then turned his focus onto Adam, who was far ahead of him, assured that he had the race in the bag.

Will cursed him under his breath, then looked around at the stands, ending at the box seats where Lord Mayweather was standing up and arguing about something with his guests. The crowds hissed and booed, for they knew exactly what happened. It was one of the oldest tricks in the book: A group of doves, trapped in a cage near the track, released when the unfavorable one was about to pass by, intended to scare the horse and stall it. Adam had friends hiding in the bushes with orders to open the doves' cage when Will neared, and only if he had the lead. Will looked for them but couldn't find them; they had possibly hidden themselves under canopies covered with real or fake grass (as tricksters like them had been known to do).

Of course it was outrageous for Adam to think he'd get away with it. Those tricksters would surely be found, and then there would be one of two consequences: The race would either be handed to Will or be rescheduled.

Unfortunately Will didn't have the time to find out what the consequences would be. He had to be at Parkinson's Temple as he promised. He couldn't stick around for a lengthy, heated debate over who was the winner—he had things to do and people to see.

He kicked Leaping Star with his spurs again and headed straight for a gate on the outside of the track. Leaping Star was a bit confused over Will's steering, for he thought Will intended on finishing the race, but he obeyed Will's direction regardless. The gate was very small, only two meters high with a steel sign hanging high above it. There were a few spectators on the other side who were mystified over why one of the riders was heading for them at breakneck speed. As he neared the gate, Leaping Star slowed down a bit and then lived up to his name when he jumped the gate as well as any hurdle. Will considered himself fortunate that the gate was made so short; otherwise, he'd have to waste time having people unlock it for him.

He raced up the gentle slope that he, Tony, and their master had reached two days prior. He then plunged into the forest, taking the same trail with a speed that the merchants would frown on.

Damn you, Adam Berryworth, he thought. *I knew you had to have a dirty little trump card; I just couldn't figure out what. No matter, though. You can have your damn victory and my Saint Helena's Star—I'm off to greater things.*

CHAPTER 5
DOOR OF OPPORTUNITY

WILL AND LEAPING STAR PLUNGED out of the forest, raced through part of the university's campus, and soon arrived at Parkinson's Temple. Tony was found near the entrance, ready and waiting to take hold of Leaping Star while Will was inside. "How did it go?" he asked as soon as Will dismounted.

Will made a crooked frown. "I hope the master didn't make all that large a bet."

"You mean you lost?"

Will nodded. "Yes, of course."

"Actually," Tony started sheepishly, "the master bet against you. He made me promise not to tell you."

Will stared at him incredulously. "He bet *against* me? Why would he do that?"

"Lord Mayweather wanted to bet for you, and he coaxed Sir Blackstone to make a counter-bet. He didn't want to do it, but the lord insisted."

Will rolled his eyes.

"Well, go on," Tony said. "Everyone's waiting."

"I'm not late, am I?" Will asked, running for the Temple instead of expecting an answer.

Parkinson's Temple was one part church and one part sanctuary. Sometimes, when the spring rains got too hard, the banks of the Alamos River flood and force people out of their homes (which made real estate around there cheap but risky). The Temple, which was founded by one Thomas Parkinson who took pity on those people, provided them shelter while they waited out the rainy season. In all other times of the year, it served as a regular chapel.

But currently, it served as part of a government program. Will and many other men were there to compete for a part in an important mission for their king and country.

Will entered the Temple's sanctum where he was approached by Sir Blackstone and Professor Roth. "Just in time, Will," Sir Blackstone said, clearly well pleased. "They're going to start in a few minutes. Have a seat."

Will sat in one of the back pews, out of breath with his forehead and cheeks slick with sweat. He looked worried despite his timely arrival.

"So how was everything?" Sir Blackstone asked.

Will smiled uneasily. "I think I made you a lot of money," he said with a hint of sarcasm.

Sir Blackstone merely nodded. "Hmm ..."

"Just what kind of errand did you send him on?" Professor Roth asked.

"Professor, I'll be honest with you. Will made a challenge with a local brat and tried to put him in his place today. I guess he lost because he now says I can pay off all my debts."

Will had been swallowing a bit of spittle as his master spoke; at that last part, he managed it down the wrong pipe. He coughed and hacked, yet tried to keep some composure. "That much?" he asked, knowing full well the master owed some fifty thousand pounds.

"An exaggeration, Will, nothing more," Sir Blackstone said with a laugh, patting Will on the back. "So he proved the better, huh?"

"No, the limey bastard cheated," Will replied. "The old doves-out-of-the-bush trick."

"I hate to say it, but I told you. Did you stick to the inside? You did, didn't you?"

"I was so *close*. I was ahead on the third lap—I was ahead the whole *race*. Then the doves came ..."

Sir Blackstone shook his head.

"You mean you were doing that horse race?" Professor Roth asked unbelieving. "I thought that wouldn't interfere with your appointment here."

Will was about to answer, but he was interrupted by the light applause at the appearance of Sir Fredrick Hamsfield, the famed former ambassador who had once been on a diplomacy mission in Carsiss twenty-five years ago. Although he was dressed much like a nobleman of Thayland, he wore on his head a hat of tightly-bound cloth called a turban, which was decorated with a golden pin shaped like a half-moon. It was said that he had spent so much time in Carsiss, he had taken on the people's accent there and had kept it ever since. It turned out to be true, although it was so soft that it was only faintly recognizable.

He stood in front of the altar at the front of the room and addressed the twenty-three students and their guardians and teachers: "Welcome, one and all, to the opportunity of a lifetime. It is my honor and my pleasure to introduce you to a world not so far away, and yet one that feels as far as the other side of the world. As you can see, you've caught me with my thinking cap on."

The audience laughed politely. Sir Hamsfield raised his hands with a mischievous smile.

"All joking aside, you might find yourself wearing such a thing if you are chosen to be one of our king's ambassadors. For it is hot down there, my friends—so hot you may feel your blood boil if you don't drink enough water. Winter may be just around the corner here, but in Carsiss, you'd never know it. It is a place of white sands and palm trees, and it never snows. In the summer, the sun is like a furnace, and the heat waves are so fierce they play tricks on your eyes. There are stories of people who were lost in the desert, where they wished for nothing but a single drop of water to slacken their thirst. Sometimes, they've said, they saw an oasis—a pool of fresh water in the middle of nowhere—just paces away, and so they ran—or they crawled faster—to get there ... only to find that it was just a mirage, a trick on the eyes.

"But Carsiss is full of beauty, too. It is a very old land, and while it is tough to live there, the people are tough, too—proud and adaptable. They make Carsiss joyous, wonderful, enlightened, and even mysterious. Even if you were to become used to everyday life there, you can always find something to surprise you.

"But ... work before pleasure, my friends. When I went to Carsiss on behalf of King James, I was in the company of Emperor Orissu, who worked with me and my Thayland friends on making peaceful and beneficial relations between our countries. We were furthering the work of past ambassadors, and while we made no great progress that wasn't made already, our talks were essential in keeping a valuable ally of ours.

"Now I come before you to ask to continue my work, to ensure that Carsiss remains a cornerstone of our future. You will do this with a new emperor. Emperor Orissu of the Kohima Dynasty has been dead these past five years, succeeded by his son, Baku. I'm afraid I don't know much about him; I've heard he is brash but wise. That is all you will have to go on. Tread carefully with this one, that is all I can say.

"Now ... to the part you've been waiting for. While there is a great many of you here, there are only three posts available. Each post is unique and we must find people who fit the criteria for each one. We must choose an aristocrat, a scholar, and a soldier. Though they each have their own parts to play, they must essentially do these things: act honorably, make fellowship, and be clever. In doing these you will paint a good picture of our country, for it is through you that our country's image will be portrayed.

"My fellows now will go to each of you with their questions. They are diplomats from the Palace who shall assess your knowledge and skills. Please wait your turn and clear your mind. You may be about to take an exciting step forward. Good luck to you all."

Nine men who were standing off on the sides came in and went around asking for certain names. They each had a list of the people they were to question; two of them went to Will and his two teachers, but only to ask if he was someone else. Will must have been second or third on one of their lists.

"I've never met any of these people before," Will said.

"You weren't supposed to," Professor Roth said. "They are here to make an honest and unbiased assessment of you and the other students. Just take this time to remember everything I've taught you. I'm sure you'll do fine."

"They won't ask questions based on my opinions, will they? Sir Blackstone's given me enough of those."

"Even if they do, answer honestly," Sir Blackstone said. "They'll want nothing but the finest candidates. Remember, Will, this may be the biggest undertaking of your life, and it means just as much to His Majesty as it does to you."

Will nodded. Long ago he had met His Majesty's uncle. James Hendricks had been an ancient man then at ninety-four years old, and while he couldn't make much of an impression, he had earned Will's respect nonetheless. He had died seven years ago, succeeded by his nephew Fredrick because he had left no children to take over—none who lived, anyway. While he had never met the current ruler, he thought he should try his best in Carsiss on behalf of his uncle—if he was chosen, that was.

"So tell me about the race, then," the professor said.

"I met a despicable oaf last week who accused me of doing something unnatural," Will said quickly. "So I wanted to take him to school in a horse race—but he cheated, and I probably lost, and so I may never show my face around here ever again. Hence my trip to Carsiss."

"You didn't *lose,* Will," Sir Blackstone countered. "He *cheated*—that does not count as a win for him. Surely everyone saw those doves being released, and as soon as they find the ones who released them, you'll be declared the winner."

"I think I know a bit more than you do, sir. It said in the rules that if either one of us should leave the premises before the other crosses the finish line, then that one forfeits the race."

"Well, yes, I do know that, but he *cheated.* I think the judge will make an exception."

"No, I don't think so, sir. They won't understand why I left. We should have told them our plans after all ..."

"I said we shouldn't have because Lord Berryworth would have tracked you down and have his jealous revenge."

"Lord *Berryworth!?"* Professor Roth exclaimed. "You challenged Lord Berryworth?"

Sir Blackstone turned to him with a look of undeserved guilt. "Adam—the son."

"Adam," the professor mused with a nod. "I actually know his father a little. Very intimidating man, looks little like his son. Adam's mother has blonde hair; his father has very dark hair."

The professor's revelation didn't strike Will until moments later, when he remembered seeing Lord Mayweather arguing with someone in his box seat. The man he was yelling at was formidable, and he wouldn't have thought him to be Adam's father due to the difference in hair color, but he may have been ...

Will groaned. He may have just gained three enemies for the price of one. First was Adam Berryworth for obvious reasons; second was Lord Mayweather for having him lose his bet; third was Lord James Berryworth who was probably very protective of his son's pride and reputation.

One of the diplomats soon came up and asked, "Are you Herman Sastroni?" Will shook his head and the man went away. A second diplomat then came and asked, "Are you Mr. Will Fontaine?"

"Yes, sir."

"Good, okay ..." The man sat next to him and glanced at his notes. "I'm Mr. Jackson, good day to you. I'm going to give you series of questions, just to test your knowledge of Carsian life and customs," he said ... at least, that was how it translated in Altrin, Thayland's native language. What he actually said was, *"Seri nar Mr. Jackson, jun renni namarre. Do akkay lonni rechhe corshlina, dedeerekke son lanna milisunnilanna eau deernekay lin tonrekka hunaregime se na Carsiss."*

Will responded, *"Sunnin don ranna shayshinna,"* which meant

"I am as ready as I'll ever be."

"Good, the first question is: What are the four *jatis?"* the diplomat asked, still speaking in Carsian.

"Brahmans, Ksatriyas, Vaisyas, and *Sudras."*

Mr. Jackson wrote in the piece of parchment he held. "And what are they in Altrin?"

"Brahmans are priests or holymen; *Ksatriyas* are nobles or overlords; *Vaisyas* are the commoners; *Sudras* are the peasants."

"Who are the Untouchables?"

"They are the *Sudras,* who are considered profane and unclean, for they must work the jobs that require contact with dirt, dust, manure, and the dead."

"If you see an Untouchable, what must you do?"

Will thought about it, believing it to be a trick question. Professor Roth hadn't given him any specific instructions on how to deal with the Untouchables, so there had to be something he could think of on his own. He thought about the nature of the Untouchables, then simply thought of their name and said, "Don't touch them."

"Correct," the diplomat said, writing in his parchment with a smile. "You wouldn't believe how many people get that one wrong."

"What do they usually say?"

"Oh, something like 'give them food' and other things like that. What are the names of the three paths to salvation?"

"The *karma-marga,* the *jnana-marga,* and the *bhakti-marga."*

"Good, and what do they mean?"

Will sighed and proceeded to describe the three paths to salvation in sparse details. Mr. Jackson then asked him for the names and dates of holidays and festivals, then for the names of the Carsian emperor, his cabinet members, and his closest relatives.

When he was done, he looked at his notes while trying to keep a blank expression, although he gave a hint of being pleased. "Well, that's everything," he said, speaking in Altrin again. "I'll bring this in for final analysis. Good luck."

"Thank you, sir," Will said.

Sir Blackstone shook his head after Mr. Jackson left. "I still can't believe the mastery you have over that language. It's remarkable."

"Mastery?" Will said. "Hardly, sir. I'm sure I'll have some problems if I get to Carsiss."

"Nonsense, I'm sure you'll do fine," Sir Blackstone said.

"There won't be any language problems you can't handle," Professor Roth said. "Just be mindful of words that sound alike."

Will nodded, and the three of them talked about how life would be in Carsiss. Professor Roth was the most helpful in describing the differences between Thayland and Carsiss, while Sir Blackstone could only make comments and conjectures. Although Will had heard many of them before, he made again to soak them all in as if hearing them for the first time. It was the only way to drum them into his head, because remembering them would make life in Carsiss a little easier if not a cakewalk.

After a while, Sir Hamsfield approached the altar again and bowed at the light applause. "My friends, your answers have been tallied, and I am glad to say there isn't a single bad egg among you. You all should be very proud. Even if you are not chosen for a post, remember that you have gained a talent and knowledge that will benefit you for the rest of your lives.

"But there is one more question I have for each of you, so clear your minds and be prepared. This question has no right or wrong answer; what you must do is think of the best and honest answer you can come up with."

Will felt a lump in his throat, and he was sure his wasn't the only lump in the room. There were no bad eggs, sure, but Sir Hamsfield's question would surely determine who would fill at least one of the posts.

"All right, are you ready?" Sir Hamsfield said. "Okay, let me give you a situation. There is a mother sitting in her quarters with her sleeping husband's head in her lap. She sees her infant child step towards a fire in the chimneyplace. If she does not intervene, her child may stumble into the fire. What should she do? Think about it as long as you like, then raise your hand if you'd like to answer."

Over a minute had gone by before someone raised his hand. Will had been racking his brain so hard he thought he'd go mad, and when the hand rose up, he felt jumpy and panicky. He had looked at Professor Roth for help, but the professor merely shook his head. "I can't help you with this one," the professor said.

The hand belonged to a stout young fellow who looked unsure of himself. He said, "She should yell at the child to get back."

"Good," Sir Hamsfield said, then pointed at another hand. "Yes?"

A gangly man with messy orange hair stood up. "She should gently slip out from under her husband's head and get to her child."

"Very good," Sir Hamsfield said with a smile that wasn't convincing. "Any others?"

The third hand raised belonged to a portly young man in a university uniform, who was no doubt dressed to impress. "She should find something and throw it at the child to make him get away from the fire."

A few laughs sounded from among the seats. Sir Hamsfield looked slightly amused. "Well, that's something. Anyone else?"

Will knew why the people answered as they did: It was because women's rights and statures in Carsiss weren't the same as in Thayland. In Thayland, women could own businesses and land, and they had the right to free speech with only a few more restrictions than men. In Carsiss, though, women were told to revere their husbands like gods, to obey their every order, and to never make their lives more frustrating and complicated than they already were. Nor could they own property; all their things belonged to either their husbands or the state. In that light, none of the questions seemed too silly or wrong. But they were all too obvious; they couldn't be what Sir Hamsfield was looking for.

Will thought of keeping silent and letting the question pass. But then he remembered something Professor Roth told him once—that women should pray to the gods even more so than men because they needed their protection more urgently.

Will raised his hand, not bothering to note the expression on both his teachers' faces. Sir Hamsfield pointed at him and he stood up, ignoring his excited heart. "The woman should pray to the gods that her child doesn't get hurt. Perhaps Rama or Krishna could come scoop the child away from harm, so she doesn't have to disturb her husband."

"Very well," Sir Hamsfield said, trying to sound indifferent. "Anyone else like to try?"

Will sat back down and waited for someone to laugh. No one did. Everyone around him knew about Carsiss and its people's beliefs as well as he. He did hear someone groan, though—probably because that someone hadn't thought of that answer himself.

Sir Hamsfield gave the students five more minutes, then thanked them for their thoughts and retreated from the sanctum. He returned a little later with two of the diplomats. He opened a scroll and said, "I am pleased to announce that we have made our decisions. The position of the aristocrat is awarded to ... Lord Samuel Harrington!"

The crowd applauded vigorously. A dark-haired gentleman stood up and took a bow. Will wondered if he had won because he had connections—not that it mattered, because only a nobleman could fill his posting.

"Congratulations, sir," Sir Hamsfield continued. "And the position of the scholar is awarded to ... Franklin Douglass!"

A tall, thin young man in a fine wool sweater stood up, looking more excited than was proper. He cupped his hands over his mouth and shrieked in a piercing tone of voice. "I won, I won, I'm going, I'm going!" he chanted.

"Yes, well—" Sir Hamsfield started, but the crowd's attention hung on Franklin, who kept shouting and cheering. It took some effort from his teacher to get him under control. Franklin sat back down, absolutely beaming in delight, grinning from ear to ear. "Well, that was a surprise," Sir Hamsfield said with a twitch of his eyebrows.

Sir Hamsfield hesitated as he looked at the scroll again. Will looked at his two teachers, who gave reassuring smiles and nods. The announcement of the soldier's post was up next, the only one that Will qualified for. Although it was true that he could benefit from his teachings under any circumstance, he had begun his lessons solely for the purpose of obtaining an ambassadorship. He drew a deep breath.

"And now, the position for the soldier is awarded to—"

Will told himself to expect disappointment so he wouldn't end up disappointed (an oxymoron if there ever was one).

But Sir Hamsfield announced his name anyway: "William Fontaine, Esquire."

Will's heart leapt in his chest. He turned to Sir Blackstone, who patted his back and prompted him to rise. Will awkwardly stood up, wearing a goofy smile and scanning the crowd with large, incredulous eyes. He couldn't breathe normally; he could only make a series of irregular gasps. He may have been laughing, but he wasn't sure. The worst part of it was his sudden awareness that he was in his dirty riding gear among numerous formal outfits.

The crowd applauded as generously as it did for the others. Although there were a few jealous looks, most of everyone looked pleased and congratulatory—none more so than Professor Roth, who could go on to tell his peers that he had taught an ambassador.

Will sat down and received more shoulder pats from Sir Blackstone. He sighed as if the air in the room had grown thin.

"Congratulations to each of you," Sir Hamsfield said. "The choices were not easy, but we feel confident that these three men will secure and strengthen our neighbor to the south—an important task seeing as how our western neighbor does not seem interested in an alliance."

The crowd laughed lightly. Thayland's western neighbor was the feudal kingdom of Thorain, who had held a rocky relationship with Thayland over the past few hundred years.

"A celebration party shall be held at the Bryant estate," Sir Hamsfield continued. "Each candidate may bring two guests. You may pick up your invitations and directions to the estate at the entrance. Good luck to each and every one of you, and I'll see you at the party."

Sir Hamsfield quietly left the room as everyone got up from their seats. Will was immediately given more congratulations by his fellow students (most of whom he had never seen before, for he had done his lessons privately).

He made to introduce himself to the other ambassadors before heading home. The first one he saw was Franklin Douglass, and from the moment he first heard him, he knew he was castrated. Castration was a common practice in the Church of Thayland, for when a small boy loses his genitals at such an early age he is bound to keep his high-pitched voice all his life, and thus be capable of singing all the high notes in church choirs. The practice also eliminated any sexual desires before they even started, which supposedly brought them closer to God. Will thought a castrated man was an unwise choice for an ambassadorship to Carsiss; the people there would never understand the reasons for a man's castration, especially since the nation's holy temples had no choirs.

"Will Fontaine?" Franklin asked. "Oh it's such an honor to meet you. Is it true you met King James when you were young?"

Will smiled. He was used to his slight celebrity status. "Why yes, I am, but that was all so long ago ..."

"I heard you made the King bounce in his bed and hang from a chandelier. Is *that* true?"

Will was also used to exaggerations of his brief meetings with King James. "No, he was bound in a wheelchair and could hardly move a muscle. I made him laugh, but that's about it ..."

"You!? Made him *laugh!?*" Franklin then laughed himself, sounding like a loon who had caught its foot in a trap. His teacher (and father, as Will later discovered), made him calm down and offered his own best wishes to Will. "I'll see you at the party!" Franklin cried as he was being led out of the Temple.

Will looked after him with a confused look.

"He seems like an odd choice for an ambassador," Lord Samuel Harrington said nearby.

"My thoughts exactly," Will said. "I'm surprised he even had a chance at all."

Lord Harrington smiled wearily. "They say the new Emperor has strange attractions ... they say he is interested in both women and *men.*"

Will raised an eyebrow. He tried thinking of something to say, but he indulged in hesitance.

Sir Blackstone responded instead: "You're not serious. That's not even possible ..."

"Oh yes, it is possible, and I believe young Mr. Douglass was chosen because of it," Lord Harrington continued. "He was a shoo-in for the posting all along. I believe the Church would frown upon the Emperor's tastes, but of course the Emperor is beyond their jurisdiction. Sir Hamsfield and the King weighed their pros and cons, and they concluded it best to send someone like Douglass over with the intention of appeasing Emperor Baku. Of course the King had the final say in the matter."

"Is he—" Will began, hardly able to bring the words out. "Is he ... Franklin, I mean ... does he have similar tastes?"

"I don't think Franklin has any taste at all. He does not feel as we do. But if he is ordered to ... *please* ... Emperor Baku, he just may do it."

"No, I don't believe that!" Will said, more loudly than he intended. "I mean, the Church wouldn't order him to do something like that."

Lord Harrington smiled knowingly. "Of course the Church wouldn't ... but the King would. He's the one in charge here, and he'll do whatever it takes to get on the Emperor's good side."

"His Majesty's a shrewd man," Sir Blackstone said.

"Well, I now know that policy of putting forth a good image for Thayland was nothing but shit," Will said. "Giving the Emperor a man to play with will only present a *bad* image for Thayland."

"It may or it may not," Lord Harrington said. "I'm sure the

King wouldn't make a move like this if he wasn't absolutely sure it was true the Emperor preferred men over women."

"The Emperor's not married, then?" Sir Blackstone asked.

"Oh, he is ... to a woman, actually. I've heard she's quite lovely, too—a goddess in the Carsian Palace. He keeps a harem, too, which he's quite known to share—"

"I can't believe it," Will muttered, refusing to hear anything unrelated to the matter of Franklin and his role in the ambassadorship. "How could the King do something like this? It's unheard of."

"And if the King has it his way, it'll stay unheard of," Lord Harrington said. "I'm sure it will be a very private affair. I apologize for upsetting you, William. Do please use discretion in this matter and take my sincere congratulations. That answer you gave was quite impressive."

They stepped out of the temple together and parted after a round of farewells. On the carriage ride home, all Will could talk about was Franklin.

"Such relationships are common in Carsiss, Will," Professor Roth said, looking up from the party invitation in his hands. "Some men flirt and get involved with other men; many others only brush with that lifestyle once or twice and then never go back."

"Why haven't you told me this before?" Will asked, sounding betrayed. He glanced once out the window, wondering if Tony was listening in from atop Leaping Star.

"Because it's all done in private, Will. You have nothing to worry about—no Carsian man would ever come onto a foreigner. I may have mistakenly said it's a common practice in Carsiss; what I meant to say is it's not unheard of. The truth is that such behavior is very rare." Then, with a dismissive tone, he repeated, "You have nothing to worry about."

Will continued to converse in the carriage, but his mind was clearly distracted throughout the ride. He didn't know how to feel about what he'd just heard—angry, upset, hopeful, or just understanding. After a while, he decided to just not feel anything at all.

CHAPTER 6
THE PARTY

SIR BLACKSTONE INSISTED THAT WILL take Tony to the party instead of him, the other guest being Professor Roth. He said he had had his fill of parties throughout his life, and he wanted to give Tony a rare chance to attend one himself.

On the ride to the Bryant estate that night, the atmosphere was melancholy inside the carriage. "I can't believe you're going away," Tony said. "I mean, I knew it was good you were studying and all, but I really didn't think it would end up like this."

"It'll only be for a year," Will said. "I'll be back home before you know it. Time is funny like that, you know."

"Yeah, I know. Remember how I didn't like you when you first came? I pushed and shoved you around, and once we got into this big fight and the master ordered us to behave and accept each other. I only agreed if you stayed out of my way."

"I thought you were a big bozo ... and I think I was right," Will said with a grin.

"But somewhere along the line, I realized you were a pretty good guy. You didn't deserve being beaten on for no good reason. I once thought I'd be happy to see you go; now it's kind of sad."

Will was uncomfortable with that kind of talk, although he appreciated Tony's earnest words. He suddenly wished to be on the boat as soon as possible in order to get his ambassadorship quickly over with. "Don't make me beat you in these good clothes," he said, shaking his head.

"You think anyone would even notice if you messed them up?" Tony asked.

When the carriage started shaking, the driver yelled at them to quit the ruckus in there.

Will and Tony's clothes were only a little scruffy when they entered the Bryant estate's manor—nothing they couldn't fix quickly in the light of the foyer. A servant led them to the ballroom, which was decorated in typical Carsian designs—curtains covered with glimmering flakes, beads hung across doorways, pottery carved with images of Hindu gods, elegant rugs under tables and chairs, and masks made of paper and clay set on the walls beside spears and scimitars—a type of sword shaped like a crescent moon. Will had his eye drawn to one such mask that looked like an angry man with a long face with stripes and polka dots all across his cheeks and forehead, its smile resembling the bridge across the hooves of a rocking horse. It seemed familiar somehow, but he couldn't quite remember where'd seen a similar face.

The main topic of conversation among the dozens of people was the appointment of Lord Harrington. Of the three ambassadors, Harrington was the only one who had been to Carsiss before, so he had the advantage of knowing the lay of the land and of the nation's capital, Nünveghett. The lord had earlier said that the best thing to do in Carsiss was go on a camel safari and see the sights of the city and desert from atop the Saparel mountain range. If the Emperor felt like traveling, he'd try to coax him into one such fabulous safari.

Will and Tony split apart in order to find single ladies who were just friends with the students who invited them (all of the students were male, for King Thayland would never consider sending a woman to Carsiss, no matter how fit for the position one would be). But much to their lament, single ladies turned out to be nonexistent in the room, and they ended up causing more uncomfortable conflicts than rousing conversations. (Tony had instead met some soldiers who thought that apprenticing under a knight was no way to be a warrior, and throughout the night they made spirited barbs at each other's professions—all in good fun.)

Will nearly jumped in horror when Franklin Douglass approached him with a dour expression. "I know what you're thinking," Franklin said. "You're wondering how a man cut below the belt could even think about going to Carsiss to confer with the Emperor. Believe me, I know—I've wondered about that myself. You see, I'm a victim of circumstance. Both my father and mother were merchants who dealt with Carsian goods. They made me learn Carsian, which was pretty easy since I've been hearing it ever since I was small. When I was five, I discovered I had a good singing voice, and I went to join the choir of the Church of Thayland. They gave me the choice of getting a snip, and I said yes on one condition: That I never go to Carsiss with my parents. I'd heard so many tales of that place it scared me. Of course I was just a kid still ...

"But alas, I got kicked off the choir for following through on a stupid dare, and so now I'm here, about to go to Carsiss."

"Hmm ... so what was that dare?" Will asked.

"Spiking the holy water."

"Ah, that'd do it to anyone."

"Yeah. So I went to go see Mr. Taylor, who's a diplomat at the King's Palace, and he put me on a kind of special mission in Carsiss ... but I'm not allowed to tell you that. I know I just did, but I want you to understand why I'm going along. There's something special I got to do, and I can't tell you what it is, except that it's special—"

"'Special,' got it."

"—and no one else can do it except me. If you're jealous of me now, don't be. This is something you wouldn't want to do, trust me."

Will nodded. "No problem there."

"Well ... good luck with everything. I may see you tomorrow. We got to get new clothes—King's orders. Bye."

Will nodded and said farewell. He then turned and took a deep breath. He supposed he'd have to tell him eventually that he knew just how "special" his task was, but he could at least put it off for the night.

Not long after, he happened upon a familiar face—a young woman with straight black hair and her mother's pair of small eyes like those of a pig. It had been years since he'd last seen her, but he could never misplace her anywhere. She was alone in one side of the room, drinking a glass of wine that she probably wasn't allowed to have (the legal drinking age in Thayland was nineteen; she was currently eighteen, if Will remembered correctly). She appeared to be waiting for someone to come by—her boyfriend, in all likelihood. She wore a dark red dress that would have matched with Will's outfit (he preferred clothes of an earthy shade of red, like that of rose petals).

"Candice Montblanc," he said to her back.

She quickly turned and surveyed him with a blank face. "Will Fontaine—a pleasure, sir. You *are* a sir, are you not?"

"Not quite, but getting there. What brings you here—you of all people?"

"I'm with a gentleman. His friend is one of the Bryants; we're invited to all the parties here."

"I'm sure. So you're not here to celebrate the ambassadorships?"

"Oh yes, I heard something about ambassadors being here. I believe they're going to Carsiss, was it not?"

She unnerved Will. Being ignorant of the cause of the party was a rather normal trait for her—a rich girl who spent much of her nights drinking and dancing and moving from one boyfriend to the next. He both envied and was appalled by her carefree lifestyle. She never wanted for money, nor did she have to work for it. She regularly had her bank accounts filled by the men who ran her vineyards, which had been entitled to her by her father. No one could buy or take away her inheritance unless she either consented to it or lost her title of nobility.

He thought of telling her that he was one of the ambassadors—not that she could care less. But instead he sighed through his nose and kept his silence. Rubbing her nose in his accomplishments would not be satisfying—a lesson he'd learned several times before with her. "Have you heard from your father recently, my Lady Montblanc?"

Candice wrinkled her nose. "No."

"Really? Any idea on when he'll come back?"

"I just said no," she said irritably. Her father was a topic she was most uncomfortable with, and he knew it. But there was a reason to ask for his whereabouts other than to upset her.

Jean du Montblanc was one of Will's greatest enemies. Many years ago, he had been part of a conspiracy group that plotted to overthrow the kingdom. Will had overheard two incriminating conversations with him, and Montblanc had found out; he tried to capture and imprison him in either servitude or a dungeon. Although all of the men in the conspiracy had been narrowly cleared of wrongdoing (thanks to a lack of evidence and willing witnesses), their plot had been thwarted, and Montblanc had disappeared without a trace. The last time Will had seen him, Montblanc had just suffered a leg injury; the fact that he had been able to escape the country with such a handicap was a testament to his power and influence, for he must have had many devoted servants who packed his things and drove him away without misgivings.

"I believe your father is an ambassador," Will said slyly. "I believe he's in the company of our friendly neighbor, King Erik of Thorain."

Candice gasped, although she didn't hesitate with a response: "You listen here, my father was never a traitor to our nation, nor is he in Thorain with its king. Whichever of your lies the courts believe is simply not true and unjustified, and I will not hear of them anymore."

"You *still* stand up for him?" Will asked with fists on his hips.

"You'll never learn, will you? He was ready to overthrow King James and—"

"Quiet!" Candice whispered fiercely. "This is not the proper place for an argument. Go and frolic elsewhere."

"I just don't understand why you're defending him," Will said with a slight apologetic tone. "Before he disappeared, he beat you until you were as blue as cobalt, and now—"

"That is none of your concern, Mr. Fontaine. Now if you would please, I don't want to talk about it."

Will grasped her arm. "It *was* my concern back then, Lady Montblanc. Your father beat you and pinned the blame on me. If he had things his way, I'd be in jail or dead."

Candice stared at the ceiling with a protruding lower lip and tapped her foot. "More lies, more deceit," she said and tugged her arm out from Will's hand. "That never happened, you bloody *cur.*"

"How can you say that? You were *there* ... then again, never mind. You want to live in denial, so be it. But I'll tell you, if I ever see your father again, I'll make him sorry he ever came back. I don't know if you know this, but—"

"Is there a problem here?" a young man said from behind. He turned Will around by the shoulder and landed an accusing finger on his chest. "Whatever problem you have, just leave her alone. Don't make me tell you again."

"My apologies," Will said with a small bow. "I was just leaving soon, anyway." He stormed away from the scene, suddenly feeling more anxious about going to Carsiss. Jean du Montblanc would never think to look for him there, if indeed he was looking at all.

Will told himself that he was just being paranoid, but there was no denying what he had been about to say to Candice: Lieutenant-Commander Kruman, the man who had requested clemency in Will's burglary trial nine years ago, had privately informed him that Montblanc had been sighted in Thorain's capital, Sempton, getting around with the help of a walking stick.

He had about to disclose that information to Candice to further upset her; she had gotten him mad, and he wanted to get her back for it. Problem was, he wasn't allowed to give her any new information on her father. Lieutenant-Commander Kruman had though it possible that Montblanc might be keeping in touch with his daughter, and Candice therefore could not be trusted. If she related to him that the Thayland government knew of his whereabouts, he would flee and become lost to them. In which case,

Candice's gentleman had inadvertently did Will a favor for interrupting.

It was okay for Will to directly ask her whether or not she and her father kept in touch, for if she had made a slipup it would benefit him. But he was sloppy when he had almost told her about the sighting. She had made him mad, and he had wanted to upset her in a deeper fashion. He needed to cool his nerves, so he helped himself to his first drink.

Will tried the rum and whiskey, and preferred the rum—he always had something of a sweet tooth. He went around, hearing petty gossip and talking about what he expected in Carsiss (such as the people's devotion to their gods). Before he knew it, it had gotten late and he thought about leaving. That was around the time Sir Hamsfield approached him. He had been chatting with a group of students who discussed what they could do with their training in the Carsian language.

"Mr. Fontaine," Sir Hamsfield said, "congratulations on your appointment. Let me tell you though, you have the toughest job of them all. You won't so much be an emissary as more of an exchange citizen. You'll be joining a Carsian military company; your job will be to train with the soldiers and be the best soldier you can. What's more, Carsiss is in a war that's slowly dying down—but don't worry, as Carsiss is on the winning side. You may have to involve yourself in several campaigns that may prove dangerous, so—"

"Thank you, sir, but I am already aware of that," Will said.

"At any rate, here are some instructions for all you must do tomorrow," Sir Hamsfield said, handing over a piece of foolscap. "You must first sign a contract which is basically a waiver of the kingdom's responsibility in case anything goes wrong. Be sure to read it in full, as well as the insurance contract which will pay a handsome amount to whoever you choose. Then you'll receive some funds for clothing. You may choose whatever you wish to wear, but it must be acceptable in Carsiss. The shopkeepers will know."

Sir Hamsfield wished him well once again, but Will stopped him from leaving. "Sir, if I may have a word with you in private?"

"Why yes, surely." Sir Hamsfield led Will to an adjacent hallway that was illuminated only by moonlight. "Now, what is it then?"

"If I may, I'd like to ask more about Franklin's role."

"So Lord Harrington told you, eh?" Sir Hamsfield said. Then, in a soft and understanding tone: "I know it's uncomfortable and it may even backfire, but it's on the King's order that he goes. I don't even like the idea myself, but the King wants to get on the Emperor's good side. Emperor Baku is said to be a cunning, manipulative man, and my boy, it's good to have people like that on your side. His Majesty believes that by, uh ... *giving* Mr. Douglass to please him, he is showing that he is understanding and sympathetic to his nature ... while a lot of people in this world may not be.

"But understand this, Mr. Fontaine: Franklin has been ordered not to do *anything* unless he is seduced, not the other way around. Emperor Baku may not be interested, or he may not want to reveal to us that the rumors of his nature are true. In that case, nothing may come out of it, which is just fine.

"Now, I'm not sure if Lord Harrington told you, but I'll tell you now—and these are orders, Mr. Fontaine, punishable by a lengthy prison sentence if broken. Do not speak of this to anyone, no exceptions. If you must speak of it to Franklin or Lord Harrington, be discreet, though it would be better not to speak of it at all. Is that understood?"

"Yes, sir," Will said, getting that rough feeling he had when his heart turned into stone.

"Good. You're a bright man, Mr. Fontaine. I'm sure you'll do well."

They shook hands and parted. Will returned to the ballroom, drowning his concerns in the expensive wine which flowed freely at the bar. He glanced in longing at the dance floor, where he spotted Candice Montblanc waltzing with her consort. She was the picture of delight, smiling and laughing at some foolish joke or other. The gentleman whispered something in her ear, and she leaned back in his arms from pure joy ... or was she faking it, trying to butter him up so he'd do her a favor? Will had heard stories of women like her, whom he wouldn't touch even with a meter-long stick.

He drank his wine till he felt lighter than air, then tried to impress his new friends with jokes he'd made about a farm boy who had wooed a nobleman's daughter and won her heart, and was then bribed by her father with a large sum of money to never see her again.

"So what did he do?" asked one of the students.

"He took the money, of course," Will said, "for that was his intention all along. Because money *can* buy you love, my friends—it can get you a puppy."

CHAPTER 7
THE VOYAGE

WILL KNEW HE HAD TO be careful; if he wasn't, he'd end up as some hateful, woman-bashing, pathetic hermit who preached of the joys of solitude and the evils of the fairer sex. His contempt for women was growing within him like a maggot in a log, and unless he kept it in check (or better yet, found himself a suitable mate), it would grow into a fly, hopping around from one person's skin to another, feeding on the salts with its tiny sucker.

The seeds of scorn were probably first planted after his breakup with his first girlfriend—a common woman named Marilyn. They met at a fair and were able to see each other for five weeks without anyone knowing. Sir Blackstone eventually found out on his own, but he didn't discourage him from the relationship. He didn't egg him on, either, but his stance was nonetheless unusual: Most vassals disallowed their pages from pursuing love.

It was Will who made the breakup. Marilyn wanted them to marry shortly, but Will wanted to finish his apprenticeship first. One night, when they were celebrating his birthday, just the two of them (Will projected his birthday to be January 5th, the day he was given to the orphanage as a newborn), Marilyn encouraged him to have booze and wine for the first time in his life (he was fifteen then, and she was sixteen). She seduced him and nearly had all his clothes off in a motel room before he figured out what was going on: She was trying to conceive by him so he would then have to marry her. Although he brashly pushed her away and left the building in a huff, he was civil when he made the breakup two days later.

Marilyn's boldness had hit a nerve, and it hadn't been mended ever since. The situation with the Lady Mayweather hadn't helped, and the foolish ignorace of Candice Montblanc had certainly made it worse (true, every young girl in Thayland was told to "stand by your man," but Candice's defense of her maniacal, homicidal father was ridiculous). Will wondered if a steady lifetime mate was all it was cracked up to be.

On the morning after the party, Will and his master made ready for the four-day trip to the southern docks where Will's boat would be (Tony was ordered to stay behind and oversee the estate in the master's absence). Seeing Sir Blackstone kiss and hug his wife goodbye had suddenly made Will hotly jealous and bitter. He buried the feelings down deep, for they were completely unwarranted. By the side of the carriage, with a luggage bag in hand, Will closed his eyes and prayed for the Lord to grant him strength.

They first arrived at Parkinson's Temple, where Will was given an insurance contract and a waiver form from a clerk from the Palace. He read both sheets top to bottom, not missing a single word or meaning.

The waiver form basically stated that he was bound to stay in Carsiss and perform his duties for at least a year, after which time he was compelled to come home and make a report. It also stressed that should he do something that would place him in disfavor or serious trouble, the kingdom would disavow any responsibility for him, just as Sir Hamsfield had said it would.

The insurance contract promised a handsome settlement amounting to five hundred pounds to each of three people he named. He chose Sir Blackstone, Tony Beckins, and Sister Amy Kaltrine, the current head of the orphanage he grew up in. (He later learned that the other two ambassadors were promised one-thousand-pound settlements, for their posts were less dangerous. "Such is the nature of insurance, where every head has a price," he quipped.) Shortly after signing the contract, he was surprised when the Palace clerk gave him a money voucher at a clothing store and a ticket to a ship named the *Desert Lily*.

Printed on the money voucher was the name DANIEL'S EXOTIC WEAR—a fine clothing store that dealt in both contemporary and foreign styles of dress. Will picked out two pieces of clothing called *lungis*, which were basically loincloths worn tightly around the body. He also got traditional trousers, jackets, and vests which he heard were common among Carsiss' elite. And although bare feet were common in Carsiss, Will made sure to get three pairs of sandals and one pair of snakeskin boots. (The total cost came to three hundred pounds, which was no light expense, but the shopkeeper assured them that the voucher would cover every pence of it.)

Before heading off to the shore, they stopped at a fancy restaurant called THE BOSCOLANES, named after an old god of nature and harvest. Sir Blackstone ordered a dish of squid ("What is it with you and hideous seafood?" Will had asked) while Will ordered a dish commonly found in Cariss: carved flying fish seasoned with hot spices, served with a side of fiery hot peppers and chili beans.

"I suppose they don't have pumpkins or squash down there," Sir Blackstone said.

"No, fertile soil is very rare, usually found around the mountains far to the south," Will said.

"How far south?"

"Farther than how the Apaches Mountains are as far from our own shore." (The Apache Mountains was where Thayland's capital was located; they could be seen from the restaurant's broad windows.)

"I can't imagine a land with no fertile soil," Sir Blackstone said, shaking his head. The slight disdain in his tone couldn't be missed. "I've been as far out as the swamplands of Diokarnissi, but I've never seen anything like this 'desert' that Carsiss has. I heard it's like the seashore only with no water. It's just *sand*—a whole helluva lotta sand. Who would want to live out there?"

"Living in such conditions can make a man and his people strong," Will said, using the same tone that Professor Roth would use in stating that same thing.

"Yes, but a man can also die in such conditions," Sir Blackstone said with a sly eye. "Don't get in over your head down there, okay?"

Will nodded, then popped a pepper into his mouth and tried not to scrunch his face as he chewed.

"Are you sure about going?" Sir Blackstone asked.

Will swallowed and breathed in through the corners of his mouth. "It's a little too late to be thinking that. I signed the waiver and everything."

"Yes, but I've always wondered if there was some big reason why you wanted to go there—some reason you've never told me."

"No, I haven't held anything back. There's no reason bigger than to expand my horizons, see the world beyond my own country."

"You're interested in being a regular diplomat, then?"

"I might ... but we'll have to see how my current trip goes first."

They made one more stop before leaving the city, and that was to shop for food to take on the road. They crossed the city limits at seven o' clock, and the driver didn't stop until they reached Santa Mona at nine in the morning. There the driver rested while Will and Sir Blackstone bought more provisions and checked the stores for any more Carsian-style clothing. Seven hours later they departed once more, this time heading for Will's old hometown, although there was yet another stop before it.

The Elf-Tree Inn, a combination hotel, restaurant and tavern, served as a regular pit stop between Santa Mona and Georgetown. Nearly every night, one could see an unusual mishmash of rabble and upscale folk indulging in the inn's luxuries, whether it was the strong brew, fine dining, or comfortable rooms and room service.

Will always visited during trips to his hometown. In early years, he had always greeted the inn's two owners, Anthony and Marian Dwight. But a few years ago, in one of the world's most true injustices, Anthony had quickly divorced Marian before their title with the inn had to be renewed; he had then left her name out of the title and gave her the boot. Will had given him a piece of his mind for that, for he and Marian had been good acquaintances ("She shed a good share of blood and tears over this place, and this is how you thank her!?"). Shortly after, Anthony married again. His new wife, like his first one, had a fiery temper and a sharp tongue, but little of Marian's good-natured hospitality and sense of fairness. After that debacle, Will never bothered to greet the inn's owners.

When they arrived at Georgetown the following afternoon, Sir Blackstone asked if Will wanted to briefly visit his old orphanage. "I can't," Will said. "I lost that pendant they gave me. It would be a disgrace."

"I'm sure they won't care about that," Sir Blackstone said. "It wasn't your fault, anyway."

"Yes, it was, in part. I put it up for the challenge, and I'm sure once old Sister Alex hears about it, she'll give me such a scolding that will put all her previous ones to shame."

Before they had left the manor, they had received another message by courier, this one informing them of Will's apparent loss in the race. It stated that while Will had clearly lost because of the doves, it was curious that he had run away with no explanation and no resolve to oversee the scandal. It made no mention of whether or not the doves' releasers were caught.

"We should have told them about the appointment after all," Will continued. "I know it would be unwise to let them think the race came only second in our concerns, but at least they would have understood my haste to leave. That would have turned things in my favor."

"I think you're wrong," Sir Blackstone said. "To Lord

Mayweather, there's nothing as important as winning a challenge and building up your reputation. He also might think your ambassadorship would be a waste of time—do you know why?"

"Because he has no stake in it?"

"That's right, and whether you like it or not, our alliance with Carsiss is a shaky and unpopular one. We beat them at war hundreds of years ago, and the only reason we didn't invade was because of their climate. Many people today still believe that we could throw away our alliance with Carsiss and nothing bad would come of it. That of course doesn't have to be *your* opinion."

They went straight through Georgetown and came upon Brussels late next morning, which was just a stone's throw away from the shore. They stopped near the pier where the *Desert Lily* was stationed and hired some hands to help with the luggage.

Lord Harrington was already onboard the ship, which was merely a cargo-holder with boxes of craftsmen's goods. "Hardly the lap of luxury, wouldn't you say, my lord?" Will asked him.

"They must be finicky with the finances," Lord Harrington replied. He looked at Will's large luggage bags. "I'm sure our free fashion wear already came at a significant expense."

"So you don't mind?" Will asked. "I'm surprised—I assumed the kingdom would be sure to escort nobles in style and comfort."

"Well there are conditions to be met, William. I would have to raise a fuss and threaten to tell everyone about how frugal the King is to have them consider hiring a liner for us."

Will nodded. He believed he would like Lord Harrington—he was proving to be more realistic and less prudish than most other nobles he had known. Of course one large piece of evidence of that was that he didn't believe Carsiss' alliance was merely expendable.

Franklin Douglass arrived sometime later, riding a shabby coach-for-hire and starved for food. Despite his celebrity within the Church's choir, he had fell on hard times, and the government spared only a small purse for travel expenses. Will frowned at that news; hauling them aboard a cargo ship was one thing, but being cheap on the carriage expenses was another.

Once Franklin and Will had all their things onboard, Will went to Sir Blackstone. "This is goodbye, sir."

"So long, Will," Sir Blackstone said with a warm smile. "Have a safe trip. Don't take any wooden nickels. Don't let anyone take advantage of you too much. Don't do anything I wouldn't do."

"Yes, sir."

"This may be the last we'll see each other," Sir Blackstone said matter-of-factly. At that, Will raised his brow and felt a lump grow in his throat. But then Sir Blackstone said with a laugh, "You might like it down there so much you'll never want to come back."

Will smiled and shook his head in reply. He had naturally thought his master was hinting at his possible death in Carsiss, but that was probably part of the joke. In later times, though, when he reflected back to those words, he wondered if Sir Blackstone really *had* meant his death, but then he suddenly turned it around into a joke so as not to distress him. Although he would have plenty of time to ask him what his original meaning was, he would never take the opportunity—he'd figure he didn't want to know the original meaning.

They firmly shook hands (for gentlemen of Thayland never embraced), and then Will climbed aboard the *Desert Lily*. The ambassadors stood by the starboard bow as the crewmen rowed the boat out to sea; shortly after the captain ordered to set sail, they stepped into the crew's quarters to eat apple slices and sandwiches of salted meat—one of several things that could stay fresh on their two-week-long voyage to Carsiss.

Franklin and Lord Harrington mostly slept on the way, for there wasn't much for them to do onboard. Will helped around on the ship, which involved spooling rope and peeling potatoes. In that latter task, he was usually paired up with a young man named Carness—a Carsian who had made it a lifelong ambition to see the Palace of Thayland. He said he finally did it a year ago, when he won a post on a brief mercantile expedition.

"And how was it?" Will asked.

"I was impressed with the double-layered defense walls," Carness said. "And the garden out front was large and very green—you can't get something like that in Carsiss. But other than that, there wasn't much else to exalt. I think the Emperor's Palace in Nünveghett is the grandest structure in the entire world—a fitting worldly testament to the providence of the gods. Once you see it, you'll understand."

Will also conversed with Lord Harrington, asking for as much of his experiences in Carsiss that he could remember. He spoke with Franklin only sparsely, mostly on details concerning his overall role in the Carsian Palace. At one point, he finally let out his curiosity of Franklin's special mission, making sure the crew's quarters were only a little populated and that their whispers were out of earshot.

"I know you've been chosen to do it because of your condition," he said, speaking in Carsian (the three of them only spoke in Carsian, for it would do them no good to get out of practice). "But I'm curious: Do you think you'll actually be able to ... to perform?"

"I've been preparing myself for it," Franklin replied. "I've been going over it in my mind, and yes, I think I'll be able."

Will took a moment to think through what he was going to say next. "I know it's not in my place to dissuade you in your mission—and I'm not going to dissuade you, really—but I really must ask this. You know the Church doesn't approve of this behavior you may be about to do, and I know you're only acting on the King's orders. But what do you think about it? Anything at all?"

Franklin made a small smile as he thought of an answer. He then said, "When I was told of my mission, someone said to me that God made Man in His own image. All of our faults, all of our strengths, they were all put into His design. If someone like the Emperor was designed to behave that way, it's because of his design, his *image.*"

"Wait, you mean the Emperor doesn't act that way on choice? That he was designed or born that way?"

"Of course, he'd have to be. No one in a right frame of mind would be a ruler of a powerful nation and act that way by choice. He'd know he'd lose face. So he must have been designed that way. At least let's give the Emperor that much credit, shall we?"

Will nodded but only tentatively. It would take some time before he completely agreed with Franklin's theory that men who bedded other men did so because they were designed to. He had always assumed that that behavior was voluntary, and that such men were of a confused and curious sort. But he would often reflect back to something Professor Roth had said—that there were men in Carsiss who experimented with that behavior only to give up on it. They must have done so because they were not designed for it, as Will himself was not. But it must take a man of a different design like the Emperor to perform that behavior and stick with it, for that was the only logical conclusion. Will would then begin to wonder on the profoundness of his attraction towards women, for it was not voluntary but instilled within him like seeds in a fruit, and it would only take extraordinary circumstances to take it out of him ... well, either that or a snip below the belt.

In other words, if men like the Emperor had their attractions as he had his, then there wasn't much anyone could about it, now was there? King Fredrick must have thought that some time ago to make him go against Church doctrine in such an audacious fashion.

CHAPTER 8
SCORPION

THE MEN ABOARD THE *Desert Lily* could not have wished for better weather, nor for a more cooperative wind. A journey of two weeks turned out to last twelve days instead. By the fifth day, Will learned why the crew had been so tightfisted with the drinking water: When the ship got a stone's throw away from the desert nation, the temperature grew like the inside of an oven. Instead of opening one barrel of water that day, the captain ordered two opened. On the last day, the captain was so pleased with their progress that he opened the remaining four.

Carsiss first appeared as a light-yellow thread on the horizon, which eventually grew into a daffodil petal disturbing the surface of a monstrous lake. He never admitted it, but Will was a little intimidated to see that the beach didn't seem to have an end, that it seemed to stretch beyond the shoreline and yet didn't welcome him to build sandcastles. It was a desert, and Sir Blackstone's direct warnings suddenly carried more weight. The master had never been in Carsiss, but he somehow knew what he was talking about.

"Now remember," Will said to the other diplomats on the starboard bow, "it's 'Carsian,' not 'Carsissian'—because no one likes being called a sissy."

Franklin was confused; Lord Harrington cracked a smile. "When I first saw Carsiss from here," the lord said, "I remarked how old it appeared, like a bone left out in the wind for a thousand years. My friend Lord Breyer said, 'Carsiss was old even when it was new. It is a land steeped in traditions and beliefs older than anything in Thayland.' I later found myself tempted to believe it."

The ship docked at the port town of Markereen. It was a modest place of considerable worth, but it mostly served merely as a gateway for the nation's capital resting two leagues away. Several young men at the docks offered to carry their bags; they were shooed away, as Lord Harrington labeled them as desert rats who would steal their luggage as soon as they grasped them. In the town center, the ambassadors hired two rickshaws (two-wheeled vehicles pulled by men) at the lord's expense and promptly went to the nearest bank, where they exchanged all of their Thayland pounds for Carsian rupees.

The rickshaws then carried them to a public stable where they hired four camels for the journey to the capital. It was the first time Will had ever seen such creatures, which in his eyes looked like bizarre horses with anthills for backs and feather dusters for eyelashes. He was told to be careful around them, for they were rascally, temperamental beasts. Will could believe it by observing how they periodically spat like snuff-chewing drunkards over a spittoon.

It took them three hours to get to Nünveghett (Will wryly noted that horses could have taken under an hour, but he admitted that horses were a far cry from camels, which could survive in the desert with only a small amount of water). While it was a very expansive city, spreading out from the northern side of the Saparel Mountains, it wasn't very impressive, what with its simple adobe dwellings and sandy streets. But its city life was nevertheless just as active as Augustine's, and more. In the marketplaces and byways, there were traveling entertainers doing all sorts of things Will had never seen before—things that no one in Thayland would ever care to do, but which were impressive and amusing nonetheless. There were men who stretched their bodies to their limits, wrapping their legs up and around their necks and then walking on their hands; there were snake-charmers who seemingly defied death by staring into the eyes of a cobra right in front of them, controlling them somehow with the music of their flutes; and there were flame-eaters who stuck blazing sticks or swords down their throats and then blew a fierce flame through their pursed lips. There were so many examples of entertainment on the streets, ranging from the familiar to the absolutely exotic. Will could hardly wait to take the time to partake in them all.

To the left was the Calkune River, which they had traveled along since leaving Markereen. It was the nation's most holy river, for the people believed that a portion of its waters went to the underworld. The people visited it frequently—there was never any time of day when it was sparsely populated. As it ran through the city, it had no banks; instead it was flanked by long stairways called *ghats,* which made it easy for everyone to observe the river and the crowds from afar. There were *ghats* made for different uses, bathing especially, but also praying, laundry-washing, and funeral services where the remains were cremated and sprinkled on the water's surface.

Everyone wore much the same sort of clothing as the ambassadors. Men usually wore *dhotis,* which were like loincloths but covered the whole legs, and women wore *saris* (long cloths that were wrapped around the body) in a large variety of styles and designs.

The Untouchables, on the other hand, were not as visually appealing. They were easily singled out by their *lungis,* which were simple, undecorated loincloths, or in the case of women, bland, undecorated *saris*. They were not found in the marketplaces, buying food and necessities, for they had to grow their own food and make their own things, holding markets only amongst themselves. They were in that part of the city only to bathe in the river, where they used no soap and had to stay at certain *ghats* that were small and kempt only by themselves. Looking at them reminded Will of the sort of place he was in.

In Thayland a lowly peasant could work hard or implement an ingenious moneymaking scheme to elevate in status and prestige; likewise, a rich and influential politician or nobleman could become corrupt and fall from grace, ending up with nothing. The social classes in Thayland were only a matter of mind and ability. In Carsiss, however, social classes were locked into place, and no one had any hope or possibility of rising or falling in their respective class. This social structure was known as the caste system.

Earlier, in Parkinson's Temple, Will had recited his knowledge of these caste classes, which were called *varnas* in Carsian. At the top were the *Brahmans*—the priests whose duties were to pray and encourage the people to follow the paths to salvation. Below them were the *Ksatriyas*—the nobles who ran government and business affairs. The third *varna* down included the *Vaisyas*—the common people who needed strong backs to handle most of the nation's hard labor. And at the very bottom were the *Sudras*, the Untouchables, called so because it was up to them to handle the nation's least desirable jobs—those that involved touching dirt, filth, dung, and corpses.

In Hinduism, the official religion of Carsiss, there was the belief that people continuously went through a cycle of life and death. Those who died with their souls marred by sin were destined to return to earth reborn as another (whether they arrived as a man or a woman made little difference). The cycle was called "reincarnation," and it was the theory and justification behind the existence of the caste system.

In Thayland sin was the name for any kind of wrongdoing; in

Carsiss sin was considered a kind of pollution of the soul caused by such wrongdoings. *Karma* was the name of the accumulation of sin. Those who died with an "unpolluted" or "pure" *karma* were bound to return to earth as one of the higher *varnas* of the caste system, such as the *Brahmans* or the *Ksatriyas*. But those who died with a considerably "impure" *karma* were bound to return as one of the lower *varnas,* such as the *Vaisyas* or the *Sudras* (assumingly as a kind of punishment). No matter what *varna* one was born into, however, it was up to everyone to do good by their fellow man and cleanse their souls of sin. Even the lowliest *Sudra* could hope to become a *Ksatriya* or *Brahman* in his next life by doing good deeds and appeasing the gods. (As a final note, there was a way to end one's cycle of reincarnation, and that was to fully cleanse one's soul of any sin and then forever be at one with the universe.)

It was a system accorded by the gods, and thus it was Carsiss' duty to instill and uphold the caste system for the sake of all souls. It did not apply to Will and the other two ambassadors, though, for they were not born in Carsiss. One could only be born into the caste system, not be incorporated into it. That was why the *varnas* were nicknamed *jatis,* after the Carsian word *jati,* meaning "birth." Carsians believed it was up to other nations whether or not to implement the caste system into their own societies and thus become a logical component of reincarnation. (However, it should be noted that the Hindu religion was very tolerant of other faiths, even going so far as to say that no one faith could be dismissed as completely false. So while Hindu holy men would like to see the caste system implemented in other countries, they never say that it was their divine duty to do so.)

Even from out in the desert, following along the Calkune, Will could easily make out the Emperor's Palace. But it wasn't until he came within a hundred meters or so when he admitted that Carness was right—the palace in Nünveghett was much bigger and more impressive than the one in Augustine.

It wasn't so much the size of it as it was the sheer imagination and the clever construction methods put into it. For one thing, it didn't seem to have any obvious corners; most of everything was rounded out so that all edges were smooth and all platforms and walls were serpentine. Numerous pillars and large towers seemed to emphasis that concept of roundness, or maybe it was that the designer enjoyed making them too much. But the concept of roundness was most exemplified by the wondrous cone-shaped spires called *sikharas* mounted atop each tower. Overall the Palace looked like something nature could have built, especially since it fit into a mountainside like a hand in a glove.

For another thing, while much of the Palace was made of marble like King Thayland's Palace, the Carsian constructors did not skimp on using gold as another working material. Of course, since gold was a soft metal, it was not used as support, only as decoration. Golden statues stared out from atop the towers and battlements; golden flowers and vines dotted the patios and windows; and things such as banisters, painting frames, and vases were made either entirely or partially of gold. Gold was especially plentiful on the walls, making up designs that complimented the elaborate engravings. Many people wondered why King Fredrick was sending ambassadors to the Carsian Emperor instead of visiting him personally; Will himself didn't know, but he thought it was good, for he would undoubtedly grind his teeth in jealously upon looking at all that gold.

What were particularly impressive (in a subtle if not astounding way) were the holy temples nearby the Palace, for they were not built by the mountainside but *into* it. Their façades looked merely like sculptures shaped on the massive rock surface, but if one were to walk through the front door of one of them, they would see that an entire building had been cut right into the mountain, with all the furnishings and necessities that any building would need—only the interior was very rocky, of course.

The Calkune made its way past the Palace's outer defense wall with no consequence, for the wall had not been built to fit snugly alongside it, nor had a moat been made to fortify the defenses. The ambassadors crossed it via a large granite bridge, from which they observed *ghats* below where commoners bathed. They met a pair of cautious soldiers on the other side by the main gate. Will observed how lightly armored they were: They wore little metal, relying instead on thick padding for defense, underneath of which they wore normal clothing. He supposed he'd have to dress like them once his army days began.

Lord Harrington dismounted and showed the soldiers a letter from King Fredrick. It was in Carsian so the soldiers could read it, and they were trained to recognize the King's signature, which was written with a flourish and had the T in "Thayland" shaped like a tall cross. The soldiers nodded and Sir Harrington mounted himself again.

The wooden doors were swung open and the iron portcullis beyond them was raised. They passed the outer wall, and Will was given another surprise about the Emperor's Palace: Within its walls was something much like a small town, with modest buildings scattered around beneath the gaze of the enormous Palace proper. The Palace of Thayland had its share of related structures in its surroundings, but only the Palace itself was worthy of the King's residence; the structures around the Emperor's Palace, however, were all grand, decorous, and clean, fit for a ruler to visit—which the Emperor undoubtedly did, discontented to sit in the Palace proper all day.

The road was paved, which the camels didn't seem to like though it made for smoother travel. They went straight for the Palace proper, where they met dozens of servants who promptly flanked them and threw pink and white flower petals on the road before them. Lord Harrington dismounted at the foot of the grand stairway and rose his hands as if to say, "Okay, enough is enough now." Franklin laughed and held his hands out while Will just observed all the petal-throwing with a kind of curious daze.

They entered the main foyer, which was much larger than the one in King Fredrick's Palace (if Will's memory was correct). It had a glassy marble floor that looked clean enough to eat off of, a number of flying buttresses across the arched ceiling, and hundreds if not thousands of designs and pictures covering everything from the walls to the ceiling and the pillars. There were images of the gods at war, the gods in peace, and the gods in lovemaking (some of those latter ones were quite graphic, which made Will flush and become not a little excited).

A tall, gangly man approached them from the side. He wore an orange turban embedded with a golden crescent moon. His eyes seemed too big for him, and they seemingly had mascara painted around them. His beard was made of wavy hairs, but it was neatly trimmed as it ended at a point. He welcomed them by wrapping a hand over a fist in front of him and bowing. No strangers to Carsian custom, the ambassadors did likewise. "Emperor Baku sends you his greetings," the man said. "I am Halicut Khan, the Prime Dieschsuch of Carsiss. If you will just follow me, I will lead you to His Eminence."

The ambassadors thanked him, though they were a little puzzled over how such an important man was appointed to lead them to the Emperor. A Dieschsuch (díce-chek) was a sort of minister under the Emperor's direct command. Unlike the Ministers of Thayland, the Dieschsuchs of Carsiss were not allowed to dispute the Emperor's orders or even suggest alternatives to them. The Emperor's commands were absolute.

Hailcut Khan led them to an upstairs hallway and invited them to sit. The chairs were rigid but comfortable enough, made of bronze and polished leather. "The Emperor will see you shortly," he said, then parted ways with them, leaving them under the gaze of two stone-faced guards with spears.

After an awkward silence, Will said, "Will the designs of this place ever cease?"

Lord Harrington smiled. "Many of Carsiss' finest sculptors and painters have made the Emperor's Palace their canvass. Emperor Orissu oversaw much of the art done here, though his son Baku has done very little so far."

"What were all those buildings out there, my lord?"

"Well, one of them's a museum, another's a smithy, and another's a cartography studio. There's even a grand hall where feasts are held for festivals or victory celebrations. Emperor Banschhek from long ago had decided once that despite all the different rooms of the Palace, he wanted more. Of course some of the functions of those buildings, like the smithy, aren't suitable to be placed in the Palace, so they are placed out there."

"Why a smithy?" Franklin asked. "Aren't there enough smithies out in the city?"

"I suppose there are. But the smithy is for the Emperor's personal use. The blacksmiths there make armor for the general army, but if the Emperor himself needs something mended or a new weapon or armor to be made, they must drop everything they are doing and get right to work on it."

"This place is so *big,*" Franklin muttered. "I'm going to get lost in here, I know it."

"Don't worry about it," Will said. "Just follow the trail of bread crumbs ... or the trail of archaeopteryx feathers," he added, referring to the Carsian version of *Hansel and Gretel.*

He then asked Lord Harrington for what he knew about Emperor Baku. Harrington said he knew only that he was twenty-six years old and had a love of hunting. The ambassadors made only little chitchat after that, waiting patiently for the Emperor to be ready to see them.

One hour dragged on to two. At that point, they were getting restless and wondered what the Emperor was doing to make them wait so long. Then two hours dragged on to three, and they began to worry that something was wrong. Perhaps their hosts had mistakenly thought the Emperor was inside the Palace, when in fact he was not. Perhaps Baku hadn't expected them to arrive two days early, and so he went out to do some errands. Still, making them wait without a reason was careless and inexcusable. Franklin said he planned on giving their hosts a piece of his mind.

"No, you won't," Lord Harrington replied to that. "Like it or not, we are at the mercy of the Emperor and his hosts. Even if they give us a bad impression, we must make a good impression, which means avoiding unnecessary confrontations."

"Maybe things will turn around once we meet His Eminence," Will said. "I suppose long waits are the least of what can go wrong in these diplomatic missions."

It was evening, and the servants were going about lighting torches around the Palace (oddly enough there were no candles around, only torches—another difference between the two palaces). The ambassadors were talking about the holidays and festivals they could expect to see in Carsiss, when they were finally brought to their feet by an unassuming servant. "His Eminence will now see you. Pray follow me."

They were led to what looked like a war room, with maps on the walls and surveying equipment scattered around. One map on the wall showed the Calkune River running from east to west—although they had approached the mouth of the Calkune from the north. Hence another difference between their countries, as mapmakers had different opinions of what direction was north. Thayland's north was Carsiss' west, and so Carsians claimed they had a western shore, though Will and the others would say they had only a northern shore. Thayland mapmakers determined their north by the location of the world's icelands, while Carsian mapmakers determined their north by the course of the sun. It made little difference, though, except for how maps were made.

Awaiting the ambassadors was not one man but three, and it wasn't hard to tell which one of them was the Emperor. He was the only one in the Empire who could bear the insignia of the sun on his turban, which was merely a golden circle with spikes protruding all around. Other than his headpiece, he wore only a pair of baggy silk pants and sandals. He was apparently no slacker, for he was healthy and fit, clearly a man not to be trifled with. His scalp appeared shaven around his turban, and his goatee was kept short and neat. He seemed to be wearing mascara, which was exclusive to women in Thayland but apparently not so in Carsiss, seeing as how the other two men also wore some. He was not as striking as Will had expected him to be, like someone larger than life somehow, but he was nonetheless quite handsome—a true heartbreaker if he wanted to be.

He wrapped a hand around a fist and bowed. "Welcome to Carsiss, sons of Thayland," he said. "You have had a long trip, and I shall see that you are made as comfortable here as we can make you."

The ambassadors bowed in return. Will noted that the Emperor spoke in a rather soft tone, but one that did not necessarily indicate a benevolent nature. He sounded a little cautious of his visitors, as if expecting them to make the mistake of insulting a high ruler. He probably had a rather highhanded view of himself, for it was believed that he appointed to his position by providence.

"Thank you for taking us into your company," Lord Harrington said. "May your nights be long and your days fruitful. I am Lord Samuel Harrington of Reckshire, and this is Franklin Douglass of Barringsworth, and this is William Fontaine of Augustine."

"Sons of Thayland, may I introduce you to Lord Darric Lamahn, the overlord of Dekla province, and Lord Hineson Bek, the overlord of Darmine province."

The ambassadors bowed at length, for they were some high-class titles in Carsiss, second only to the Dieschsuchs.

"Please have a seat, all of you," the Emperor continued. "There is just one more thing I must take care of before I join you."

Will and the others did as told. They found pitchers of wine and water that were surprising fresh, as well as melons, sliced coconuts, and green peppers.

Emperor Baku proceeded to the other side of the room, where he plucked something moving within a jar with a pair of tongs. Will couldn't quite make out what it was until the Emperor moved into a torch's light. It was a spider, and a big one at that. He brought it to a glass bowel that was unusually broad and filled with large sand grains; crawling over those grains were scorpions, which Will had his eyes on since he first entered the room.

The Emperor turned to them with the spider in front of him

twitching its legs as if it could grab a foothold on the air around it. "My friends, in Thayland your personification of evil is the snake, who slithers its way into your homes and makes false promises through its poison-filled fangs. In Carsiss it is the spider, who crawls and bites whatever is warm and soft, like flesh. It creeps into our homes and lies silently, subtly, waiting for its time to strike.

"The only enemy it has other than man is the scorpion. True, the scorpion is much like the spider, for it also crawls and is filled with poison—but its deadly nectar is found in its stinger, not its fangs. By having it in its stinger, it gives a clear warning to anyone who strays near it, giving them no question as to what it is capable of. Not so with a spider, which kills with what it also uses to eat with."

The Emperor dropped the spider into the scorpion bowel, where it was immediately attacked by the inhabitants. After one swift strike and two more for good measure, it was killed and feasted on by the larger arachnids. It didn't even have a chance.

"Carsiss is like the scorpion," the Emperor continued. "We give clear warning to anyone who dares to threaten us ... and our allies."

He gave a small bow. Lord Darric lifted a glass of wine, said, "Excellent show, Your Eminence!" and then polished his drink.

CHAPTER 9
THE OLD AND THE NEW

THEIR INITIAL CONVERSATION WAS not of nation-related issues but of each other, as Lord Harrington suggested it should be. Lord Harrington told little of himself; instead he went on about his son who was well on his way to becoming the next dean of the university he was attending, what with his excellent grades and social-climbing. Franklin merely said he had been an esteemed singer in the Church's choir, and that he was not married nor willing to marry anytime soon. He made no mention of his castration, which was not only for politeness' sake but was also to avoid any conflict with the Carsians, who might take offense. His hope (well, the *ambassadors'* hope) was that his nature would be self-evident and the Emperor would act accordingly.

Will said he was an esquire—a knight in training. At that the Emperor took a keen interest in him. He asked, "I've heard of your esquires: They are not only students, they are like indentured servants. Am I correct?"

"Yes, Your Eminence," Will replied.

"Your parents must be very strong to let you go at such an early age."

"Actually no, my parents are unknown to me. I was raised in a sanctuary for orphans."

"So you are a bastard then?"

Will took offense to that, but all he showed for it were raised eyebrows for a split second. "I don't know if I am or not, Your Eminence. My parents are unknown."

"I see ..." The Emperor sipped from his wine glass. He was probably one of those drunks who couldn't help saying the first thing that popped into their heads. "Is it true that part of a knight's training is to run through a course filled with giant swinging hammers?"

"Why yes, Your Eminence, that's true."

"Have you gone through it?"

"No, Your Eminence."

"So you are not a knight?"

"No, Your Eminence."

"So why do you want to join our army? Is this part of a knight's training?"

"No, it's nothing to do with my training."

"His Eminence makes a good point," Lord Darric said. He was a rotund fellow who was by then dangerously swinging his wine glass around, spilling some of its fresh contents on his expansive robe. "Don't you know we're at war, son of Thayland? We're up against the Mulvars, a tribe of bloodthirsty savages who rape our women and steal our babies in the middle of night. There's no hope we can be rid of their barbaric filth, but we'd be damned if we don't try. So why would you want to join our army and go up against them? Got something to prove?"

It *was* a good point, and Will knew he couldn't use the same old "to broaden my horizons" excuse he had used on Sir Blackstone. "I had a friend suggest it to me. She said it would be in my best interest to go to Carsiss."

"Do you love her?" Lord Darric asked. "Do you want to marry her someday? I know that marriages in Thayland are not arranged."

"No, it's not that kind of love. It's just that I trust her implicitly, and she's never steered me wrong before."

He couldn't tell them any more than that without starting to make up details. Fortunately the men in the room seemed satisfied enough with what he gave them. Will nodded and drank more of his watered-down wine.

He couldn't tell them that the girl in question was Marie the ghost girl—the phantom who had given him the seeing glass and sent him on a journey that had taken him inside the King's Palace and even to the King himself (King Fredrick's uncle, King James). Ever since that ordeal nine years ago, he'd been seeing Marie every so often in that forgotten basement on the edge of a plantation.

Eight years ago, she had told him that he should go to Carsiss, but not right away. She said he should take his time, learn about Carsiss and its language first and apply for an ambassadorship. He asked why he should do that, but her reasons were muddled and oblique. She just said there was something there he had to see, something that the whole world should know. Knowing her tendency for puzzling statements, he took her word that he should go to Carsiss, even though he had no clue what he was looking for.

"The *Brahmans* say women are a hair closer to the gods," the Emperor said, "so the gods can whisper into their ears better than they can with men."

"The *Brahmans* who said that must have imbibed more than

we have!" Lord Darric cried.

"Don't dismiss the *Brahmans* so easily like that," the Emperor said. "They are our superiors after all. And the gods must surely be listening, for *I* am listening."

Lord Darric appeared shamefaced. Will meanwhile thought about what the Emperor said: To an ignorant son of Thayland, the Emperor's remarks would have meant that the *Brahmans* had more power than the Emperor, and that they could order him around, take control of the nation's future. But their superiority was actually theoretical, not actual. The *Brahmans,* being priests who were closer than anyone else to *moksha*—the final emancipation of the soul—were more favored in the grand scheme of the universe, but it was up to the *Ksatriyas,* such as the overlords and the Emperor, who made the laws and enforced them. Even the *Brahmans* had to obey whatever order they were given—although it was unwise to cross them, for they were highly favored by the people.

"Is there a woman in your life, William Fontaine?" the Emperor asked.

Will was suddenly uncomfortable with all the attention. The Emperor was asking him more questions than he had asked either of the other two diplomats. The Emperor might have thought his station in life was more fascinating, or perhaps it was because of his dark skin, which was closer in color to the Emperor's bronze skin (which was what he had expected even before his voyage) ... or perhaps it was the Emperor's rumored sexual orientation that made him take a shine to him. "No, Your Eminence," he said. "Well, there *was,* but not right now. I wouldn't be opposed to it."

"I see," the Emperor said with a chuckle. "Well, not to worry, William—you'll find a mate someday, and a good one at that."

"Your Eminence, I've heard that the gods have blessed you with one of their own," Lord Harrington said. "When shall we have the pleasure of meeting her?"

"Ah, she is away on matters of diplomacy," the Emperor said. "She is trying to patch up relations between two tribal leaders in Darmine province, where she will also be on vacation."

"The two tribes are fighting over a mountain spring," Lord Hineson said. He was a tall man with bushy eyebrows and a prominently narrow chin. "I say to you, sons of Thayland, would it be possible to increase shipments of your water and have them delivered straight to my province?"

"That is a matter for another day," the Emperor said. "And besides, that may not help things, for the water must be charged and levied, while the spring water is always free. Let us call it a night, and then we shall get to business tomorrow."

The Emperor and the two overlords sat cross-legged on the floor and said the *Gayatrimantra*—a Hindu prayer recited at the beginning and end of every day—followed by a recitation of a part of the *Rigveda*—one of four holy scriptures called the *Vedas*. The ambassadors were not invited to attend and were free to leave for their rooms, for they were not of the Hindu faith which one could only be born into.

Will had thought he'd have to stay in a barrack or a tent like all the other soldiers, but a room for him was prepared in the Palace. It was of a modest size but just as beautifully decorated as the rest of the building. At the bed Will found satin sheets and a mattress full of fluffy down—perhaps goose feathers. It was the most comfortable bed he'd ever been in, but he thought he might still have trouble sleeping. He just couldn't get used to the blasted heat which he couldn't escape from, even within the deep confines of the Palace. He was sweaty all over, and he understood why people were willing to bathe in the same river that they put ashes in; it was because the heat made you sweat so bad you stunk like an animal after just half a day. He could probably frolic with pigs in mud and couldn't come out less unclean than he felt just then.

Well, Marie, I'm here, he thought before he lied himself down. *I know you'd never send me on a wild goose chase here, but I hope things go more smoothly than last time.*

Shortly after daybreak, he discovered why the Emperor's Palace was built where it was: There was a large spring bursting from within the mountain. The water was said to come up hot and bubbling, but it cooled down considerably by the time it reached the pools near the inner garden. Will had learned that the Emperor had given the ambassadors permission to use his personal bathing pool as he made his morning offering to the deceased and his recitation of the Gayatrimantra. He found the other two diplomats there and joined them to complain about the heat.

"It's not so bad once you get used to it," Lord Harrington said. "Unlike some places, Nünveghett has an abundance of fresh groundwater, so be sure to drink your fill every day, as there's plenty to go around."

"Groundwater, huh?" Will mused. "So I won't have to fill up jars at the river, then."

"You made quite an impression last night, Will," Franklin said. "The Emperor seemed more interested in you than either of us."

Will merely shrugged and said nothing. Even in the morning light, he was still uncomfortable with the attention.

"Perhaps it's not like you think, Will," Lord Harrington said. "The Emperor seems like a warrior himself, so he'd naturally want to know more about a warrior from Thayland. If you play your cards right, flatter him without overdoing it, you could find yourself in a favorable position here."

"I don't plan to stay here," Will said. "Carsiss may be a good place to visit, but it's not home to me."

"No one's expecting you to stay, but if you make good allies here, you could be more indebted by the King than you could ever dream. Just think about it and look for opportunities. It's what you're here for, though you may not know it."

They met the Emperor in the dining hall, joining him for a breakfast of roasted duck served with vegetables and *chapati,* a type of flat white bread. They talked of Carsiss' state in foreign affairs, with Lord Harrington making questions that tested the nation's loyalty to Thayland: "As you may well know, Your Eminence, nations have always used exports as a way to reward and punish other nations. Would you adhere to a policy of controlling exports when making demands?"

"It would depend on the demand," the Emperor said. "If you refused to help with a life-and-death situation, then I would cut off all trade with Thayland. However it would not be wise to simply lessen or increase exports for trivial matters, for that would affect the merchants as well as me. The merchants don't like being played like pawns, and I must respect that."

"What if a shipment of water or some other essential item was stolen by pirates, and the King said a new shipment couldn't be made until after a week. Would you decrease your exports to balance the trade between our nations?"

The Emperor shook his head with a sly smile. "Why would I do that? Imports bring in supplies; exports bring in money. Even if we could not have that water, at least we would have money. This rewards-and-punishment system you speak of seems like a game for children."

"Indeed it is," Lord Harrington said.

"Forgive me for asking," the Emperor said, "but is that your king's policy? Would he go so far as to punish me?"

Lord Harrington thought about it. "Situations vary so there is really no telling, but over trivial matters I know His Majesty would never decrease exports. He has his own merchant community to think about."

"A very wise man, I'm sure," the Emperor said. "I have met him before, but I could not judge him well. He is interesting but ... unreadable."

After breakfast, they walked in the halls (always under the watchful eyes of armed guards awaiting any bold assassination attempts) and discussed Thayland's relation with Thorain, and what Carsiss could do if Thorain were to suddenly invade again. "My father sent soldiers there when Thorain last invaded," the Emperor said. "I shall follow his example and send soldiers whenever they are needed."

Franklin, who seemed eager to stay one step ahead of Lord Harrington in his questions (as if they were in a popularity contest), asked, "But Your Eminence, you are in a war right now. If Thorain were to attack right now, would you be able to take away soldiers from your own nation's war?"

"Luckily for you, my war is almost over. We are winning single-handedly. But even if not, I would still send whatever soldiers I could spare."

"That seems very generous of you, Your Eminence," Lord Harrington said. "But in your war you have never asked for any assistance, which we've always been curious about."

"My war is not so great, for we have been lucky in that the savages have not grown more in number than us, the true Carsians. We could do without support from Thayland; to bring in support would be an insult to my people."

Lord Harrington nodded. Will meanwhile had made a mental note: The Mulvars whom the Emperor fought were not considered true citizens of Carsiss.

The Emperor continued: "Thayland on the other hand does not nearly outmatch Thorain, and since we wish to continue our support for your country, we would gladly send soldiers and weapons across the sea."

Lord Harrington voiced his relief and flattered the Emperor by commenting on his "deep wisdom and stimulating intellect." Franklin tried making similar sentiments but ended up with rather awkward ones, such as "The fire in your eyes is like the heat of your nation," and "Your palace shows that you have nothing to hide or anything to make up for." Will and Lord Harrington both cringed at that last one.

Will in the meantime had little to say, for he felt he hadn't had much to offer to a conversation with a great ruler. However the Emperor managed to find one activity they could both eagerly share in. He had invited Will inside his *dojo*—a large room with padded flooring and a large array of weapons gathered on the walls. There were axes and spears, staffs and bows, and nearly any type of sword he could think of.

But despite the impressive selection, the Emperor chose to practice with a bamboo stick. He threw one to Will, who couldn't help remarking that it was a plant he was holding—some sort of segmented stem nearly as thick as his forearm.

"It comes from the eastern jungles," the Emperor said. "It is so strong they use it for construction there. But here I use as thus." He then proceeded to whack a leather-bound dummy three times in under a second. He then challenged Will to do the same, but to hit it four times instead.

Will imitated the Emperor with impressive skill, but his four strikes did not happen fast enough for the Emperor's liking. The Emperor then had a go at it, making four strikes instead of three, and it was easy to see that his strikes happened faster than Will's ever did. He then pulled some fancy footwork, revolving around the dummy while striking it continuously, hardly faltering between his hits, and ending the dance with a decisive blow to the dummy's padded head.

"How many broken bones is that?" Will joked.

The Emperor invited Will to have a go at it. Will performed admirably, but though he could match the precision of the blows, he could never match the speed no matter how hard he tried. When the Emperor noticed his frustration, he said, "Don't concern yourself with replicating my ways. I too had been at your level; of course, I was fourteen then and was just starting my training. From what I see, I can tell you that you are a fine warrior, an excellent addition to my army."

"Forgive me, Your Eminence," Will said with a bow. "In truth I am more used to training with a sword, and I have underestimated the usefulness of something so light in my hands."

"A sword, yes—you are training for knighthood of course." The

Emperor went to a wall and brought down a broadsword from its pegs. "Your smiths insist on sending blades like this to Carsiss. I know these blades are designed like the Cross of your beloved Christ, but we have no interest in them." He then fetched a scimitar—a sword shaped like a crescent moon. "Now these I can handle. It makes cleaving your enemy feel so much more natural, because you are not required to bend your wrists so much. A narrow and straight design is only for arrows and spears. Tell your smiths that if they can make these as well as any Carsian smith, they'd make themselves a fat purse."

Later the Emperor invited the ambassadors to a beautiful garden outside of the Palace proper. It stood beside the outer defense wall and was held in by the rear of a building. It contained all sorts of exotic flowers, vines, and bushes, as well as fruits so rich and juicy they were named after some of the gods in exaltation. Spring water flowed in channels as if it came from a lake, feeding a grassland that grew and prospered like it was in Thayland. In the middle of the grassy plot was a large marble statue of Siva, one of the main gods of Hinduism, one half of his face smiling and jovial, the other half frowning and scowling.

The ambassadors learned that many of the last Emperors had used the garden as a spot for thinking and meditation; Emperor Baku, however, mostly used it for target practice. He never hit the fruit, for fear of angering the gods they were named after; instead he set up three bulls-eyes painted on squares of hay. He used a bow of silver and tin with a string made of fine horse hair. There were three other bows made of cherry wood which he allowed Lord Harrington and Franklin to use, but he insisted that Will use his own personal bow. Will was shocked and nearly wanted to give the bow back, but knowing it would be insulting he instead accepted it graciously. The Emperor explained that he had impressed him so well in the *dojo* that he was willing to let him use some of his more finer instruments.

Will had always been a decent shot, though the Emperor proved the better one. Lord Harrington also demonstrated his adeptness and bragged about how good he was shooting from horseback. Franklin merely got an A for effort.

"Your Eminence," Will said during his turn, "you lead so many people's lives. I can hardly fathom myself with such an undertaking, but one day I may find myself leading many others. Please tell me, what does good leadership involve?"

"Leading by example," the Emperor said. "You must follow the mantra that you insist your men follow as well. You must 'take your own medicine,' as they say. As we say in Carsiss, a leader is 'the first one to enter and the last one to leave.'"

The Emperor suddenly turned, took a few steps away, and then faced Will with his arms outstretched, all while Will was trying to concentrate on aiming an arrow. "But let us not kid ourselves. You do not see *me* doing this. I call for war, but I do not take up a sword. When the people starve or become thirsty, I claim to feel their pain, even if this palace sustains me throughout it all. That is because a leader cannot die, cannot be expendable. The people need a leader for guidance. If I should die now, no one can replace me for I have no heir yet. Carsiss would be left with no direction, and everyone would suffer. A great leader cannot die, Will Fontaine—not when there is something to be done yet. One day, when you see the faces of men who look to you for guidance, you will understand."

Will tried not to let his concern show, for he had much the opposite opinion. He had loosened the string of his bow to hear the Emperor's speech; when the Emperor was done, he drew the arrow back and let it fly. It hit the target three rings away from the bulls-eye, the furthest one.

"You are so wise, Your Eminence," Franklin said. "Your wisdom easily outshines even those in Thayland's Palace—except for the King's, of course."

The Emperor slightly wrinkled his brow, both in embarrassment and in concern over Franklin's tendency for strange compliments. "I know. It is my burden as well as my blessing."

Once Will's turn was over (he had three hits in the outer ring and two in the middle ring), Lord Harrington had a go at it. After his first shot, the Emperor turned thoughtful again: "A good leader must also strive to make new things and learn to bury the old. Nothing ever remains the same—it a constant and sometimes painful lesson history teaches us. We must make new things, and I don't mean just products but ideas, philosophies, techniques.

"Take for example your feud with Thorain. You do not just fight for land but for ideologies. Thorain has its serfs and overlords; Thayland has its freemen, its middle class. Your society is more desirable to live in, so Thorain's people immigrate to Thayland in the hundreds, even if it is illegal and they risk their lives for it. Thayland, which has once had its serfs, has strived for something new, while Thorain clings to its old ways like a crabby old hermit. And who is winning? Thayland, of course. I confess that is one reason why I and my fathers have chosen Thayland to have relations with.

"Carsiss, meanwhile, has its caste system. It is an old way, and while neither I nor my people wish to dispose of it—for it is something the gods themselves had made—I believe we must look for something new to work for, something new to believe in. Thus I make my war with the Mulvars, for once it is over we shall finally have our peace with them."

Will and Franklin bowed, as was customary when the Emperor reflected his wishes. Lord Harrington bowed after he let his arrow fly, which landed only a few centimeters away from the bulls-eye.

That evening the Emperor invited the ambassadors and the two overlords to an entertainment hall. It was one of the more lavishly decorated rooms in the Palace, complete with bead curtains, satin pillows, oil lamps, and even a chandelier with tallow candles. There were large leather bags filled with hardened beans used as seats; Will found them odd at first but could not deny how comfortable they were. Off to one side were small tables holding hookahs—beautifully ornate glass pipes that were used to smoke tobacco. On another side was a shale statue of Brahma, the creator of the world who had four arms raised up, each hand making different gestures. There was also a statue of a lesser-known deity, which Lord Harrington recognized as Kama, the god of desire.

One portion of the room was dedicated for musicians, who kept going a light but lively tune even before the main guests arrived. Among the instruments were two flutes, a fiddle, a sitar, a pair of clappers, and two sets of bongo drums. Their music increased the energy level in the room and rose Will's anticipation as to what was going to happen there.

"What are we here for?" he asked Lord Harrington. "Are we going to dance or something?"

"Something like that," Lord Harrington said. He kept licking his lips and looking around himself. "You'll be pleasantly surprised, trust me."

Wine and rum were passed around, which Lord Darric and Hineson wasted no time drinking. Will was quick to grab a glassful before it was all gone. His rum was heavily spiced, and he wondered if some ingredient was added to alter his senses. Franklin was hesitant to drink anything but had some wine anyway so as not to be left out of the festivities.

The Emperor helped himself into an extended chair and downed the rest of his rum, then ordered more from a servant. "A toast!" he shouted to make himself heard over the music and careless laughing of the overlords. "To our new guests from the north. My father always remarked how good it was to have sons of Thayland over ... and to see their faces at this!"

He set his glass down and clapped his hands. The music suddenly became louder and faster, more lively and sultry. For one awkward moment, Will wondered if he should get up or not ... and then, from the far side of the room, the dancers came in. They rushed about, light on their bare feet, and stepped into formation in a vacant part of the room in front of the guests.

They were eight of the most beautiful women Will had ever seen. They wore clothing consisting of laced satin with beads and jewels, although any coverings were scant and small, hugging tightly to their curvy forms. Their makeup was wonderfully done, adding degrees to their already sumptuous beauty. Their mascara and lip-coloring were deep shades of black that went well with their shiny hair, which was put into styles that any man would wish to run his hands through (the woman in front of the formation had an exceptionally irresistible style with one wave of smooth hair covering her left eye). And they were bare-breasted, which made for a sight Will could only have imagined before.

They performed a dance in which they moved in perfect synchronization, moving back and forth and side to side with delicate arm and leg motions. It was a dance that made use of their beautiful forms and liquid agility. Banners of thin silk were attached to their wrists and legs, which flowed through the air like streams of rainbows, adding a sort of surreal element to their dance of desire.

The music eventually became faster as well as the dance. Will felt his senses and worries melt away, his growing contempt for the opposite sex split into two and dissolved into dust. He felt senses he had never known were there, and an impulse that nearly made him uncontrollable (although he did manage to control himself, and admirably). For the longest moment, it was just him and the women—those vivacious vixens who eyed him with a certain amusement and an understanding of what he was going through.

With a final strong note, the music and dancing stopped. The

Emperor and his guests applauded (Will and Franklin joined in only after they snapped to their senses). The dancers bowed, each with one leg crossed over the other and one arm upraised. The music then started again, more slowly but just as sultry. The dancers ran here and there among the men, each one dancing to their own design. Will had a particular eye on two women who stood together and moved their bellies like waves in the sea.

And then, one at a time, they began to sit with the men. The Emperor was flanked by two ladies who each crossed one leg over his lap and helped themselves to the wine and rum. Lord Darric was seen with his hands on a dancer's back and belly, who fed him grapes from a bowl; after a time, he couldn't help but to bury his face into her neck and smother it with kisses. Franklin was also fed grapes from one of the more petite dancers. The dancer grew worried over how shy he was and how he refused to touch her smooth skin; she got the attention of another dancer and asked for assistance to help break him out of his shell.

Will was the last one to get attention, which he later learned was because the ladies weren't sure if he was a son of Thayland or a Euthasian, what with his dark skin (Euthasians were known to look down on such erotic activities). A dancer with short, bulbous hair and green clothing sat in his lap and laid an arm around his neck. He was at first hesitant to do anything, but then his hands sought for some flesh to feel and he formed a smile that grew brighter like the morning sun. She smiled like an angel in return, the contrast of her white teeth and dark lip-coloring exquisite and inviting. Will found he had eyes only for her, though his ears were picking up sounds from around him that conjured some disturbing images to mind.

He knew he should say something, though he had little idea what. So he merely said the first thing he thought of: "Come here often?"

CHAPTER 10
TRAINING

THAT NIGHT HE HAD A dream the kind of which he hadn't had in a long time. He dreamed of his old nemesis, Jean du Montblanc, sitting in a throne of smooth stone. In his lap was a huge Doberman pinscher, curled up and fast asleep. Will was only a few paces away, and he stooped down to make out Montblanc's face more clearly, which was concealed in shadow.

Montblanc ran his fingertips along the Doberman's head. Will steeled himself in case the dog should wake up and attack him, but for a long time, Montblanc made no motion to stir it awake. "What do you want?" Will asked.

Montblanc didn't respond right away, but then said a curious thing: "You're blind."

Will shrugged. "I'm blind, huh? How so?"

"As I am." And with that, Montblanc leaned forward into the light to show what he meant, for his sockets had no eyes in them nor any lids to cover them up.

Will awoke with a start, as well as one monster hangover. He pressed a hand up to his temple. Memories of last evening flooded his mind, both pleasurable and disconcerting. He remembered a pair of soft lips pressed against his, warm hands on his back and shoulders ... and more. Oh by all the Hindu gods, was there ever more. He pressed his fingertips against his lips and then looked at them. They had marks that were undoubtedly lip-coloring.

It was conduct unbecoming a knight's apprentice, so he should have been ashamed ... but then again, he was in Carsiss, and in the Emperor's hospitality. He could temporarily forget some of the responsibilities of his apprenticeship and instead partake in all that Carsiss had to offer.

Not that it was going to be all fun and games. At first light, he was scheduled to be part of an infantry unit headed by one Commander Tanalac. His army days were soon going to start while the other two ambassadors went off to do some cross-country traveling to scope out the nation's economy and welfare.

Will looked around him. He was back in his room, although he couldn't remember how he got there. He checked the space beside him ... and saw no one. He sighed in relief, for he had heard some horror stories of men who had gotten too drunk only to awaken with a mistress beside them in bed.

But that girl was no mistress, he thought to himself. *She was a harem dancer—a piece of property owned by the Emperor. King Fredrick would abhor such a thing in Thayland—but of course this isn't Thayland. You're going to have to accept that.*

He sighed, fell back down, and drifted again to sleep.

Five hours later he was in an outfit consisting of leather leg- and shin-guards and a pair of baggy pants. On his head was a kind of hood attached to his head by a girth, so as to keep the sun off his forehead—a deceptively simple trick that worked more than it appeared to. Attached to his belt was a leather loop which a scimitar's blade went through (he preferred to have a sheath, for it was awkward walking with a bare blade against his leg, but the Carsian army had no such things).

A Palace servant directed him to a training hall in the city, where he began to meet his new comrades. But soon after his arrival, everyone was down to business. They organized a three-square formation in a courtyard (which had no roof, to Will's dismay) and awaited their commander to begin their exercises.

After nearly ten minutes of standing around (something that would never happen in Thayland), a trio of horses suddenly rushed into the compound and ran startlingly near the head of the formation. Will was intimidated, fearful that the horses would balk at the sight of all the men, but they were kept under control. The men whom the horses ran alongside never flinched, never even gave any signal that the horses were there and were kicking up a cloud of sand into their faces.

The horses went up and around to one of the courtyard's front entrances. One of the riders got off and saluted the other two, who appeared to be generals by the looks of their leather-and-steel armor and the armoring of their steeds. The single man then headed to face to the infantry. He was no doubt Commander Tanalac, a formidable man of a tall height and a wide, muscular form. He hadn't a single unshaven hair on his head, and unlike his men he wore no hood. He had a pair of blazing eyes and an ugly scar running from temple to jawline.

"Baree-DA!" he cried, which meant "attention" in Carsian. The men uniformly brought their heels together and their arms straight at their sides. Commander Tanalac then drew his sword and everyone followed suit. *"Takee-NA!"* The commander thrust his

sword forward and everyone followed suit. He had them follow the same movement thirty times, and then went onto slices, swinging the sword in a swift vertical motion.

Will had previously wondered why everyone had so much space between them, but at that point he figured out why, for they were not at a shish kabob stakeout. The exercises were very different from those in Thayland, which did not involve sword motions but merely marching routines; swordplay was practiced in different formations and in fewer numbers.

Will didn't mind this new method of training, but only at first. He was always good with a sword and was familiar with the movements Commander Tanalac was teaching ... but then the commander had everyone do jumping routines, which Will had never heard of or seen before. As soon as the commander demonstrated a twisting of the body in midair, everyone followed suit except Will, who was perplexed. Doing such motions in their current formation was dangerous, for there was no telling if someone would become disoriented and accidentally poke someone beside him. After everyone jumped two times in synchronization with the commander, Will followed suit but found it hard to keep his footing. He couldn't stay in one place, though everyone else seemed to have no trouble doing that. He often skipped jumps just to prepare to do another.

Commander Tanalac moved on to another jumping exercise, one that involved striking his blade down on the ground. Will found that one to be a bit easier, but he grew fatigued very fast in the sweltering sun and soon found it hard to concentrate. The third jumping exercise involved another twisting of the body, one that had the blade doing a horizontal slice.

In the middle of that exercise, the commander stopped everyone short by howling a single command: *"Kara-ad!"* He returned his scimitar to his belt and marched straight into the center square. Will muttered a prayer hoping that the commander wasn't coming for him, and he resisted the urge to keep an eye on his progress. His prayer went unanswered, for the commander turned right in the center square and made his way to the left square, where Will was stationed. As Will heard his footsteps grow louder, he felt his heart being strained like a wet dishrag.

Commander Tanalac stopped with his face two decimeters away from Will's. "You!" he shouted. "State your name!"

"Will Fontaine, sir!"

"Fontaine?! That is no Euthasian name! Are you a son of Thayland?"

"Yes, sir!"

The commander hesitated, then stated, "You jump like a heron on its two wobbly legs! Are you a man or an ostrich?"

Will wondered if it was a trick question, then replied, "A man, sir!"

Commander Tanalac struck his left ear with his palm, as fast as if he was swatting a fly. Will staggered a bit, holding his ear in disbelief; he then remembered he wasn't in Thayland anymore and stood up straight again, trying to ignore his battered ear.

"What sort of man fights like that?" Tanalac cried. "You are as graceful as a clipped vulture, and as ugly as one, too! If you want to stay in my unit, you will have to do better, and do it now!"

Will wanted to breathe heavily, not in exhaustion but in rage. If any average commander in Thayland's infantry had seen their jumping exercises, he would have called them ridiculous. But Will had been more accepting, and he gave them his best shot—but was it his fault he hadn't been training for them ever since childhood like the other men? Of course not, and it was unfair for one to assume he had and then throw him to the dogs.

And how dare the bastard strike a foreign emissary!

"Yes, sir!" Will said, though it pained him to.

Commander Tanalac promptly returned to the front of the center square and continued the exercises. With the pangs of outrage throbbing in his mind, he begrudgingly admitted that his concentration and focus had improved, and he found himself keeping up with the rest of the unit. He glanced at the two generals watching from their corner. He couldn't read their expressions from his faraway vantage point, but the fact that they didn't stop and question Tanalac proved that they didn't consider his actions disgraceful.

Will began to seriously reconsider his decision to come to Carsiss. It had quickly turned out that he had more to worry about than just the harsh climate, and he quietly cursed Professor Roth for not warning him of some of the army's more extreme customs.

He thought of taking the matter to the Emperor, spelling out his grievances ... but he couldn't do that. It wouldn't be wise to have his commander lose face in front of the Emperor, and even if the Emperor's goodwill held up, such grievances would make Will appear weak. It was not only a matter of honor and personal relations, but also one of pride and dignity. A commander striking his men was not unheard of in Thayland, and the fact that he was a diplomat wouldn't make him appear any less of a hypocrite.

Once the exercises were over, it was time for them to march through the streets—a custom as old as Carsiss itself, Will was told. They belted their swords and took up spears, for they were more intimidating to the eye. Then the front doors of the training hall were thrust open, and the men poured outside and into the public.

Most of the streets of Nünveghett were too narrow to march through, but there was one route wide enough for a line as wide as five men. The people had apparently been expecting them, for the route was cleared of pedestrians, vehicles and animals. One exception was a cow, which the soldiers took relative care to avoid touching. In Carsiss there was a social movement called *ahimsa* that preached of the virtues of nonviolence. It told of the glory of cows, which gave food without having to be killed; eventually the people began to think of cows as exceptionally holy creatures favored by the gods, and their slaughter became strictly illegal. Even touching a cow was discouraged and considered a profane act, for it was unwise to distress them. And so cows were able to travel freely anywhere in Carsiss, even in city streets, and it was up to the Untouchables to clean up after them.

Will took the march as an opportunity to observe the condition of the city. Most of the buildings were in good condition, and the street sweepers had done well to keep the streets clean and in repair. People kept to the sides of the streets, and for the most part they gave the soldiers only cursory glances, not as if they feared them but as if they wanted nothing to do with them.

The overall view of the city seemed satisfactory, and Will was already planning the good points he'd put in his ultimate report to the King—but then the soldiers went downhill towards the river, and the view took a drastic turn. He often saw groups of men walking or hanging out at street corners; such groups ranged from three members to as many as twelve. They were disturbing to look at, for they often had some clear distinction that separated them from other groups. Some groups had members who each wore red bandanas; other groups had black bandanas, or yellow armbands, or similar tattoos. It was like each group had its own signature, unmistakable and displayed like some kind of warning sign.

Gangs, Will thought. *They're like the roving gangs in Thayland who either go on mass thieving sprees or make public destruction for political causes. Except these people aren't just roaming the countryside; they're right here in the city where everyone can see them. And it's not as if they're here to threaten and molest the honest, hard-working people; in this part of the city, they* are *the honest, hard-working people, in a sense.*

Will wondered if the gangs were formed because of class warfare or craftsmen rivalry, which wasn't hard to imagine with the caste system placed in the city. They obviously disliked and distrusted each other, for no two different gangs were seen within thirty meters of each other, each one holding onto their supposed territory. They apparently held no great love for the soldiers, either, for they often turned a malicious eye at them, regardless of what colors they wore.

When they returned to the training hall, they went into their training formations again and were faced by their commander. Will expected a speech or something from Tanalac, but all he did was say a brief word about diligence and then promptly dismissed them.

They gathered inside a huge mess hall where they made plates of fresh fruits and vegetables handpicked from baskets. They also grabbed little plates of water and sesame they used as offerings to the gods to honor their descendants.

Will made a few acquaintances, such as Tamaro Dulglen, who had a son in a local university, and Bihar Ollesun, a reserved young man who already had his share of facial scars.

Will asked them about the gangs. Who were they and what did they do?

"No one's really sure," Bihar said. "They have their turfs, which they guard like animals, and they watch each others' backs. Sometimes a dead body shows up, and it's obvious that rival gang members killed him. This happens maybe twice a month."

"Why aren't you sure?" Will asked. "Surely someone has to investigate them, find out why they've gathered like this."

"Sometimes the government plants a mole in a gang, but then they just wind up dead," Bihar said soberly.

"Do you think they're formed according to their castes?"

"Yes, somewhat," Tamaro said. "Some gangs are made up only of *Vaisyas* who wear bandanas and tatoos; other gangs are made up of both *Vaisyas* and Untouchables."

"So perhaps this gang activity began with caste rivalry," Will mused, "but then the castes split into different factions over petty disputes."

Bihar and Tamaro fell silent at that for a moment, then Tamaro said, "Look, Fontaine, it's not really something we talk about. We leave talk like that up to the *Ksatriyas,* let them handle it. It's none of our concern."

Will wrinkled his brow at that. He thought that was no way to deal with a problem, especially when it was laid right on your doorstep. There had to be something the *Vaisyas* could do about those gangs, not just leave it as a government problem.

A few minutes later, two soldiers approached. "William Fontaine," one of them said, saying his first name with some difficulty. "The commander wishes to see you."

Will thought for a moment, then said, "Tell him I'm busy. Eating is hard work, you know." All faces upon him gaped in disbelief. But then Will stood up and said, "I'm kidding, of course."

Commander Tanalac was outside, just under the long overhang of the building's roof. The messenger soldiers took positions behind him. "William Fontaine," he said, also having trouble saying his first name. "Now that you are in my unit, you had better consider some things. First of all, are you willing to obey all my orders?"

An interrogation, Will thought. *I love this guy already.* "Yes, sir," he said simply.

"Are you willing to march into battle with me?" Commander Tanalac asked.

"Yes, sir."

"Are you willing to die for me?"

Will nearly wrinkled his brow, and he wondered whether he actually did or not. "Yes, sir."

"Are you willing to die for your honor?"

"Yes, sir."

Commander Tanalac stepped a hair closer. "To a Carsian warrior, nothing is more important than his honor. It sustains him and keeps his safe, for there is nothing that makes the gods angrier than a warrior who dishonors himself. An honorable warrior upholds what is right; he respects his duties to his commander, his countrymen, and his Emperor.

"Now that you are in my unit, your actions are a part of my honor. If you do anything wrong and unjust, I will have to answer for you ... and we don't want that to happen, do we?"

"No, sir."

Tanalac tried on a sneer. "But you sons of Thayland are

nothing but worms who indulge yourselves and grow fat. You live only for drink, and you take orders from women. You don't believe in honor any more than the jackal believes in hunting for itself; like the jackal, you just pick up others' leavings. You come from a sorry lot, and while I don't know what the gods will make of you, you had better not make me sorry for letting you into my unit. Dismissed, Fontaine."

Tanalac turned on his heels and marched off with the two messenger soldiers following. Will returned inside and reclaimed his seat. "What did he want with you?" Bihar asked.

"He wanted to remind me of the mistake I made in coming here," Will said.

To ease his growing tensions, he wrote a letter to Tony and Sir Blackstone. He claimed that the climate in Carsiss was so hot and austere that the nation could have been sharing a border with Hell. But they shouldn't worry, for he was drinking lots of water and mostly stayed in the shade. The people were friendly enough, and their customs were strange but fascinating. He seriously thought about including Commander Tanalac's remarks about the people of Thayland, just for the sake of rumor-mongering, but he figured no responsible emissary would write about something like that. It was up to him to keep on a good face while he was overseas, and any unpleasantness could be related later back home.

CHAPTER 11
BEHOLDING GREATNESS

THE FOLLOWING MONTH WAS a trying time for Will. Although the jumping exercises were easier to do since he knew what to expect, Commander Tanalac kept holding his thumb on him like he was a tiger that might turn on its master at any moment. On some days, he merely glared at Will with those hawklike eyes of his; on other days, he made a public display of him, yelling that he wasn't doing good enough, wasn't working hard enough, or hadn't bathed properly even if the man next to him was filthier than he was. Tanalac's job was apparently to make his life a living hell, but if he expected Will to buckle, Will fully intended to disappoint him. He imagined Tanalac had a wall in his office or war room that had scratches on it, and each scratch represented one soldier who cried like a baby under his tyranny. It was a silly idea of course, but if it was true, Tanalac's fingers must have been aching to make a scratch for Will.

Will vowed to strengthen his resolve and to make it through Carsiss with his dignity intact, even if he had to return home with a patchwork of scars. He did his duties and exercises to the best of his abilities and steeled himself for his encounters with the commander. He expected anything to happen in those encounters, for he never really could tell what Tanalac would do in each one. Sometimes he just yelled at him; other times he boxed his ear again. And he'd find any excuse to harass him, even if it was a small mistake that a Thayland commander would turn a blind eye at.

It's a game to him, Will thought. *It's all just a game to him, and I'll be damned if his honor has anything to do with it.*

Most of the soldiers were sympathetic with him, understanding that Tanalac was a virtual slavedriver. But a few who were more loyal to Tanalac started to harass him, too, although their skirmishes never came to physical blows. Whenever they called him names and hurl insults about his mother, Will would just keep his silence and his cool. He wasn't going to give Tanalac's little pets a bone.

The only instances of joy Will had in that period were during his time in the Palace. He could no longer stay in his old room there (he slept in the barracks next to the training hall), but one duty as an ambassador was to the keep communication going between him and the other diplomats whenever he could. Lord Harrington told him boring details of Carsiss' economy (their main export to Thayland was fish, while silks and dyes were close behind), and Franklin Douglass told him of the fascinating customs and foods he saw in the nearby town of Nakardijhad, which was further down along the Saparel Mountains. It was a thriving community despite how they had no springs there, only the waters of the River Calkut.

"Next month there is going to be a festival there," Franklin said. "It's a celebration of a decisive victory in the Five Year's War where the Carsians won. They founded Carsiss after that. There's not only going to be parties but also serious ceremonies worshiping the gods Vishnu and Siva. Those are the two most important deities in Hindu, you know that?"

"Yes, I do," Will said, hoping that Franklin wouldn't go into another tireless tirade of trivia, one of his more annoying habits (another was biting his nails, although he never did it in front of the Emperor, thank God).

Twenty-four days after sending his first letter back home, he received a reply which he read while strolling in the Palace halls. It was a bit disappointing since it was rather short and straightforward. The letter basically said that everything was fine and that Carsiss sounded exciting. Strangely, it was written only by Tony. Will figured that at least part of it would be in Sir Blackstone's tall, sharp script, but it was all in Tony's short, blocky script. The master might have either been out or busy when Will's letter had gotten there.

A few days after, Will was walking with Lord Harrington in the Palace courtyard, discussing Tanalac's attitude and behavior towards him. Lord Harrington was shocked and appalled, but Will acted as if he couldn't care less what Tanalac did: "He yelled himself so hoarse that he couldn't give out commands anymore and had to cancel the rest of the exercises. You should pity a man who has it so hard."

"But Will, he hits you on the ear," Lord Harrington said. "He's no worse than a rogue. You have to tell the Emperor of this."

"No, and you won't either, begging my lord's pardon. Believe it or not, the other soldiers say this kind of abuse isn't uncommon with Carsian commanders. They have to keep their troops in line." That was an exaggeration, for no Carsian commander singled out one particular man for harassment like Tanalac did to him.

"But surely you want to put a stop to it, don't you?"

"It's really no big deal, my lord. I came to Carsiss fully knowing what to expect, and I expected this." That of course was another exaggeration.

A little further down their way, Lord Harrington stopped them and said, "Say, Will, are you feeling up for a challenge?"

"What kind of challenge, my lord?"

"Just a little race. I'll bet you that I can beat you to the blacksmith's from here. There's only one condition: You must go up those stairs while I go around the bend."

Will raised an eyebrow. With that condition, Lord Harrington had given him the upper hand. They were standing in front of a large shrine dedicated to the god Siva, which held a marble statue of the deity. The canopy was built into the side of a slope; to the right of the shrine was a stairway leading almost right up to the blacksmith's; to the left was no stairway, only an unpaved part of the slope. To reach the blacksmith's from the left side, Lord Harrington would have to go up the slope and then turn right and run along the upper side of the shrine. Lord Harrington should have been aware of Will's unfair advantage, but since he was the one giving it to him, he was practically asking to lose.

"Okay, I'll take that challenge," Will said.

They took up positions and Lord Harrington counted from three to one. Both men started like the hare against the tortoise, Will heading straight for the stairs, Lord Harrington heading for the bend leading to the slope. Lord Harrington was Will's elder by twenty years, but he was fit and still worthy of a race.

Will rushed up the stairs, breathing hard under the desert sun. The stairway had two landings in its path, for the hill was uneven where they were built, but Will didn't consider them a major hindrance. He was bound to reach the blacksmith's and claim his reward, whatever it was. He'd then bet he could hit the blacksmith's and then turn around and reach the starting point before Lord Harrington even saw the blacksmith's himself.

After the second landing, Will told himself to keep moving, keep breathing, keep pumping his arms, so he could prove to the lord just how foolish he was to make a challenge like that. Of course he wouldn't rub it in his face, but he'd at least—

He saw Lord Harrington reach the blacksmith's just after he cleared the stairs. The building was to his left, only ten or so meters away. The lord placed a hand on the front entrance and waved to Will.

"How did you *do* that?" Will asked when he caught up.

Lord Harrington tried to appear innocent and reserved, which didn't work. He was obviously keeping himself from laughing. "Well, I've been running in marathons before you were even born. It's no wonder I have legs like a gazelle."

"No, it's impossible for you to beat me, and you know it," Will said, more amused than annoyed. "So how did you do it? There has to be something you're not telling me."

Lord Harrington let loose a smile, and he laughed almost like a kid with candy. "All right, I guess there's no pulling the wool over *your* eyes. I'll show you—" he glanced at their surroundings, "—if you keep quiet."

Will nodded and looked around. There were a few servants and soldiers around, but none of them seemed interested in the two sons of Thayland. Lord Harrington ambled over to the back of the shrine where there was a small booth made of red-painted wood and paper windows, with a broad roof of red shingles like that of the shrine. Inside was a small altar with a small statue of Brahma, creator of the world. Lord Harrington stepped behind the altar, and to Will's amazement, he stepped down into the ground. "Follow me," he said, "and watch your head."

Will went behind the altar and saw a square hole in the ground with a sandstone lid lifted off its top. He saw no ladder but there was no need for one, for Lord Harrington handily jumped down and landed with his shoulders still aboveground. The lord then stooped down and went further inside. Will followed suit, and then the lord went past him and closed the lid, enveloping them in total darkness.

Will forgot Lord Harrington's advice and tried to stand up straight, instead hitting his head hard against the low ceiling. "Oh, watch yourself," Lord Harrington said. "These walls are made of limestone or some other kind of sturdy rock. Must have been mined from the mountains or something."

"Where the hell are we?" Will asked.

"We're in a tunnel. I got inside from a booth on the shrine's west side."

"This is great."

"Yeah, well, if the Emperor knew we were here, he'd deport us for sure. Come, take my hand."

Will did, and Lord Harrington took him around a bend and turned right. Will kept his head down and felt along the ceiling to keep tabs on its level. He also checked the width of the walls and estimated that three men could fit between them. The walls were indeed very sturdy, made of some rock alien to the immediate region. It couldn't be sandstone for it wasn't porous; Lord Harrington's guess of it being limestone could be right on the mark.

They traveled perhaps twenty meters or more until Lord Harrington stopped. "We're not getting back up here, but here's the exit beside the museum. It's not inside a booth; it's behind a display of old bones belonging to the Emperor's ancestors."

"How did you find this place?" Will asked.

"Last time I was here I made a friend out of a soldier. I did him a favor by being the nursemaid to his child while the appointed nursemaid was out sick. It's something no Carsian man would do, but I'm from Thayland so I was exempt. The man was humiliated by his peers, but he was grateful enough to show me this tunnel. It's known only to the Emperor, the dieschsuchs, and the highest Imperial Guards ... and some people who happened to see it being used. And now I've shown it to you. That man said it might be useful to me someday, and I think it may be helpful to you."

"My lord, do you imply that it'd be easy for me to fall into danger here?"

"What do you mean?"

"I mean, look at what my new commander's been doing to me. It's like he's trying to provoke me. So what if he frames me for something I didn't do? Would I have to use this as an escape route?"

"Indeed, Will. I don't know if you know this already, but the court of Thayland's Royal Palace is a dangerous place itself. Jealousy runs rampant, not only among the nobles but among the servants, too. Everyone's vying to get the top bids, the big contracts, the sweetheart deals—and must I mention the adultery that goes on there? Desperate situations call for desperate measures in the Royal Court, and the same goes for the Carsian Imperial Court as well. Be careful that you don't fly too high, Will, or the sun may melt your wings. In that case, maybe it's not such a good idea to agitate your commander by snitching him to the Emperor."

Will tentatively agreed, and the two of them turned back and went out the exit by the west side of the shrine. Will then thanked Lord Harrington and left for the barracks.

Whenever the Emperor had the chance to see and chat with Will, he took it. He seemed genuinely sincere in securing a friendship with him, inviting him to some of his important gatherings as well as some moments of free time.

One day when Will and the Emperor were doing target practice in the garden again, the Emperor said, "In every dilemma we have, there is always a right choice and a wrong choice. Only one choice does the most good, while the other does the most evil. Some may say that there is always middle ground to reach, but I disagree. Any decision where people have reservations is no good. It has to be either one side or the other."

"Do you have an example, Your Eminence?" Will asked.

The Emperor pulled back an arrow. "In Darmine province, the Halmar tribe has taken control of a spring, which had belonged to the Makune tribe." He released the arrow, which landed on the second ring from the bulls-eye. "The Makunes are dying of thirst, and they have no chance of winning their spring back. They do what they can with purified ocean water, but the purification process is a long one, and they cannot hope to slack their thirst with only ocean water. So both sides turn to me for help; they want me to make a final decision."

"Surely the spring has an endless flow of water," Will said. "Why can't the tribes share?"

The Emperor gave him a shrewd look. "Ah, you are an idealist. Good for you, but idealism cannot work here. The Makunes and the Halmars are blood enemies; their feuds go back generations, and in respect to their ancestors they must keep the thirst for revenge running hot. To them, a Makune and a Halmar drinking together would be a travesty, and the gods would turn away from them—perhaps even curse them. There's no hope for peace, Will Fontaine.

"So what am I to do? I must decide who the spring belongs to. It's a simple choice of either the Halmars or the Makunes. And going back to your suggestion, what if I were to say them to them, 'share?' What if I were to even go to them, join their chiefs' hands together, and say, 'peace?' It may work for a while, but their hatred runs deep to a level even I cannot reach—I know this for a fact."

Will looked troubled. Were all the Emperor's concerns put in terms that were so black and white?

But then the Emperor surprised him: "The only leverage I have in the conflict is the water from Thayland. I could give the water to the Makunes to let them slacken their thirst without the spring. But the water is not free, as you may know. We have a good deal with your kingdom in which Thayland picks up the bottling company's fee, while we just pay for travel expenses. But why must the Makunes pay for their water and the tax imposed on it while the Halmars drink their fill for free? Water is life, and in Carsiss it is as precious as gold and silver. Though they may survive on Thayland's water, their resentment towards the Halmars may strengthen.

"So answer me this, Will Fontaine, though it may not be fair: To whom should the spring belong to?"

Will didn't want to make that decision; his answer might influence the Emperor's judgment, and then he'd have a share of the blood of those tribesmen on his hands. On the other hand, it was good for him to win the Emperor's approval. He thought about it for some time (through at least three turns at the bulls-eye), and he then asked, "Are you with the Vaishnavists or the Saivists, Your Eminence?"

"As Emperor, I must be with both sects ... but I confess, I am more inclined with the Saivists. Siva is the god of both creation *and* destruction; I like that conflict within him, for it seems rather human."

"So Siva knows what it is to both create and sacrifice. I suppose it's time for the Makunes to know, too. I assume they've had the spring for a long time before the Halmars got it for themselves. For that time they had it easy; now they must move aside and let the Halmars reap the spring's wealth. But the Halmars had better watch out, because while they may have the advantage now, the Makunes will be sure to multiply, and one day they will fight and reclaim their spring."

The Emperor nodded. "That was just what I was going to say to them. I hadn't figured Siva into the equation, though, but somehow you have. Very good, Will Fontaine. I may be in your debt." He pulled back an arrow but then slowly slackened the bowstring and looked back at Will. "*May* be in your debt."

Will nodded and smiled, but he couldn't help but swallow back a lump in his throat.

Will had apparently made a greater impression on the Emperor than he'd thought, for what the Emperor did next for him was totally unexpected and was perhaps a right exclusive to him.

After a day of exceptional torment from Commander Tanalac (the commander had "accidentally" stepped on his foot during one of the speeches he made right up in his face), the Emperor invited him that evening into his study—a room no one was allowed to intrude on penalty of twenty lashes. It had a high ceiling suitable for two bookcases that could only have been built right there in the room. Nearly each cover had a title in the strange, cursive style of the Carsian language, but a few of them had Altrin titles. "You can read Altrin, Your Eminence?" Will asked.

"I can do more than just read it," the Emperor said, speaking in Thayland's mother tongue.

Will showed pleasant surprise and then laughed. "I should have known. Forgive my ignorance."

"That's okay," the Emperor said, still speaking in Altrin. "I forgive your king for being ignorant, for he do not speak Carsian. He was almost not the king, true?"

Ignoring the Emperor's lack of grammar skills, Will said in Carsian, "His uncle had died without an heir, so it was up to the Archbishop—Thayland's chief holy man—to choose the next man in line. The Archbishop was gracious enough to choose King James' esteemed nephew, Fredrick."

"That way the king can still be chosen by Providence, I see," the Emperor said, reverting back to Carsian. "Will, I have something to show you. Here ..."

The Emperor went to a simple wooden table. On the table was a beautifully-ornate hourglass, decorated with fine jewels yet not overly so. It seemed to be mostly made of gold with some pieces made of tin or iron. Around each circular end was a ring which looked like silver, but he didn't know for sure, for platinum hadn't come to mind. The ring was embedded with a language he didn't recognize; it was cursive like Carsian yet had sharper points and more pronounced loops. The glass chambers seemed to be made of two layers, as if one layer had been blown over the inner one. The bottom surface of each chamber had half of a globe made of beautiful, shiny obsidian. Unlike most hourglasses, which had three handles, the one in the study had two, which were flawlessly shaped and looked like two arms holding a piece of jade in place.

"Magnificent, isn't it?" the Emperor asked. "I have actually seen better, and believe me I would rather have one of those if not for one thing *this* hourglass can do.

"This glass has been in my family for many generations, at least six. My forefather back then never told how he came of it, but today it matters not. It has a name: *Las Bouseaux L'Amsouis."*

"Unusual name," Will said. "It's not Carsian, is it?"

"Not at all. Carsiss used to be dominated by a people from the south called the Lenores. They called their nation here Amsouis." The Emperor pointed to the upper platinum ring. "The glass' name is inscribed here. Its name means the Sands of Amsouis; today we call it the Sands of Carsiss."

Will couldn't help but stare at the sands lying in the bottom chamber. He expected the Emperor to turn it over for him, but the Emperor pointed an open palm to it, inviting him to do it. "By all means."

Will shook his head. "No, I can't do that," he said, trying to sound as polite as possible. "This is a great national treasure; it would be, I don't know ... improper for me to touch it. Only a Carsian—"

The Emperor said nothing, only politely smiled and nodded at the glass. Will didn't know how or why, but he got the idea that if he should refuse a second time, the Emperor would surely lose his patience and goodwill.

Will sighed and grasped the hourglass with both hands. It was heavier than it looked, but he managed to carefully rotate it and center it on the table. He thought there would follow an awkward moment where it would be him and the Emperor merely watching the sands fall, but the Emperor told him to peer in close at the falling sands. With little hesitation, Will did so ... and then he saw one of the most curious things he'd see in his life.

It took a while for him to catch it, for his eyes had to adjust, but once they did there was no mistaking the faint image that appeared around the falling sands. And it was more than just an image, for the people inside were moving, seemingly as alive and real as Will and the Emperor. There was at first one man; he had on a collar shirt with no frills, with a broad string of cloth hanging from the collar like a rope dangling from a welcome bell; a dark jacket was over the shirt with no vest underneath, forming a V-shape from collar to navel. He was not a Carsian but of a fair skin like most people in Thayland. Four more people dressed much like him came in from the right (one of them had skin as dark as Will's), and the first man promptly sat at a desk in front a large window with unattractive curtains. He picked up what looked like a quill but couldn't be for it had no ink well, and he started to write on what may have been a charter, only it was on a small sheet of paper instead of the traditional sheepskin scroll. For the next three minutes, they did little more than talk and shake hands, and to Will's shocked surprise, hundreds of flashes of light constantly beamed on them as if from tiny, powerful explosions, but the men didn't seem to mind them in the least.

And then the image disappeared. Will tried to adjust his eyes again, for he thought he had merely lost his focus, but the image never reappeared.

"What did you see?" the Emperor asked. Will stood up and tried to describe the scene as best he could, barely able to contain his excitement. "Ah, the men in the jackets," the Emperor continued. "I have seen them as well."

"Do you know who they are and where they are?" Will asked.

"In all my life, I have never seen a style of dress as theirs. All I know at least is that the Sands show only what *will* happen, not what *is* happening. I believe these people are from the far future—a future we will never live to see. They are rulers, with the man at the desk being the head chief. He appears to be signing something, isn't he? It is either a law or an approval for an operation of some kind. Whatever it is, it may lead to something great ... perhaps even ominous, in which case the Sands are trying to warn us to never let it happen. Of course, since we have no clue as to what they are signing, there is little we can do about it."

After a moment of thought, Will said, "If we had someone who could read lips, we could find out. Surely they're speaking a language that is used today, like Altrin or Sarnic ..."

"You surprise me, Will Fontaine. I didn't think you'd be so eager to believe in what you just saw."

It took another moment of thought for Will to grasp what the Emperor implied, and then he understood. Any other man would have had his sense of reality shaken by the image in the Sands, but Will had already had his shaken when he was only eleven, when Marie the ghost girl had appeared before him and given him the "seeing glass," which revealed one's truthfulness and inner desire. The Sands of Carsiss were just as fascinating, yet weren't more extraordinary. "I suppose I easily take things at face value," Will said.

The Emperor merely nodded, a little confused. "Well, the Sands will not show another display until after they have all run through, and you cannot cheat by turning them again so early.

"Over the years, I have seen into the Sands many times, and yet they show me only two images. One of them is what you have seen just now; the other is the one closer to my heart. It shows me running the head of my enemy—the head chief of the Mulvars, Marsoon Diachhe—through a spike and displaying it from atop the gate of the Palace wall. It shows me victorious, you see, and I know it leaves me able to build a glorious future for Carsiss. The Sands, you see, allows you to behold a future greatness, but one you and I must work to achieve."

"What conflict do you have with the Mulvars?" Will asked.

"It is an old and sorry history between our peoples, Will Fontaine, and I do not wish to go into it tonight. Perhaps some other time, my friend—if you continue to display the same wisdom and courage that you have already."

Will was surprised to be called friend by the Emperor, but he hid it well. He thought it was good to not show surprise in order to express a sense of confidence. It was nothing but a deception, true, but one that had served him well often enough times.

Strolling in a hallway, talking lightly with the Emperor about the Sands, Will spotted the harem dancers clad in heavy *saris* of elegant flower designs. He could hardly take his eyes off them, remembering that one night in their company. True, their companionship may have been pleasurable, but it had also been empty with little meaning. He wished he could talk to them, get to know their hopes and dreams just as the Lady Mayweather had wanted to know his. As he and the Emperor approached them, they glanced at the men and held a bow, clutching at their *saris*.

"You like them?" the Emperor asked once they passed the women. He then added with a laugh, "Perhaps you more than like them?"

"They are certainly attractive," Will admitted.

"They are mine," the Emperor said matter-of-factly. "They have made vows to the gods that they are to remain in my possession. But don't worry, Will Fontaine, you will see them again, I promise."

"Are they trustworthy?" Will asked, but he then became flustered. "Forgive me, Your Eminence—it's not in my place to question that. Please forget I said anything."

"Ah, but it shows more wisdom from you," the Emperor said.

"Indeed, you should question their loyalty. Men and women cannot live without one another, and yet it is like they are from different worlds. A man under my rule can easily pledge his loyalty to me, but a woman cannot since she has different duties to perform."

Will thought that was another example of the Emperor's rash black-and-white thinking, but he merely nodded in agreement.

"Be careful of them, Will Fontaine, for they are heartbreakers and look only to themselves ... and they become easily jealous. Perhaps I should tell you the story of one such woman who died after becoming my father's favorite ... but I think you get the picture."

CHAPTER 12
TO WAR

FOR THE NEXT THREE DAYS, Will hadn't seen the Emperor. He still visited the Palace to talk with the other ambassadors, but the Emperor was nowhere to be seen. There were no signs of his whereabouts and no invitations to more fighting or archery practices. It was as if he was actively avoiding him. He asked Dieschsuch Halicut how the Emperor was, and the man said he was well and in high spirits. Will then asked if he was doing anything important, and Halicut strangely said, "He is *always* doing something important, son of Thayland. A regular busybody is he, with no time for fun and games."

"Well is he doing anything *specifically* important?" Will asked.

"Hmm ... well yes, he is."

After a moment of waiting for a longer answer, Will asked, "Anything meant for my ears?"

"Yes ... and no."

Will nodded. "I take it he's doing nothing, then. Good day to you."

Will wasn't sure why he was so interested in seeing the Emperor again. It was perhaps because he wanted something to report back to the King, or it was perhaps because he was fond of their little talks in all of their significance. One thing for certain was that he had been thinking of how he could take advantage of their bond, as simple as it was. There was always the chance he could use it someday, especially if he was in serious trouble.

His hopes of seeing the Emperor anytime soon were dashed when Commander Tanalac had important and unexpected news for his unit: "A report says the enemy has gathered in the eastern canyons! We are to head out immediately and attack. Start preparations!"

The men all went on the move, each one knowing his purpose from the get-go. There were also murmured protests, for their new campaign would mean they'd miss the festival celebration of Carsiss' national holiday, though no one dared to say so to the commander or to fall short in their duties.

To Will fell the job of setting saddles on the unit's camels, which all didn't like the process very much. Getting the saddle on their backs was no problem, but snapping the bridles on them was a real pain, for they often tried to fit their enormous lips around his head like it was a lollipop. Will was told to smack them hard should they ever do that, and so he did, though he could never imagine doing that to a horse. Nasty creatures, those camels.

The cavalry soon marched out of the city with the soldiers right behind. Despite all of Will's troubles, he never found himself mounted on a camel, which he couldn't figure as either a curse or a blessing. There was much fanfare on the army's part, but the citizens mostly observed the soldiers' departure with disinterest. There were always some patriotic soul who cried out wishing them luck, but for the most part their leaving was greeted with mere apathy, as if they were being sent out to pick up dinner instead of to meet hardened barbarians waving swords and spears in their bloodstained hands. *Something like this would never happen in Thayland,* Will thought. *This is certainly a discredit to the nation.*

It was a four-day journey to the eastern canyons, and it might take another day or two in searching for the canyon the Mulvars were holed up in. As expected, it was more exhausting than any march he had endured in Thayland. At times he felt a little silly in the billowing clothes he had on, for they did not seem to befit a warrior, but he told himself that he should be more grateful for the clothes than anything. In Thayland it was common for a man to be bare-chested in the summer months, but Carsiss was a different story. In Carsiss the sunlight beat down on you like a tangible fist, threatening to sear and tear apart your skin like it was so much rubble. Its hot kiss was like that of a vampire's, robbing you of your energy and fluids greedily and mercilessly. Although everyone was glad the sun was there, they also realized it was a double-edged sword, both generous benefactor and bloodthirsty parasite. Will's new army uniform was designed with that in mind, both hiding his skin from the sunlight and allowing it to breathe without relying only on sweat to keep it cool.

The journey consisted of just one step after another on the coarse landscape. Once the city was out of sight, all there was to see were the yellow ground, the flying sands, the soaring mountains, his fellow soldiers, and the charming backsides of the camels up ahead. He told himself he should be thanking his lucky stars that he was not traveling over the hot, shifting sands south of the mountains, which were said to have claimed the lives of many travelers who tended to wander aimlessly from lack of food and water. Will had never seen such a landscape, which he imagined was just a big beach with no water. And such a land seemed so daunting and forbidden (especially in that ungodly hot sun), he didn't even *want* to imagine it. If he ever saw a genuine sand dune, he thought, it would be too soon.

They rationed their food and water under meticulously strict guidelines. Each man could have only a quarter gallon of water a day, and they had to hold any water in their bladders until the unit was done marching for the day (in Carsiss, it was considered a true crime of nature for the body to waste good water in such an undignified manner, and if one's mouth went dry while their bladder ached for release, that was their body's own damn fault).

Food consisted mostly of dry rice, *chapatis,* and sun-dried beef jerky (always a favorite). But Will quickly learned that their food stores were not meant to be their only source of sustenance. He often saw groups of men jump out of line and cut the heads off rattlesnakes, and then rejoin the formation and eat the snakes while marching, its blood dripping on their clothes and staining them a dark red. He was naturally horrified and disgusted at first, but after trying it himself he had to admit it wasn't bad eating. He had to bite down hard into the skin (which was not slimy as it appeared but smooth and dry) and pull the tender meat out underneath, taking care not to ingest any bones or funny substances. Rattlesnakes were an especial favorite of the men, while the king snakes and cobras were eaten only out of necessity, for their meat was stringy and foul.

They sighted the canyons at dawn. The unit stopped about half a league away and set up camp, which involved building their tents and reining the camels together. During all the runabout, Commander Tanalac sent his scouts to the canyons to look for the Mulvars. He said to be careful for they were armed, sent by their chieftain to invade Nünveghett. They were not to show themselves, only to determine their location and report it back.

The men took turns at sleeping in the tents, and on that particular day the privilege fell upon Will. He was half-asleep when he faintly heard the order to move out. He sat up and hastened to get his boots on (boots were very rare in Carsiss, commonplace only on soldiers and the *Ksatriyas).* The others in the tent made their way out before he did. Just as he had slipped his hood on, the last man went out and a stranger barged in. "Will Fontaine," he said.

"Yes, sir, I was just heading out."

"No, you are to remain behind while the unit advances."

"What? Are you serious?"

"It's the commander's order."

Will stepped closer. "No, I've got to be on my way now."

"You are to stay in here, Will Fontaine."

"Why? What's the commander thinking?"

The stranger sounded a little sympathetic but remained firm in his stance. "It seems you are a favorite of the Emperor's, and the commander does not want you to come to harm, as it would make him lose the Emperor's favor."

Will pointed at him. "You tell him to get that ridiculous notion out of his head! I came here to serve and that's what I'll do!"

"Remain here, Will Fontaine!" the man cried, then abruptly left. Will followed him out but only took a few steps from the tent. The man mounted on a camel, gave Will a last look of warning, and took off, his mount trotting more like a dog than a horse.

Will watched him go, more confused than ever about Commander Tanalac's intentions. Not wanting to displease the Emperor was understandable, but since when had he ever given a damn about that as far as Will was concerned? He had maimed his ear and stepped on his foot with impunity, but currently he didn't want the Emperor's favorite diplomat to fight their vicious enemy despite all the way he had marched to get there? It was utterly absurd. He sneered and nearly cursed the gods, but he then realized he shouldn't say the gods' names in vain in Carsiss. Who knew who might still be listening?

He watched the unit go till the camp had no one but himself. Having just eaten and with nothing else to do, he went back inside and went back to sleep (with his boots on, for he didn't want a scorpion or centipede to crawl in them). He didn't sleep well but managed to stay down for a good forty minutes while the men were down in the canyon doing Lord-knows-what to those barbarians.

When he became fully awake, he decided he had had enough. To hell with the commander's order, he was going to go down there and survey the situation. He may have missed the fighting, but at least he had to gather details for his final report to the King. There was no one around to force him to stay, anyway. He downed most of the water in his snakeskin bag and rushed out of the tent and down to the eastern canyons. For one he wished he had a camel, foul beasts that they were.

He expected only two things at the battle site: dead bodies on the ground and the Carsian unit victorious. The Carsians had to have been victorious, because if they hadn't been the Mulvars would have surely invaded and decimated the Carsians' camp with Will right inside it. His expectations did not disappoint him, except that the dead bodies were not as he had pictured.

Will carefully climbed down in the canyon, and the first body he saw was of a man wearing only a *dhoti* and a necklace of beads and lizard bones. He had died from a deep puncture in his neck by a spearhead, not far from the stream running through the canyon's depths. There was no weapon lying nearby him, so Will figured that a Carsian had taken it as a spoil. The next body he came across was a woman—at least, it looked like a woman, what with the colorful *sari* and the long hair. He wanted to be sure, so he turned the body over to see her face. She had died from arrows to the heart and belly; her eyes were frozen in a look of shock and pain. As if seeing a dead woman in a battle site was not horrifying enough, two children lied nearby, her hand still clenched around one of theirs. Arrows that had missed their marks lied all around as if from a hailstorm.

Will slowly stood up over the woman and peered further down the canyon. The canyon curved to the right, so there wasn't much more to see—except for more bodies scattered around. Once his eyes were adjusted to the shadow of the canyon, he could spot more women among the dead.

He went into the heart of the canyon, where the Mulvars' camp lied—or at least what was left of it. The Mulvars had settled themselves in numerous tents of elephant and tiger skins, most of which had been either torn down or burned by the rampaging Carsians. The sky was murky with smoke, the air pungent with the acrid smell of fire and burnt flesh. The place was alive with wild yelling and stomping feet, sounding more like a circus than a battleground.

More bodies were everywhere, scattered lifelessly about like sandbags. There seemed to be an equal amount of men and women, not to mention boys and girls, their young innocent lives ripped from them with indifference. Some of the people were killed with decisive strokes; others seemed to have been toyed with, their wounds numerous and indirect. Blood flowed freely from each body, staining the sandstone ground as red as roses and spilling into the flowing stream, turning into trailing ribbons of dark scarlet in the water.

Will moved in a state of shock, somehow managing to keep his breakfast from reaching his gorge. He had his scimitar at the ready on his belt, but he barely acknowledged it was there, holding his arms straight at his sides. He peered at nearly every body he came across, looking for a soldier among them. There were none. Some of the men had swords and spears, but a good many of them were unarmed, and none of them wore full body armor (there was a pair of gauntlets here and there but that was about it). They were not fighters; they were merely commoners who made their living through crafts, such as blacksmithing, pottery-making, tailoring, and farming. Judging by their state and by the presence of the women and children, the Carsians did not encounter an invasion force; the Mulvars were most likely simple nomads who made the canyon a temporary shelter from the sun. They were probably hoping to avoid a battle with the Carsians, but the Carsians had dragged them into one, anyway.

No, this was no battle, Will corrected himself. *This was a slaughter.*

There were hardly any Carsians among the dead. The Mulvars had no chance against the raging, armored Carsian soldiers. That especially went for the women, who were forbidden from seeking combat skills, and that of course went doubly for the children, who likely had no taste for blood and could not hold any decent weapons.

Will's mind boiled with rage and confusion, threatening to make him wild with anger and guilt. They had been expecting an invasion force, not a gathering of families. Why hadn't the Carsians first recognized who they were dealing with and then proceed to capture, not massacre, their enemies? Wouldn't that have been what the Emperor wanted?

And where was Will's place in the fighting? Why had he been brought along across the desert flatlands only to be left behind in the fighting?

You now know why you were left behind, he thought to

himself. *Commander Tanalac knew you wouldn't approve of the slaughter of these innocents. He probably never even meant for you to see the carnage being left behind, only the heads of these "fierce barbarians." It's a curious thing, though, that he didn't order his messenger to stay behind and ensure you stayed with him.*

He ventured further into the Mulvarian camp. Carsian soldiers romped about like madmen, seemingly searching for something. Spoils probably, and also survivors hiding among the burning tents and supply stores. Will had been training with those very men for about a month, and he wasn't surprised by their actions. The soldiers in Carsiss (or at least those in Commander Tanalac's charge) were prone to fits of violent behavior and ruthlessness. They occasionally got into fistfights with each other, which everyone would gather around and wager on. At nights of particularly hard drinking and roughhousing, they would find two dogs (either off the streets or from a soldier's residence), provoke them into anger, and then let them loose on each other in a pit, usually someone's enclosed backyard. That is not to say they were all uncivilized, for they often paid respects to each other and each other's wives and lovers, and they never faltered in paying respects to their ancestors nor in reciting their daily prayers.

But one would not know that judging by their apparent thirst for blood in that canyon. At one point, twenty feet away from Will, a Mulvarian man ran out from a burning tent where he could not hide in any longer. Soldiers threw rocks at him, and one struck him in the knees, causing him to fall. He rose to his feet, but he had hesitated long enough to allow a soldier to catch up to him from behind. The soldier ran past him, slicing his sword across the man's neck. Blood sprayed out and fanned across the ground; the Mulvarian man tried to touch his wound in disbelief, but he didn't have the strength to even bring his arms up. He fell to the ground, becoming just another statistic in the pages of history. He had slightly fairer skin and trimmer eyebrows than the Carsians, as did the rest of his people; those were the only differences Will could make out between the two peoples.

Will suddenly wanted to see Tanalac; he had to see just what their bold and noble commander was doing amid all the lawlessness. He found him in a clearing, the skies above him tainted with the smoke of nearby fires. Will could have expected to catch him doing a thousand things except for what he was doing just then: holding a baby high above his head as if proclaiming it to be a sacred creature or something.

Strangely enough, there were about thirty Mulvarian people gathered around, whom the commander was addressing: "Is there anyone who will claim this child? Anyone at all?" No one said a word. "You know what this child's fate will be. Confess and at least have the dignity of joining him."

The soldiers around him stomped their spears and looked around menacingly, daring any of the Mulvars to claim parenthood of the child. Still no one spoke.

"Good, then let us be done with it," Commander Tanalac said. With that, he laid the baby on a birch wood table (gently, not roughly as if handling a fresh fish), and took out his scimitar.

Instead of getting right to it, he starting making another speech. Will could hardly hear him, for his blood was rushing in his ears. Without much thought, he ran up to the gruesome scene and snatched the child up from the table. It was wrapped in a hole-riddled blanket, which made the child easy to handle. "What are you doing!?" he cried, though he damn well knew the answer.

Commander Tanalac looked outraged at first, and Will thought he'd go into one of his exhausting tirades about how he was a worm of Thayland. But the commander got sensible and gave Will a shrewd look. "No one is claiming custody of this child," he said. "Its parents are probably dead. It is better that it leave this world and go into *brahman,* the universal force, and undergo *samsara* and be reborn—perhaps even reach *moksha* and be forever pure of soul."

They were ideal conditions surrounding the child's death—too ideal, and the commander knew it. Plus he was leaving out his promise that the child's parents would die along with it, which would topple his argument over why the child should die and be relieved of being left an orphan. But somehow Will didn't think it was wise to point that out.

"You can't kill him," Will said, holding the baby in the crook of one arm and using his free hand to open the blanket to have a better look at it. It was crying its lungs out, occasionally coughing on the faint traces of smoke. "It's just a *child;* it can't even hold a sword."

"It *will* hold a sword," the commander said. "He'll grow up and kill twenty Carsians before he's taken down. Is that what you want?"

"It's a girl," Will said matter-of-factly, his voice shaking. He found himself wanting to look at the child more than he did Tanalac, and he forced himself to gaze more at the commander. "It's a *girl*. She'll probably never hold a sword." He wanted to say more—things like how much of a coward Tanalac was to execute a baby and make a show of it, and how it took no bravery or guts to kill helpless women and children with a band of armed and fit soldiers. But he thought it wholly unwise to say such things—not because they weren't true, but because he was in no position to do so. Tanalac was the one in charge, the one in command of the soldiers, the one who had their absolute loyalty. Will was the odd man out, the one who was leaving himself in a precarious and extremely dangerous position; it didn't even matter that he was an ambassador. Later, thinking back on that moment, he would compare himself to a chess player. His argument was the board, his points of reason the pieces. If he had merely upset the commander with barbed convictions, it would be akin to merely lifting his chess opponent's pieces off the board and claiming victory—which of course would really be no victory at all.

Will kept his mouth shut and let the conviction in his eyes do all the telling for him.

Tanalac shook his head in contempt and said, "If you really care so much for it, *you* go and find its parents. If you do, I swear I'll spare it and the father and mother."

"Will you spare these people?" Will asked. It was a risky question, and he really had no hope for their safety, but the question needed asking, anyway.

"I will. I'm going to send them free to deliver a message to Marsoon Diachhe: 'Do not let any of your people go anywhere near Nünveghett, for our patience is nearing its end.'"

Will couldn't see what was so wrong with the Mulvars being near the capital. They had weapons, true, but they couldn't be blamed for wanting to protect their women and children. It was always the women and children who flashed in his mind, and though it was unfair for the bodies of the men to linger as an afterthought, that didn't mean their deaths were any less unwarranted.

"Fine, I'll go and—" He couldn't continue, for his voice had cracked from an overflow of emotion. He steeled himself and said,

"I'll find the parents, and I'll make sure you set them free."

"Good, do that," Tanalac said. "But if I were you, I'd just drop it. There are plenty of fine spoils to go around—why waste the opportunity to find some?"

Looking for spoils was the furthest thing from Will's mind, not that he'd let Tanalac know. He turned and went to the surviving Mulvars in the clearing, personally asking each one if they owned the child and assuring them that both the child and parents would be safe. The Mulvars' use of the Carsian language was spotty, but thankfully they had enough mastery of it to understand him.

He kept wondering if Tanalac really meant to free them. Letting them live for that long while his men scoured the canyon to kill more was a good indication that he was sincere; on the other hand, it was possible that he was just staging a show, getting their hopes up merely for his amusement. He had already proved to be a monster beyond Will's initial reckoning; if he was capable of any more cruel and twisted operations, Will wouldn't be surprised.

None of the survivors claimed ownership for the baby. They were probably afraid that Tanalac would follow through on his promise to slay her and her parents. Will couldn't blame them for that, but he vowed to himself that if he was in their position, he'd be glad to take his child back, if only to take her away from the wolves.

When it was clear the baby would find no salvation in the clearing, Will went about the unlikely task of finding the parents elsewhere. He didn't mean to search the bodies, only to find a surviving Mulvar to claim ownership, whether he or she was actually a parent or not. It was an impossible task, he knew, for the Carsian soldiers did their own tasks well, clearing the camp of all traces of life. But Will had nothing else better to do until the commander ordered the unit to return home, so he took a shot at it.

The rampaging soldiers noticed him with the baby, and soon a crowd formed around him, taunting him and stomping their feet. The child's crying had intensified, and Will worried about her health. The antagonizing went on for about a minute or two, and Will knew it was only a matter of time before someone snatched the baby from his arms and did some ungodly thing to her.

But Tanalac approached the mob and ordered it to disperse. "The child is his spoil, and any man who does wrong by it will have to answer to me." The soldiers sobered up and retreated, most of them looking back at Will and either sneering or frowning. Will was hardly grateful for the commander, for he was sure the order was for his own amusement. It was somehow funny for him to see Will search desperately for the child's parents.

Two hours later, Will was found with the baby still in his arms. He was hungry and thirsty, but what he was most concerned about was the welfare of the child. Her crying was almost continuous, and she took breaks only in order to catch her breath. Finally the commander ordered the soldiers to gather in the clearing (which was impossible, for the clearing was not big enough for all of them) and ordered them to return home in an organized fashion. He sent them back to camp except for six men whom he handpicked. Will stayed behind on his own, making sure that the survivors were let go. They were, as Tanalac ordered them to run down the path of the canyon opposite his men—but to Will's horror, he had his six men release arrows at them. Two more Mulvars died in that canyon, and Will could only be grateful that they were the last to do so.

Tanalac led his men out of the clearing without so much as looking at Will. Will gazed down at the child, who had calmed down and was half asleep for the moment. It was actually the first time Will had held a baby in his entire life, and he had little idea of what to do with her. He could only hope his resolve and his wits could allow her to survive the way back to Nünveghett.

Soon after Will returned to the Carsian's camp, he was summoned by Tanalac. He stepped inside the commander's tent and stamped a fist over his heart just centimeters above the baby's head. The baby was thankfully quiet during the procession.

"That child is your spoil," Tanalac said matter-of-factly, "but I warn you: I will not recognize its presence here. I will only give you *your* share of the water, not a drop more. That goes for the food and blankets as well, and you're also not getting another turn inside a tent. We'll be heading out within the hour, and if you need to stop and tend to the child, no one will wait for you. If anyone does, they will be punished. You will not be punished, though, and that is all the leniency you'll get from me. Now get out of my sight, son of Thayland, and do not expect that child to survive: It's still barely off its mother's teat, and you can be no substitute."

Will obliged and was promptly ordered to feed the camels. He immediately feared for the child, for he expected to be handed more than his fair share of the unit's odd jobs. Fortunately, during the trek back home, that was not to be.

He couldn't simply put the child down somewhere and get to work, so he always had to hold it in the crook of one arm. Doing that while leading the camels to bushes they could feed on was trickier than he expected. He first had to search each one's bridles and make any adjustments, then pull them away to the nearest group of bushes, which happened to be a fifth of a league away, or roughly two hundred paces. Some of the camels came willingly enough, but others were stubborn, as if they didn't want to be led by a figure carrying a crying and shrieking baby. He could hardly blame them, for the crying got to him, too, and he grumbled over how the camels weren't fed earlier. It was true that they could go for days without feeding, and so they didn't need to feed until after the job was completed—but dammit, he had a helpless child in his care, so whose needs outweighed the other's?

Feelings of dread and unease had been festering in Will's heart, constantly warning him that his salvation of the baby would come to naught, for she would die if he didn't care for her properly or if he took too long to get back to the city. He wished he had a covered wagon, like the ones the Mulvars used to carry their families in, protecting them from the sun—but there was no such luxury among the unit. Soon after the unit got moving, those feelings quieted down, for it seemed the other men were bound by Tanalac's orders to do the child no harm. The warning in his heart still applied though—there was no getting over it. Will had been prepared to sacrifice his own health and conveniences for the child's sake, but he had little idea of how far his sacrifices would go.

The main thing he had to look after was the child's hydration. Her small frame could barely hold enough water for itself, and in the desert's intense heat, water ran through her like a filter. It was the same conundrum that adults had: The water she would intake would leave her through two of the usual channels—her waste disposal and her sweat. Will's water skin could hold three quarters of a gallon, which seemed enough to last the child throughout one day, but her mouth and lips became dry more often than he thought they would, and he found himself taking his water skin from his pack at least three times each hour, and fed her water till she refused any more. Periodically he had to unclothe her and hold her straight up in the shadow of a bush so she could do her natural business, and he fretted over how that waste could have been used to cool her off instead. In the middle of the first day, he took to gently washing her chest and forehead with fresh water, hoping it would help her to not rely on her sweat so much.

Feeding her was quite a different challenge. Snake meat was out of the question, nor did he think any kind of meat would be adequate; he had to rely only on his share of the food stores, which included things like beans and apples. He at first cut up his food into small bites, and then forced them into the child's mouth. It quickly became apparent, though, that she could not chew well enough for her to ingest whatever he gave her. Remembering what some animals did for their young, he took to chewing the food himself first, grinding it into a soft pulp, then spitting it into a bowl and spooning it with a finger. The process disgusted him, but the men around him made a bigger show of it: They pretended to gag and retch and vomit, and some of them offered to do some of the chewing themselves, even spitting their food on the ground and pointing it out as an offering. Will told them that if they really wanted to help, they could do that for their toothless old mothers.

By only the second day, his liberal usage of his water and food on the child started taking a toll on him. He walked much of the day with his mouth as dry as a bone, and he was prone to periods of dizziness and confusion. His wits were becoming dull and he wasn't as fast on his feet as he usually was. Plus his skin was peeling and blistering, and his eyes were becoming red and irritated. He took on a habit of taking a mouthful of water and holding it in as long as he could. It didn't help much for his hydration, and his mouth still became dry soon after he swallowed, but at least for a time he could forget how dry he was getting.

By the forth day, he began to seriously fear for his own health and safety, not just for his sake but for the child's, too. If he had to rely on someone to take care of her should he become unable to do so, he would find no one willing or capable. She would die among uncaring strangers, and that would be a fate Will wouldn't be able to tolerate.

CHAPTER 13
A SHAKY COMPROMISE

THE UNIT'S RETURN TO Nünveghett was as uninteresting as its departure, except for how some people noticed the single dark-skinned soldier carrying what looked like a baby in a dirty blanket. Those people usually told others about the remarkable sight, either right away or later in the day, and they wondered what to make of it. Whose child was it, and where did it come from? Was it perhaps a Carsian child who had been kidnapped and just been rescued?

Will heard none of it; he only hoped that the child's presence wouldn't make waves within the community, especially if word got out that the baby was a Mulvar. He was somewhat relieved to get back inside the training hall, if only to get the child out of public, but his relief was short-lived when the commander ordered them to get into formation for regular exercises. Will thought about leaving the child somewhere safe, somewhere no one would find her—but he was certain that there was in fact no such place in the training hall. He wasn't simply worried about scorpions or lizards; he was more concerned that some bastard would take the baby and dispose of her—a vile rogue that had no qualms about skipping exercises to do it, or one who was ordered by Tanalac to do it.

Will skipped the exercises instead, slipping outside while everyone formed up on the training ground. He knew he'd be severely punished, but he pushed the thought to the back of his mind. The child had to be at the top of his priorities, not his good standing in Commander Tanalac's unit.

The Palace wasn't very far from the training hall, but in the condition he was in, he couldn't run nor did he want to walk anymore. He flagged a vacant rickshaw in the street and paid the driver what little money he had on him. Inside the vehicle, Will touched the child's forehead, trying to comfort her and gauge her temperature. Despite his sacrifices and dedication, he was afraid the child was dying.

The driver was generous enough to drop him off at the Palace bridge. The two guards at the main gate trusted him well enough not to insist on seeing the child up close, giving her only a passing interest instead. Once past the gate, he felt his strength returning, for he knew he had taken the baby into a virtual lion's den. He had to keep his guard up.

Walking in the hallways of the Palace proper with the Mulvarian baby in his arms, he felt more conscious of himself than he ever did in his life. He prayed that the child wouldn't cry and draw attention to herself. Someone may then insist on seeing her, offering Will to help, then see that the baby was a Mulvar and start what would undoubtedly become one of the biggest scandals in Carsian history. Will realized that the Mulvars were more different than the Carsians than just by name; they were of a different race, and while their differences were subtle, they could easily be recognized if you knew what to look for. Will didn't think to question the race of the Mulvars when he first heard of their conflict with the Carsians, and since his discovery of it, he thought their differences were trivial and could be easily overlooked. If dark- and fair-skinned people could live together in Thayland, why not Carsians and Mulvars?

Apparently the Carsian soldiers were of a different opinion, and in that case Will thought it safe to assume that the rest of the Carsians were, too. And yet he had to rely on Carsians to help him take care of the child, and there was only one place he could think of where he'd find people inclined to do it.

He had been on a stroll with Lord Harrington in the Palace halls when the lord pointed out the living quarters of the Emperor's harem. He never thought he'd ever pay a visit there, but he made a note of its location. With the baby in his arms, he rapped on the door and prepared for anything—especially rejection.

The woman with the wave of hair over one eye answered the door. She looked only passing surprised to see both him and the baby. "Yes?"

"I'm Will Fontaine," he said, trying hard to keep his voice steady. "I have a favor to ask you. Can I please come in?"

The woman took a moment to think. She was not allowed any men inside who were not with the Emperor, but the baby in Will's arms piqued her interest. She replied only by stepping back and gesturing for him to enter.

The harem's quarters was as elegant as the rest of the Palace, remarkable only in the distinct beds which were large and plush and brightly colored. He found the women either sleeping or sitting around; they wore colorful *saris* of extravagant designs, including jewel-encrusted patterns and brocaded hems. There were also housemaids with rags and feather dusters; they were easily singled out from the harem members, for they were plain and elderly, and their *saris* were of simple design.

All conversation stopped upon his arrival; the sleeping ones were awaken, and they all tentatively drew near. He was uncomfortable in addressing all of them at once, so he turned to the one who had answered the door. She gracefully took the baby from him and brought her for the others to see. The baby started to cry, but she was silenced by the woman who shushed and rocked her. It had been a while since she had heard a woman's voice.

"My unit went to battle," Will said, "except it wasn't a battle. They were going to kill her, so I took her away from them and brought her with me."

There were gasps as the women gradually recognized the baby for what she was. The woman holding her turned to Will. Her voice was rather husky, somehow making her seem wiser beyond her years. "How many others know of her?"

"Just the men of my unit."

"No one else? And they allowed you to bring her?"

"Yes. The commander didn't think she would survive the journey."

The woman looked back down at the child. "I see."

Another woman asked, "Why did you bring her here?"

"I couldn't think of anywhere else to bring her. I can't leave her with just anyone. I was hoping you would look after her for me."

"That's not fair!" one of the women cried, a little louder than Will had liked. Similar words of protest cropped up, some more heated than others.

"The Emperor will never allow this," the woman with the child said, silencing the others.

"Are you the one in charge here?" Will asked.

"I am."

"I know it wouldn't be fair for you to be responsible for her, but I'm not asking you to be. I'm only asking you to look after her awhile; it'll be up to me to plead the Emperor to allow her to stay."

There were more protests, all of them claiming it was impossible that the Emperor would give allowance. "You brought her here, it is only right for you to ask," the headmistress said, not unkindly.

"Yes, but you'll have to promise that you will look after her ... and *keep* her, not throw her at the first soldier you see. I'll not leave her with careless strangers."

There was a brief moment of silence which Will took for outrage. The headmistress then said, "You have my word, she will be taken cared of. I will look after her ..." She looked down at the child with tender and concerned eyes. "If no one else."

It was good enough for him. "Thank you."

The headmistress closed her eyes and made a slow nod. "You'd better hurry."

"Is the Emperor still in the Palace?"

"I believe he is."

Will turned to leave but then faced the headmistress again. "What is your name?"

"Jonoli."

"Thank you, Jonoli."

Will marched through the adjacent hallway as if the devil was on his heels, pleased that his gambit had paid off. The harem women were not allowed to bear children while in the Emperor's service, so he assumed they secretly desired a child in their lives—it was only natural. What he was not so sure of was whether or not they'd accept a Mulvarian child, let alone one not from their wombs. Though many of them had opposed taking the child in, the headmistress at least was all too gracious and accommodating.

But he had a new problem, one he had not factored into his plans. Those housemaids, three in all, who were only there to clean the place—they were not bound inside the quarters for most hours of the day like the harem girls. They were sure to leave and spread word about the baby like the gossiping hens they were. Will had preferred the Emperor learned of the baby from him first.

He stopped at the nearest corner and kept an eye on the entrance. Within minutes, the housemaids left the quarters, talking to each other at a fast rate, at times throwing their hands into the air as if they were being attacked by bugs. Will thought about asking them to keep their gossip to themselves for a time, but they might take it as a threat which would not reflect well on him. He turned and headed away instead, intending to beat them at their own game.

Will didn't see the Emperor right away; he wanted to speak with

Lord Harrington first, and quickly before the housemaids' gossip spread too far. He had been thinking of what to say to the Emperor, but he thought Lord Harrington might give him a new perspective with some better ideas.

The servants he passed directed him to the hot springs, where Lord Harrington was getting a massage and was apparently flirting with the young masseuse (his wife had died six years ago, and therefore he was a very eligible bachelor). "Lord Harrington," he said. "Forgive the intrusion, but this can't wait."

Lord Harrington sent the perturbed masseuse away and sat up on his marble table, wearing only a towel. "Yes, Will, what is it?"

Will sat beside him. The humid, crisp air and the sound of flowing water soothed his nerves and gave the impression that time had slowed down. He hesitated a moment, then told of the horrible massacre in the canyon, of how women and children were killed along with men who were barely armored. He told of how different the Mulvars were from the Carsians, and his theory of why they were killed.

"They wanted to exterminate them, as many as they could. They're not at *war,* or at least they are no longer. Now the Carsians just do extermination campaigns. We didn't go there to win; we went there to kill every last man, woman and child. The commander let some go free to talk to their chieftain, but I think it's only to drive them out of the nation, not out of pity."

Lord Harrington looked troubled, taking Will's word as fact and never questioning his perspective. They'd been whispering in Altrin the whole time, for their words were not for Carsian ears. "You never knew the Mulvars were a different race?" Lord Harrington asked. "I had always known, but if their war has become a massacre, this is important news. I'm certain the King wouldn't approve."

"There's something else, too," Will said. He quickly told of the baby he had rescued and of where he had left her.

"Will, that's a terrible idea," Lord Harrington said. "The harem is the Emperor's property, and giving them a child to look after may distract them from their duties, which is to clean house and please the Emperor and his guests."

"'Clean house?' I never thought they were housemaids."

"I'm sorry, 'cleaning house' is political slang for 'spying.' They're often sent to nobleman's estates so they can spy on them for the Emperor."

"And what about the child? Do you think the Emperor might take her away because she's a Mulvar?"

Lord Harrington thought it over. "Will, I'm not sure the Emperor is prejudiced against the Mulvars. He may not even know about the massacre; he may think it was a battle between warriors, nothing more."

"How can he not know what happened? He's the Emperor, he's supposed to know everything that goes on in his nation."

"But it's possible his generals only tell him what they want him to know. Let me give you an example: Fifty years ago, there was a battle in the Saffrice Sea over a misunderstanding; it was between a Varnis merchant ship and a Creian warship on patrol. The King of Varnis was told by his generals that the fight was a clear act of war from the Prime Minister of Creia; they even falsified evidence and eyewitnesses to support this. The King fortified his defenses in the Saffrice Sea. He could have gone to war at any time, but instead he demanded an explanation from the Prime Minister. The Prime Minister invited the King to his country to talk, but the King refused. The next offer was to talk in the closest thing to a neutral territory: the middle of the Saffrice Sea. The King accepted, and there they got their story straight: The Varnis merchant ship had been using a map with out-of-date boundaries, and it had wandered into Creian waters. This was said to them by the sailors onboard their ship. The story and new evidence discredited the 'evidence' of the generals, and they were all demoted with no chance of promoting again.

"So you see, Will, it's possible the Emperor doesn't know about the massacre and that he's too careless to see for himself."

"I don't believe that," Will grumbled. "I don't think the Emperor's so foolish."

"All I'm saying is that it's possible. For now, you must think of why the Emperor should allow a child to stay with his harem."

"Because at the end of the year, I'll take her home with me."

Lord Harrington nodded. "That's good for a start. But you'll have to assure him that his harem will not be distracted. And remember, their specific activities are kept very confidential, so he can't go into details about their work. In other words, you can't get a clear picture of whether or not they'll be too busy to look after the child. Have you given her a name?"

"No, not yet. My lord, what if he asks where the baby came from? If he doesn't think the battle was a massacre, he'll think I stole her somewhere."

"Tell him she is an orphan. But Will, remember, and please listen very closely: Don't tell him what happened in the canyon."

"But he *has* to know," Will suddenly burst out, his voice just a hair above a whisper.

"The *King* must know of it before the Emperor does. If you go and tell him everything his generals don't want him to know, your life may be in danger here. It'll be better to wait until you can tell His Majesty, so that His Majesty may take the matter into his own hands. It is in fact your duty as ambassador to inform him of this. Let the King talk with the Emperor of the massacre himself, for it will be less dangerous for him to do so. Do you see what I'm saying?"

"Yes," Will muttered, and then more clearly: "Yes, my lord, it makes perfect sense."

"And don't include this information in your monthly letters to the Ministry of State. Those letters are read and deciphered by imperial officials before they get sent out. As for the baby, it may be better for you to take her to a household in the city."

"No, I can't trust anyone else with her. The harem girls don't care that she's a Mulvar, but the citizens probably will. They hate the Mulvars just as the soldiers do."

"Then you should send her away. Give her to a Thayland ship, and have someone deliver her to your master. I'm sure he'll be pleased to look after her."

Will shook his head. "I'll do that as a last resort. I'd rather not let her out of my hands."

"Then you'll definitely have to convince the Emperor to let her stay with the harem. But Will, please don't let this jeopardize your duties. I don't want to see you deported like Mr. Douglass."

Will drew closer, his whispering grown softer but more fierce. "What? Franklin's being deported!?"

"So you haven't heard yet? Yes, Mr. Douglass is being deported. He's lucky he's a Thayland ambassador or he might have gotten beheaded."

"What the hell happened?"

"He's been accused of trying to poison the Emperor. Can you believe it? I've had a dickens of a time trying to convince the Emperor that the King didn't put him up to it. They thought his castration was done to somehow make him a better assassin, so I had to carefully tell them the real reason why he was cut. It's unbelievable!"

"Dammit," Will muttered. "This will look bad on both of us, won't it?"

"I'm afraid so, but don't you put yourself in his position. You wouldn't be executed, but you'd find yourself in a Thayland prison sure enough. In fact, even if you leave here on your own, you'll be arrested and thrown in jail—that's the cold reality of being an emissary.

"You should go see the Emperor now. Remember what I said, and you'll do fine."

"I will, thank you, my lord."

"I still think you should send the child to Thayland. At least try to consider it. And thank you for the information—I'll look into it sometime."

Will went to the office of the Prime Dieschsuch and asked his assistant—a man of about forty with a crooked turban and a generous beard (a typical Carsian, in other words)—where to find the Emperor. "He's usually out in his garden at this time of day," he said. "Or he's taking a bath, one or the other."

The bath was out of the question, so Will went to the garden. It was vacant, but by a stroke of luck, he ran into the Emperor just outside the building, exiting the museum with two overlords. Upon sighting Will, he ordered his servants to escort his guests to the dining hall and went straight for his troubled ambassador. "Ah, Will Fontaine, it seems you have fallen in love with my harem," he said, not angry at all but very amused. "But you seem to be mistaken, my friend. You give women flowers, jewelry, or even sweet tarts ... you do not give them *babies,* especially other people's babies." He drew out that last part at length so as to put Will's intellect into question, humiliating him.

"My apologies, Your Eminence," Will said with a bow. "I just didn't know where else to take the child."

"There are plenty of households to take her, Will Fontaine; my harem is not the only one."

"But I do not trust anyone out there, Your Eminence. I do not think anyone would take her in so willingly."

"And why would you trust my harem and not anyone else?"

Will thought carefully of a response, but the Emperor then bade them to retreat to the shadow of the museum's portico. "I think your worries are misplaced," the Emperor continued. "If you would but look, you'll see there are more compassionate people in Nünveghett than you think."

Will thought back to the first woman he had seen in the canyon, who had died from arrows to the heart and belly. She was no warrior, and she had not died because she was prepared to invade the city.

She had died because she was a Mulvar.

"Forgive me, Your Eminence," Will said, "but good, compassionate souls are hard to find even in my nation."

"It cannot stay with my harem," the Emperor said flatly. "My ladies are involved in more things than you may know, and they cannot be confined to watch over a child. Many of them are against it themselves."

A chill ran up Will's spine. The Emperor had implied that he had recently been to the harem's quarters; the thought of him seeing the child there was disturbing, to say the least.

"But I promise you, Your Eminence, the child will not be a distraction; if I am wrong, then I will take her elsewhere. I also plan to take her home with me next fall. But please, for now let her stay with the harem. I trust no one else."

The Emperor shook his head. "I have guests over, did you see? The girls must entertain them this evening, and I am not sure they can do that if they have a baby on their minds."

"Then the ladies may leave her in the care of a handmaiden, Your Eminence. Surely at least one handmaiden can be spared."

The Emperor was slow to reply, but he then nodded. "That may be so. But if my guests believe, even for a moment, that they do not have the ladies' full attention, then they will complain and the ladies will not be able to perform ... further duties."

You mean sleep with them and get them to talk in bed, Will thought. *Dammit, why does it have to come to this?*

He said, "Your Eminence, if you would allow me to talk with your harem a little, I'll see to it they will not be distracted from their duties. If your guests end up complaining or worse, then I will admit to your wisdom and take the child away."

"A bargain, then, Will Fontaine?" The Emperor gave him a shrewd look, almost as if he expected an answer; then he turned and paced about the museum's porch. Will stayed where he was, keeping silent yet thinking of all sorts of things to say next. After a minute, the Emperor asked, "Is the child an orphan?"

"She is, Your Eminence."

"Very unfortunate. I see why you care for her. I have much respect for you, Will Fontaine; I see in you the makings of a great man—a great leader and debater. Tonight will be the first test. If my plans do not go as I want, the child will be taken away from the harem. But it may not have to leave the Palace; I'm sure other arrangements can be made to your liking."

Will nodded, hoping that the Emperor didn't mean the Palace dungeon. "Thank you, Your Eminence. I am in your debt."

"Be careful when you say those words," the Emperor said with a wry smile, "for the person you say them to just may remember them."

"Yes, Your Eminence," Will said with a low bow.

"Your friend, Franklin Douglass, shall be deported," the Emperor suddenly said matter-of-factly. "He tried to poison me, the horrible little man. He should thank the gods for our treaty with Thayland, for he shall keep his head—although at that insolence, I would suggest that King Fredrick take off his head himself." Upon noticing Will's ill face, he nodded in apology. "I am sorry, Will Fontaine, I am being rude. He is your partner of a sort, and I'm sure you'll be sorry to see him go. You may see him in the Palace dungeon if you wish."

Will thanked the Emperor a second time. On their walk back to the Palace proper, he noted to himself that the Emperor did not ask where exactly the child had come from. He did ask if she was an orphan, which meant he assumed Will had come across civilians, but he did not ask what had happened to those civilians. He strongly wanted to ask him about the status of their war with the Mulvars, but he kept Lord Harrington's advice in mind. There was no need to put himself in danger; he needed to inform the King of what had happened in that canyon—and he especially needed to bring the child back to his home in Thayland, where she'd be safe.

CHAPTER 14
CONSEQUENCES

WILL SLEPT POORLY THAT night. Despite how he had his comfortable Palace bed back thanks to the Emperor's permission, he couldn't stop worrying over how the harem girls were performing for the guest overlords, for the child's life possibly depended on it. It was ridiculous when he thought of it in a certain sense, but it sure wouldn't seem so if the child was ripped from his arms like so much luggage.

He had done his best to explain the situation to the ladies and to persuade them to forget about the baby when pleasing the overlords. He wasn't sure if he got through to them, especially since he and Jonoli seemed to be the only ones who truly cared for the child—although that may have been a blessing in disguise, for if they didn't care for her, why would they think of her in the entertainment hall?

Jonoli the headmistress had kept her word and looked after the child; he was afraid he had misjudged her, but his fears thankfully proved unfounded. Jonoli seemed to care for her like she was her own. She had even given her a name: Ambri. It was derived from *ambriva,* the Carsian word for "hopeful." Jonoli said the name was inspired by him, for hopeful was what Will was for the child. Will said there couldn't be a more fitting name.

His time with Ambri was short, for he was very tired from his long and frustrating trek. He wanted to stay as long as he could, but the ladies insisted he go to bed early and eat all that he could at sunrise. "I understand the toll you have taken to get Ambri to safety," Jonoli had said. "Hopefully, you will not have to suffer for her anymore. You must rest, for you have an important day tomorrow. You can leave the rest up to me."

Will gave her a funny look that was one part gratitude and one part confusion. It seemed too good to be true for the harem's headmistress to be as equally dedicated to the child as he was, even though the child had just been laid into her lap.

When he woke up at first light, what he first wanted to do was see Ambri—but there was one thing to be done before that.

Will had once been in the dungeon beneath the King's Palace in Augustine nine years ago. It was a dark, dank, and desolate place that he wished never to see again. The dungeon of the Emperor's Palace was slightly brighter, for it was aboveground with plenty of windows for sunlight to get in. That was hardly a blessing, for the sunlight of Carsiss' blazingly hot desert warmed the dungeon like an oven, cooking its porous flagstones like a flame to a piece of coal.

Will found Franklin Douglass in his cell sweating buckets, his shirt and pants stained from the moisture gathered around his armpits and crotch. He was asleep when Will arrived; the guardsmen who escorted Will banged a tin cup along the cell's bars to rouse him awake.

"Franklin?" Will said. Franklin got up quickly at Will's voice and drew near the door. The guard pulled out his sword and ordered him to step back. Will said that it was all right, but the guard insisted that Franklin had to follow his orders.

"Are you here to get me out?" Franklin asked from his bed.

"Sorry, but no," Will replied, speaking in Altrin. "I just wanted to see you before you get deported today."

"Oh," Franklin said, looking more sorry for himself than he ever had. Reverting to Altrin, he said, "I'm glad to keep my head, but a prison in Thayland is no picnic, either. I'm damned either way."

"What happened, Franklin? I heard you tried to poison the Emperor."

Franklin's eyes grew large with outrage. "No, I didn't! I was told to give that cup of wine to him by a cook, so I did, and the Emperor gave it to his food taster, and he sniffed it and sipped it, and the next thing you know he dropped on the floor shaking all over. The Emperor told his guards to arrest me, and only me! I keep telling him it was the cook, one of the damn cooks who gave me it, it was *his* fault it was poisoned! But I heard from one of the negotiators who visited me here that the Emperor trusts his cooks implicitly, so it had to be me who poisoned the wine!"

"Is the food taster dead?"

"Yes, what do you think happened?"

"Did he taste everything the Emperor had that evening?"

"Yes, of course he did."

Will thought about the evening when the Emperor entertained the ambassadors with his harem; he hadn't needed a food taster on the wine and rum then. And yet on all other occasions when the Emperor ate and drank, a food taster was there to ensure his food was untainted. So why hadn't a taster tested the wine and rum on that night with the harem? Will tried to make a connection that would uncover someone's guilt, but he couldn't, not without asking all the food tasters of who should have been the taster that night.

"Where did the cook give you the wine?" Will asked.

"Out in the hall when all the cooks brought the food in," Franklin replied.

"And you didn't think it was strange that they treated you like a servant?"

"No ... well, they knew I was trying to make a good impression on the Emperor."

"You mean you told them about your mission?"

"No ... but it was obvious to everyone I've been trying to impress him. I mean, I'm not a good talker like Lord Harrington, and I'm not a good sword-practice buddy like you. All I've got are my charms, so I thought ... maybe if the Emperor really liked the wine I gave him, he might take a shine to me. It was foolish, I know that now. Never trust a wine you don't know about!"

"It still seems odd," Will mused. He asked Franklin a few more questions, such as what did the suspicious cook look like and why he thought the Emperor completely trusted his cooks. He then gave Franklin his condolences and promised to write letters to the King and the Royal Court asking for clemency in Franklin's case, seeing as how there was little evidence to incriminate him.

In the following days, Will would question the cook and the imperial food tasters, but it was to no avail. All the cooks denied giving Franklin the wine, and the food tasters couldn't remember who had tasted the Emperor's wine and rum on that night with the harem (one of them said that it was not unheard of for the tasters to neglect their duties from time to time).

Finally Will talked with Lord Harrington, hoping to get a new angle on the case, but he was of little help. "I've said before, this place has its share of corruption," Lord Harrington said. "If the Emperor chooses to live in denial, then there's nothing we can do ... not unless we catch one of the cooks with a bottle of rat poison in his hands."

"The cook should have known the poison would go to the taster first," Will said, "which makes me believe that he was trying to frame Franklin for the crime."

Lord Harrington nodded. "I'm afraid so, and may he rot in hell in any case."

"But why would he do that?" Will asked.

"Mr. Douglass was the weakest one of us, Will. He couldn't talk shop with us, only try for attention. Maybe that one cook realized this and thought he'd do the Emperor a favor by getting rid of him."

"That's a pretty weak motive, begging your pardon."

Lord Harrington smiled helplessly. "I know, but it's the best I can think of."

Will never came to a better conclusion on his own, so he was forced to admit that he could not crack the case unless he did some inside investigating or brought all the cooks and tasters to trial for serious interrogation. But seeing as how the Emperor seemed relieved to be rid of Franklin himself, any such service might be lost on an impossible customer.

Will didn't see Franklin's deportation; he was too busy getting his forearms whipped by Commander Tanalac.

Right after his visit in the dungeon, he returned to the barracks where he was immediately chided by the commander for missing his exercises yesterday. Tanalac claimed he was making a bad example for the men and that he should expect no special treatment just because he was an emissary. He then went on to say that Thayland citizens were spineless worms who did not know discipline and honor even if their lives depended on it. Will took it all with a set jaw and a calm demeanor, and he agreed to everything the commander said.

Will had just gotten through exercises and was about to eat in the mess hall when the commander and two of his sidekicks came up to him and brought him into custody. In the middle of the mess hall, in front of most of the unit's men with plates of food, Will's hands were bound together, and he was then forced on his knees so his arms could be bound to a small wooden table. Tanalac was handed a small whip that was little more than a riding crop and lashed it across Will's forearms. Dark weals abruptly appeared on his skin like shadows on the back of a grizzly bear. The commander looked around at the men and reminded them that any absence from their mandatory exercises were dealt with punishment. He brought up the whip again and lashed it across Will's flesh. Will grimaced and took in a sharp breath, telling himself not to cry, not to scream or beg, for that was what Tanalac undoubtedly wanted.

The lashings went on for five minutes. Tanalac often took the time to speak to his men, reminding them of procedure and discipline and telling them axioms such as "A man who pains to do good is more enlightened than one who pains to do nothing." He said it was unfair for Will to be regarded as an exception to the unit, yet that was just what he, Tanalac, was doing—for if it had been any other soldier who skipped his duty, Tanalac would bring out the full whip and crack it on the man's back. But since Will was a special guest of the nation, bruised forearms were all he was going to receive.

When Will was finally released from the table, he had suffered twenty blows. Streamlets of blood ran down his arms and hands, and the table was covered with fans of crimson specks. He was promptly ordered to clean himself up in time for the unit's march through the city.

Will let the commander have his moment, his little victory, for as much as Tanalac needed to do it, the commander felt no satisfaction from it. What he had wanted was not wounds and weals across Will's forearms; no, what he really wanted was to see the child from the canyon dead, either from dehydration or starvation thanks to his insistence that he'd spare it no water or food. And yet Will didn't give him the satisfaction, for Ambri was alive and in the Palace, safe from the commander's wretched claws. Will had scored the greater victory, and in whipping his forearms, Tanalac had admitted defeat.

A little later on, however, Will saw something that absolutely infuriated him. Shortly after the unit's march through the city, he noticed Tanalac not far from the barracks. A woman with a infant girl approached him. The girl was let down and she walked towards Tanalac with awkward steps. Tanalac swept her up into his arms and gave her cheek a firm kiss, and then went to the woman—his wife—and gave her lips a gentle kiss.

Will's hands formed into fists, and he grew so ill he couldn't keep his eyes on the three of them. *You're a family man, huh?* he thought. *I'll bet you didn't think of your daughter when you ordered your men to fly arrows into women and children; I'll bet you didn't think of your wife when you held Ambri up to the sky like a sacrificial lamb. You're holding your daughter with bloodstained hands, and you kiss her with a filthy mouth that ordered your men to kill innocents. You may be a family man, but you're still a bastard, still a monster, and I swear, when the King discusses the canyon massacre with the Emperor, he'll have your name on his lips.*

About the only good thing to happen that day was the pleasant surprise that everything had went well with the harem and the overlords, and so the Emperor gave his permission to let Ambri stay in the harem's quarters.

"You are very lucky, Will Fontaine," the Emperor said. "I still do not like the idea of this child in my Palace, but out of respect to you, I will allow it." Will tried to say thanks, but the Emperor interrupted. "But if there are any outstanding instances concerning that child, I may pull the child out of there. I do not want it to be any more trouble than what it is worth. My generosity can extend only so far."

Will bowed in humble agreement, and then did so again when the Emperor said he was allowed to see Ambri and the harem whenever he was free from his duties.

Will felt lighter than air as he went to the harem's quarters. Remembering his manners even though had no mother who made him remember (it was nuns in an orphanage who had done that), Will knocked on the door and stated who he was. One of the girls answered and let him in with a blank face. Will hesitantly went inside, knowing full well that he was a kind of outsider both in nationality and gender. He looked around at the women's faces and found nary a welcoming expression.

The only friendly faces were in the far end of the room, which had been made into a makeshift nursery. There was a table with bookstands shaped into a square, a pillow inside of it. Bottles of goat's milk and plates of *chapatis* were laid in one corner alongside three piles of satin blankets. Jonoli stood there with Ambri in her arms, flanked by four women who didn't mind Ambri being there. She greeted him with a sly smile and handed Ambri to him when he neared. Will stared into Ambri's big brown eyes and smiled. God, it'd been a long time since he felt like doing that! It was an almost alien feeling, and it seemed all the more delicious because of it. He noticed how Ambri was drooling from her mouth, and he laughed and wiped the drool away with a finger. It had only been yesterday when he feared she would completely dry out.

"Be welcome, Will Fontaine," Jonoli said. "Our home is your home, for as long as you like."

Will flashed her a small smile and grateful eyes ... but a second later he grew suspicious. Was Jonoli really as saintly as she appeared? Or was there something she could get out of their arrangement?

For the first time in Carsiss, Will was truly happy. He had found something to live and work for, and he counted his blessings every day. But with that happiness came the strong desire to leave, to just pack up and hit the sea back to Thayland. He wanted to get the hell out of Carsiss, for he wanted no more part in a people and an army that freely killed helpless others, no matter what the reason.

One week later, though, Will began to reconsider his impression of the Carsian people.

He had been going through the daily routine of first performing his duties as a soldier, then of retreating to the Palace and spending time with Ambri. The Emperor was away on emergency business, so Will didn't feel the weight of his gaze on his shoulders. Unfortunately Lord Harrington had gone, too, so he couldn't provide much advice about babies (he had reared a son and a daughter, and had purportedly not left all the work up to his wife).

The daily exercises were, Will had to admit, the most exciting and rewarding part of each day. All of the jumping and swinging and thrusting were honing his reflexes and building up his muscle tone. He felt more energetic and aware than he usually did in Thayland, and he wondered how well his fighting prowess would prove to be once he got back to his homeland.

The marches through the city, however, were the most dreadful part of each day. There was something vaguely unsettling about watching those different gangs on the streets with their bandanas and armbands; he always expected them to start tearing into each other at any given moment. He still had little idea as to what the gang societies were all about, and he had the feeling he didn't want to know. He just wanted to get the hell out of Carsiss and leave them behind, anyway.

On the sixth day since he had brought Ambri to the Palace, people started taking a keen interest in the unit's daily march. They would leave their houses and alleyways and clutter the streets and sidewalks to get a good look at the passing soldiers. Their expressions were hopeful rather than forlorn as they had been before. Something had raised their spirits, although Will couldn't see what. For all he knew, it could have been the clouds that were promising rain.

That next day, the crowds did one better: they cheered.

Mothers came out of their adobe dwellings with their infants in their arms and cried out in clear voices. Smiling youngsters who would have ordinarily been rampaging the streets stealing fruits and loaves of bread instead filled the sidewalks and cheered at the soldiers, who would have ordinarily been helping the local police chase them down. And although the gangs of armbands and bandanas kept apart from each other, for that day they were united in doing the same activity: hooting and hollering at the soldiers, which was quite a sight to see.

Back in the barracks, the soldiers all wondered to each other about the cause of the celebration. They had had no warning that it was forthcoming, nor any idea as to what they did that warranted such jovial voices on their behalf.

The day after that, the cause became clear. Many of them had discovered it beforehand, when they had gone out and questioned people. But Will, who had been mostly keeping to himself ever since bringing Ambri to the city, was absolutely shocked and immediately curious.

It started just as the day before with the cheering and yelling as the soldiers moved through the city. But gradually, as like a firefly emerging from the dark, two words became clear amid the white noise: a name.

Will didn't catch it at first because there wasn't enough people saying it. But once the name began to ring clear from the citizens, he couldn't help but turn his gaze towards them as he was not allowed to do. He could hardly believe his ears nor his eyes, but there was no mistake that the people were looking at him as he passed by, his dark skin making him easy to spot in the unit. He felt a rush of blood to his face, not sure what he should say or do, for the name they were all crying out was none other than his own.

It started with "Will Fontaine," which many Carsians he knew called him. When the unit progressed to the river, though, the crowds shortened their chant to just "Fontaine." The same mothers and hoodlum youngsters who had filled the sidewalks yesterday cried out that singsong chant, giving no clear reason for their worship other than that he was their hero. Will wondered if it all had something to do with Ambri, the child he had informally presented to the city when he arrived back from the canyons, but it seemed too good to be true. Surely they couldn't be cheering for the sanctuary of a Mulvar, one of their sworn enemies.

Whatever he had done, the acclaim for him transcended

genders, generations, and even gang memberships. Men in both bandanas and armbands chanted his name. Old men with walking canes and snot-nosed brats who probably didn't know what they were saying chanted his name. There was even an elderly fellow who had his genitals attached to a sandstone block with a rope who chanted his name. He had been crawling on the ground in that fashion in order to purge himself of sin, but for that moment his sin was forgotten, and he propped himself up by his elbows and cried, "Fontaine! Fontaine!"

Will hadn't been put on the spot like that since he was chosen for ambassadorship, only he had been partially expecting it that time. On that day, there was no forewarning, no signs of some kind of uprising. He knew he was partially responsible for that, for he hadn't been going out in public and checking on the status of the people. He hadn't wanted to for fear of retaliation against him bringing a Mulvar to the city, but after that eventful march, he fully intended to.

He expected Tanalac to summon him, and Tanalac did. The commander was fuming over the chanting crowds, and he expected Will to answer for it.

"I'm as much in the dark as you are, sir," Will said.

"You made that happen somehow, Will Fontaine," Tanalac said, pointing an accusing finger at him. "And by the gods, you have to know. Answer me!"

Will choose his words carefully. "I've done nothing outstanding lately, other than bringing that child into the city. If it is not because of the child, then I have no clue, sir."

"The child," Tanalac said mockingly. "What the hell is so special about that child?"

"I do not know, sir."

Tanalac snickered. "I ought to request for that child to come into my custody, then we'll see what those people think."

Will gave a brief look of disgust and outrage, but he kept his cool. "If I may ask, sir, what does this have to do with my duties as an officer?"

"What does *what* have to do?"

"The child ... and those people."

"They're a distraction, both to you and to me. I don't need—"

"Sir! I shall do my duties no matter what!"

Tanalac struck him on the right ear with the back of his hand, then drew his face near Will's. "Do not interrupt me when I'm talking! I don't know how they do things in Thayland, but here the commander owns a part of all his men's spoils. You know what that means, do you? That child is mine as well as yours, and if those people do not quiet down, I will have to quiet them myself by taking the child away from here. That is all, dismissed."

Will thought about calling him the greatest fool he's ever known, for taking the child away would only incur the people's wrath. He even thought about making an idle threat against Tanalac's daughter, but that was just his rage getting the better of him—plus he'd never sink to Tanalac's level. No, if Tanalac made good on his promise, it would have to be the Emperor to put a stop to him ... and if the Emperor refused to get involved, Will promised himself he'd take desperate measures, even if it killed him.

The following night, Will went to an inn-and-pub near the barracks, a favorite hotspot for a group of friends that included Tamaro and Bihar. Will was sorry for missing out on seeing Ambri, but he had to figure out the real cause of the people's celebration.

He covered himself as much as he could, dressing in a hood and cloak which made him look like some sort of wizard or parlor magician. Not long after he sat in a booth and threw back the hood, he was recognized and surrounded by admiring fans. They constantly barraged him with questions, many of which he could have done without, but he had to answer them as a way of saying, "Thanks for the free drinks."

"Is it true that Thayland is full of witches, and that people are dunked in water to see if they are witches?" asked a man with half his teeth remaining.

"No, those stupid witch hunts ended years ago, before I was born," Will said.

"Is it true that Thayland women are kept indoors until they turn sixteen, and then they're set loose to marry any man they like?" asked an elderly woman with shallow eyes and large crow's feet.

"I don't know about the marrying part, but that first part might damn well be true, for all I know."

"Is it true that you have no camels, but you do have horses as big as elephants?" a lanky young man with thinning hair said.

Will, having never seen an elephant, shrugged his shoulders. "It might be true, but you still need two such horses to pull a wagon with twenty bales of hay."

The young man opened his eyes in astonishment. "You must make *everything* big in Thayland!"

There were a few more questions he answered about Thayland, but eventually someone let loose with the whopper—the one question that turned the whole topic of discussion around: "Why did you save that baby?"

Everyone had been talking all at once, but at that question they quieted down, eager for the answer. Will thought about it, conscious of the soldiers nearby who had been there that day in the canyon. "The baby was orphaned," he said.

"How did the parents die?"

Will shook his head. "I didn't see them."

"Well the soldiers must have killed them."

At that, the discussions arose once again, and the soldiers looked into their drinks as if they might rediscover their dignity in them. For his part, Will tried to pay attention to all the talking going on before him. It was hard to keep track of what any one person was saying, but one man stood out with his loud, booming voice, his generous belly filling out his loincloth, and his yellow vest getting more beer stains from his shaking mug. "The Emperor wars against those Mulvars without our say-so! He doesn't care what happens to them or what happens to us, just as long as his soldiers spill their blood and we don't say anything against it! Well shame on him and shame to our country. Here's to the Mulvars, and to their baby in our Palace!" He raised his mug and downed the rest of its contents.

Will returned to the barracks feeling haunted and betrayed. If what that man said was true (and it very well might be, for no one disputed what he said), then the Emperor knew all about the massacre in that canyon and had no confusion as to Ambri's origin. Will felt he had put himself into a tighter box than he'd thought, and that Ambri's safety hung by a thread thinner than he believed. It was for Will's sake that the Emperor showed leniency for the Mulvarian child, but it was still remarkable that he showed any leniency at all. He had wanted her and her people dead in that canyon, so letting Ambri stay with his harem showed a conflict of interest.

Or perhaps the man in the pub was mistaken; perhaps a lot of Carsians didn't really know much about their emperor. People in Thayland said all sorts of things about their king, even though none of them knew anything about him or what he did. Still, that didn't keep Will from shuddering at night with images of dead Mulvars and of Ambri racing through his mind.

Three months after arriving in Carsiss, Will was put on night patrol. It was Commander Tanalac's way of trying to separate him from Ambri. But thanks to a favor from Prime Dieschsuch Halicut, the order was rescinded. Will was put on daytime patrol instead, which suited him fine because the weather was growing mild in Carsiss, the strong sunlight becoming no problem as long as Will wore full clothing and a hood.

Thanks to Halicut's favor, Will continued to see Ambri at nights, plus he could sleep in his plush Palace bed. He played with her whenever he could, amusing her by twirling yarn around his fingers and making shapes, playing peek-a-boo, and playing got-your-nose, among other strange and silly things. But mostly he helped feed her, buying her crushed food and fresh juice and milk with his generous salary. Oftentimes he could be found in the makeshift nursery in a new rocking chair, holding her in his arms and carefully feeding her from a bottle. It was a most unmanly sight, and if word ever got out to the soldiers as to how he looked in that chair, they would have piled endless layers of shame on him. That never happened, but even if it did, Will would have hardly given a damn.

He bought her necessities such as a brand new crib, clothes, and earthenware utensils; he also liked to spoil her with new toys such a top, a rubber teething ring (as opposed to wood), dolls of different sorts, and a small magnifying glass ("her seeing glass" he liked to call it). He even bought a large teddy bear as tall as his arm was long; the ladies voted to be rid of it, saying it was in bad taste and wouldn't look right in their quarters. Will reluctantly conceded and gave it to a poor family whom he found washing in the Calkune.

Jonoli proved to be a doting surrogate mother who cared for her as well as any new mother would (Will could tell because Ambri was comfortable and happy in her arms). She admitted that she never had to look after a baby before, but she got by on her instincts and by seeing what methods worked and what didn't. In no time, she could pick Ambri up with no discomfort on either part, and she could feed her without overdoing it. She could tell when Ambri needed to eat, spit up, or have her diaper changed. She kissed the child goodnight and got up in the middle of morning whenever Ambri started crying. It was as if Ambri had come from her own womb.

Will made sure to show his appreciation. At times he'd give her bouquets of daisies, tiger flowers, or cactus flowers. She always took them graciously with a friendly kiss, then settled them in a vase he had gotten. One day he brought her a rose, and she chided him for getting it, for they were rare and particularly expensive in Carsiss. That next week, he surprised and infuriated her by bringing three more.

The ladies of the harem were usually not allowed out of their quarters except for two evening hours, and only if they traveled all together. The only exception was if one lady could find a male escort she could trust. Jonoli took Will as an escort, and they were sometimes seen roaming the Palace halls together, talking the night away. Will talked of his master's estate back in Thayland and of how he had gotten there. That little tale led to the greater one of how he had met King James, fudging the details a bit so that he didn't mention Marie the ghost girl or the magical seeing glass she gave him. Jonoli found the story charming, but she admitted disbelieving it.

Jonoli in turn told of how she had been sold into indentured service when she was sixteen, for her father had died and her mother could not look after her. "It was to a dastardly *Ksatriya* who took advantage of me," she said. "Not all the time, only some of the time. He was married and had to hide it from his wife. He promised me death if I should ever tell her. A year later he had to sell me as a payment for a debt. It was to a wealthy weapons marketer who was skilled as a fighter. His wife taught me how to use a sword without his knowing."

"Really?" Will asked. "You can use a sword?"

"I've grown rusty over the years, but give me a sword and it can all come back to me. I ran away from that man and left Carsiss for a while. When I came back I ... *fell* into indentured service again. Then Emperor Orissu had his eye on me and wanted me with a sick desire. He bought me and forced me into his harem. Not long after, he died and left me in his son's possession."

Will remembered that Emperor Orissu had died five years ago, so that would make Jonoli definitely older than him, perhaps by three or four years.

"Do you regret it?" Will asked.

"I suppose I am. I don't know, it's been a long time since I've resigned to my fate. If I were to go free, I'd be a slave to no man, perhaps never marry. I've seen and done many horrible things—no man would want me with such a *karma.*"

Will frowned. He supposed she meant the spy-work the Emperor made her do. She'd had to sleep with many men, and perhaps even kill those who proved to be an enemy of his. And yet she was so caring when it came to Ambri, it was hard to imagine.

Although many of the ladies had resented Ambri's presence in their quarters, in time most of them grew to like her. They all wanted to have a turn at feeding and holding her. Will was pleased over how Ambri had grown on them, but on his visits he oftentimes had to force his way through the women to see Ambri himself. Some of them started to resent him in a new way, saying that they took the most care of Ambri, so it wasn't fair that he should have her in what little time he was there. Jonoli tried to defend his long absences, but it was like talking to barking dogs.

The Emperor was getting more prone to taking long trips, being away for weeks at a time, always accompanied by Lord Harrington. Whenever he returned, it was only for a short interval. On one of those visits, the Emperor decided to hold a victory celebration, for he had just had two warring overlords sign a peace agreement. It wasn't a particularly great victory, for the agreement was little more than a ceasefire, but Will suspected the Emperor wanted to enjoy some comforts of home.

One of those comforts was his harem, and he invited Will, Lord Harrington, and a few of his *Ksatriya* vassals for another gathering with the ladies. Will feared that the ladies would be awkward around him, but on the contrary, the whole ordeal with Ambri seemed to have increased their desires for him. All the ladies in the room stole at least a short glance at him, even if they were with the other men; that may have made the other men a little jealous, but it fortunately made little effect. Will especially had the eyes of Jonoli, who had been prone to touching him those days—usually with just a hand on his shoulder or arm—but in being the headmistress, she was only allowed to sit with the Emperor.

The day after the gathering, Will tried to talk with Lord Harrington about Ambri and the canyon massacre. But the lord shook him off. "Believe me, Will, I'd like to talk, but not now. I'm looking into the matter, but I haven't seen or heard enough. And I wish to investigate without the Emperor noticing. Just a little longer, Will, after we get back from Dekla province—then we'll talk."

"At least come and see Ambri," Will said. "She's gotten so much bigger since I first saw her."

"Sorry, maybe another time," Lord Harrington replied, then made a hasty farewell and headed down the hall as though he had a hot date.

Before Will knew it, it was the middle of December. The temperature dropped dramatically, the scorching sun having lost its teeth. The citizens broke out their heavy clothes and kept fires going at nights.

He sadly thought of the people of Thayland getting ready for Christmas and the new year. In Carsiss there was no Christmas and the new year didn't come until the spring equinox. Will bore his bleeding heart to Jonoli, saying that he was missing out on spiced eggnog and roasting chestnuts and Christmas trees. (He had to explain the concept of Christmas trees to her, and she thought him mad to talk of a fat man in a red suit going down a chimney for the sake of an indoor tree).

"But what I especially miss is the annual winter jousting tournament," he said. "We don't have much snow in Thayland, but the blistering cold makes it more challenging for the knights in their steel armor." He then had to explain what jousting was, and she compared it to fencing, another sport prone to serious injury.

One night when Will was low in spirits, Jonoli broke away from the harem when the ladies passed by him. He was standing by a banister on the third-floor landing, eating a green apple. Jonoli stood beside him and asked what was the matter.

"Nothing," he said. "I was just thinking that this can't last—you know, with you, me, and Ambri." He made it sound as if he wished their arrangement could last longer, when in fact he couldn't have it last shortly enough. He was anxious to leave Carsiss with Ambri in tow, but he couldn't say that out of courtesy to Jonoli.

"You do not like it here, I know," Jonoli said. "You long for home, just as you should. There are things happening in Carsiss that you cannot abide ... nor can I."

"Can you tell me what is happening?" Will asked, lowering his voice to a bare whisper. "Just what is going on with Carsiss and the Mulvars?"

"We are at war, which the Emperor and his colleagues would tell you. But these days, it is not so much a war as it is a termination. They kill innocents just like they would Ambri."

"But why? Why do the soldiers do that?"

"Carsians usually honor their ancestors by keeping old blood feuds alive. A disagreement over land that had happened hundreds of years ago may be remembered by their descendants today. It is a flawed way to settle things, and I do not commend it, but that is the way it is. Carsians may believe in *karma,* but we also believe in ageless revenge."

Will shook his head. "But the Emperor doesn't believe that, does he? He just celebrated a peace agreement between two overlords. He can't agree to the killing of innocents, whether they're Mulvars or not."

Jonoli drew in closer to him. "I am sorry, Will, but I do not know where the Emperor stands on this. I am too afraid to ask him. I just believe there is nothing I can do about it. But there was something *you* had done about it, and it does you more credit than anything any ordinary soldier would do. Truly, the gods hold you in their favor."

Will was about to say that what the gods favored was open to interpretation, but then thought better of it. "The people seem to regard me as a hero. It's all because of Ambri, so not everyone abides by the killing of innocent Mulvars. So why do the soldiers do it anyway?"

"City-living is something new in Carsiss," Jonoli said. "Nünveghett was a fishing village at first, but over the past two hundred years, it has grown into the heart of a mighty empire. City-living gives people new things to live for and new duties to uphold. This has made them grow soft in holding old blood feuds. City people are not interested in blood feuds, and so the people in this city do not care about the traveling Mulvars. They prefer to leave them be, or perhaps to even take them in as brothers and sisters."

Will was surprised at that. He was beginning to think that blood feuds were the reason for the gangs in the city, but if Jonoli was right, then that theory was thrown into question.

"I am a quarter Mulvarian," Jonoli said. "My great-grandfather was a Mulvar, though he never married my great-grandmother, a Carsian. When I was told about it, I did not understand the implications. My mother and father had to explain to me about the blood feuds between the Carsians and the Mulvars. They are numerous, Will, more than I can remember. The generals and possibly the Emperor would do horrible things to me if they should ever find out."

"I won't tell," Will said. "So, you mentioned the generals. Are they definitely responsible for the war?"

"Yes, they are in complete command."

"Is it possible that the generals are killing innocent Mulvars without the Emperor knowing?"

"That is not likely. The Emperor has a keen interest in the war. He wishes to know everything that is going on."

Will wished he could take her word for it, but she couldn't convince him. He had to wait until he could talk again with Lord Harrington before he could be certain.

"I think I'm at a loss, Jonoli," he said. "I want to bring peace to this land, but saving a baby won't do it alone. And I was only sent here to keep the peace between our two nations, not tell the Emperor how to run his state."

"Do you believe there can be peace between us and the Mulvars?" Jonoli asked.

"Well, look at me. Do I look like a son of Thayland?"

"But you *are* a son of Thayland."

"No buts—do I or don't I?"

"You look like a Euthasian, but it matters not."

"That's right, it matters not. But the truth is, my distant ancestors were from Euthasia. They were brought to Thayland against their will and sold as slaves. The fair-skinned men treated the dark-skinned as property, and this lasted for hundreds of years. It was not until the dark-skinned converted to Christianity when they were treated as equals, and when the serfs were freed, so too were the slaves. It was not thought possible for a time, when riots and lootings were common. Now fair-skinned and dark-skinned work side by side, and we are all the better for it.

"It may be different here, because I don't know the differences between your two peoples, but if you find something in common—something *strong* enough—then there can be peace. But not right away, maybe."

"But you will leave us before that happens?" Jonoli asked. If she had been any of the other women, she would have sounded scared or fretful. But Jonoli was calm and collected, almost unnaturally so. Her cool demeanor combined with her husky voice made her seem older and wiser than a hermit atop a mountain; it was no wonder she was chosen as headmistress, and there was little doubt that she could handle a sword as she had claimed.

"I don't want to, but I have to as ambassador," Will replied.

"But maybe I'll come back. Perhaps the Emperor will invite me back in, and then we can talk. We can put all the bullshit aside and get to the real details. We can talk about where I found Ambri, and *how* I found her. Did you know I first saw her in the hands of my commander? He was about to execute her in front of Mulvars, probably as a warning, or probably just to show how crazy he is. He's a monster of the worst sort, Jonoli; you'd do best to steer clear of him."

They both fell into a comfortable silence, Will lying his scarred forearms on the banister, Jonoli standing beside him. Jonoli then said, "Even if you lose a chance at peace, there is one thing you have won here."

"What's that?" Will asked.

Jonoli placed her hands on his shoulders and forced him to stand straight and face her, then put a cool hand on his temple. "You have won my heart."

She drew in and gave Will the most sensual and provocative kiss he'd ever had. He found her lips warm and smooth, thanks to the moisturizer she always put on them. His hands wanted to slip beneath her billowy *sari* and feel the skin underneath, but he tamed them by remembering they were still in a semipublic place.

When she parted from him, he was left wanting more, thinking it was over too soon; then he realized it had been longer than he thought. She quickly took his hand before any rebellious juvenile thoughts crept up in his mind and began to lead him away. She brought him to his quarters and opened the door as if it was her very own. Once inside she did the locks herself, and then he had the idea of pulling a table in front of the door, just to be safe.

Will had thought that all their talk of slaughter and blood feuds had raised his guard up, but instead it seemed to have lowered it, for he surrendered all his senses to her that night. In his bed, Jonoli showed him sensations and bodily desires he'd known only in dreams. She seemed to know all his pleasure points, functional limits, and carnal preferences, all the while letting him only *think* he was in control—an illusion she had perfected over the years and could perform with minimal effort.

For that one night, Will's concerns melted away, spun into earthly ecstasy and lost among its many colors. He felt as if caught in a thunderstorm with no safe place in sight, but that was okay for he was thirsty and yearned for all the rain in the world. Jonoli was his thunder, his partner, his captor, and his mystery. He was indebted to her, but yet she was an enigma he was leaving unsolved.

At daybreak, Will was roused awake when Jonoli climbed out of bed. She hurriedly dressed herself, claiming she had to get back to the harem's quarters before anyone noticed her missing (or at least to let the women know she was still safe). Will got up himself and made ready for his morning patrol. At some time in the process, he said, "Jonoli, I'll not forget all you've done for me, but I have been betrayed before ... and if you should betray me, I'll make you sorry for it."

For a moment, Jonoli pretended as if she didn't hear, instead putting the finishing touches on her *sari* with her back to him. But she then turned and said, "You'll have nothing to worry about."

It was quite the understatement, though she couldn't have known that. Two days later, Will experienced another night he'd never forget—which Jonoli had nothing to do with.

In the two days between, Will had started a regular routine of doing his morning patrol and then seeing Ambri at night. He was sometimes followed around by curious citizens during his patrol, but such instances were becoming rare as people noticed that he acted much like a regular soldier and not some heavenly saint.

Meanwhile Ambri was getting rebellious, growing fussy and discontent with staying in her crib, even at night. One of the ladies who knew about children warned that Ambri was bound to have a sense of independence, even if it was best for her to be more dependent.

Will and Jonoli grew closer, touching each other whenever they pleased and giving gentle reassurances. But they were slightly afraid to show affection in front of the others, for the Emperor would not like to hear that his harem's headmistress was more interested in another man. They kissed only in private and discussed the Emperor only between themselves.

"What do you think he would do if he found out?" Will asked once.

"It is hard to tell with him," Jonoli said. "He might not care as long as we don't do anything in front of him. He might not care for me so much since he often uses me on his guests. Or he might disown me and throw me into the dungeon, for I know too much. If he should become angry, he might be coaxed to do nothing if I should ... well, if I should tell him an important secret about you. Which I never will."

Will felt a pang of dread despite the reassurance. Jonoli was a smart cookie, but she could be *too* smart. She could have him tied around her finger if she wanted to. "Have you ever ... been with him?" he asked.

"He's been with all the harem. He does not prefer one over any other, even me. It is just my job to keep the other women in line; other than that, I am not so special."

Will wasn't so sure about that, for the Emperor might have been more particular than she realized He wondered how the Emperor could sleep with his whole harem and keep a wife at the same time. The answer, which was all too obvious, came to him: The Emperor could do that because he was the Emperor. On the other hand, if his wife should leave him or cheat on him, he could place her under the axe or guillotine. It was the same with Thayland's king.

On the evening of his second unforgettable night, Will had tried to send Ambri to his home in Thayland. He went to a cargo ship in Markereen with a Thayland crew and spoke with its captain. The captain shook his head and strolled down the dock, keeping an eye on his men as they unloaded crates. "Sorry, young man, but I can't do it."

"I'll pay for everything," Will said as he kept in step. "I'll even give you all the food she'll need on the way."

"We're all working men here, with no time to look after a babe. If the little one dies on me, then ..." He turned and looked at Will with apologetic eyes. "Well, I don't want it on my conscience. If you were coming along, then maybe we could work it out—or maybe you could find someone else on passage to Thayland to take the babe. But today I'm taking no passengers; you'll have to look elsewhere."

Will considered the advice, but as he looked around the harbor, he could find no Thayland citizens waiting for a ship. Tourists from the north were becoming rare in Carsiss, and Will might have had to wait all day to happen upon one. Instead of taking that chance, he returned to the Palace, feeling sure that Ambri wouldn't leave for Thayland until he did.

He kissed the sleeping child goodnight and turned in for the evening. He locked his door as he always did but left the window open; he liked the cold evening breeze and thought it left no security risk.

In the middle of the night, a gag was placed over his mouth. It took him a while to realize it was not part of a dream. He awoke with a jerk and tried to take a deep breath, but the only air he got was from the folds in the black cloth. He grabbed one of the arms holding the gag and pushed it away, sitting up in bed at the same time. He was mother-naked but had no qualms about rising from bed to meet his assailant.

He turned out to have not one visitor but two—men dressed all in black, their clothes mostly made of cloth but also consisting of leather belts and gauntlets. They had hoods that enveloped their entire heads, except for slits they could see through.

The nearest man jumped onto the bed and kicked Will in the belly, then gave a few good blows to the head and chest. Will grabbed hold of his arms and spun their bodies around, making them fall off the bed and knock down a table with a vase. Both men got up and exchanged punches and kicks, Will having the more difficult time because of his bare feet stepping on shards of the broken shale vase.

The other man was near the window, standing with his feet wide apart. He decided he'd had enough of watching, so he climbed on the bed to get involved. Will tried to pay attention to him, but he had his hands full dealing with the first assailant; he let the second man grab him underneath the armpits, lift him up in the air, and heave him over the bed. Will crashed on the hard marble floor, getting a good smack on the head and twisting one foot badly. He quickly crawled over to his sword and drew it from his belt. He pointed it menacingly at the men while getting back up on his feet. His foot wasn't broken and he didn't twist his ankle, but they felt fragile and couldn't allow him stable footing.

The men risked getting closer despite the sword in their faces. Will swung his blade when they got close enough, not bothering to give warning. He thought he'd surely hit them, perhaps slice off a finger or two, but the men were too fast for him and jumped out of harm's way. It was true even for the second man, who was of a considerable depth and height. After just a moment, once his aching head cleared up, he thought who that second man could be: Commander Tanalac.

Will had his name on his lips, but he never spoke it. He growled instead and swung his blade as he neared the men. They avoided his blows at first, then the second man blocked a strike with one gauntlet and struck Will's elbow, effectively crippling it for the moment. Will dropped his blade and was at the assailant's mercy, taking in punches like a raw steak. He struck at the man's chest, but he had armor on underneath his black outfit, so he went for the head instead, which was considerably higher up than his.

The first assailant then drew a dagger and swiped it. Will thought he'd be dead for sure, but the swings were only halfhearted attempts which never touched him. He decided to risk his foot and barrel-rolled past the larger man, getting to his sword on the floor. He planned to take the larger man's head off, but the man kicked him in the gut before he could stand and planted a double-fist between his shoulder blades. Will somehow managed to keep his footing, though he dropped the sword again. He neared the bed, hoping to get higher ground again and turn the tides in his favor. But the larger man then drew his own dagger and made swipes that scratched him on an arm and shoulder. But scratching was all he did, and Will wondered if he was intentionally giving him love taps or was merely incompetent.

Will climbed up on the bed and tried to put all his focus on punching the living daylights out of the larger man. It was a decision he'd later regret, for he was a little successful. He had intended to disorient the man, take his dagger, and then bring it to his throat. The man was disoriented, but he still punched and slashed like a bucking mule, and in one of his throes his dagger leapt out and slashed across Will's right eye. The eyeball exploded, and since there was no initial pain, Will at first didn't realize what had happened. He knew he had gained a blind spot, but he thought it was from the blow to his head. He then brought a hand up to the wound and made a voiceless cry. He stepped back and eyed his assailants with hatred and spite, letting his feelings be clear before they paired up and ended his life.

But apparently their job was done. They sheathed their daggers and abruptly left through the window, rappelling down the ropes they used to enter the room in the first place. Will tried to lift one of the grappling hooks that anchored the rope, but it was too heavy with the man on the rope. He had uncovered his erupted eye, but he was repelled at the idea of anyone seeing him that way and placed a hand over it again. He then noticed how bloody his hand was and told himself not to be foolish, for he was bound to catch an infection if he kept touching it. He left his room and ran to get the Palace physician, who would surely be in bed but was used to house calls, what with the Emperor being a bit of a hypochondriac.

CHAPTER 15
THE TRUE STATE

HE DIDN'T KNOW WHAT was the worst part: his socket being wiped out or the disinfectant in said socket.

The physician—a man pushing sixty who would have been called a "cranky ol' wanker" in Thayland—was brutal in getting the ooze and blood out of there. He had Will lie down, pushed a hand on his forehead and cheek, and used his fingers to keep the eyelid open while the other hand wiped around the inside with a clean cloth. It took minutes that seemed like ages. He then tossed the cloth on a nearby table and dipped another cloth into a short bottle of something like alcohol. He held the eyelid open again and dipped the wet cloth in and out in a flash. It stung like a sonuvabitch.

"Ouch!" Will cried, rising from the couch.

"'Ouch' is a woman's word," the physician chided.

"Then I guess I'm not a man," Will snapped. "And I'm not a woman, either—just call me *'it.'*"

The physician insisted he had to do more with the disinfectant, or else Will would get an infection that could not be chopped off with an axe. Will conceded, and the torture continued. But his pain was nothing compared to the humiliation of returning to the harem with his new cloth eye patch. Everyone demanded to know what had happened. Will joked that he fell and landed on a pebble. Jonoli approached him cautiously and let him go past her without a word. He settled in his rocking chair and made a deep sigh.

"Whoever did this to you, we shall find him and kill him," Jonoli said.

"There were two men in black," Will said. "I couldn't make out their faces."

"I know who they are," Jonoli said. "They are your fellow soldiers. They've always hated Ambri."

"Have any of them said anything to you?" Will asked, suddenly concerned.

"No, but from what you've told me, I know they hate Ambri—*still* hate her."

One of the ladies picked up Ambri from her crib, who started crying. "You want to hold her?"

"No, please," Will said. On some days, when he had had to deal with a lot of trouble on patrol, he found it hard to slip into a compassionate and fatherly mood for Ambri; after the attack in his room, he found it impossible to do that.

Jonoli retrieved Ambri, who then stopped crying, especially when Jonoli started her diaper change. The other women understandably gave her a wide berth. "You said there were two men?" Jonoli asked.

Will explained that they didn't seem to want to kill him. They made only lame attempts to wound him, and when one finally did wound him and had him cornered, they ran like the cowards they were. Most of the women fawned over how brave and lucky he was; Jonoli merely moped about, craving revenge for what was done to her man.

Will was granted a reprieve from his soldier duties, thanks to a decree from both Prime Dieschsuch Halicut and Qadeem Duraslim, the Dieschsuch of Military—a large and hard-bitten man who was nonetheless all too happy to tend to the needs of a wounded Thayland ambassador. Tanalac was not pleased, for he thought Will was still fit for duty, which made him vie for the title of "most hard-bitten."

The healing process progressed to the physician's satisfaction, though that did not mean that more disinfectant was not necessary. After the turn of the year in Thayland, Will replaced his cloth eye patch for one made of horse leather. He had to admit, it made him look tougher, but Jonoli didn't care for it. "You should not need it at all," she muttered. "This should not have happened. We cannot let those men get away with it."

Jonoli was more dead set on revenge than Will was from the very start, but Will was not decided on the matter until his first meeting with Tanalac since the incident. He had to present himself to the commander to let him judge whether or not he was fit for duty.

Tanalac did not look his best: His cheeks were yellow from fresh bruises, and he favored his right forearm which Will's blade had hit (the gauntlet must have been made of cheap iron, which the sword easily dented). He couldn't help but give Will knowing eyes and a sly smile from time to time. "So, eager to come back, are you? After a little poke in the eye, you come crying to me, wanting to come back? You spineless worm of Thayland."

Tanalac eagerly had Will sign a waiver and scheduled him for the next day's exercises. He told Will he'd better not slack off, though Will wouldn't dream of it.

Will later told Jonoli what he had suspected all along—that Tanalac had been one of the intruders.

"Why didn't you tell me this sooner?" she asked.

"Because I had no proof," he said. "But I do now; I'm sure of it now. Still, no one would believe me."

"So what do you want to do? Curl up and take it like a dog? Is that it?"

"Well he's given me shit before, but I've never complained—thought it'd do no good to complain. And now I still won't complain—I'll do one better. I'll go eye for an eye, make him sorry he did this."

Jonoli commended him, then said if he wished to kill Tanalac, she wanted in on it, too. Will said he wasn't a cold-blooded monster like him, so there'd be no killing; instead, he'd give him a warning—a notice that he was not as helpless as Tanalac thought.

"I know," Jonoli said, "we'll steal a horse, cut off its head, and leave it on his bed for him to wake up to."

"Holy shit, you serious?" Will asked.

Jonoli shrugged. "Here in Carsiss, it happens all the time."

Will thought about it. "Or for better effect, we could use a cow's head, make him wake up to *that.*"

Jonoli was shocked. "A *cow's* head? Are *you* serious? Will, a cow is a *sacred animal,* you can't—"

Will raised his hands up. "Hey, I'm only kidding, only kidding. I'd never hurt a cow."

Jonoli gave him a haughty look. "Just kidding? You'd *better* be kidding, or you won't get any of *this* ever again."

Will and Jonoli soon started to make their plans. They wrote a list of equipment they'd need and even had their measurements taken for black outfits of their own. What they next needed was a map charting Tanalac's daily activities. Their plan was simple: Kidnap the commander, strip him naked, and leave him in the outskirts of town. It was more humiliating and sanitary than dragging a horse's head around.

But their plans hit a snag when the Emperor returned. Will and Jonoli had vowed not to go along with the plan as long as the Emperor was present, for there was no accounting how many eyes and ears he had around.

With the Emperor came Lord Harrington, and Will made it a

point to talk with him right away. But before he could, he had to make a show of greeting the Emperor in the foyer and assuring him that he had kept his Palace safe and unspoiled.

But to his credit, the Emperor was not very concerned with his Palace. "By the gods, what happened to you?" he asked.

Will rose from his bow. "I was attacked two weeks ago in the dead of night. Two unknown figures made an attempt on—" Before he finished, the Emperor laid his hands on his head and lifted the eye patch. He frowned and wrinkled his brow, then dropped the patch with a look of pity. "But I am alive and well, Your Eminence," Will continued, and then ended with a lie: "That is all that matters."

"I am terribly sorry for you," the Emperor said. "I'm sure an investigation has taken place?"

"Yes, Your Eminence, but there has been no clue as to who those men were."

"No, I was thinking of how these men could have gotten to you past security. Was someone sleeping on guard?"

"No, Your Eminence—no one was sleeping, but no one saw anything, either. The intruders used ropes and grappling hooks to climb up to my window; to do that, they had to climb over the outer wall somehow." Of course, what Will didn't say was that Commander Tanalac could very well have knocked on the front gate to get past the wall, then slipped into his outfit and asked any nearby guards to look the other way, as implausible as it sounded.

The Emperor angrily shook his head. "We will find the guards who should have been watching over you, and they shall receive a hundred lashes—no, *two* hundred lashes. No one ignorantly allows intruders inside the Palace; those intruders could have come for *me,* you understand."

Will hastily agreed, then accepted an invitation to a welcome home feast for the Emperor and parted ways with him. Lord Harrington then approached him and said, "Will, I'm so sorry what happened. We should talk about it later, but after the feast. I'll see you then."

The cooks slaved over ovens and stoves for the next few hours, and they presented a meal that barely left any room on the long dining table. Will hadn't been hungry earlier, but his fasting caught up to him and he had generous firsts and seconds. It was like a feast from Heaven, especially since lobster was never served in the soldiers' mess hall.

Will later followed Lord Harrington to his quarters and finally had his second chance to talk with him since the canyon massacre. Lord Harrington offered Will a seat and said, speaking in Altrin, "Will, I've been asking around, everywhere I've been. It seems the war against the Mulvars was waged with no warning, no special circumstances—it just happened. The Emperor waged his war and the Mulvars have been fighting for their lives ever since.

"The Mulvarian state—or what little state there is, since they're mostly nomads—had armies at that time, but the Carsians have whittled them away. They're now defenseless and can barely get any weapons or armor. Carsiss has them cornered and desperate, but the nation's still pressing on. Nowadays the true state of the war is a genocide—an extermination of an entire race of people. It's just as you've said. I had my doubts at first, but I've kept hearing the same thing from all over the nation."

"The King won't like this," Will said.

"No, of course not," Lord Harrington said with a wry smirk. "We're talking about innocent people being slaughtered like cattle. No decent person would approve of that. Not only is it inhumane, but it doesn't reflect well on Carsiss. Who's to say they won't kill civilians in Thorain—or Thayland even—should they be called there? That's how the King will look at it, you know. Now tell me something: Have you asked around about the massacre?"

"No ... well, the harem knows of it. I had to tell them why I took Ambri."

"Ambri? That's the child's name? How is she?"

"She's good. I'm afraid she's cooped up indoors all the time, but she's healthy and well fed."

"You know, it's possible those intruders attacked you because of her."

"I know that, but to hell with them. What I really ought to do is appeal to Thayland for asylum."

"They'll never grant that—it's specifically in your contract. They don't want to acknowledge that relations with Carsiss have been slipping."

"If I'm sent home in a pine box, they'll slip even more."

Lord Harrington nodded. "Good point. Don't let me stop you, then. Now about the Mulvars, they've been having blood feuds with the Carsians for hundreds of years—"

"Yes, I know about that," Will quickly interjected.

"—which is the entire basis of their extermination. But the

people I've talked to don't seem to care about those feuds anymore. They've seen the killings, and they're as human as you and me, so no one approves of the war. There have been movements to stop the war, and they've mostly been underground—but that's just conjecture, because almost no one wants to tell me about them. There have been public outcries, but they've usually been shut down by the soldiers and police." Lord Harrington added ominously, "The Emperor wants no one to question his war."

"What about your theory that the generals are keeping him in the dark?"

"I think I was mistaken in that. This 'war' has been going on for four damn years—you'd think it would've come to a head by now. And the Emperor makes speeches—he really likes making speeches—and he gives subtle hints that he knows the Mulvars are helpless. He keeps calling them 'the scourge,' and he's admitted that the soldiers' spoils don't amount to much replacement armor and weapons. There are rumors that the Mulvarian leader, Marsoon Diachhe, has petitioned—hell, has *pleaded*—the Emperor for peace, but the 'war' is as strong as ever."

"What about those people in the canyon? Have you heard anything about them, like why they were there?"

"Yes, there had been people in Markereen who told me this: They were refugees who were expecting a boat to arrive and take them to Thayland. They had sent a scout into town to look for the boat while they hid away in the canyon. But the scout was found by guardsmen, and they beat out of him the location of the refugees. I suppose they killed him then. The Emperor claimed they were an invading army and thus justified the reason for sending his troops—but nearly everyone knows the truth, for they know the true state of the war. It's no mystery to anyone, anywhere."

Will swallowed hard and solemnly looked into his lap. He seemed to have been the next to last one in Carsiss to know, and it seemed he had totally misjudged the Carsian people.

"Many Mulvars aren't sticking around for it, of course," Lord Harrington said. "They've retreated to surrounding nations such as Rozimi and Alquin. Carsiss usually has only cool relations with its neighbors, but in some places like Alquin and Bune, the troops can actually cross the borders and pursue the Mulvars. But much of Carsiss is sacred ground to the Mulvars—you know how that goes—and many of them don't want to leave. God help them, they're just standing there down south, waiting to be killed."

Lord Harrington finally fell into prolonged silence. He'd been keeping his tone of voice cool, casual, betraying little concern in case prying ears were listening to his foreign words. It was admirable, but Will could see the cost it took him in his contorted features. He then continued:

"Speak of this to no one, not even the women of the harem. Send your petition if you must, but remember that letters can be opened and deciphered—and then sent right back to the Emperor. And don't get close to any of those women, God save you; they are a part of the Court, and you know what I've said of the Court. It's best if we ride out our stay of diplomacy and then make our full, uncensored report to His Majesty. I look at your eye patch, Will, and I know we're in too much trouble as it is. God be with you, young man."

The next day, the Emperor made a stunning announcement. He was in his throne room, standing atop his high dais with three of his generals kneeling before him at the bottom of the steps. Spread out across the room were commanders, lieutenants, and two Thayland ambassadors, all kneeling with their heads to the floor.

"As I journeyed through the province of Sancrat," the Emperor said, "I heard rumor of a new resident in old Sancrat Palace: a mighty dragon that has been terrorizing villages and cities. They call it Kojari. It is possible it has a nest there, breeding a new generation of fear and carnage in our great empire. For our safety—and for our *honor*—this dragon must be slain, its head brought to my Palace as a great treasure—a treasure greater than any jewel, for it is a treasure that attests to the bravery and capability of our nation's forces.

"It is my honor to send you to the dragon, to have you prove your skills and mettle, and to display to the whole world that the forming of our mighty empire was not just an accident. You shall gather your forces and leave by month's end."

The Emperor tapped a fist over his heart and cried, "To glory and honor!" Everyone followed suit, even Will who suddenly felt sick. First a mission of genocide, then a mission of dragon-slaying? It seemed too incredible to be true, plus he felt like campaigning as much as he did poking out his other eye. He was going to leave Ambri behind and put himself in danger—and for what? Honor and glory and the head of a dragon. It was ridiculous and too much needless work—but unlike what he did to a heckler one day, he was going to keep his mouth shut.

It was a long month full of drills and equipment checks. Will had to spend more time at the barracks and see Ambri less. Troops from within the immediate area of the capital were gathering in Nünveghett, and it was up to Will to help organize them and arrange their lodging. Most soldiers were able to stay within private homes, but a good many of them were left to stay outdoors. Thirty days after the Emperor's announcement, nearly nine thousand men were gathered for the dragon hunt.

On the day he and the entire division were set to leave, Will made his goodbyes to Lord Harrington, the women, and Ambri. Lord Harrington took it hard, but not as much as Jonoli. She was a steel magnolia, but rather than cry out against the Emperor's foolishness, she let her tears flow while doing her best to stifle her sobbing. He wiped her tears away with his thumbs, and she wrapped her arms tightly around him. They made a final kiss even though they were in front of the whole harem. Hiding their personal affection from them seemed of little importance in that dire hour; and besides, the other women suspected of their close relationship, anyway.

Will looked long and hard at her, thinking of a way to say sorry for putting her in such a predicament, but he knew she would just chew him out for it so he let his silence speak for him. He could have once more lain with her that previous night (all he had to do was ask), but he didn't dare with the Emperor's presence in the Palace. Having sex without it was risky enough, but it seemed even more unwise with it.

Parting with Ambri was even harder. Sitting in the rocking chair and feeding her milk, he remembered their hellish journey through the desert flats, his struggle to keep her alive and healthy, and how he had nearly failed. On the day of his return to Nünveghett, Ambri hadn't been very responsive, simply breathing for the sake of it and not taking interest in anything he or others did. Thinking on that, Will sighed through his nostrils and shed a tear. He quickly rose and gave Ambri away, unable to finish feeding her. Ambri cried in the harem woman's custody until her new bearer sat and resumed feeding.

He turned to Jonoli and said, "I don't care, do whatever it takes to keep her safe. Without me around, who knows what the hell will happen." He kissed her once more and abruptly left.

Will had had his share of strange conundrums since arriving in Carsiss: Though he was excited to serve both his country and its ally, he was sickened by the last mission of his unit. Even though saving Ambri was not in his best interest, it was what his conscience wanted and what his homeland would want. And then, just before he left on the dragon-slaying mission, he wanted both to stay in the Palace and to get the hell out. He wanted to stay because of Ambri and Jonoli, while he wanted to leave because of the Emperor's wife.

Her name was Annell. The Emperor had visited her in Dekla province and brought her with him on his visit to Sancrat province. Will had first seen her at the Emperor's welcome-home feast. She was every bit the goddess that Lord Harrington had joked her to be—a physically flawless woman who easily outshined her husband in terms of looks and personality. Will didn't think she was any more beautiful than Jonoli, but there was something about her that was very compelling, very intriguing. She had a soul of mystery and spark, easily the life of any party, and had a persona that demanded respect in any form. She both repulsed and fascinated Will at the same time.

At the feast, she asked a lot of pertinent questions to all the guests, including the dieschsuchs, the local *Ksatriyas,* and the two Thayland ambassadors. She seemed interested and knowledgeable of everything they were interested in, be it camel safaris, blacksmithing, hunting exotic animals, or local politics. Her engaging conversation coupled with her pleasant laughter had them all eating out of her hand.

Once she turned her attention to Will, it was clear she had taken a special interest in him—one that was on the edge of perverse. She first asked him his name. Once she got it, she said, "Fontaine—it rhymes with Futin, the Nebanese god of masculine desire. His wife is Fantin, the goddess of the ocean waters. Alas, they cannot mate, for they have been cursed by Carnel the Black Witch, doomed to have ugly offspring should they conceive."

Will couldn't help but widen his eyes a few times. "I assure you, I'm not Futin in disguise," he said jokingly.

"Ah, but you look like him," Annell said. "Even with your eye patch, you're as scrumptious as chocolate cake. Everyone can see that."

The Emperor smiled serenely as if he was used to her publicly flirting with other men. "Will Fontaine believes in only one God, my dear, so he'd never claim to be one himself."

Annell made a laugh that sounded like a gasp, as if the Emperor's wry observation was hysterically funny. "But surely, Fontaine could be a god if he wanted to. He could be ... the ruler ... of us *all.*" She whipped her head down, letting her plume of hair bounce a little, which was probably an intended effect. She then picked up a carrot stick and stuck it between her teeth while looking at Will from the top of her eyes, smiling like a court jester.

"Lord Fontaine is a valued member of our military," Dieschsuch Qadeem said. "He is showing how splendidly Thayland disciplines its troops."

Will was about to argue that he was no lord, but Annell bounced in her seat and asked, "Are you married?"

"N-no, my lady."

"Then it is good you are in Carsiss; you should marry a Carsian woman. Thayland women keep themselves so pent-up; they are like dams ready to burst open. I just don't understand why they don't let themselves go. Now, Carsian women, we devour men's hearts and ask for seconds. Doesn't that sound more exciting to you, Will Fontaine?"

Will's mind drew a blank on how to reply—it *did* sound exciting, yes, but he wasn't sure such a woman was right for him. And then he remembered that Jonoli might be such woman, and reconsidered that opinion. And then he realized that saying no to that kind of question from the Emperor's wife was really no option, so he nodded and smirked.

"I *knew* it!" Annell nearly cried out. "Thayland men are missing out on so much!" She continued to ask him a number of potentially embarrassing questions, all of which Will gave an answer that he thought she wanted to hear. But soon the Emperor put an end to it by saying how rude she was for completely ignoring Lady Kemmel, who was surely dying to know how Annell applied her makeup with such finesse. (Lady Kemmel actually *didn't* seem interested, but she asked the question anyway for the sake of the Emperor.)

Since then, Will had seen Annell only three times during his short visits to the Palace. She never made conversation with him, but whenever she spotted him she waved and flashed him a winning smile. It did not even matter if she was with her husband, she always gave him a greeting that suggested a bond of familiarity and mutual fondness. He prayed that their meetings would continue to be infrequent and would not upset the Emperor too much.

After seeing off Ambri and Jonoli, Will went to his quarters to collect some essentials he'd need on the way to kill the dragon, such as his uniform, his water skin, his compass, and an extra pair of boots. He put on the uniform, put his other things in a pack, and headed out for the barracks where he was expected.

He walked down a third-floor hallway that looked down on the Palace foyer. There were a handful of people in the foyer, coming and going to wherever their businesses took them, while Will's hallway seemed totally devoid of life. His footfalls were loud and lonely, his presence the only infringement in the floor's mirrorlike reflection. It was as if everyone was generously giving him some space to think in, even though he didn't like to think in that dreadful moment.

But suddenly, a woman stepped out from a niche that led to a guestroom door. She wore a gray woolen robe with a hood that wrapped her head and effectively concealed her features. She said nothing, only gestured for the startled Will to follow her into the niche. Thinking she was Jonoli, he shook his head in disbelief and did as asked with a smirk.

Before he could properly put his pack down, she embraced and kissed him. He welcomed it gratefully, thinking he could squander a little more time for one last pleasurable goodbye. But it wasn't long before he realized something was wrong: The woman didn't tend to suckle his lower lip as Jonoli always did.

He drew back and pulled back the hood—although he knew already who she was, for he recognized the plume of frizzy hair beneath.

"Why did you stop?" Annell asked, partly in outrage.

Will could hardly speak, only utter a few syllables. Annell tightly embraced him again and kissed more forcefully. Will pushed her back and tried to stoop down for his pack while catching his breath. "Annell, you shouldn't do this!" he cried under his breath, but Annell wouldn't have it—she grabbed and pulled at him, even as he stumbled back into the hallway. She begged him to come back to her before anyone heard or saw them—but it was too late, as the sound of footfalls echoed in an adjacent hallway.

Two guards rushed out and faced them with pointed spears. "Who's there?" one of them cried.

Annell gave up her fussing and stood there looking at them,

defeated and ashamed. "It is I, the Emperor's wife," she stated moodily. She opened her robe to reveal the elegant dress she had on underneath. "There is nothing to see here—be on about your way."

The guards pointed their spears to the sky and bowed. "Forgive us, Your Ladyship," they said, and retreated back in the second hallway.

Will said nothing, only gave Annell a look of betrayal and confusion. He slung his pack over his shoulder and left at a quicker pace, not daring to look behind him for fear that she'd think he missed her.

He wondered what had gotten into her, then blamed himself for simply being a Yes-Man to all her questions a month ago. He questioned the wisdom in that, for it was as if he had led her on. And yet she was the Emperor's wife, and she knew she could be forfeiting her life by seeing another man. He also wondered what the Emperor would do with him as soon as he heard about the scuffle from those guards; whatever it'd be, it wouldn't be pretty. It seemed that the dragon-slaying mission had come just in time, for he could either win the Emperor's forgiveness by bringing home the dragon's head or escape his earthly concerns by burning within the dragon's belly.

He was ready to go out the front door when he was stopped by a servant. "Will Fontaine," he said, "the Emperor wishes to see you in his study."

Will's heart leapt, and he awkwardly stood and stared down the foyer. The Emperor was the last person he wanted to see at that point. There was no chance he had sent the servant because he'd heard about the incident with Will and his wife (there was no time for that), but it was possible he would hear about it with Will right in front of him. His head would be on the block for sure. He thought about not going, wondering why the Emperor hadn't requested to see him earlier in the month. But curiosity won over reason, for he sincerely wanted to know what the Emperor wanted with him.

He jogged to the Emperor's study, sweating in the Palace's chilly air thanks to him lugging his pack around. He slung the pack down at the door and ordered the nearby guard to watch it for him. He entered with an unassuming air, pretending that everything was all right with the world.

"Will Fontaine," the Emperor said warmly. "It has been a while since we could talk in private. How are you?"

Will bowed . "I am doing well, thank you, Your Eminence."

"And how is the child?"

Will hesitated, for he did not want to talk about Ambri with the Emperor. "She is fine and well, Your Eminence."

"Is that all? She is not happy, then?"

"No, she's happy. I'm sorry to see her so confined, but I and the ladies keep her very happy."

The Emperor made a smug nod of approval. "Good. Have you given her a name?"

For one crazy moment, Will thought about giving him a bogus name, thinking it was none of the Emperor's business to know her true name. He quickly told himself not to be foolish, and he told the Emperor the truth.

"Ambri," the Emperor said. "Beautiful name. I have been away for so long, and I have many stories to tell you, but we do not have the time for that now. Will Fontaine, I have invited you here for a second look through the Sands of Carsiss."

Will was pleasantly surprised. Ambri had been taking up most of his thoughts recently, but thoughts of the Sands of Carsiss were always strong whenever they came. He'd been craving a second look and had been wanting to ask the Emperor for one since he got back. "Thank you, Your Eminence. This is an honor that words can't describe."

"You are a very interesting man," the Emperor said almost forcefully, "and trust me, I am as curious as you as to what you will see. Go on ahead."

Will turned over the hourglass as carefully as he could, trying not to let his exhaustion get to him. If he dropped the damn thing, he may as well have told the Emperor his wife had taken him as a new lover, his life was just as forfeit. When he stooped over to look into the falling sand grains, he suddenly grew worried. What if he saw his own future, and that it was not as pleasant as he hoped it would be?

It took quite some time for an image to appear. Will wondered if he had to focus his eyes in a certain way, even though he never had to before. The Emperor grew impatient at one point and asked if he saw anything. Will merely shook his head and continued staring. He was starting to grow impatient himself since he had to get to the barracks, but eventually an image finally appeared.

It was of him in very fine Carsian clothing—a red, buttonless vest made of silk, its hems lined with golden thread, paired with pants of a similar design. He wore a turban spotted with flecks of gold, with a gold emblem of the sun attached to the front. Over his blind eye was a special eye patch lined with gold and centered with a golden half-circle. He climbed a set of broad stairs and then seated himself in a throne made of silver and gold and embedded with countless jewels. He had been leading a woman up the stairs with him, and at the top she sat in a similar throne beside him. He could see her face once she was seated and when it came into focus. She was exceptionally beautiful, almost heavenly, but to his surprise, she was not Annell, or Jonoli, or even any of the harem ladies. She was a complete unknown, with large, starry eyes and a square jaw that would surely complement her smile. Will gazed down from the dais at some unseen entity, his expression serious and unforgiving; his wife (for that was what she surely was) looked much the same but a little more composed.

The image ended there. Will slowly stood up, not sure what to think of it.

"What did you see?" the Emperor asked, slightly revealing his anticipation.

Will looked at him and almost panicked. He did not want to lose his semblance of composure, for that would tip the Emperor off that something was amiss. There was no mystery as to Will had seen, and it was something the Emperor could not know about. He had to come up with a false story, and quickly before the Emperor grew suspicious. "I saw myself in Thayland," he said, secretly congratulating himself for making a good start. "I was in His Majesty's throne room, and he was laying his sword on me—knighting me."

"Is that so?" the Emperor asked. "Well, I am sure it will be so. Perhaps on your next look into the Sands, you will see yourself doing some stupendously brave deed ... such as slaying an ogre." The Emperor burst out laughing, and Will joined in hesitantly. The Emperor then led him out, patted his back and said, "Even when you are knighted, do not forget your friends here in Carsiss. If there is anything I can do for you within my power, let me know."

Will bowed low. "Thank you, Your Eminence. I am truly grateful."

"And Will? When you face the dragon, do try to stay alive. Do whatever it takes."

Will wrinkled his brow momentarily, wondering what would make the Emperor say that. He merely nodded, picked up his pack, and headed out.

At the front door, the same servant who stopped him before stopped him again. "A gift from His Eminence," he said and held out a water skin with fresh water inside, probably from the Palace spring. Will slightly groaned at the new load he had to carry, but he thanked the servant nonetheless. The servant smiled widely and said, "Pleasant hunting, Will Fontaine."

Will nodded and stepped outside. *That's good of you to be so courteous,* he thought as though speaking to the servant. *When I become Emperor, maybe I'll remember it.*

CHAPTER 16
DRAGON HUNT

AS LUCK HAD IT, WILL WAS one of the first to sleep in a tent in the military division sent for the dragon's head. Among the nearly nine thousand troops, there were only enough tents to house a seventh of them each night. The fortunate few who had them on that first night picked the short straws from the hands of attendants.

But despite the comfortable enclosure, Will slept poorly. He couldn't get the image of him as Emperor out of his head. He wondered what events could lead to such a thing, and a string of possibilities lit up his mind. There could be a public uprising born of unrest and resentment, ultimately led by him by whatever reason and means. Perhaps the Carsian people would be fed up of unnecessary military actions towards the Mulvars, and they chose to regard their families and the public welfare above their emperor. Or perhaps the Emperor would grow so fond and respectful of Will that he'd name him his heir apparent, and then he'd die without leaving a child.

But Will wondered whether he really wanted the throne or not. Being the ruler of a nation was a huge responsibility, and he wasn't sure he'd be up to it. He'd like to be a leader someday, perhaps of a military unit or a public committee, but not a king or emperor. He was an orphan who was raised by nuns and volunteer teachers, not a noble who traveled the world and gained a mind for politics. True, he was educated, but he had only a basic education and not the personal rearing that great leaders had. He honestly didn't think great leadership was for him.

And yet the Sands seemed to say otherwise. They showed him in fashionable clothes and seated in an impressive throne (impressive in Carsiss at least—no King of Thayland would be caught dead in such a gaudy seat). Perhaps Will had a greatly underestimated view of himself, or perhaps he misunderstood the image, since it only showed that he'd be Emperor, not necessarily a good one.

Or perhaps the image was not what he thought it was. He remembered the Emperor saying that the Sands showed him his future, but one that he must work at to achieve. Of course there was no denying that he'd have to work to be Emperor, but perhaps he meant something else by it. Perhaps the image he saw—as well as any image portrayed in the Sands—was not an inevitable state of things to be, but only of a possible state. Perhaps he *could* be Emperor, but only if he *wanted* to. It made more sense, but still, it was hard to imagine himself as Carsiss' big cheese.

It was a month-and-a-half's journey to Sancrat Palace, the course bearing south-by-southeast. They crossed the Saparel Mountains using the paths used by camel safaris, sometimes going in single file which slowed them down. After that, it was clear sailing all the way.

Every day put Will on edge. The path was not like the desert flats that led to the canyons—it was pure desert, full of sand dunes and dangerous wildlife such as snakes, lizards, scorpions, and hornets. Special emphasis should be put on the snakes, of which rattlesnakes were few in number. There were mostly cobras and a type called "sidewinders" which traveled by writhing their bodies and traveling sideways, which always left wondrous wavy patterns on the sand. The soldiers still killed and ate snakes raw, for it was practical and encouraged, but the practice wasn't any safer (if anything, it was more dangerous, for only rattlers made audible warnings whenever a person approached them). Will at least gave soldiers credit for avoiding their venomous fangs by approaching them with a shield out in front of them while an accomplice stood nearby and cut the head off after the snake sprang and bounced off the shield.

But the worst part of the journey for Will was not the wildlife but the unstable footing. Wherever he landed his feet, they sunk into a few centimeters of sand, making an eerie shifting sound that was sort of like crunching snow but worse. And the going was really bad uphill, where each step sunk a bit further and the loose sand made his feet slide downhill a few centimeters. He wondered how many meters of pure, uninterrupted sand there was under his feet, going on and on like the ocean waters. He never really dwelled on how deep the ocean went, for he always knew that if he fell into it, he could swim and bob on the surface. But in the desert, there were phenomena known as "sand pits" or "quicksand," where the sand was so loose you could sink into it, and how far down you could go no one knew. Of course, there had to be an end to all that sand somewhere, brought about by solid earth, because the thought of sinking into quicksand and falling straight to hell was too ridiculous—unless some of the Church's more radical preachers were right.

The convoy had one general and forty commanders at the head. One of the commanders was Tanalac, who looked about as happy as a pig in shit to be going on such a glorifying mission as a dragon hunt. Will stayed clear of him, not just for his own sake but for Tanalac's as well. Whenever Tanalac looked at Will, his usual stony expression faltered into a look of knowing. He usually put on a sly smile and raised an eyebrow, and at one point he even tipped him a repulsive wink.

Will often thought of challenging him to a fight, justifying it to the other commanders by pointing him out as the one who took his eye. But he knew he would do no such thing. Although taking risks was a part of life, he could not endanger himself any more than he had to for the sake of Ambri. Her life depended on him, and he could not let her down. He prayed that he'd quell his anger long enough till he returned to Nünveghett, where he could leave all dragon-slaying foolishness behind and look after Ambri again. The Emperor might have been praying for that, too, which was why he told Will to stay alive.

He also prayed for Jonoli. In his absence, she was sure to take a lot of flak for seeing after Ambri, and she'd have to be strong and clever enough to work around it. He might even have loved her, but he really wasn't sure. His affection for her ran deep, but actual love may not have been in the cards. It was possible their relationship was merely one of mutual interests with benefits. As for a serious commitment, he wasn't sure one would work. It wasn't that Jonoli wasn't interesting or capable of being a good wife and mother; nor was it that he was intimidated by her strong and independent spirit (in fact, he liked strong women, while so many other Thayland men only approved of docile and submitting women who never questioned orders and never showed much willpower). It was the simple fact that he wasn't sure whether or not Jonoli would follow him to Thayland. As much as he liked the exciting customs and interesting people—not to mention his commitment to return and start peace talks—he did not want to stay in Carsiss. The massacre in the canyon may have helped with that decision, but it was mostly his upbringing and his love of Thayland's society and climate. Jonoli would either have to leave Carsiss or kiss any commitment between them goodbye.

Along the way, the men amused themselves with the usual games and fireside stories. Whenever Will was in new company at the nightly campfires, he impressed them with his story of how he and twenty others uncovered a secret gambling hall in the city. Gambling in Carsiss was looked down upon, for it was thought to hinder the economy. Gambling between two or three people was tolerated, but gambling done in crowds was strictly prohibited. Once soldiers heard that Will was involved in a casino bust, they wanted all the details, such as the layout of the building and the types of games being played (and they always seemed excited to hear them, as if they wished they'd been there off duty so they could place a couple of bets). Will always told the truth (the place was a rat's nest with stained walls and flooring and too much dust in the air), but the soldiers who'd been there with him felt free to exaggerate (there were hot table games as far as the eye could see, free tobacco and pipes, a large pit for cock-fights, and of course, dancing girls).

The most exciting part of the tale was when the soldiers broke open the makeshift vault (it was merely a steel box, and very rusty at that) and dumped out its contents—fifty thousand rupees, all in unmarked bills. As was customary and allowed by law, the soldiers split the money between them (which greatly upset the casino's proprietors, though they could do nothing about it while under arrest). Will came away with just over two thousand rupees, a part of which Will donated to a medical care facility for *Sudras*. The rest greatly helped with his care of Ambri, a fact that he kept his comrades in the dark about.

Will also asked the soldiers for any dragon-slaying stories they'd heard. He was dismayed to learn that most tales of past conquests were so grossly exaggerated that one couldn't tell apart the fact from the fiction. Each tale involved some kind of swanky larger-than-life hero who often single-handedly killed the beast in question. One dragon, which was said to be as big as the Emperor's Palace, was slain by a warrior with a blade of a momentous length. He drew back his sword so far that it reached the Saparel Mountains, then swung it with such force that the dragon's head came clean off and typhoons were created across the globe. Another tale told of how a great magician confronted a dragon which had taken over a temple dedicated to Vishnu, and defeated it by uttering the One Mighty Word—a spell that turned the dragon's insides out and kept the temple's custodians cleaning up for weeks.

Will couldn't help but roll his eyes. He had wanted some useful information as to how they could kill Kojari, the dragon of Sancrat

Palace, but instead he had gotten nothing but bullshit. Whenever he refused to humor the teller of a story, the teller would always insist all his details were true. It seemed all dragon-slaying expeditions were meant to generate a new tall tale or two, and their current one would surely be no exception. Will could only hope that the commanders knew what they were doing and that conventional weapons such as swords and arrows would be sufficient.

In the last quarter of the journey, Will started getting odd receptions from the men, ranging from extra-friendly to icy-cold. His comrades either gave him accusing glances or hearty cheers whenever he approached a campfire. Such people were often mixed together, but at one point he found a fire surrounded only by accommodating people. With no critical glares amongst them, they felt free to relate the story of how he had rescued a Mulvarian child. Just like with the story of how he had met King James, there were exaggerations, but none of them were grossly farfetched. A general consensus was that he was hiding the child in a cave somewhere (one man claimed that an intelligent eagle was looking after her; another claimed it was an intelligent goat). Will never corrected them, but did agree that she was in hiding. Talking about Ambri was uncomfortable, though, for it brought back disturbing memories. At least it was good to know that there were many soldiers who would not have pranced around and burned down a Mulvarian camp, relishing in the ensuring bloodshed.

Halfway to Sancrat Province, they stopped at a town called Mankat. There was a spring there, so they all filled up their water skins and barrels. In a surprise move, the commanders decided to stay there for the night, even though the town was hardly big enough to accommodate the whole division. The men were ordered to make camp outside of town and to keep away from the taverns and other pleasure spots. The men grumbled, but many of them found nomadic liquor merchants and bought nearly all their supplies. For that one night, they drowned their troubles in the sweet escape of wine and rum (and even whiskey, which was rare in Carsiss). Will was offered some but declined, worried that he'd start blabbing about his concerns for Ambri and Jonoli in his intoxicated state.

Twenty-two days later, they came upon the village of Naramet, the town which had been ravaged by the dragon. It was a pitiable sight: Many buildings were destroyed with no chance for repair, rubble and craters were scattered across the ground, and the people lived in a constant air of paranoia, afraid that Kojari would return and start trouble again. Everyone was delighted to see the soldiers there, but the soldiers didn't come to lift their spirits; they came for the shipment of catapults that had arrived only days before from a nearby city. The commanders accounted for all of them, commandeered some horses to pull them, and then ordered the men to march to the palace posthaste. They had a dragon to kill and wanted to get it done in time for dinner.

In the middle of the next day, the message got out that Sancrat Palace had been sighted. All the men cheered and broke into song, which aggravated the commanders who didn't want to draw the dragon's attention outside of the palace. They figured their only chance to kill Kojari laid within the confines of her new home, where she would be less mobile and more open to flying arrows.

The men's spirits picked up, and they marched with more vivacity. That didn't stop a few souls from killing snakes for lunch, but it did decrease the number of such reptilian snacks. Even Will felt a little refreshed, and he joined in the songs of dragon-slaying and enemy-conquering, no matter how gruesome they were.

Sancrat Palace was an impressive sight. It was taller than the Emperor's Palace, and its location was incredible: a massive cylindrical mountain that seemed to have no business standing in the middle of a barren desert. The palace seemed to have been built to overcome the mountain's mighty size, as if meant as a display of man conquering nature, but the mountain still won in terms of sheer size and solidity. The palace had a rather tall defense wall to protect it from arrows and projectiles, but the palace still dwarfed it being over six stories high. It had numerous towers sporting *sikharas,* making it resemble a massive pincushion, and it stood remarkably straight despite the bumpy mountaintop it rested on. A most striking piece of architecture no doubt, but certainly nightmarish for acrophobes.

Will looked for signs of the dragon amid the palace's towers and walls, but there were none. It might have been resting inside, which might have made it tired and sluggish by the time they reached it. As they neared the mountain's base, Will grew anxious and excited. He'd never seen a live dragon before, only illustrations. They were said to be in a variety of forms and sizes, ranging from as large as a house to as small as a horse.

The company stopped at the beginning of a trail that led up the mountain and spent the night. The commanders met together in their usual tent and pored over maps and strategies. At his campfire, Will joked that the commanders were planning to make a gigantic shield which the dragon would bounce off of so a team would behead it from the side, just like the snakes. Some of his comrades took him seriously, so he spent much of his time insisting he was just kidding.

The next morning, the company started up the road. It mostly spiraled around the mountain, but at some places it made a sharp V-turn, which was difficult to get the catapults around. Everyone could climb in files of four men shoulder-to-shoulder, making the trek easier than crossing the Saparel Mountains, but no less taxing. One of the path's major dangers was the number of archaeopteryxes that lived on the mountain. They were creatures half-reptile, half-bird, with mean dispositions and ruthless tricks up their sleeves. They were often seen climbing the mountainside with their talons and claw-tipped wings. When agitated, they swooped down on a man and bit at his neck with their sharp beaks perched on their scaly, snakelike heads, then glided away before the man could retaliate. They were also prone to irritate the horses and rummage through supplies like messy bandits. Many were killed for their tasty meat and rainbow-colored feathers, both of which were highly-sought market items.

By the time people started reaching the top, they were exhausted and in no mood to work. The commanders gave everyone a break but insisted that they stay in formation. Will was one of the fortunate ones who made it to the mountaintop while most of the others were stuck on the winding trail. That moment of kneeling before the incredible structure surrounded by a sea of soldiers seemed surreal and impossible somehow—but it was probably just the light mountaintop air getting to him. Plus, he'd been traveling through a hot desert landscape for about forty-five days, doing little more than walking and eating, and he had thought many times that they'd never reach Sancrat Palace, it was too damn far away. He thanked God that the camels survived and their water had lasted, as well as how the journey had started in winter, when the temperature was much more tolerable.

Only four commanders made it to the mountaintop. One of them was Tanalac, who traveled through the formations on horseback, barking orders and informing everyone that their day had only just begun. Will never told his comrades that it was he who had nearly killed Ambri, so he kept his growing resentment to himself. He instead glared at the despicable bastard as though he was the dragon itself.

He also observed two others who rode by. One of them was Commander Tavachhe, a barrel-chested man with a big, shaggy beard and bloodshot eyes. He may have looked like a raving barbarian, but he seemed competent and attentive to his soldiers' needs. And there was Commander Naveran, a tall, gangly man who did not look as strong as the others but still had good muscle tone. He was the more quiet of the bunch, more content to observe before throwing out orders. The general, whose name was Taniko, was nowhere to be seen. Will assumed that he was staying off to the side, too busy licking his chops in anticipation at getting that dragon's head that would undoubtedly make him a famous Carsian hero.

After two hours, the commanders made their first move against the dragon, which they assumed was already inside. Two infantry units and three archery units were picked to be led by the division's fourth commander—a man called Gonchere who was a professional wrestler back home and who had often gotten into bouts while on the journey. He was a greatly respected man, especially by those who bet for him during his matches, but Will was grateful that he wouldn't accompany Gonchere in the initial assault.

The main gate had been greatly damaged in a long ago battle, and there was little trouble in swing the wooden doors open. There was also a portcullis with an opening wench that was thankfully unharmed; it was lifted with no problems. The damage wrought was the first sign of the palace's bloody history. It had once been the proud home of Sancrat overlords and was regularly visited by Carsian emperors who were usually envious of it. It had also been regularly attacked by enemy armies who lusted after it as an important gateway to an all-out invasion of Carsiss. But for two hundred years, the Carsian denizens had successfully fended off those attacks ... until fifty years ago, when an Alquin force delivered such massive blows and used such effective strategies that half of the Carsian defenses were wiped out.

The irony of it was that the Alquins didn't even come to invade—they merely had a dispute over illegal drug trafficking. The overlord of Sancrat had refused to investigate the existence of opium fields, which led the Alquins to suspect that he was growing the opium himself (which very well may have been the case). After Emperor Tamil (the father of Orissu) had made very real threats against them, the Alquins ran back home with their tails between their legs. A reconstruction operation on the palace had never gotten off the ground due to asinine political reasons, and the place stayed vacant until its most recent reptilian squatter moved in.

Commander Gonchere marched his troops—nearly four hundred men in all—into the courtyard and straight into the palace, holding a red flag from atop his horse as a national sign of malevolence towards the enemy. From that point on, all that Will and the division could do was wait. Will expected nothing to happen, for he had been sure Kojari would have made her presence known as they climbed up the mountain. She might have been away somewhere, snatching cows from their herds or burning down another village in order to eradicate more humans—her deadly and *only* predator.

He was proven wrong, and with tragic results. A booming, thumping noise came from inside, and the entire outside division fell silent. The men inside were faintly heard, yelling frantically, apparently on the verge of losing all control and discipline. Then came an intense pounding as Kojari jumped into the fray. Her roar sounded like two boulders being ground together, probably by some infantile giant. There was the flickering of bowstrings as arrows were released, and yet they seemed of little consequence as Kojari roared and rampaged without either slowdown or acceleration. The men's yelling intensified when the pounding did likewise and some horrible crashing accompanied the chaos. Many of the outside men ran to the palace, but the commanders furiously ordered them to stand down.

The battle took all of five minutes, though it seemed much longer. At the end, there were great flapping sounds as Kojari took to the air, plus thumping coming from far up. After that was nothing but the sound of misery coming from the men inside.

It was a very sobering moment for the division. All the energy and thoughts of glory derived from their earlier war songs were drained in a flash. So it was a little of a shock to hear the commanders picking out more units to head inside. "Time is of the essence!" Tanalac cried. "If we are to slow it down, we must freshen our forces inside and attack before it recuperates! This is only the beginning!"

Will rolled his eyes and prayed that the damn dragon hunt

wouldn't spell an end to his hopes for Ambri's future, as well as that for her native people. He prayed again for strength when his unit was picked out for the second assault.

They wasted little time in getting inside, all of the men chasing after Tanalac on horseback like ducklings after their mother. While cutting across the vacant and spacious courtyard, Will's eye was caught by something very bizarre and unexpected: Spread across the front of the palace, on either side of the front entrance, were carved murals made up of about a hundred illustrations. Each illustration depicted human beings engaged in various forms of sex. The diversity and imagination of each mural was impressive and captivating, and it brought to mind pleasant but disturbing images of his one night with Jonoli. He quickly snapped to his senses, though, fully aware that it was no time to start reminiscing about better days. Still, he wondered if the previous men had had their resolves shaken by those very murals.

The inside of the palace was both a wonder and a nightmare to behold. Despite how the building had been falling into ruin, it was still a beautiful and magnificent piece of architecture. Each of the palace's five upper floors had a U-shaped landing above the entrance hall; looking up at them was like gazing into a tunnel leading to the heavens, where angels gracefully swooped from one floor to another. There were a great many windows lined up along each floor which could capture the sunlight no matter where the sun was throughout the day, not the least of which was the open ceiling whose glass domes had been broken long ago. Although the overall design may not have been practical, the palace was certainly the very definition of luxury and earthly beauty.

On the other hand, the ground floor had been turned into a disaster zone. Dead soldiers and separated body parts were strewn everywhere; blood was sprayed and splashed across the floor, walls, and pillars, forming lines, fans, and puddles; spent arrows lied around without a hint of blood or any other sign that showed that they served a useful purpose in wounding Kojari. The marble floor itself was cracked and crushed in a thousand places, indicating where the mighty beast had stepped. What was especially jarring were the two craters that formed where Kojari had landed from above, each one roughly two meters in width.

Among the initial assault team were plenty of survivors, many of them seriously wounded and hanging by threads; those who made it through with only scratches were either tending to the wounded or going about in a trance, severely traumatized. Some of them hysterically told the new arrivals that it was hopeless, Kojari could not be defeated, their mission was all in vain. Will wryly noted that Carsian soldiers could gleefully spread hopelessness by killing women and children but couldn't handle being hopeless themselves.

Tanalac dismounted from his horse and demanded to see Commander Gonchere. He was led to his body, which had nearly been torn into two. Tanalac muttered something about what a tragic loss it was, then turned around and started barking out orders again.

Will and many others wanted to help the wounded, but Tanalac ordered everyone to ignore them and get into formation. He placed archers on the second- and third-floor landings, while infantrymen were stationed on the ground floor. He also ordered men to move about the palace, the idea being that Kojari would have nowhere to hide once the palace was completely occupied. In an act of partial cowardice, Will dropped the scimitar on his back, picked up a bow and a quiver of arrows from one of the corpses, and blended in with a unit of archers, so as to put himself into an relatively safe place.

Near the front entrance was a gong that was left remarkably intact. Tanalac picked up the club attached to it and banged it against the bronze plate, its ringing echoing throughout the hall. He ordered Kojari to show herself, claiming that he would restore honor to the Carsian soldiers she had slaughtered.

Kojari was slow to answer, but answer she did, not with a roar but with the whispering of the air that filled her wings. She glided from one landing to another, one floor to the next. Although her weight must have been great, the flooring held up remarkably well, though they could not handle repeated mistreatment for very long, judging from the dust and debris that fell on each respective lower floor.

Tanalac looked up at her grimly, then turned his attention to his men and cried, "Any man who lets up fighting will receive twenty lashes, not a single less!"

In a moment of misplaced sarcasm, Will thought, *I'm sure Kojari will give them all the lashes they could ever want.*

When Kojari landed on the third-floor landing, archers from the opposite side of the U aimed their arrows and sent a volley at her. Kojari huffed hot air through her nostrils and pounced on them like a lizard on a battalion of ants. There was a sickening squash when she landed on a number of men, then a terrible whoosh as she swiped her claws and drove men back in a display of tossed limbs and flying blood. She opened her mouth to reveal a pair of jaws made of incredibly large teeth, each one shaped like the beaks of woodpeckers of various sizes.

Will was frozen with shock for a moment, then remembered himself and got an arrow ready. He missed the initial volley from his unit, but his aim was true despite his one good eye, though the arrow pitifully bounced off Kojari's scales like it was a toothpick. Kojari paid his unit no mind, instead going after the archers across the way who had fled back farther down the landing. She caught up to them in no time, thanks to the considerable height of the floor that accommodated her own great size. She made another terrible display of violence and chaos while pounding and stomping on the floor. Predictably, the floor gave way beneath her, and both Kojari and many of the archers fell to the ground floor along with marble debris.

Tanalac just as predictably ordered his infantrymen to attack. They did so with an admirable effort, hoping to make an impression while Kojari was still shaken from her fall. But Kojari was shaken for only a moment, her survival instincts easily overcoming any awkwardness at the unexpected drawback. She pounced on them, pinning more soldiers under her claws and crushing the life out of them. She moved about the floor with incredible agility and speed, repeatedly swiveling her body around to keep tabs on the mounting forces around her. Quite a few men came right up to her only to be disappointed that their swords couldn't even make a dent in her solid hide; many more who managed to get within a few paces of her never even touched her, either driven back by her claws or transformed into a mess by her flashing jaws. Anyone approaching from her backside were usually met by her tail, which continually swept them away and broke their bones like so many loaves of bread.

From his vantage point, Will had a clear and isolated view of the carnage. The soldiers seemed to have no chance against her; they were outmatched in capability and defenses. Each soldier had thick padding on, either made of tightly-woven cotton or leather, but with Kojari's sharp and quick claws and teeth, they might as well have been made out of paper. The only weak spot he could point out was the inside of her mouth. Kojari wasn't an entirely mindless beast, though, for she often kept her mouth closed, opening it only when there was minimal danger nearby. She breathed mostly through her nostrils, which could have proven to be weak spots themselves except that they were shielded by plated skin and turned at an angle so that no arrow could reach the nasal passages.

Kojari much resembled an iguana, except for her head, legs, and enormous pair of wings. While an iguana dragged its belly along the ground, Kojari's limbs were thick and strong enough to lift her belly up off it. Her claws resembled those of a wolverine's—large nails on small toes. Her head had a snout similar to an iguana's, but her eyes were set lower and she had a number of quills lining along her jaw and eyebrows. Her wings were broad and tall, which was necessary for such a mammoth creature to take to the air. Whenever she landed on the ground and intended to stay awhile, they folded neatly across her back, the right one lying over the left, making her look as if she wore a cape.

Will had expected her to have mostly yellow skin with some black spots or a black underbelly, but she turned out to be mostly black with bright yellow splotches lined up along her spine, shoulder blades, and snout, all complemented by her yellow irises. It didn't make for good camouflage, which explained the reason why she chose to be pent up in the palace, which matched her color scheme better than anywhere else in the desert.

Kojari was nearly backed up into a corner, but before anyone could think they had her trapped, she splayed her claws as best she could, pounced forward, and charged through the men as if they made up a hay field. It was an astounding and gruesome scene, seeing those men getting hammered and thrown into the air like string puppets. Seeing such a display could almost make Will forget that there were about eight thousand soldiers left outside, ready to take her on as soon as they were needed. With that number, one would think defeating Kojari would be no problem—unless she was a being that didn't lose stamina easily.

The rampage seemed like it could go on forever, but Kojari had had enough. At the end of her charge, she unfurled her great bat-like wings and took to the air, leaving behind a small whirlwind that threw about blood and loose equipment. She landed on the third-floor landing, then pounced again and flew to the fourth-floor, and so on till she reached the sixth.

It was time for the men to recuperate—although recovery

seemed impossible in light of that terrible loss. The ground floor was filled with more bodies, arrows, and debris than before, and it was hard for anyone to walk around. The mortally wounded lied on the floor completely helpless, while the injured moped around with fractured limbs and broken spirits. There were very few who had not been untouched, one of them being Tanalac, who had stayed safely off to the side despite his bold promise of whippings earlier. He must have thought he was the only nonexpendable person in the palace—and as infuriating as it was, he was probably right. According to the Carsian rules of combat, at least one commander had to be present on the battlefield at all times; if each commander fell to the dragon, it would then be up to the general to bring the men home, tired and shamefaced.

In the aftermath of that horrible battle, Will could finally see why stories of dragon hunts were grossly exaggerated. Exaggerations were needed to sweeten up those stories, because the reality of dragon-hunting was deemed too terrible to relate. Dragons weren't brought down by men of superhuman strength and cunning; they were brought down with the blood, sweat, and tears of many soldiers like the division currently at Sancrat Palace, and the losses sustained in such battles were staggering. And yet younger generations couldn't hear of those details, for they would lose all faith that dragon hunts were indeed glorious and righteous undertakings.

Commander Tanalac rallied his troops together as best he could and took a count. Out the four hundred men he had brought in, two hundred were killed, fifty were dying, and ninety were unfit for further combat. Tanalac didn't seem daunted, though, as he didn't order more reinforcements. Instead he ordered a clearing to be made in the middle of the room, making space for another fight. Some of the men grumbled, but most followed their orders dutifully, so much so that Will thought of them as automatons—men who put aside all sense of self to get the job done. He didn't know whether to pity or envy them.

After a half-hour's work, the clearing was only half-made, but it suited Tanalac just fine. He ordered his men into a bare formation and gave them a few bits of strategy to work with. He then hit the gong again and yelled for Kojari to show herself. Kojari didn't come as quickly as before; she took her time, probably tending to some business elsewhere. Twenty minutes and forty-four hits of the gong later, Kojari returned, first emitting a roar that echoed down through the hall, then gliding from one floor to the next until she landed on the ground ready for more combat. She didn't seem bothered by the lack of fresh soldiers; she just charged into the spread-out formation eager for more blood to taste.

Once again the archers released volleys from the second floor (Will was among them, thankful that Tanalac didn't notice he had the wrong weapon) while infantrymen charged fruitlessly at Kojari's virtual storm of claws and teeth. That time, though, the swordsmen took their time, scattering around Kojari as she swiveled about and going for her side and underbelly just as Tanalac had earlier suggested.

A few brave souls (or at least suicidal ones) leapt from the second floor and landed on her back on top of her wings, eager to sink their blades into the back of her exposed neck. But Kojari had thick plating across her back that was made of the same substance as her scales, and their blades merely bounced off it as if they were striking a piece of mortar. Kojari usually just shrugged them off, although one man managed to hang on long enough to get her angry; she furiously writhed her wings and body until the man was propelled into the air and then snapped her jaws into him. With her new prize, she took to the air again and retreated to the sixth floor.

The men may have been hopeless before, but they grew more so after that third attempt. Only a handful of people got near Kojari's underbelly, and they reported how well reinforced it was—not as much as her back, but enough to prevent any blades from sinking into her heart. One man spoke of it as if he was revering Kojari as a god, and Tanalac smacked him across the face with the back of his hand.

Soon after Kojari left, Will discussed strategy with his fellow archers. He didn't speak as if they were in a formal group session; rather, he looked at the men on either side of them and pointed out something he had observed about Kojari, and then suggested a simple plan around it. He didn't think his suggestion would come to anything real, but it became more popular than he thought and it went down the grapevine all the way to Commander Tanalac. The commander was enthusiastic about the idea because he had no other ideas himself.

Tanalac sent someone to bring in a unit of archers and ordered a number of dummies to be made. Many of the men stood dumbfounded at that last order, wondering how they could made dummies. Tanalac yelled at them to figure that out on their own, and that he needed them within the hour. The men scattered and ran through the palace looking for raw materials.

Will and some others were able to find bags of ancient rice and grain. They stuffed them into suits of armor and made them stand by erecting a simple cross made with wooden stakes. They ended up making three dummies in that fashion, none of which would be mistaken for a real man except for perhaps a dragon looking from afar. Tanalac was pleased with the dummies, but he was even more pleased with the notion of using corpses as dummies. Many of the men disapproved of the horrid idea, but most of them agreed that as long as the corpses were used for a good purpose, nothing was wrong. For his part, Will never agreed with that, and his resentment towards Tanalac grew ever more.

The plan was simple. Kojari had tended to pounce on the slow and unmoving, which was only natural. So in theory, Kojari should put her full attention on the dummies, leaving the living men free to fly arrows at her safely from afar. The hope was that she'd open her mouth long and wide enough to let a few arrows slip inside , for it was agreed that that was her only weak point.

The men got into position and Tanalac banged on the gong. Kojari was slow to respond once again, but like Pavlov's dogs, she came salivating at the ringing soon enough. When she reached the third-floor landing, the archers all ran away from the center of the hall, leaving behind the dummies and standing corpses.

In theory, it should have worked: Kojari should have gone after the dummies, leaving herself open to volleys from the archers underneath and above the second-floor landing. But there was one thing that Will or any other man couldn't have figured: Kojari's vision detected heat, and since the dummies emitted no heat, Kojari could not mistake them for being alive. Instead of landing near the dummies, she landed in the thick of the archers, tearing into them with her claws and pummeling them with her tail. It caught everyone by surprise, increasing the chaotic moment that would end up as the greatest blunder of the dragon hunt.

The only good thing about the battle was that a sword had managed to puncture the underside of Kojari's right claw. The blade was held by a dying man lying on the floor, keeping it vertical and sturdy enough for Kojari to break the layer of scales and sink her claw into it. She huffed through her nostrils and backed away, swinging her tail furiously. She soon after took to the air and retreated to the sixth floor.

Tanalac was a mixture of anger and hope. He hated how the plan had been an abysmal failure, but he'd seen how Kojari had been wounded and related it to everyone on the floor. He then ordered the mess to be cleaned up (even though the corpses were starting to resemble a mountain) and organized a party to search for Kojari's eggs. Everyone had suspected she had eggs, which explained why she never left the palace to attack the men outside. With the eggs in their possession, Tanalac reasoned, Kojari would be hesitant to attack.

Will, who had heard about the operation from a comrade, thought Tanalac's reasoning was ridiculous. He had half a mind to tell him that Kojari's fury would only increase if her eggs were taken away from her, but he wanted to avoid contact with Tanalac as much as possible, not trusting himself to deal with the man who had surely taken his eye. If Tanalac wanted to make another blunder, that was fine with him. The longer the battle dragged on and the higher the corpses mounted, the sooner the entire division would raise a mutiny against its commanders and general. The resulting execution list would be long, but Will had a feeling he would be left untouched.

Commander Tavachhe soon came in and demanded to know what the men's progress was. Tanalac was clearly ashamed to say that so far the men were only able to wound Kojari's right claw, his earlier excitement over that feat totally gone. To Will's satisfaction, Tavachhe assumed command of the operation, saying to an arguing Tanalac that it was the general's order. Tanalac left in a huff, claiming that he would make the general see things his way and have him back inside before nightfall, which was fast approaching.

Tavachhe wasn't content with sticking around the main hall. It was only partially because he was sickened by the corpses; what he mostly wanted to do was personally seek out the hiding place of Kojari's nest. However, he thought the main hall shouldn't be unattended by command, so he brought in Commander Naveran to look over the hall in his absence. Naveran was just as adamant about the hall being cleared of corpses, so he ordered more men to haul them outside (a morbid operation that resulted in many men losing their lunches).

When nightfall came, there was no word on Kojari's nest and no Tanalac returning inside. There were no sounds of battle anywhere in the palace, and Commander Naveran wasn't pushing for more battles. The men were all tired, hungry and frustrated.

They ate little and didn't talk much. They took short rests which were mostly plagued by nightmares, and no one built campfires to keep the night's chill away for fear of attracting Kojari. At one point, a man stood tall and yelled out a suggestion: The men should draw a *yantra* on the floor, which was a kind of diagram used to control things such as snakes, sand dunes, and atmosphere (the idea was that anything placed on a *yantra,* such as Kojari, would be held under the designer's complete control, just like magic). The idea was shot down by Commander Naveran, who ordered the man to stay outside and keep his ideas to himself.

Will spent much of the night resting and clearing the floor of corpses—a job that no one had thought to do in the canyon, he sourly noted. He tried to keep thoughts of home out of his mind, though such thoughts were pleasant and intoxicating. He remarked to himself that if the massacre in the canyon hadn't happened, he wouldn't have had Ambri and Jonoli in his life at that moment—the two things he wanted the most to return to. It was yet another conundrum he had since arriving in Carsiss, and it was the most horrible of them all. It had to take numerous deaths for Will to feel more alive and satisfied than he'd ever been—but if he could sacrifice his newfound happiness for the lives of each of those Mulvars, he would have gladly done it.

At daybreak, there was another battle, one unprovoked by the men. Kojari came down the hall like an angel of death, rousing unprepared men to their feet and their wits. From the start, it was clear that Kojari had been worked up into a rage, as she came down quickly, roaring out her displeasure. She landed hard on the third-floor landing, and since it was in a spot she had landed on many times before, it gave way underneath her, sending her down to the second floor. She landed on a good many men, adding to yesterday's horrendous body count and the confusion of the moment. Kojari regained her footing and shrugged off flying arrows, many of which had met her tough hide before. She jumped and landed on the ground floor, and the bloodbath began anew.

Will was in a far point on the ground floor, releasing arrows at her without stop within an archery unit. The volleys were unorganized, and many arrows either collided in midair or hit the wrong target, but the archers made their presence known to Kojari judging from how she turned and charged at them.

It was the first time Will felt he was in immediate danger, and he was too shocked to move. He got moving once a retreating comrade pushed him on the shoulder. Kojari would have plowed in the archers no matter where they ran had not a daring soul jumped onto her head from the second floor. He caught her by surprise and tried to use her moment of hesitation to drive his blade into her left eye. But Kojari recovered quickly and whipped her head from side to side, sending the poor man airborne. He landed on the second floor, breaking several bones. She immediately went after him, eager to make him pay for his insolence.

Commander Naveran tried rallying his forces together, but they couldn't hear him over Kojari's carnage and their own yelling and screaming. He had to contend for them making a wild charge at her, swinging their swords into the air and yelling at Kojari to come at them. She was happy to oblige, although their battle with her didn't last long. Eventually, Kojari had had enough of fighting in the enclosed hall and retreated to the third floor, where she crawled through an opening to the outside world.

The men at first wondered why she had gone ... then they heard the cries coming from outside. They rushed to the entrance and threw the doors open. Although they couldn't see the men past the defense wall, they saw what Kojari was doing quite clearly. Their worst-case scenario was being played out: Kojari was diving into the outside mass of soldiers, landing only long enough for a quick slash of her claws and a swing of her tail, then retreating to the air again to prepare for another dive. After a lot of wondering of how they could be fitted through the palace's front doors, the catapults were finally being put into use, tossing boulders into the air which usually missed their mark. Before long, the field was littered with numerous flaming boulders that had flown and landed fruitlessly. One of the catapults was destroyed when Kojari dived at it and slashed it into so much firewood, leaving four catapults left available. Arrows filled the skies like rain, but none of them hit a spot of any relevance nor made any holes in the dragon's wings, which were made of a strange substance than was very lightweight and yet was as tough as steel.

It was another sobering moment for everyone. Despite all the men's efforts, absolutely no one could stop or hinder Kojari. The wound in her right claw was clearly healed, the muscle having been cinched together underneath clotted blood. It had been their only hope of bringing her down, but it was there no longer. It was as if some god had decided to give mankind a challenge it never had before, and so he molded the finest and toughest killing machine to ever walk the face of the earth.

Will set his back against a wall and slid down to the ground. He had had enough fighting and secretly wished the general would have sense enough to return his troops home without Kojari's damn head.

Commander Tavachhe soon returned to the hall and made his report, which explained why Kojari was acting erratically: He and some men had found her nest on the sixth floor while she was away, and in a fit of passion three men went against his orders and broke open the three eggs. They quickly retreated and feared for the dragon's retaliation. Since no might could make right, the men responsible were free to act on their own, but Commander Tavachhe secretly singled them out for imprisonment once the mission was over.

Over the course of twenty minutes, Kojari exacted her revenge, but she soon grew tired and retreated to the top of the palace to recuperate. Four commanders led a small squadron of men to scour the palace's sixth floor in search of her, but strangely she was never found. They deduced that she had transferred to a tower in back of the palace, wisely staying away from the men. They saw little point in searching the towers, since their forces would be spread thin if they did. They had no choice but to wait for her to come to them, not the other way around.

The commanders ordered no clean-up job to be done; instead they directed everyone to tend to their armor and weapons, especially the catapults. They saw the catapults as their only chance to bring her down, hoping that the flaming projectiles would prove effective against her impossibly tough plating. They organized units and taught them how to get Kojari's attention, which would draw her near a catapult and get her open to fire. None of those men, of course, took their job with much pride and gratification.

Although he tried to deny it to himself, Will was experiencing severe mental trauma. He was upset over how the dragon hunt was failing miserably and how the commanders were not entertaining thoughts of returning home. Out of all the missions he'd been on over the years, the dragon hunt easily outweighed them in terms of foolishness, destruction, and loss of life. Some may have said that in light of all that negativity, the mission had to be successful in the end in order to justify it. It would be the ultimate story of perseverance conquering despair, like in the story of the

Ramayana, where the god Rama is exiled from his father's kingdom and goes on to rescue his wife, Sita, from the evil King Ravana.

But Will saw no hope for success, not with their current plan. The Emperor was just in enacting a strike against Kojari, but he had had no clue of the dragon's capabilities. Throwing hundreds of men at her—a plan that sounded good a month ago—was simply not working. They needed more than strength of arms; they needed a plan clever enough to pierce her steely scales without putting many men in danger.

At the rate their current plan was going, a mutiny was inevitable. The men were despairing, and after a little more fighting their resolves would break. The commanders pushed ahead in blind pursuit, but the men were seeing no point in it. Kojari had become a sort of demon in their minds, and everyone knew that demons were beings that man alone had no hope of crushing. To bring down Kojari, they would need a miracle on their side.

CHAPTER 17
TO DIE YOUNG

IT WAS JUST PAST evening when Kojari returned to the hall. Despite her recess, she didn't seem well rested. It wasn't a weakness that the men could exploit, though, for she was still faster and stronger than they could handle. The arrows flew to no avail, and the swordsmen couldn't even scratch her hide. It was a nightmarish scene that had been played so times before that the men had actually grown used to it, even the fresh units who just came in from outside.

Still, everyone had hope because they'd heard of the sword that had pierced Kojari's claw. They aimed for the claws, confident that they had the least covering of scales. They weren't entirely wrong, but they didn't account for the fact that no amount of human strength could pierce the skin there without help.

After about nine minutes of slaughter and the end of three units of fresh recruits, Kojari was starting to slow down. She was probably on the verge of retiring when she spotted a soldier that stood out from the rest. All the soldiers who were around her usually ended up covered in blood, but only in splotches. The one who caught her eye was absolutely drenched in it, a result of standing next to a man she mutilated with a claw stroke. Despite what many men thought, Kojari certainly had her weaknesses, and one of them was the sight and smell of blood. It was irresistible to her, and the aroma from that soldier was especially invigorating.

The man could tell he was being singled out, so he turned tail and ran. He was completely hopeless until he spotted a large piece of rubble shaped like a V, standing as if it was a tent. He ducked and ran under it, barely having enough room to turn around. Kojari neared the building fragment and slapped it with one claw. She could have been strong enough to lift it up and expose the soldier, but she was more tired than she knew. Instead she continued slapping it around, sliding it across the floor. The man did not fare well inside: He was safe from Kojari's jaws, but he couldn't take the moving of the fragment around him. His head banged against the insides, and his left foot was crushed by the fragment's underside.

Kojari grew frustrated, not just by her prey who laid half-dying inside the fragment, but also from the gang of men attacking her tail and ribs. She opened her jaws and banged her teeth and gums against the fragment and periodically slid her tongue inside, hoping to push the man out the other side while also tasting the blood on him. When that didn't work, she roared, hoping to scare him out. But the man was trapped with his calf caught under the fragment, crying in pain and begging to die.

Suddenly, a rather intrepid archer saw his chance and took it. He ran out from behind a pillar, stepped partially inside the fragment and drew back an arrow in his bowstring. He aimed carefully, waiting for Kojari to move her tongue into just the right position, then let it fly.

It didn't catch her in the major artery the archer was aiming at, but Kojari felt it all the same. She stepped back and roared in surprise and agitation. She shook her head a few times, then snaked her tongue around to get at the arrow. She managed to snap the shaft into two, but the arrowhead was still lodged inside. She quickly became irritated and made weird, high-pitched cries that rang painfully in the men's ears.

In her throes of pain, Kojari forgot where she was, and the soldiers took advantage. A good many archers, Will included, stepped in front of her and let fly at her open mouth. Finally, after more than twenty-four hours of fighting and bloodshed, arrows hit home onto soft skin. Kojari roared louder than she ever had before, but the men were undaunted and kept the volleys coming. Soon the inside of Kojari's mouth resembled a porcupine, each piercing running red with blood. She backed away and fluttered her retracted wings, but the damage had already been done. There was no going back for her. Not even closing her mouth seemed to help because the blood would then rush down her throat and cause her to retch.

Commander Tavachhe was seeing the whole thing, and his energy picked up at the first sight of blood. He ordered his archers to keep sending volleys; when their quivers started to run dry, he ordered his swordsmen to get near Kojari and throw their blades into her mouth. "The blood has to keep running!" he cried, little knowing he had made a partial prediction of things to come.

The blades were thrown as ordered, some of them cutting deep into Kojari's tongue. Three of them reached her tonsils, and when she shut her mouth again she could hardly help but to swallow them. The writhing of her body must have let them tear her stomach lining, because before anyone knew it she opened her jaws wide and let out a river of blood and guts that was comparable to the corpses she'd been leaving behind.

As much as it was terrific, the sight was also incredibly sickening, and many men lost their breakfasts. Will felt his own gorge rise but managed to keep it down. He kept his attention on Kojari, who was still on her feet and still a threat. But there was nothing to worry: She swayed a few times, looking around the room, staring in anger and hatred at the creatures responsible for destroying her eggs, then let out one last phlegm-clogged breath and let her belly crash on the floor.

It was finally over. The men cheered so loudly that the division outside heard them, and so they cheered as well. Everyone, even those who had become the most desperate and despairing, became totally elated, and a celebration began that lasted for half of the day. Will, who had dutifully awaited his inevitable mutiny, couldn't help but join in, gladly opening the barrels of mead and rum that had been saved for the occasion. Soon everyone began getting wild and out of control; General Taniko wasn't exactly pleased about the men's behavior, but since he had also been expecting a mutiny (which he predicted would happen one or two days from then), he let them have their fun, hoping that they'd forgive him and the Emperor for all the lost lives.

It was quite a day to remember, not just for the division and Sancrat, but for all of Carsiss. The Emperor would soon have his dragon's head, and he'd show it off to his citizens proudly. People in taverns and bedsides would start to tell of the single man who had launched an arrow of flame and death at Kojari, which then traveled several leagues through the air and hit her square in the mouth, cutting her tongue clean off and setting her head ablaze. They'd say that she fell to the earth leaving a trail of smoke and blood from above the clouds, then made a great crater that nearly leveled all of Sancrat Palace. It was truly a kill for the ages.

But for Will, the day would be filled with terrible memories—not just for the running of Kojari's blood, but also for his own.

As predicted, Kojari's head was hard to get off. The thick plating that protected her for years on end was nearly impossible to crack. The men had to resort to using swords and saws that ran through a fierce bonfire until they were red-hot; the temperature of their blades did half the work for them as they slowly turned the plating around the neck into ash. To prevent their skin from being singed by the hot handles, the wielders wrapped the handles with rags drenched in water. At the first sight of fresh blood brought on by one of the blades, the men cheered, relieved that their work was not being done in vain.

The men outside were busy getting things ready for the trek back home. The camels were fed and all the equipment was put back in their carts. A large census was held to determine who lived and who died, and then search parties were conducted to look for the bodies of the missing. The bodies were stripped of their gauntlets (for those were what would be sent to their families), then placed in piles and burned. Those whose bodies were not found were presumed to be deserters, for there were plenty of sighting of men fleeing the mountain soon after Kojari made her presence known. Executions were grimly promised for them.

When Kojari's head finally came off, it was pulled out of the palace by ropes, then hoisted onto a cart and meticulously driven down the mountain path by men and camels, who even pulled from the backside when gravity did the work for them coming down.

Will was preparing the camels as usual when he spotted the head on ground level. He sighed in relief, still unable to believe he had survived over a day's worth of facing the monster. The sentiment was shared with some of the others who also faced her and lived to tell the tale.

Eventually the division slowly started to move back to Nünveghett. Will's unit was near the back of the division's linear formation, so he and his comrades had a while to go before they could start moving. But before that happened, he was paid a very unexpected visit by Commander Tanalac. Will didn't want to see him of course, but he was in such a good mood he would have done anything short of hugging and kissing him and forgiving him for his eye. He stood up straight and saluted with his fist over his heart, as did his immediate company.

Tanalac came and stopped barely a meter away from Will. Will expected him to say something right away, but Tanalac hesitated, not seeming like his usual self. Will was a little concerned that he had brought four gruff-looking men with him, for he didn't know what to make of it.

It was done a little too quickly to be proper, but Will broke the ice first: "Commander Tanalac, sir!"

Tanalac quickly drew a fist back and smacked Will in the cheek, then used his other hand for an uppercut. Will could have kept his balance if he'd seen it coming, but the element of surprise make his feet slide in the sand and he toppled over. He was never one to stay on the ground, though, so he scrambled away and hurried back onto his feet. He approached his commander with his fists up, ducked under a roundhouse blow, and landed a few blows on Tanalac's exposed belly before making his own uppercut.

Tanalac was thrown back, but his thugs were quick to step in. One of them wrapped his arms around Will's shoulders while another head-butted him, punched his face, and knocked the wind out of him. Will kicked him in a kneecap, but he was hardly phased as he continued his array of brutal blows that left Will weary and helpless.

The attacker was replaced by a third man, whose new assault was even worse than his predecessor's. His specialty was in crippling limbs, which he did with a perverse sort of pleasure. He twisted Will's left arm so that the elbow pointed up, then wrapped an arm around Will's forearm and brought his other elbow down on Will's own, snapping it like a twig. Will howled in pain—a death cry he never equaled even as his fingers were being broken one by one.

The man behind him eventually let go, and the limb-breaker charged at him and delivered a leaping kick to his midsection. Will went flying down, kicking up sand on impact. He looked around, expecting at least one of his comrades to come to his aid, but Tanalac was warning everyone to stay away and let the proceedings commence without interruption. Everyone obeyed like the mindless sheep they were.

Will could later remember the awful moment when the gang surrounded him and started kicking and stamping their feet on him. But as the beating went on without mercy, his consciousness swam away along with the intense pain. He fell into a deep sleep, either from a few hits to the head or from the shock of so much pain all at once. Once he woke, he found the division was gone.

He tried to move, but only succeeded in getting halfway into a sitting position before his ribs and head protested. He hit the ground again and laid there, gripping his torso, clenching his teeth, and breathing hard. Dry blood was caked over his face and limbs, layers of sweat enveloped him, and there were patches of skin as dark as the new moon. He didn't trust himself to inspect his wounds, for touching them would only make them worse; plus he didn't really want to know how fully injured he was. He already knew his left arm was useless; he didn't want to know what all else those bastards had done to him.

He slipped in and out of consciousness, trying his best to stay in because he didn't want to stay in that spot and wait for death to come. He slowly tried to get up, testing his limits first and acknowledging the pain he'd feel upon movement. When he managed to get himself to sit, he inspected his legs, moving them around. They were covered in blood and felt like acid was splashed on them, but they seemed fully functional. He thanked God for small favors and slowly got back up on his feet.

He felt no better standing up; he still felt dizzy and was bound to fall back down again. He had a better look around him, but what he saw wasn't encouraging. He was stranded in the middle of nowhere; the only nearby thing of any significance was the mountain, and that was of little use. He could have used its shadow to hide from the sun, but that was only if he was committed to his death and accepted his defeat at the hands of his loathsome commander.

But he didn't want to die, not after that calamity he went through. There were also Ambri and Jonoli to think of; he had to get back to them, even if he was too late and could only learn of their fates.

The division soldiers had left thousands of footprints in their wake, but the wind would soon sweep them away. He started on the trail, wondering if a black line in the far distance was the division marching ahead. He kept a hand on his left rib while his left arm dangled as if on a butcher's hook. His pace was slow but regular without hint of a limp. He was bleeding only a little, grateful that his long rest had at least given his blood time to clot.

The company had done a good job of loading up the equipment, but they still left some things behind. He looked around for food and water, but found none. The only thing he found useful was a cloak of loose and stringy wool; he put it on for protection against the sun and gave thanks again for another small miracle.

It may have been winter, but the sun was still harsh and overbearing, especially in overlong exposure. Among the immense sand dunes, Will had no hope of finding shelter; he had only his cloak which served admirably. But he still sweated like a roasted pig after a basting, and he found himself worried about his hydration all over again. He had no child to look over, but he would have happily exchanged his injuries for one, even if a barrel of water wasn't included as a bonus.

That first evening, his legs felt rubbery and his head was pounding. He came across a sparse number of cacti and felt hopeful. Cacti held considerable amounts of water, he'd heard, which just may save a thirsty desert drifter. He took out his knife (which he wished he had thought of when Tanalac first attacked him) and tried to cut a hole into the first cactus he came to. Unfortunately his focus wasn't as sharp as he'd hoped, and he ended up slipping the blade and bringing the meat of his palm on the thorns. He cried in pain and then started sobbing, suddenly sorry for himself and the loved ones he was desperately trying to reach.

He didn't give up, though, and when he finally pried out a piece of the cactus's skin ... there was nothing. He had expected water to gush out like Kojari's blood from her jaws, but there was only a trickle instead. He hastily cut some of the surrounding thorns off and set his tongue on the small but precious stream. It lasted a good while, but once it slowed down to mere drops, he was left unsatisfied.

He cursed his luck and cursed the man who left him for dead, and then cursed the hundreds of men who had just walked on by him as though he wasn't lying bleeding and unaware. He then cursed himself for letting Tanalac get so close to him, and finally cursed Carsiss for being so damn inhospitable both in and out of civilization.

He then grieved for Ambri, who never asked to be kept in the care of strangers who might wish her harm; and for Jonoli, who had willingly went against the wishes of her peers by first caring for Ambri and then caring for Will. He was deathly afraid something had happened to them immediately once he left Nünveghett, and then he cursed the Emperor for making him go on that foolish dragon hunt.

Ever since witnessing the massacre in the canyon, he'd been doing only what he thought was right, but it seemed his noble actions had earned him only an early death. To die young was a tragedy he thought he'd never earn nor seek; but unfortunately that was only his opinion, and it conflicted with those of people in power in that contemptible nation he'd once proudly been an ambassador in. He swore that if the heat and dehydration didn't get to him first, he'd die of shame instead.

By the next day's first light, the footprints were mostly gone, only a faint shadow of them remaining. He'd have to rely on his sense of direction from that point on, hoping that it would take him back to

Naramet, where the company was headed to drop off the catapults. Once he reached Naramet, he'd probably be restored to health by some kindly people, and then he'd eventually return to Nünveghett with a caravan as an escort. He wouldn't bother seeing the Emperor; he'd get the next ship to Thayland and make his full report to the King, probably less one arm.

But it looked hopeless. The aching in his head and all over his body was becoming unbearable, and it didn't seem to go away. His mouth held barely any moisture, and his skin was darkening and peeling off, especially around his left elbow, which was showing signs of gangrene and infection.

He was becoming emotionally unstable, at times despairing for himself and his loved ones, and at other times growing angry at his enemies which included Montblanc (the father, not the daughter) and the Emperor (who had obviously cared more for his harem than for Ambri). He kept blaming himself for his situation, his excuse being that he was too full of euphoria over the dragon's defeat to realize Tanalac had brought the gang to finish the job he started in Will's Palace bedroom; plus he never thought Tanalac would dare start a no-holds-barred fight with him in front of the other soldiers. If some of those soldiers blew the whistle, would the Emperor have Tanalac skinned for his vengeful rage?

All for a Mulvarian baby, Will thought with a shake of his head. *Tanalac did it because I took Ambri away from him when he wanted her dead. It's as if he doesn't have his own child to look after.*

On the third day, Will couldn't believe he was still alive and walking. Well, *barely* walking: He was prone to falling down and staying where he was for undeterminable lengths of time. He was growing to enjoy those moments, for they were respites from forcing his weary legs from working; plus he didn't have to think so much about how thirsty he was. He could think about how Ambri greedily drank her milk as though she hadn't forgotten her time in the desert, and how she laughed delightfully when he and the women played with her. He could also think of Jonoli—so patient and understanding, with such smooth skin and soft lips that he found himself desperately missing.

There were times when he thought he didn't deserve her, not after witnessing the dead people in the canyon and proving unable to stop their slaughter (Ambri being the only exception). And there were times when he thought about Tanalac's order to have him stay behind as the other men rushed the canyon. He wondered if it was really because he didn't want to put the Emperor's pet into danger—or if it was because he didn't want Will to know the truth of what was really going on in that canyon. It was a ridiculous thought, though, for Tanalac didn't seem at the time like someone who had anything to hide.

As pleasant as it was to think about things, Will always got back up and went on moving, pressing ever onward toward Naramet, where safety and life awaited. But as the day passed by, his falls became more frequent, and he was afraid he'd eventually go tumbling down a sand dune and wreck himself beyond repair.

He remembered running his raspy tongue across his peeling lips before taking his last fall. His knees gave out with no warning, and he planted his face into the soft ground. He turned his head aside and spat out sand. He decided he didn't want to think just then, so he tried to push himself back up. He got his head only as high as a quarter-meter off the ground when his right arm collapsed. He planted his face again in the sand and spat more out. He decided a little rest was what the doctor ordered after all.

He waited five minutes that felt like hours, then tried to get up again. He made no more ground than last time, and after that failure he started to panic. *This might really be it for me,* he thought before trying again. He failed a third time, and his passing conjecture seemed more real to him. Rather than dreaming of home or wasting more strength, he fell into the sleep of the dead, not moving a muscle or rolling his eyes. He imagined he'd get some strength back upon awakening, and then he'd get up and start moving again. Better yet, it would be nighttime, and he'd be able to move without sunlight as how he should have been doing all along.

But his heart wasn't doing so well. Throughout those weary three days of no water or food, his heart had been beating gallantly, keeping him alive long enough to dream and hope of escaping the hellish desert. It was strong and healthy, the product of a lifetime of rigorous exercise and a diet full of protein. But it could only last so long with so little food and so much tribulation. One of the reasons Will had been falling was because his heart hadn't been able to supply his muscles with enough oxygen to sustain them, and in his final fall it was nearly at its breaking point.

As Will slept, his heart still managed to keep beating. So bold, so brave, and so strong it was that it wouldn't quit just because it finally had a chance to. It gathered as much oxygen it could and continued pumping Will's lifeblood—but once his lungs gave out on him, his heart soon made its final beat and ended its futile efforts.

Will's hooded cloak was able to conceal his bare skin from the sun's harsh rays. When he died, only a thin web-like pattern of sunlight laid out across his head and hands. From afar, he might have been only an inanimate piece of clothing discarded by someone in the division ... but that didn't stop the vultures from coming down around him. They'd been following Will for quite some time, and they were delighted to finally have their feast.

CHAPTER 18
RENEWAL

IT WAS NIGHTTIME WHEN the division set its sights on Nünveghett. Since it was customary for a victorious army to return home in daylight, General Taniko ordered camp to be set up a league away from the city. The soldiers waited until daybreak, then collapsed the tents, mounted the camels, and returned to the city amid throngs of cheering crowds.

They proudly displayed Kojari's head while marching in the streets—the head that had taken a lot of time and manpower (not to mention trial and error) to kill. As soon as the head crossed the city border, people tried to climb aboard the cart to touch it; the soldiers showed no tolerance for that behavior, gripping the fools by their ankles and tossing them onto the ground like they were sandbags. The people in one immediate area grew wise and never tried the stunt themselves, but as soon as the head got to another area the painful lesson was repeated.

The division was ordered to stay in and around the city's barracks, while the head and the general went straight for the Palace. The head was to be mounted atop of the front wall for a while as a sign of national pride. Over the past forty-plus days on the road, the blood had drained out, the meat had rotted terribly, and the eyes had sunken in—but the skull and scale plating had held up remarkably well. Even so, it still weighed nearly a ton, so having a team of men move it atop the Palace defense wall would prove interesting, even with the help of cranes.

General Taniko had the high priority of seeing the Emperor, and he wasn't to do it alone. Tanalac went with him, nearly bursting with pride over the gutless act he had committed after the monster's kill.

They were led to a high balcony that offered an expansive view of the city. The Emperor was there with his wife, but he sent her away as soon as his new company arrived. "General," he greeted simply. "And Commander Tanalac. Congratulations on your prize—I'm sure it wasn't easy."

"There is no job your army cannot do, Your Eminence," General Taniko said with a bow.

"Hmm," the Emperor sounded with a tone of uncertainty. "Any dead?"

The general hesitated. He knew he'd have to give the number of dead some time or other, but that didn't mean he'd like to. "Nine hundred," he said. It was actually an underestimate—over two hundred more were missing and presumed deserters.

Understatement or not, the number was able to give the Emperor a horrible pause. Nine hundred men—very close to one-tenth the number of the whole division—was a very inflated price for a dragon head. He hadn't even thought the total division was necessary; he had just got that many men together because he wanted to get their hearts thumping, to fuel their thirst for battle and blood, as well as to arouse national pride within all the people and inspire more men to enlist.

He looked down and shook his head, suddenly having doubts as to whether the mission had been a good idea or not. The people were not going to like how one dragon head had cost nine hundred men, and they would rightfully blame their grievances on him. He made a fist and banged it against the railing, crying out a curse. "What of Will Fontaine!?" he burst out.

The general motioned for Commander Tanalac to speak. "Your Eminence, the son of Thayland is dead," the commander said, hiding his nervousness rather well.

"By what means?" the Emperor asked. His tone suggested he was in no mood for embellishments or exaggerations—just the straight facts.

Tanalac cleared his throat. "I gave him a good beating, then left him alive. I made sure he didn't get up until the entire division had passed him; then I left him to rot in the desert. If he awoke, he'd be too injured to cover much ground; he'd be—"

"So he's dead then?"

Tanalac's nerves were so high-strung that he did not fluster at all. "Yes, Your Eminence."

"But you didn't confirm it?"

"I confirmed that the division left him behind."

"You should have chopped off his head."

Tanalac said nothing. He knew he was in hot water with no way out—the best thing to do was to make no excuses and accept any punishment.

But the Emperor surprised him. "Do you think he suffered, at least?"

"Yes, Your Eminence."

The Emperor nodded. "Good. Very well done, commander. I

have another job for you." He pointed at the city behind him. "Somewhere out there is a child—and you should know what child I mean. I want it found and brought here alive ... but dead will be just as good, I don't care. Matter of fact, dead might be better, just bring it back *whole*. I'll give a thousand rupees to the man who delivers it to me personally."

"Was it not with the harem?" Tanalac asked. "That's what I heard, anyway."

"I've dealt with the harem, and they're not talking. One of them gave a false lead, so I'm not sure we should trust them anymore. It'll be up to you to find it. I'm not even sure it's in the city now, so the search must spread to Markereen, Dallan, and Navalut."

"Excuse me, Your Eminence, but have all the boats been checked at Markereen?"

"Yes, yes, the boats are being checked." The Emperor paused for thought, then said, "A thousand rupees for the child's return, but really, it's not very important. It's a matter of pride, and if it gets away it won't really matter. I'll give the search two more weeks ... then I'll give the speech we've long been waiting for."

Tanalac flashed a smile and bowed. The general followed suit, and the two men were dismissed.

The eight thousand soldiers fanned out across the city in search of Ambri. No home or business was considered unsuspicious, even the estates of the *Ksatriyas* (though they were given a milder treatment than the commoners' dwellings). They stormed through houses, turning over furniture and threatening the owners, and many were not above slipping a trinket or two into their pockets.

Although many citizens let the manhunt be conducted with little complaint, a good number of them did not stand idly by. They held secret rallies and small personal meetings, thinking up plans and strategies that would finally get them the results they'd been waiting a long time for. After many failures, they finally decided to come to more drastic measures; problem was, they needed many more volunteers, and there was no man among the underground groups charismatic and accomplished enough to convince so many to join their cause.

Actually, they had thought of one man who could probably do it, and they'd be willing to kidnap him if they had to. But this man hadn't been seen since the soldiers returned, and everyone presumed he was either dead or missing ...

Actually, even Will himself didn't know which one he was—dead or missing. He could have been both—missed by his loved ones and dead in the middle of nowhere. But in the strange place he found himself in, he certainly didn't *feel* dead.

He felt lighter than air and eternally free. He was free of the containment of flesh, blood, and bone; free of earthly wants and needs, and of responsibilities owed to his king and country. He didn't have a care in the world, and though he knew that was no way to go through life, life had decided it had no need of him anymore and he felt sublimely happy.

He was in a place that was no place—a place of nothingness, of shadow and a profound depth. There was no water or land, no trees or rocks, no skies or clouds—such earthly things had no business there. It was a place beyond the earth and the mortal coil containing love and war and suffering and hope. It was the perfect place to be, where he could be anything and anyone he wanted, free of what he was before and the boundaries that had defined him.

And yet he was confused. The place was not what he expected. He expected to go either to Heaven—a place above the clouds where everyone was pleasant and wanted nothing but God's love—or to Hell—a chasm of fire and smoke and boundless suffering, where evil beings ripped wicked souls to shreds and made them wish they'd never in life done anything bad so much as swatting a noisy fly. But instead there he was, just floating along in a land of nothing, all alone and yet lonely not one bit. He was confused, and yet he was not distraught—such negative feelings seemed to be impossible there, and he was grateful for that much.

He could have been falling, or he could have been rising, or perhaps even standing perfectly still. There was no gravity or points of reference, nor any air for him to feel rushing by (not that he had skin to feel air with). He suddenly wished he was going somewhere, though he didn't care where or what it was. He wished to see and hear things again, even if it meant returning to his mortal flesh again.

But suddenly, a thought occurred to him, and he was surprised it didn't come to him sooner (not that he had much sense of time in that place). Perhaps he was wrong in his assumption that he was headed for either Heaven or Hell. Perhaps he was in fact within the energies of the universe, and that his stay in that dark place was merely a transitional period before he was reincarnated as someone or something else—a human, a horse, a deer, a fish, or *anything*. It would mean that the idea of death and rebirth that was preached by Hinduism was correct, and if that meant returning to the face of the earth, then he could hardly wait.

But waiting was what he did, what he had to do. At least it was a wait without much longing or torment—it seemed that a soul without a body could endure nearly anything. He was delighted to think of returning to the earth, and that feeling stayed with him.

An undeterminable time later, he finally saw something, just as though he had his earthly eyes again: a single ray of light, made of many colors that were constantly changing, as if it was a piece of a broken rainbow. It rotated around as if it was a clock hand, then it broadened at one end while narrowed at the other, gaining a sense of depth. Will longed to reach it and touch it, but it always seemed out of his grasp. All he could do was watch, unable to swim towards it like in an ocean. It tantalized him like a bone to a dog, although it was by no means an unpleasant experience.

He had no idea how long it was before it finally came to him. There was no great ceremony involved—it simply drew closer like a ship's bow heading into dock. He became enveloped within it and instantly regained the sense of flesh and earthly feelings he had thought were forever lost to him. He was excited at first, but that feeling quickly turned to doubt and despair. He suddenly remembered the conditions of his death and the matters he had left behind. He wanted to return to the infinite state of bliss he was in before, and he tried to swim or fly out of the ray of light—but the light held onto him like the tentacle of an octopus seizing its prey. It was relentless and merciless, and it let him know that his fate was not in his hands but its own, whatever it was. Will tried to scream but he had no mouth to do that (not yet, at least), and he relented and agreed to let him fall into its jurisdiction, praying that his fate would be swift and painless.

He found himself traveling down the ray at an infinitesimal speed. He almost felt as if he had a stomach, which lurched as he sped down the ray—an odd sensation since there was still no air to blow through his hair. He oftentimes closed his newly-formed eyes to fight the queasiness, but he mostly gazed at where he was going, which was apparently nowhere. He expected to soon see the grassy knolls of Thayland or the rolling dunes of Carsiss—either of which he hoped for instead of some foreign land he knew little about. But he wondered if he had the wrong idea—perhaps he wouldn't see the earth but the body of the being he was going to be reborn as, or maybe even the womb of his new mother. The thought of having a new mother was especially exciting, since he'd never known the mother from his previous life.

When he reached the end of the ray, the end of his journey came not with a bang but with a whisper. The world of nothingness suddenly grew terribly bright, though it was probably just his eyes being manipulated by the light. He shut his eyes tight and waited for the next step of his rebirth—his *samsara*—and he prayed to whatever God or gods there were that he'd return to earth as a human, so that he could think, work, and love intelligently, and make a fresh start not as an orphan but as a young man who would grow more self-confident and well adjusted.

Or a young woman, it mattered not.

He was fully immersed in water and curled into a fetal position. It was totally dark and hardly any sound reached his ears except for the drone of water pressure and the occasional swish of a wave. He felt more secure than he had for a long time, and he was happy beyond what words could tell. He supposed he was in his mother's womb, an innocent newborn-to-be who had just had a horrible fate and was probably about to have an interesting future. He could hardly wait to be out and about, to be cared for and to grow up and see what he (he thought he was a "he") looked like.

But something was wrong with that picture. For one thing, he was fully grown; and for another thing, he was fully clothed.

He opened his eyes and became aware of himself more than any fetus had right to be. He tried moving his left arm, and yes, it was healed and whole. He was indeed reborn, just as he thought ... but what was he doing clad in his former soldier's outfit? And with a sword to boot?

He opened his mouth and water rushed into his lungs. He started convulsing, straightening his body and regaining his proper balance. His knees bumped against a level stone floor, and he quickly planted his feet on it and stood himself up. He emerged from the water and tried to get a breath of air, but of course his flooded lungs were incapable of that. He found a wall in front of him that reached up to his chest, and he placed a hand on it and began retching. He was acutely aware that he was not alone, as a woman and her two children gave out blood-curdling screams and ran away in terror.

It took a while, but he finally vomited the water and began taking deep breaths. Once he got his wind back, he wasted no time in hauling himself over the wall and out of the water. As he stood in the faint moonlight, letting water drip from his clothes, he was aware of two things: First, he had his right eye back—it was as if he had never lost it. To see properly again was a great relief, but it was also unsettling. He wasn't sure why right away, but it later dawned on him that not only was he brought back to life, but he had been tinkered with, too.

The second thing he was aware of was his heart. He could always have been aware of his heartbeat before, but only if he concentrated on it. But upon his resurrection, every heartbeat made itself known, because each one caused him pain. He was only dimly aware of it when he was in the water because he had more pressing matters to tend to, but there in the moonlight he clutched his chest with one damp glove, bent over, and took sharp breaths while giving voice to his suffering. The pain wasn't great, but it was shocking in the same sense that his broken left arm had been.

He glanced behind him at his makeshift womb, which was nothing more than a fountain being filled with spring water. He then took in his surroundings with uncertain eyes. He seemed to be back in Carsiss—at least, it could have been Carsiss. He was in an alley between two adobe structures, the ground made of well-trodden sand. He headed out of the alley (being careful to walk with his wobbly feet) and came upon a market lane, where all the stores were closed for the night, though a few carts and rickshaws could be had on the street. It was unfamiliar territory, but it could very well have been somewhere in Nünveghett.

He wandered down the lane some way, then made a series of turns that brought him nowhere. Of course he didn't know where he was going nor what he should do next. He ambled along in a state of confusion and exhaustion, trying hard not to keel over and avoiding the late-night pedestrians. He prayed that robbers didn't find him, for even though he had a sheathed sword on his belt, he was too weary to defend himself.

The memories of his death in the desert were still fresh, as if it had happened just the other day, as well as the memories of the black void and the ray of sparkling light. He concurred that whatever will that had brought him back from the dead did so for a certain reason, only it never bothered to tell him or give clues as to what it might be. He was immensely grateful for what it did, and he felt that he should do whatever it wanted of him, though the idea was daunting. He only wished he knew what the hell it was that he was brought back for. Surely it wasn't out of pity or spite—he hardly thought that any powerful being would have such trivial motives.

There was also the matter of who or what he should be grateful to. He knew he should pay respects to whatever the being was, but did it have a name—perhaps one he was familiar with? Was it the One God whom he'd been worshipping all his life? Or was it actually one or more of the Hindu gods that the Carsians looked up to? Hinduism held the fundamental belief of resurrection—that souls returned to the earth. And wasn't that what just happened to him? Of course it was, so did that mean that Hinduism was right on the money while resurrection's naysayers were sorely mistaken?

Whoever had resurrected him did the job admirably but with a catch. His right eye and left arm were miraculously restored, and the blade he was given was a brand new longsword that could have come straight from Thayland. But his painful heartbeats were a price he could have done without. They drove him crazy, feeling like small bursts emitting shrapnel within his chest cavity. He could think of only one reason why that was: The resurrection process must have put such a toll on his heart that it was left tainted somehow. He couldn't guess as to any specifics, but who could? Were there any people who could call themselves experts on the process of resurrection without being quacks?

In his travels, Will rarely looked up, keeping his eyes mostly peeled on the ground. At one point he rubbed the top of his head and noticed yet another difference in him. When he was young, he kept his hair as dreadlocks; in his later years, he kept it mostly shaved off. He had shaven his head only a few days before the dragon fight had started, and he didn't have much hair when he had died. But upon his resurrection, he was clean-shaven once again ... but there was more to it. He actually had no hair to speak of, as if the will behind the ray of light had pulled all the hair out of his head. He no longer had to worry about shaving, but nonetheless it was very unnerving to undergo such a dramatic change.

When he reached a small clearing that served as a sports field, he cut across it and gazed at the distance. Jutting from the horizon were the dark forms of mountains, barely seen against the starry sky. He recognized their shapes as the Saparel Mountains alongside the Carsian capital, and off to his left were the lights surrounding the Emperor's Palace, making him positive he was in Nünveghett.

He suddenly heard loud voices from the nearest buildings. He dropped and laid on the ground, correctly assuming they were soldiers' voices. They appeared briefly, carrying lanterns and looking around as if searching for something halfheartedly. They then headed into an alley and disappeared from sight.

He wondered if it was him they were looking for. Perhaps that woman who screamed earlier had told them about him, his crime being that he had defiled the fountain water—a serious offense in Carsiss. He'd have to avoid any soldiers while making his way through the city—and he wouldn't do it just for his earlier incident. He would do it because he was afraid of bumping into a former comrade. He didn't want his presence being known. He planned on getting to the docks and stowing away on a ship bound for Thayland, and being noticed by the authorities might prevent him from doing that.

He got back up and removed the leather armor from his outfit, leaving on the basic shirt, pants, and cotton vest. He then continued across the clearing, staying hunched over so that he might be mistaken for a dog or a coyote.

Reaching the docks was easy since he used the mountains as a reference point and found a familiar portion of the city. On the way, he worried that stowing away might not work—then he reached into a pocket that was making a racket and pulled out a wad of bills amounting to five hundred rupees—enough to give a family of four a modest but comfortable wardrobe.

He didn't remember having money when he died, but then he didn't have a longsword, either. Both items must have been gifts from whoever had revived him. He thought it was kind of creepy, as if he had partly wished his revival was caused by natural forces instead of an intelligent being who did the task purposefully.

He inspected the bills, wondering if the water had damaged them. They were wrinkled, but the bills were made of tightly-woven cotton and imprinted by hot presses, so there was no ink to run when they were wet. He whispered a prayer of thanks for his incredible fortune, and soon bought a cloak from a fabric merchant. Such cloaks were common in Carsiss at night, so he wouldn't look too suspicious.

It was getting to be daybreak when he rented a horse and made off for Markereen. The ride took about ten minutes (a vast difference in the time a plodding camel took), after which he turned the horse in and reached the docks, where he would confidently pay the fare for a trip back home. He was sure that whatever reason why life was breathed back into him was not for him to get killed in more foolishness in Carsiss. He would make his report to the King and let matters fall into *his* hands. That way Tanalac's treachery and the Emperor's poor oversight would not go unpunished.

He was strolling on the wooden planks, searching for a passenger ship heading to Thayland and clutching his chest in pain, when he was approached by a young man wearing a hood and shirt made of heavy cloth. "Pardon me, sir," the man said, "but are you the son of Thayland in our army?"

Will smiled. "Sorry, you must be mistaken. I'm from ... Euthasia."

The man nodded and then spoke in an alien tongue. Will turned nervous, then made a small nod and headed away. The man smiled and stepped into pace with him. "Euthasia, huh? Why did you say nothing, then? Why are you here?"

"I'm going home," Will quickly replied. "Your people don't seem to want me here anymore."

"That's not true—not true at all. Everyone's been awaiting your return, but you were not with the others. Whatever happened to you?"

Will stopped. "Who do you think I am?"

The man looked apprehensive. "The son of Thayland."

"No, what's my *name?"*

"Will Fontaine, sir. I meant no offense."

"I know, but you're wrong. I heard this guy Will Fontaine lost his eye. Do I look like I lost any eyes?"

"You do not ... but you must be Will Fontaine."

Will sighed. "And why is that?"

"Because you are the only dark-skinned son of Thayland around here. You must be him."

"I'm a friend who's looking for him."

"You will not find him here—he's in Nünveghett. Come, and we'll look for him together."

"No, I just said I'm going home."

"Some friend you are."

Will grunted and the man laughed.

"Look," said the man a hair above a whisper, "I think you should come with me. There are some people who want to meet you."

"Who, Tanalac?" Will snapped.

"I don't know what you mean, sir. I cannot say his name here, but if you would come—"

"No, no, I'm not going anywhere unless you say this guy's name. Is he really so damn important that his name is like a holy word?"

"No, sir, but you never know who might be listening."

"But I'm not going to go see some nobody or walk into a trap. If you want me so badly, you'll tell me his name—or you can stop wasting my time right now."

"Madick Treyboia," the man said in a lower voice. "And I am Sen Lanachhe, a member of the resistance. Madick is my leader."

"The resistance to what?"

"The Emperor."

Will let slip a look of horror, but then thought there was little to worry about. He'd never heard of any resistance movement, either through official channels or the rumor mill. So he had no reason to believe this Sen Lanachhe. The idea of a resistance was nonetheless intriguing, but he said, "I have no major problem with the Emperor."

"No problems with the Emperor?" Sen asked. "I heard you saved a Mulvar baby from a mass slaughter which the Emperor commanded to be done. I'm sure you were appalled by the slaughter, for no other soldier would take a baby as a spoil. But now you say you have no major problems with the Emperor?"

Sen had a point. "I guess I stand corrected," Will replied.

"Then if you want to end his tyranny, I suggest you come with me to see my master. You will not regret it."

Will supposed that if there really was a resistance with a capable leader in charge, it was worth looking into. It would make a good addition for his report to King Fredrick. "Okay, but I'm warning you, if this is a trick, you'll have more than just the Emperor to worry about."

Sen looked unsure of himself for a moment, then said, "I'm sure you'll like him—Madick will see things your way."

CHAPTER 19
A NEW RECRUITMENT

WILL AND SEN TOOK A rickshaw to a impoverished part of the city, which led Will to wonder if Madick was a bold *Sudra*—an Untouchable—who was stepping beyond his station by taking on a position of leadership. But Sen said he was a *Vaisya* who made his temporary headquarters in the shantytowns because the soldiers usually don't march through them.

They stopped about half a league away from their destination and walked the rest of the way. Will was very nervous in the shantytown, for whenever he took a good look at the harsh conditions the Untouchables lived in, he felt guilty and helpless. Dwellings mostly consisted of tents that had already been well used by caravans. The men wore little more than loincloths while the women wore *saris* covered with mud and food stains. The children merely went around naked, their swollen bellies hanging over legs that were nearly as thin as sticks. In fact even the adults were too thin to be considered healthy; they ambled about like zombies, taking their time probably because they didn't have the energy to hustle. Trash and dung littered the ground, and while Will and Sen moved carefully to avoid it, the citizens made only passing efforts to move around it.

Sen turned into an alley between two adobe buildings, which were among the only ones in the shantytown. They went behind one of the buildings and went through a ground-level door to the cellar. Will supposed Madick was the kind of spoiled leader who demanded luxury even when hiding from the authorities.

They went down a short passageway and met two guards flanking a door. They wore rusted armor that was pilfered from Carsian soldiers. "Password?" one of them asked.

"Come now, you know me, Mennic," Sen said.

"Of course I do ... and I know you know the password, so let's have it."

"Tenrana," Sen said at length, making a show of it. It was Carsian for "retribution."

Mennic opened the door, and Sen led Will inside. They found a man sitting at a table, reading a scroll. He greeted Sen, then gave Will a curious look as if he already suspected who he was.

"Madick, you are not going to believe this," Sen said proudly. "I have brought to you Will Fontaine."

Madick smiled broadly, but then let it falter at Will's pensive and unenthusiastic expression. Will had thought he would get a slap on the back and a hearty handshake, but Madick took his mood into consideration and wisely slipped into a sullen manner. He appeared to be a formidable man, strong and sagacious, much like the Emperor. He was a little tall and wore only a white pair of trousers and a tattered vest. He was at least clean, having bathed earlier in the day unlike the numerous *Sudras* outside.

"Will Fontaine, it is a pleasure," he said. He offered Will a seat next to a lantern, one of only four pieces of unattractive furniture in the small room. The air was dank and the walls were dirty, but at least there was a bowl of water where one could wash his hands. "Anything to eat? I have fresh fish and some mangos."

"No, thanks," Will said. He was actually very hungry, and some food would have calmed his nerves, but he didn't want to be calmed.

Madick gave him a pondering look. "We were looking for you, but you weren't around when the soldiers returned. We were worried about you."

Will nodded, not at all surprised. There was no mystery about his celebrity status in Nünveghett.

"The people all look up to you," Madick continued. "It takes more than just guts to rescue a Mulvar, even if it is just a child. I'm sure you are very proud of yourself--everyone else is."

"I don't care," Will said with a blank tone. "She's probably dead, anyway." He hadn't really been thinking of Ambri until he reached Markereen, and all thoughts of her had no hope. Without him to watch over her, someone such as Tanalac would have made sure that Ambri no longer stayed in the Palace. The return of the soldiers meant that Will had come back about forty days after his death, which left his enemies plenty of time to have their way with Ambri.

"The soldiers are all looking for her," Madick said, which got him Will's attention. "Baku wants to publicly execute her. He knows the people wonder why he would let a Mulvar stay in his palace, and he wants to show them that he'll tolerate it no longer. He wants to affirm his resolve to see all Mulvars dead. Don't you see? He wants to take whatever good you have done and trample it--all for his own foolish ambition."

"So you want me to join you--in this resistance of yours?" Will asked.

"Yes," Madick replied, trying on his most winning smile. "The people are skeptical about me—about *us*. If they see you side with us, they may be more willing to join us in our cause to overthrow Baku. No one approves of Baku's policies anymore, but not enough people are willing to take a stand against him. The will of the Emperor, no matter who he is, is always—"

"Wait, wait," Will interjected. "If you're going to turn this into a thing about honor, you can stop right there. I've had my fill of 'honor'—I've had to stomach it from my former commander long enough. Truth is, Sen caught me trying to catch a ship out of this place. It's something that may yet get me flayed in Thayland, but I don't have much choice."

"You do have a choice," Madick said pointedly. "You don't have to flee from whatever Baku put you through; you can stand up to him, tell him that you have had enough of him. If you're concerned for your safety, my men will defend you with their lives if need be. Believe me, I need you alive—I need everyone to see you stand beside me.

"As for honor—I don't care much for honor, either, believe me. I don't do this for honor; I do it for what I think is right. I have no ambition to be Emperor; I haven't forgotten that I'm but a *Vaisya,* and the throne is beyond my station."

Madick spread out his hands as if making a public speech, which he had undoubtedly done many times before and probably with the same words he was currently saying. He probably had a love for speeches, which was another characteristic he shared with the Emperor. "I don't care much for honor. What has honor gotten us? Blood feuds! If my father hated his brother, does that mean I must hate my cousin? No, only a fool would say that. So what does that make the warrior-kings—the *Ksatriyas* who send their vassals to join Baku's Mulvar-killing campaigns?

"You have done something extraordinary during your stay in Carsiss, though you may not know it. You have defied Baku's stubbornness by letting a Mulvar stay in his palace. I would not have thought it possible if it wasn't for the strong rumor throughout the city. Many have said it was false, but there have been no such word from the Palace or the soldiers. And when I saw the people cheering at you as you marched in the streets, I knew we had a new hero in Carsiss—someone who has brought sense and a new ideology to the Palace. But you think too low of yourself. Believe me, you could be like Marku Berasei, who stood up against Emperor Bansel the Terrible, or like Junkel Halimoor, who stopped Lord Gentrick's invasion of his village. You could be like them, who fought not for honor or glory, but for what is right."

"You mean to stop the killing of the Mulvars?" Will asked.

Madick nodded gravely. "You may not know, but there are Carsian villages in the south who must house soldiers and pay high taxes for them. The soldiers are shameless—they take whatever they want and give nothing in return. Baku encourages such behavior—he thinks it fosters their killing instincts and makes them willing to kill unarmed civilians."

"And you think overthrowing the Emperor is going to end all this?" Will asked.

"Yes," Madick replied in a half-whisper, almost as if he was in awe. "The Emperor is always seen as a god, whoever he is. He is considered the embodiment of Carsiss, the heart and soul of the people. Whatever his wishes, it is for the good of the nation. It's just more foolishness I wish to absolve. Baku is just a man, and once we show the people that, they'll realize how absurd it is to kill the Mulvars just for him.

"Baku once admitted that he holds the god Siva in the highest regard. Siva is the god of both creation and destruction, but Baku only respects the destructive side of him; he doesn't care about the creation side. He is no worse than a hyena, killing and maiming and looking for carcasses to eat. And he has no heir yet, so once he goes, the dynasty ends with him. Our land may no longer even be called Carsiss anymore; we can make anew, starting with the abolishment of blood feuds."

Madick fell silent, giving Will time for his meaning to sink in. Will then said, "In all my time with him, I've never thought the Emperor was that bad. I mostly thought ill of the generals—I heard they are in total command of the war on the Mulvars."

"But we are not at war—not anymore," Madick said.

"I know that, but ... I've always thought the Emperor had little idea of what was going on, that only the generals and certain commanders knew about the situation with the war."

"Have you ever asked him about it?" Madick demanded. "Have you ever asked him how the war was going, or if he expected the Mulvars to surrender soon?"

Will was about to say something, but quit after a second thought. He had in fact never asked the Emperor about the war's situation, but not because he was ignorant; it was because Lord Harrington explicitly told him to keep silent about it. It was not his duty to put the Emperor in the wrong; he was only in Carsiss to uphold favorable diplomatic relations. Once he reported to the King the situation in Carsiss, it could then be left up to him to respond to.

"You're asking me to go against the wishes of my country," Will said. "I was only here as an ambassador, not some crusader for justice."

"Will Fontaine, you must stop deluding yourself. Baku is the worst leader in Carsiss' throne since Bansel the Terrible. He is no better for Thayland than he is for Carsiss. You don't want him for an ally, not since you're from such a noble country as Thayland. If you stay with me, I can prove that to you."

Will nodded, partially admitting to his own ignorance. He had chosen to stay ignorant at Lord Harrington's request, and it may be that Madick knew more of what was going on in Carsiss than he did. He briefly considered joining him, trying to weigh the negatives and the positives. Staying with Madick a little longer might make him able to give a thorough report to King Fredrick. And he might find out more about Ambri—where she was and how she was doing. He did not want to abandon her, no matter what the cost. He also worried about Jonoli and the other harem ladies, wondering if they were punished for looking after Ambri.

There was also the grave matter of Tanalac. Will was still in the curious glow of having been resurrected after death, as if he was somehow so important that the world refused to let him go. As wondrous and spectacular as it was, it should not have happened. Tanalac was the one responsible for it, and Will didn't think a mere prank would alleviate the heavy grudge he held for him.

"All right, I might consider joining you," Will said. "But I have my conditions."

"Name them," Madick said, clearly expecting Will to say as much.

"First, I want you to understand that I may not stay with you all the way. If you're going to lead an attack on the Palace like I think you are, I may not stick around. Actually, I'll probably leave long before. What I'll do for you is stay long enough to give the *appearance* that I'm on your side. A month or two should do it. In that time, you should have no problems in getting recruits—if I'm as important as you say I am.

"The second thing may be more difficult, but it's very personal to me. I want you to capture Commander Tanalac of the Carsian Infantry in Nünveghett. I want to see him alive and caged. If you can't get him—that is, if you think it would be too risky to capture him in the early stages of your resistance—then at least promise me you won't let him get away."

"He did you wrong?" Madick asked.

"You'd better believe it."

"Commander Milrin Tanalac is one of Baku's most trusted men. I heard he could have been made captain some time ago, but Baku wanted him to keep training the troops. I guess he's a really good drill instructor."

"Yeah, but he's got no tolerance for foreigners."

Madick shrugged. "Neither does Baku. He has little patience in foreign relations."

Will was about to ask if he had heard right, but decided to forget about it. Madick could act like he knew the Emperor well all he liked; as long as he was serious about ending the slaughter of the Mulvars, that was all that mattered.

CHAPTER 20
DISILLUSIONMENT

THE NEXT TWO WEEKS WERE enlightening, to say the least. Will had been skeptical about how influential Madick was—for all he knew, Madick suffered delusions of grandeur and was important only in his mind and with a handful of others. But it quickly became clear that that was not the case: Madick was able to bring small crowds together in enclosed buildings, who listened to his speeches with full attention. The crowds held no illusions as to the risk of holding such meetings, as Madick was a man wanted by the state, and so they kept cheering and roughhousing to a bare minimum, bringing little attention to themselves. Will noticed the gapes of awe and nods of agreement during Madick's speeches, making him realize that Madick was a greater threat to the Emperor than he had first thought.

Whenever he traveled, Madick went in disguise, often changing his outfits in an inconsistent manner. For example, sometimes his clothing and accessories marked him as a devoted follower of Vishnu; at other times, he was marked as a follower of Siva. There were times when he wore a loincloth and dirtied himself to disguise him as an Untouchable, but mostly he went about in more complete attire, with pants and a vest. He never wanted to overdo a disguise, so he shunned hoods and cloaks, instead resorting to fake beards and moustaches, which actually looked quite realistic even when looked on up close.

Madick had an assortment of bodyguards that always followed him, albeit not too closely. Sometimes, once they made sure an area was clear of soldiers, Madick would rip off his false facial hair, shimmy up a lamppost or a statue's pedestal and yell out a defamatory comment about the Emperor, criticizing his war against the Mulvars and attacking his claim to the throne. The crowd would cheer more often than not, and then Madick would make a hasty retreat before he could gather a crowd around him, usually hiding out in the dwelling of a confidant until things quieted down outside.

"I think you're placing too much faith in the people," Will once told him. "They aren't all of one mind, you know. One of them might point you out to the soldiers, and they might get you before you can make a new headquarters."

"It'll make little difference," Madick said with a laugh. "Do you think I am an island, Will Fontaine? I have friends as arrogant as me doing the same things I am doing. If I am captured, it will be up to them to continue the resistance. The only thing that will change is that my friends will be more reserved."

Will shook his head, hardly believing the tenacity and resilience of the man. Madick seemed too good to be true at times, laying down his life for the sake of a people whose fate bore him little consequence—unless of course he had relatives who were Mulvars, but he claimed he had none.

Whether he was reckless or not, there was no doubting Madick's magnetism. Whether he was at a gathering or doing one of his public hijinks, people gave him looks of admiration and respect, whether they were man or woman, carpenter or blacksmith, clansman or free agent. Even the Untouchables paid him their respects and gave him tributes that they could afford to part with. It was all despite the fact that Madick requested the men to take up arms at his command and promised times of hard work, bloodshed, and sacrifice—all to dethrone a man who was said to have the gods' favor in whatever he did.

And of course, Will was getting a good part of the people's attention. The grim soldier who had been ignoring their cheers as he marched their streets was finally giving them their dues, making short speeches about how the future of Carsiss was in their hands, giving them handshakes, and answering their questions. One question that made its way into every gathering asked about the whereabouts of the Mulvar child. He said he had left Ambri in the care of people he trusted, but since he could not return to the Palace due to a treachery he had undergone, he couldn't find out where they had taken her.

After one such gathering, Will asked Madick why he hadn't heard of his resistance movement while he was a soldier.

"We haven't been active until the soldiers left for the dragon hunt," Madick replied. "With all those soldiers gone, I and my friends had decided it was time to act. But it's been slow-going since we haven't been getting the number of recruits we need. Asking Carsians to engage in civil war is not as easy as it looks, believe me."

"Taking out the Emperor is all you want to do, right?" Will asked. "Why not send assassins?"

Madick gave him a shrewd look. "We've tried, trust me. Even with the dragon hunt going on, the Palace has been kept heavily fortified. I'm afraid they're aware of us already, and they're waiting for us to make a mistake. We may even have moles in our midst, which is why we've got to hurry and act soon."

Will also noticed at the meetings that both men with bandanas and men with armbands were present, although they maintained a good distance away from each other. "What's with the gangs?" Will asked Madick. "What are they about?"

Madick was confused at first, so Will had to point out the bandanas and armbands. Madick sighed and thought of an answer. "They are not 'gangs,' more like political adversaries. Those with bandanas work closely with the *Sudras,* and those with armbands do not. Those with black bandanas work very closely with the *Sudras,* while those with red bandanas work with them at a distance. It is necessary for them to identify themselves this way, because even though they are all *Vaisyas,* those who do not work with *Sudras* do not want to touch other *Vasiyas* who do. It is obscene to touch a *Sudra,* but that does not stop everyone from working with them."

Will began to laugh. He couldn't help himself, even though he knew it was inappropriate. Madick asked him what was so funny. "I thought there was a lot more to it than that," he said. "The soldiers I worked with had no clue what they were about. I wonder why that is."

"They probably *did* know, but feigned ignorance," Madick said. "It's usually not something we discuss with foreigners."

"Why not?"

"Because it draws a thin line between what we want and what the gods want. We do not want to upset the gods, but many of us do not want to ignore the potential of the *Sudras,* either."

"I see ... so what would you do about it once the Emperor is overthrown? Get rid of the caste system?"

"Absolutely not," Madick replied, a little louder than he intended. He then talked about how the caste system was designed by the gods and that no mortal man should interfere with it. Rebel or no, Madick still held some faith in the status quo.

"But I heard that sometimes gang members were found dead, killed by rivals. Isn't that true?"

Madick nodded gravely.

"Then don't you want to put a stop to that?"

"I know this is going to sound bad, but it's not my problem. Sometimes gang members get heated in their opinions, and they take drastic measures. It's a pitiful way to prove one is right, but there's nothing I can do about it ... not unless I or the Emperor proclaim that no one shall work with the *Sudras* ever again, and that wouldn't be right."

"And no one can order them to behave themselves? Or would that just make them appear weak?" Will shook his head helplessly. "I guess there are hypocrites no matter where you go."

All in all, things progressed smoothly, even if problems arose with people claiming the resistance was doomed to fail. Will tried to convince them otherwise, but secretly he gave them credit—he also was uncertain about the future of the resistance movement, not quite believing that victory was imminent.

Nonetheless, he did his part to convince people to join the resistance, because he deeply believed that Madick and his forces were doing the right thing, even if it meant the death of a man who was clueless about the state of the war. The images of the dead Mulvars in the canyon were still clearly etched in his mind, haunting him in his thoughts and dreams. If more bloodshed was necessary to prevent more massacres like that, then in his opinion it should be so.

After ten days of accompanying him to gatherings and giving little speeches of his own, Will's presence was having a noticeable impact. People who were skeptical before were beginning to voice their dissent to the Emperor and their loyalty to the resistance. That led Will to start thinking about heading back to Thayland, never minding missing the chance to see Tanalac as a prisoner. He also thought of asking around for Ambri, finding her before the soldiers did and bringing her to Thayland.

But then two things happened that made him think about hanging around a little longer. The first thing came about after flyers were posted announcing that the Emperor was going to make a speech at the Palace. Madick said he wasn't going to attend, and he forbade Will from attending himself, claiming it was too risky. Instead he deployed some of his men to listen to the speech and report back.

On the night after the speech, Will was summoned to a cellar that Madick had just made into his new headquarters. Madick offered him drinking water and fresh *bajra* to eat. "What's the occasion?" Will asked, half-jokingly since it seemed Madick and his men were holding a small party.

Madick, however, was very grave and forlorn. "We have details of Baku's speech. He named three men as traitors to the nation: Franklin Douglass, Vincent Harrington, and you."

"Traitors?" Will asked. He was so startled he couldn't think of anything more to say, so he merely repeated himself.

"He said the sons of Thayland betrayed his trust, coming not to make peace but to assassinate him."

"Assassinate him? Wait, hold on—all I know is that Franklin was deported because he was accused of trying to poison him. But Franklin said he was framed by a cook who gave him a cup of poisoned wine. It was the damn cook's fault, and it happened when I was away!"

Madick raised a hand, trying to assuage Will's sudden hot temperament. "I believe you, Will Fontaine. But Baku seems to think otherwise. He said you and Vincent Harrington conspired together to kill him, and that he was lucky to realize it in time."

"What did he do to Lord Harrington?"

Madick sat up straight. "He's a lord? Hmm, he didn't say. What he did say was that all the traitors were dealt with."

"We are not traitors," Will hotly muttered. "Whoever the hell told him that is going to pay, I swear it."

"It gets worse," Madick said, not sounding like he was enjoying being the bearer of bad news. "Baku went on to say how all sons of Thayland were treacherous dogs with no sense of honor or loyalty. In the 'best interest of our country,' he's revoked all maritime rights of Thayland ships in Carsian waters and docks."

"Why the hell would he do that?" Will asked, even though he already knew the answer: The Emperor assumed all Thayland citizens were traitors out to get him.

But Madick gave another answer entirely: "He's prepared to go to war against Thayland."

"What?" Will half-yelled. "Don't be absurd. Losing Thayland as an ally would be the worst thing he's ever done. Carsiss is no match for our army, begging your pardon, Madick. I don't think he'd be stupid enough to go to war."

"What if he were to ally with Thorain, your closest enemy?"

"We keep tabs on Carsian travelers in Thayland. Part of my training in the Carsian language and customs was to guard the trade routes and make sure no Carsians got into Thorain, where they wouldn't be wanted, anyway. I know the methods used to do this, and they're very effective."

Madick shook his head. "There's always a way around

everything. Who do you think you're talking to? I've had to avoid soldiers all the time lately; I bet I could find a way into Thorain *and* disguise myself pretty well. But anyway, we're getting off topic. You're in hotter water than you may believe. If Baku discovers you're still alive, your head will be even more coveted than that damn dragon's. You'll need to stay low for a while, maybe not even attend public meetings. Ever considered getting a moustache? You can borrow one of mine."

The next thing Madick said convinced Will that he had to see the Palace at least once more. He had said a group of Mulvars had been raided recently, and that their heads were mounted atop the outer wall of the Palace. There was little reason not to believe Madick, but Will had to see those heads for himself. He had to see just how far the Emperor was willing to go to show his resolve in eliminating the Mulvars.

He and three of Madick's bodyguards approached the Palace from along the Calkune River. They got as close as they dared, which was far enough to clearly see the heads atop the wall. They were stuck on pikes standing erect, wavering slightly in the strong wind. In the direct sunlight, he could see there were heads of both men and women. The women's long hair flowed with the breeze, which could have been beautiful if the women were still alive. But hair flowing from heads separated from their shoulders was sickening and terrible, for it was an inherent human belief that vessels of the dead were best kept motionless, unable to give any impression of life other than the appearance of sleep.

It was hard to tell if they all belonged only to Mulvars, since Mulvars and Carsians were hard to spot from a distance; for all Will knew, some of them had belonged to the Emperor's Carsian political enemies. There was one lone exception—a head whose origin was quite clear. The head had fair skin and short black hair, and upon recognizing it, Will wanted a closer look just to be sure. He thought better of it, though, deciding to trust his eyes only from his vantage point: The head was definitely Lord Harrington's, planted not far from the head of Kojari down below. (The massive head had proven too heavy to lift atop the wall, so it was instead placed at the bottom atop a sandstone block.)

Will tightened his hood which the wind was threatening to blow back. "Is Marsoon Diachhe up there?" he asked one of the bodyguards—a man named Laniko.

"We don't think so. Baku would have said if he was."

Will nodded and turned back to the wall. It was a gruesome sight, the likes of which he'd hoped he would never see. Setting heads on pikes had been a regular practice long ago in Thayland, but at the behest of the Church it was abolished. Still, Will wasn't surprised to see it alive and well in Carsiss, especially since the Emperor told him of a vision he'd seen in the Sands—that of him placing Marsoon Diachhe's head atop a spike.

Will fixed his gaze on the head of Lord Harrington's, whose eyes were shut and slightly slanted. He wondered what the lord had done to convince the Emperor he was an assassin. Whatever it was, he began to question the advice he had given—to stay silent and wait until he returned home to Thayland. The wisdom in that started to seem moot. If they had only voiced their concerns instead of appearing shifty and pretending everything was all right, then the Emperor wouldn't have suspected them of treachery. They were probably fools to think they could keep avoiding the issue of the war on the Mulvars without the Emperor detecting that their goodwill was not with him.

Will clenched his fist and felt frustrated tears ready to surface. He abruptly turned and said, "I've seen enough, let's go."

The second thing that made him stay longer in Carsiss happened only four days later. By that time, Will's resentment towards the Emperor had reached an all-time high. Lord Harrington's execution was inexcusable, as King Fredrick would surely certify. But Will needed to know specifics as to why he was executed. The Emperor said both he and Will were involved in an assassination conspiracy, but he didn't support his claim with evidence. Something had to have happened in the Palace—another frame job, perhaps—and Will needed to know what it was in order to give the King a full report.

He asked Madick to use his spy network to find it out. But intelligence from the Palace was hard to come by, especially since they had no moles working inside. But the spies discovered something that could serve as a doorway to all the answers they needed—if they played their cards right.

Prime Dieschsuch Halicut had urgent family business in a town south of the mountains. His carriage was due to take the main mountain road leading back to Nünveghett. And so, resistance loyalists made the boldest move they'd done since their campaign started: They captured the Prime Dieschsuch.

It was the middle of the night when Will and Madick were escorted to a small building that was once a home but fell into ruin after being struck by lightning. The ceiling had caved in, but there was little damage to the walls. Madick assured Will he could question him all he liked, but he would have to wait until he was through with Halicut first. Madick's interrogation took nearly ninety minutes, during which time Will chatted with guards outside about home life and how awful spoiled children were. Their conversation was sometimes interrupted by sudden yelling from inside the dwelling.

When it was finally Will's turn to see Halicut, he was solemnly led inside. Halicut was bound to a chair; he had a table in front of him where a glass of water stood, the only luxury he was afforded. The room was illuminated by several oil lamps that gave the place a ghostly atmosphere. Halicut greeted Will with a look of disbelief, opening his eyes wide and parting his lips like a fish. "You're alive?" he stammered after taking a moment to gather himself. Will nodded with a sardonic look, his arms crossed. "I heard you were dead."

"Greetings, Dieschsuch Halicut," Will said. "How did you hear of my death?"

"The ... the Emperor told me. There was no body, but His Eminence said he didn't need one. He said—"

"Who told the Emperor, my lord Halicut?"

Halicut hesitated, probably thinking that the Emperor would have his head if he talked. But since he had talked too much already ...

"Commander Tanalac—he told him."

"And what did he do with Tanalac?"

Halicut shrugged. "Well, he didn't give him a medal, I think. He just sent him to look for the Mulvar child."

"A medal?" Will asked. "Why the hell would he give him a medal?"

Halicut stammered something incoherent, shaking his head all the while.

Will relaxed himself and said, "Hey, it's okay, my lord Halicut. I have nothing against you. You have always proven to be a gracious host. I won't harm you, but I can't guarantee my friends won't if you don't give me some answers. So, was Tanalac *supposed* to kill me?"

"Yes, Master Will Fontaine," Halicut said after swallowing.

"Please, no 'Master' or 'Will Fontaine'—just call me Will."

"Yes, Will ... the Emperor ordered Tanalac to kill you. But apparently you escaped, I'm very pleased to see."

Will approached him, hunching himself over. "Say that again? Are you sure?"

"Of course, Master Will. I didn't like the idea, because you and the other sons of Thayland were quite courteous, I didn't think it right for—"

"No, of course you didn't. You're no monster, are you? But why would His Eminence do that?"

Halicut swallowed again and sighed. "Oh, Master Will, the Emperor was so frustrated with you. Out of all the others, you gave him the most trouble. That skinny guy, the one with the high voice—he was easy. He wanted to please the Emperor so much he didn't even think twice about giving him that wine."

"You *knew* about that?" Will cried out.

"Of course ... and so did the Emperor. He knew he wasn't in any danger—so long as he gave the wine to his food-taster. Franklin Douglass was blamed and was the first to go, because he was the annoying one."

"Because he was annoying? But what do you mean he was the first to go?"

"Well, uh ... the Emperor wanted to frame you all for wrongdoing. Franklin was easy, and so was Harrington."

"What happened to Lord Harrington? Why was he executed?"

"Well, His Lordship Harrington was framed for murder. One of the Emperor's personal guards was killed in the night. It was done by another guard who then put the bloody knife in Lord Harrington's room. The Emperor took His Lordship to his room—just making conversation, that is—and discovered the knife, right there on his desk. His Lordship was imprisoned and forced to sign a confession. The confession said that the guard was killed to get to the Emperor, who was actually away from his room at the time ..."

"You liar," Will said, letting his shadow fall across Halicut's features. "Lord Harrington would never sign a false confession."

"Oh, please pardon me, Master Will, but you are wrong ... or rather it would be true if his life wasn't at stake. But he was told he would remain safe if he signed it, and he'd be killed if he did not in two days. He signed it but was killed, anyway. His head is atop the Palace's defense wall."

"Yes, I saw it," Will muttered, stepping away.

"He was easy, too, but you were very difficult. I admire you, I really do. It is not easy to defy the Emperor and get away with it; I don't think there was ever anybody—"

"Get to the damn point," Will snapped.

"Yes, well ... we all expected you to gather spoils at the Mulvar raid. You were supposed to stay behind like a coward, and then go the raid and grab all the spoils you wanted. But no one expected you to get a baby instead. When the Emperor heard what you had done, and that you had left it with the harem, he went to the harem, and we were all so afraid he would take it and kill it. But he didn't; he looked at the baby and thought about it. He decided he did not want to upset you. So he ordered the harem not to tell you he was there, and then he agreed to let the baby stay with the harem."

"Because he didn't want to upset me?"

"Yes, Master Will. He wanted to stay in your favor. He had other plans for you, but he held them off for a little while. But things got worse when the people learned about the baby, and when they cheered for you like a hero. I think the Emperor went on holiday because he was so upset and didn't want you to know."

"Did you know about the assassins that came into my room?"

Halicut nodded enthusiastically. "Oh, yes, yes, Master Will! The Emperor wanted you to get angry so you could slip up and do something horrible. So he sent Tanalac and Bartund to your room to attack you—"

"The *Emperor* sent them?"

"Yes, but not to kill you. They were supposed to hold back and make you angry. I heard they took one of your eyes, and I could have sworn you did ..."

"I was supposed to be angry so I would 'slip up?'"

"Yes. You were supposed to take revenge on Commander Tanalac, because you would recognize him by the gauntlets he wore that night. But you never did. The Emperor waited and waited, but you never did anything. You were supposed to do something before the dragon hunt, but you didn't."

I nearly did, Will thought, *but 'nearly' doesn't count.*

"The Emperor decided to just send you on the dragon hunt and have Tanalac kill you on the way. But before that, he tried one last chance to frame you for something: He ordered his beloved wife to seduce you."

"What?" Will cried, hunching over again. "*He* made his wife do that?"

"Oh, yes. She was supposed to seduce you and take you to her room, and then she would scream, and the guards would see both you of ... together, you know."

Will took a moment to think about that day. He remembered how the Emperor invited him into his study for one last look into the Sands of Carsiss. If Dieschsuch Halicut was being truthful about everything, the Emperor must have wanted Will to see himself dead in the middle of the desert—the destiny that he, the Emperor, was sending him to. If Will had instead said that he saw himself as Emperor, then Emperor Baku might have raised a knife or sword against Will himself. Of course, the Emperor might have done that even if he *didn't* plan to have Will killed.

Will surprised himself and everyone in the room when he grabbed Halicut's vest and pulled his face up near his. "You're not making any sense," he cried. "Why would the Emperor do all these things?"

"Oh, please, Master Will, I'll tell you, please let me go!" Halicut said while blubbering. Will did as asked and allowed Halicut a moment to compose himself. "The Emperor wanted to frame you sons of Thayland for acts of dishonor," Halicut continued. "He wanted to accuse you of staying behind while the other soldiers attacked the Mulvars, and then arriving after the fighting ended to collect spoils. He wanted to accuse you of attacking a superior officer for no good reason. But once he couldn't do that, he wanted to accuse you of laying with his wife. You upset him a great deal by not falling into any of his traps, acting only with honor and gaining the hearts of the people.

"He knows the people do not favor him; he knows the people do not favor the war. He has nothing personal against the Mulvars; he only wants to make his mark in the Kohima Dynasty by being the one to kill them all. He is going to do that no matter what—but he doesn't want to stop there. He looks at his land of sand and dust, and he is not pleased. So he has set his eyes on Thayland, his nation's longtime ally."

"You're lying," Will said halfheartedly.

"Please, Master Will, I do not lie. He wishes to convince the people that the sons of Thayland are nothing but dishonorable dogs who deserve to have their rich, emerald land taken away from them by a people more honorable and commendable."

Halicut fell silent, letting his words sink in.

"I think I know what he means," Madick said. "Baku wants to influence public opinion in favor of invading Thayland."

"Why ... why would he have to do that?" Will asked. "The people will do whatever he tells them to. If he doesn't have enough men, he can just draft all the men he needs."

"It's not that," Madick said. "The people simply don't favor him—you've seen that every day with me. He can order them around all he wants, but if their hearts aren't into it, an invasion would probably fail. So he used you and the others as examples of how barbarous sons of Thayland are, framing you for crimes you didn't commit."

"Yes, yes, it is all true," Halicut said. "But please, Master Will, I was against it, I even said so, but the Emperor ... he threatened to kill me and my family if I got in his way. Please forgive me, Master Will, I beg your mercy ..."

Will nodded irritably. "Yes, of course. You've done us a great service, Prime Dieschsuch." He looked at Madick, not wanting to say his name in front of Halicut. "I think our prisoner deserves to be as comfortable as possible, don't you agree?"

Madick nodded. "Okay, let's take him away," he said as Halicut started muttering in thanks.

Will wandered outside, keeping to himself and staring at the night sky. Madick joined him momentarily. "I had no idea," he said. "I didn't know what to think when he listed you as traitors, just that he wanted to wage war against Thayland. At least now I know I'm doing this for more than just the Mulvars. Any time you want, Will Fontaine, you're free to go back home. Of course, you never needed my permission, anyway."

Will looked at him from the corner of his eye. "I don't know—I think I could still be of some use to you."

CHAPTER 21
THE BREAKOUT

WILL HAD BEEN SERVING MADICK with a coolness and slyness that nearly matched Madick's, but after interrogating Halicut, anger began to mar those features. His speeches became more passionate, his drive more purposeful, which Madick was glad to see; but he was also losing his focus and showed more disapproval of dissent from the citizens. He was becoming less charming and more menacing.

Madick confronted him alone one time, three days after the interrogation. "I'm glad to see you're now seeing things my way, but this is a bit much," he said. "Please remember that people see you as a child's savior, not a warmonger."

"I know, it's just—" Will paused, struggling to find the right words. "I love Thayland; I'd do anything to protect my land. But there's more to it than that. I've just learned the Emperor have been playing us for fools all this time. Franklin and Lord Harrington did not deserve what they got, and he nearly got *me* killed. I see now that my fights in the Palace and in Sancrat had nothing to do with Ambri, and it just ... it *infuriates* me."

"I understand—I was like that once," Madick said. "Twice I saw innocent people killed, and I couldn't understand why ... not until someone told me. It opened my eyes. I finally understood and the reason made sense ... and that was why I was so angry. But yelling at people to follow me did not become me, and so I learned control and focus—two things you are losing. You understand."

Will nodded. "Any word on Tanalac?"

"I'm sorry—it seems he's pent himself up in the Palace. He might have gotten word we were searching for him, and that means they are on to us. We must be more careful from now on, and that means stopping the search for Tanalac."

"I see," Will said in a sobered tone. "If that's the case, stopping the search really is necessary. It can wait another day."

Madick nodded and soon parted with Will. When left alone, Will put a fist over his heart and breathed deeply. The pain of his heartbeats had gotten worse since the interrogation, and headaches arose frequently. As much as he didn't want to, he worried about his health and wondered if his resurrection had encountered problems during its process. If all he had to look forward to was a life full of agony and doubt, he wasn't sure if his amazing comeback was worth it.

Ever since Halicut's kidnapping, Madick worried that that may not have been the best move to make. It drew attention to the rebellion's existence, and soldiers were noticeably searching for any signs of their activities. They asked the citizens questions, posted up wanted flyers on the streets, and began to frequent secret meeting places. Madick knew their time grew short.

Six days after Halicut's interrogation, one of the rebellion's leaders was captured. Will was always kept in the dark about the identities of the other leaders, so he was confused when Madick said, in a weary tone, "Hondrun's gone."

It happened at night. Hondrun Duleney was staying in a tent that was like any of the hundred others in a shantytown. The soldiers surrounded the area and stealthily killed many of Hondrun's guards. They captured whoever was left, one of whom valued his life enough to guide them to Hondrun's tent. Hondrun was a strong and proud man, and he didn't go without a fight, but a blow to the head knocked him out, and he was then brought to the Palace by being dragged on a line behind a horse. The next day, flyers went up announcing his execution.

"We won't stop the meetings," Madick said, "but we'll have to cut them short and disallow questioning. We need you now more than ever, Will."

Will merely nodded and went back to the scroll he was reading, one of Madick's many documents concerning battle strategies and historical fights. He had always been trained in close-quarters combat, and needed some guidance in large campaigns.

The next day, Will gave Madick another task to work with. "I want you to find Jonoli—she's the headmistress of Baku's harem."

"Is she your lady-friend?" Madick asked at length, sounding like he was against the idea already. He naturally wanted to avoid any tasks that would prove unbeneficial, and finding Jonoli only because she was Will's lover might be one of them.

"Yes, she is," Will said guardedly, "but that's beside the point. We once discussed about how Ambri could get out of the Palace without the guards knowing. She said there was actually a way in and out of the Palace that wasn't guarded, but she didn't tell me where it was. She said it was forbidden knowledge, and that not even I should know about it."

"She may not trust you very much," Madick said.

"Probably," Will said with a sigh. "We got closer after I gave Ambri to her—she was very devoted to that child, you know—but I could tell she didn't trust me fully. Maybe because I'm a foreigner, or maybe just because I'm a man."

Madick said he was sorry Will didn't tell all that to him earlier. Will claimed that he had other things on his mind—but the truth was that he had little hope that they could capture Jonoli. She was mostly likely still in the Palace, perhaps held in the dungeon for hiding Ambri. He sincerely expected to never see her again, not even her corpse if that was what she had become.

But two days later, Madick surprised him.

"I've heard she is still alive," Madick told him. "But Will ... she's in the worst possible place."

"What?" Will asked in a low voice.

"She and the other ladies of Baku's harem are held in the *Qualini Durakur.*"

Will furrowed his brow. The closest Altrin translation for the name was "Soul Breaker," which could only be appropriate for a limited number of things—none of them good.

Madick related the story of how Emperor Bansel the Terrible had added a few touches to the Palace dungeon, bringing in torture machines that he put to use at once. He was said to love hearing the cries and screams of those poor souls coming up from the small air shafts that connected the dungeon to various parts of the Palace. His wife put up with it for a while, but she eventually complained of nightmares, which got so bad that she often awoke screaming and stirred Bansel awake, too. He tried to shut her up by reprimanding her, and when that didn't work he slept in a separate room. But the screaming from the dungeon continued to cause his wife grief and torment, so Bansel had no choice but to build another prison and move his precious devices there, which he sometimes visited for his sick enjoyment. That place, nestled in the Saparel Mountains to the west of the Palace, was *Qualini Durakur.*

A lump was brought to Will's throat when he imagined Jonoli held up in such a hellish place. Madick had said she was alive, but in what condition? At that point, Will could only pray that it was a condition that left her still able to speak.

"It'll take a while before we can get her out of there," Madick said in an apologetic tone. "Perhaps two or three days—maybe even a week."

"Why?" Will asked. "Don't we have enough troops? We can

take the place tonight if we wanted to."

"It's not that. Capturing the Prime Dieschsuch brought us attention we didn't need, and it got poor Hondrun captured. If we're ever going to take *Qualini Durakur,* it'll have to be on the eve of the Palace invasion. Your lady-friend will have to tell us what she knows as soon as she can so we can draw up plans right away. Do you see what I'm saying, Will?"

Will nodded.

"I'll need to speak with the other leaders. I'll tell them about your lady-friend and how she can help us. We'll then change our plans in positioning the troops to accommodate the breakout. This means we'll get only one try at it, and if it doesn't work, the invasion will go as originally planned."

Will was suddenly very apprehensive. Most of those "troops" Madick spoke of were merely townspeople who had to get their armor from their own means. Thanks to Will, the resistance movement's funding had increased, but much of it could only afford weapons that were passed out indiscreetly on the streets.

He also worried about Jonoli—not just for her condition but for her cooperation. If she either refused to speak or was lying or exaggerating about the secret path, she and the resistance were put in precarious positions.

The next day, the resistance leaders met in a cellar owned by a confidant. Will was there, accompanying Madick. He was greeted very graciously by the other leaders; they said they would have brought him gifts if they knew he was coming, but Will said that was quite all right. Besides Madick, there were five of them—three elderly men and two men of around middle-age. Three of them, he learned, had been soldiers who had participated firsthand in early stages of the war on the Mulvars. When the war started becoming a massacre, they had separately protested, only to be discharged and threatened with imprisonment if they continued protesting. They were currently acting generals for the resistance.

Madick explained the situation to them. They were naturally skeptical—perhaps even believing that Will was only interested in rescuing his lover—but they ended up agreeing on giving troops to Madick to invade *Qualini Durakur*.

Three days later, as messengers went door to door spreading the first orders of the Palace invasion, Will and Madick led their five hundred men to the valley where *Qualini Durakur* lied. It was a cold early morning in April, a time when one could see his breath in the air despite the low humidity. The two men rode their horses to a high vantage point overlooking the valley, which was strangely shaped like the larva of a housefly, allowing a lot of level ground for buildings.

The prison wasn't nearly as large as Will had expected: It was broad but had only floor and was guarded with minimal forces. The main obstacle was the defense wall made of sandstone blocks, but with only a few guards around, an invasion force of five hundred seemed like overkill.

There had been no enemy scouts, so the resistance's approach had been a stealthy one. The prison guards appeared to do their business with no hint of knowing they were being watched. No one had anticipated the importance of the current prisoners, other than how the Emperor himself had them sent there.

When Madick concurred that his forces were in their positions, he took out his whistle and blew a few notes on it, sounding like a songbird from Thayland. The men, divided into three units, ran from the cliffs and charged at the outer wall. On the outside were only six guards, two of them on horseback. They were besides themselves upon seeing the enemy advance, not knowing what to do. A few of them went to the main gate and begged to be let in, while the others bravely charged the enemy to no avail.

A bell was rung from a watchtower by the time the resistance reached the wall. The wall was only one story tall, so they handily tossed grappling hooks over it and climbed the ropes. From there, it was only a matter of eliminating the small defense forces that gathered outside the building. It took no longer than ten minutes, after which the limestone ground was stained with crimson, and a handful of the resistance members sheathed bloody swords and held dripping spears.

Will shook his head, sincerely ashamed that the breakout had to resort to so much bloodshed. He had asked Madick for leniency towards the prison guards earlier in the day, but Madick insisted he wanted no chance of a guard escaping and telling his superiors what happened. Will suspected Madick had a low opinion of Imperial guards and soldiers, anyway.

Will and Madick got down from their vantage point and approached the prison. They wanted to monitor the men, making sure they understand their orders. They were to swiftly locate the harem women, get them out, and have them ready for the road. Will expected to see Jonoli momentarily, but instead a panicked messenger approached. "Master Madick," he said, "there's a problem inside. We've found the women, but one of them is holding a man hostage."

"What?" Madick asked. He clearly hadn't anticipated the situation. He looked at Will for help.

"I'll go look," Will said. "I think I know what's going on."

"What's going on?" Madick asked, but Will had already begun riding for the prison. He darted through the open gate and dismounted. The men had amassed around the building; he dove into them, squeezing past them and pushing them aside to get to the front doors.

Inside, the men were searching the place, opening drawers and overturning tables, looking for any spoils that caught their fancy. Will had to continue squeezing past them in the entrance hallway, but in the first large room he came across, he found plenty of space. It wasn't hard to see why: It was the torture room, filled with unnatural-looking machines specifically designed for human suffering. Will pulled down the scarf over his face and gave the place a cautionary look. There was a rack, which stretched out a person's limbs, a thumbscrew, which clamped down a person's thumbs, and a strappado—a rope on a pulley system that hung a person by his hands—among numerous others devices. He imagined the guards using the harem girls on the machines, and his arms and neck broke into gooseflesh despite his warm clothes. He was caught off guard at the sight of an iron maiden—a kind of sarcophagus with long nails lining the inside surface. Its lid bore a design of an insane-looking man with wide eyes and a long tongue. The device was left open, and in the light of a torch set in a sconce, Will saw that the nails were darker in color than the steel of the inside surface.

The next hallway was lined with prison cells. It was full of nervous-looking men so cluttered together that Will couldn't squeeze past them. He ordered them to clear into the torture room and slowly made his way to the scene. He heard one of the resistance commanders up ahead—a levelheaded man by the name of Aman. He sounded like he was pleading to someone. Will cursed under his breath, hoping the situation was not as he imagined.

When he only paces away from Aman, he heard Jonoli's voice from inside an open cell: "What's going on? Don't get closer!"

"We're not doing anything," Aman said. "Don't panic, everything's all right."

Will slowed down and cautiously moved beside Aman, peering into the cell. Four women were inside, clothed only in loincloths. Jonoli was one of them, holding a man in front of her with his back to her, one hand clutching his chest and the other holding a knife to his throat. The other women were behind, looking on in either fear or hard determination.

"Jonoli, it's me," Will said.

Jonoli was surprised but still cautious. It took her a while to recognize him, then tentatively said his name.

"Yes, it's me. *I* brought these men here. We want to rescue you, nothing more. I promise if you let that man go, no one will harm you." He looked at Aman and firmly punched his shoulder. "Isn't that right, Aman?"

Aman, who may have had other ideas, briskly nodded. He was a good commander and a married man, but Will wondered about his aesthetics. It was a common practice for armies to capture woman prisoners and enslave them for the use of the men. It wasn't hard to imagine the resistance continuing that practice since the women were harem members and Aman and his men were only human.

Jonoli must have imagined it as Will did, so she had taken the knife off the first man who entered the cell and held him hostage.

"Please, Jonoli," Will said, "let him go."

Jonoli pressed her chapped lips together, then hesitantly released the man. He hurried out of the cell and went down the hall, stopping only to look back and give her a hateful look.

Will quickly surveyed the area, then turned to the men behind him and said, "Get some blankets and cover them up, then get them out of here on the double."

Aman told them to move it, reassuming his command. Will dropped his scarf and took off his overlarge shirt. He gave it to Jonoli and told her to put it on. Jonoli took it, looking plenty ashamed to, and did as told.

"Come on, let's go, Jonoli," Will said, holding out a hand. Jonoli hesitated to take it, still the pensive one. It seemed her faith in all men was shaken, and she was not making Will an exception. He couldn't blame her, but if she refused to go with him, he'd have no choice but to force her.

Fortunately, she did take his hand, and then drew herself close to him for support. He wrapped an arm around her back and led her down the hall. "You must be freezing," Jonoli said.

"That doesn't matter," Will said.

"I thought you were dead."

"I was," Will said, then quickly added, "I *almost* was, but I couldn't leave you and Ambri behind."

"Ambri ..." Jonoli mused. "Is she still safe?"

"I'm not sure, but I think so," Will replied. "Let's just worry about you for now."

Will carefully inspected how the women were treated, making sure the men didn't have any funny ideas. He had a brief word with Commander Aman, letting him know that mistreatment of the women would be met with severe punishment. He thought of the harem as sort of a second family to him, as odd as it seemed, and he did not want to regret saving them by throwing them to the dogs. Lord knew they must have been through enough torment already in *Qualini Durakur*.

Jonoli gave Will his shirt back once she had gotten a blanket that covered her full body. She kept it tightly wrapped around herself as she marched through the mountainside with sandals on her feet. Will didn't want to talk to her in such a state, so he asked Madick for a recess in the march back to Nünveghett. With the army stopped, Will set up a tent and put down sleeping bags inside. Once some men got a fire going, Will invited Jonoli in the tent and offered her hot water. "Sorry, I don't have anything stronger," he said.

"It's fine, thank you," Jonoli replied, holding the bowl in her hands and letting the steam reach her face ... then asked something that had been on her mind since she first saw him in the prison: "What happened to your eye?"

Will was caught slightly off guard, but he recovered quickly. "Oh well, I ... I was faking it."

"Faking it? Truly?"

"Yes well, I really didn't have any evidence that I was attacked in my room, so I pretended that I lost my eye."

Jonoli gave him a look of disbelief that could have cut right to the bone. "But the doctor treated you, and you had a scar over your eyebrow ... and the men left their grappling hooks behind! You didn't need more evidence than that!"

Will felt a flush over his face, and he tried to think fast. "Well, I

... I have my secrets, and I managed to fool everyone, didn't I?"

Jonoli eyed him suspiciously, but then shook her head and said, "I don't understand, but no matter, I suppose."

Will nodded, both in agreement and relief. "I'm glad you got Ambri out of the Palace. Did Baku look for her right away, when I was gone?"

"No, but I knew he would. I took Ambri to a safe place on the night after you left." She was about to bring the bowl to her lips when she suddenly said, "Why do you call him 'Baku?' He is 'the Emperor' to you."

"Not anymore," Will said with a tone that suggested he did not want to argue about it. He related to her what Prime Dieschsuch Halicut had said. "I have no doubt he told the truth, and since then I've lost all respect to Baku. Do you realize why all these men are assembled here? They are rebels, ready to overthrow Baku. They've had enough of his 'war' on the Mulvars, and now they plan to be rid of him."

"Don't be a fool, Will," Jonoli snapped. "There has to be more than that. That man you ride with–is he their leader? He is doing this so he can take the throne himself."

Will nodded. "I've thought of that. He said he's not interested in the throne, and I've little reason to believe him. But Jonoli ... I was nearly killed in Sancrat. Halicut said Baku ordered my death. So if I must choose between Baku and Madick as Emperor, I'll choose Madick. At least *he* seems sincere."

"I suppose you're right." Jonoli looked down at her bowl wearily.

"Did you have any idea what Baku was planning?" Will asked.

"No," Jonoli said forcefully. "I would have told you if I did. Have some faith in me."

"Okay," Will said with a nod.

"So you are a rebel, then? What happened to your plan to return and make peace between us and the Mulvars?"

Will made a sly smile. "Sometimes the world sees a tyrant who just can't listen to reason ... and when that happens, there's little you can do."

Jonoli sighed. "No, there isn't. But many will die ... perhaps even you."

"I won't be the first," Will said morosely. "Lord Harrington was executed, did you know that? His head is above the Palace gate, among those of about twenty Mulvars."

"And Bensha ..." Jonoli suddenly grew disturbed and dropped the bowl in her lap, the hot water soaking into her blanket. She cried out the name again and began sobbing, burying her face in her hands.

Will recognized the name, Bensha. She was one of the harem members. She was somewhere in her mid-twenties and was one of the more petite girls. She had long hair and let it hang over her ears. She was rather sullen, sharp-tongued, and not too quick to smile, but when she did it brightened her features considerably. When Jonoli's sobbing subsided, he asked, "What happened to Bensha?"

"They ... they killed her," Jonoli said in a sad voice that sounded so unlike her usual self. "It was my fault, all my fault. I thought we could escape—I thought I could find some way out of there. They were always asking me where Ambri was, and one day they threatened to kill one of the girls. I gave them a false location—I thought it could buy us time to figure an escape route. But we couldn't do it by the time they came back ... so they ... they drew straws ... and the man who picked Bensha drew the short one ... *and they killed her.*"

Jonoli broke into more sobbing. Will brought a hand up to his forehead and shut his eyes. He remembered the spikes in the iron maiden, dark in color because they were covered in old blood.

"And we were whipped," Jonoli said after suddenly looking up. He didn't need to be told, though: The evidence was all over her back and ribs. They were covered with stringy scars, running both vertically and horizontally. It was the same with all the girls, some of them having felt the whip as recently as yesterday.

"Every day I heard the others screaming as they were lashed," Jonoli continued. "They did it every day when we were first brought here. But *I* didn't scream. I cried but I never screamed, because that was what they wanted. I just kept it all in." She paused then, bringing her head back down. "They still hate me, though. They wanted me to confess, but I never did. They are no longer my sisters. At least I know Ambri is safe still."

"I'm sorry, Jonoli," Will said. "I'm so sorry for what you went through."

"It is not your fault—"

"No, I brought Ambri to you, so it *is* partly my fault ... but it is mostly Baku's fault. What do you think he would say if he knew Bensha was dead and the others have turned against you?"

Jonoli kept her head down, but Will could tell in the faint light that she grimaced.

"Do you wish to defend him even now? Do you see why it's best to be rid of him?"

Jonoli shook her head and sniffed. "I just thought he was chosen by the gods. You cannot overthrow a decision made by the gods."

Will hesitated, thinking back on his resurrection. "I don't think the gods chose Baku," he said. "Baku just happened to be born into the throne. That doesn't mean he's beyond *karma,* does it?"

"No, Will—no one is beyond *karma.*"

"And if you believe the Mulvars are the gods' subjects, then they must be very angry with Baku, wouldn't you think?"

"I don't know ... but if I were a god, I would be furious."

"That's why we need to get inside the Palace. Jonoli, do you remember how we talked about a way to get Ambri out of there? You never told me where that unguarded path was, but I need to know it now. It might be a great help to us."

Jonoli paused, appearing contemplative. She then shifted herself, wrapping her blanket more tightly around her ... and she told him of the unguarded path. "You have to be very careful," she concluded. "If they see you entering it, they'll catch on quickly. It is not like they don't know about it."

"I see."

"Will ... " Jonoli looked at him squarely in the face. "Will you kill him?"

"I don't think imprisonment will do," Will said. "After all he's done, it's the only thing I can do. Why do you ask?"

Jonoli waved a dismissive hand. "It's nothing."

"What's nothing?" Will asked at length.

"Well, it's just that ... I could have been his wife, once. I was just brought into the harem and ... he chose me because he said I was special."

"Are you saying you loved him?"

Jonoli shook her head firmly. "No, I was desperate. I wanted to get out of servitude and make a better life for myself. But I was scared he would find out I was a quarter Mulvarian, so there was really no chance. Like I said, it's nothing."

Will nodded but he didn't quite buy it. In all his years of undergoing puberty, he had learned at least one thing: Women's hearts were not easily swayed.

"He's a monster," he said. "If everything about him is true, he's no worse than Commander Tanalac. Remember Tanalac? He tried to kill me in Sancrat province. I escaped only because he didn't sic the whole army on me."

"And he was *supposed* to be the one who took your eye," Jonoli said accusingly.

"Yeah, yeah, he took it all right ... and I faked it so well, even *he* believed it."

"So, are you going to march on Nünveghett? With what army?"

Will gave her a briefing on how he had making speeches.

"So you're going to lead *townspeople* to the Palace? That's mad!"

"You said it yourself: The people are tired of blood feuds. Overtaking the Palace is the only way to end them, to make the Emperor see reason."

"Yes, but I thought ... well, it doesn't matter what I thought. The Mulvars are being killed—that's all that matters. So you're going to be a commander, huh?"

Will suddenly turned solemn. "I think so ... but actually, I believe the resistance leaders would rather be rid of me now."

That belief turned out to be justified as soon as he made his report to Madick in the leader's tent. Madick congratulated him on the job well done ... and then promptly said that Will would not be joining him in Nünveghett.

"Why not?" Will asked, feigning ignorance by sounding outraged.

"Your job with us is over," Madick said firmly. "We don't want you killed; it's best you left us as a living hero while you still can."

"But I deserve to be there! And I'm not going without Ambri!"

"Hasn't the woman told you where she is?"

"I didn't ask her because it didn't matter—I planned on getting her after the invasion. And besides, you need me there to lead the men. After all that convincing I've done, I owe it to them!"

"No one's questioning your bravery, and no one will. We'll tell everyone that we kept you safe, even against your will."

Will snickered. "Listen to yourself: That would just make you sound like an ass."

Madick smirked in spite of himself. "Perhaps, but at least I'll get what I want in the end."

Will thought about telling him that he sounded like Baku just then, but then thought better of it. The two of them exchanged more barbs, and then Will left the tent in a huff, the clear loser of the debate. He retreated to Jonoli's tent and told her what to expect: "Madick will lead most of the company to Nünveghett, where he'll tell the other leaders about the passage. We, however—along with the other women—will be escorted by fifty men to Markereen, where I'll be forced aboard a boat and sent to Thayland."

"Those fools," Jonoli said. "They think that by getting rid of you, they can get all the glory for themselves?"

"I don't think so," Will said bitterly. "At least it could be worse—they could just kill me."

"And what if you try to escape? What would they do then?"

"I don't know, but I've got to give them the slip and get to Nünveghett on my own."

There was a thoughtful pause, then Jonoli searched the inside of her blanket and pulled out a small vial of colorless liquid. "I got this when I went back into the prison," she said. "It's something the guards used on us to keep us under control. They used only small doses, but if you use the whole thing, it will knock you out for a long time."

Will took the vial, took a whiff of the contents, and quickly drew it away from his face and closed it. It was an incredibly acrid smell, and he could see himself passing out from smelling it too long. He looked at it approvingly, but then said, "I can't use this on Madick."

"No, I was thinking you could use it on someone else," Jonoli said.

As promised, Madick quickly gathered a squadron together and brought it under the command of Aman. He told the women where they were going and assured them of their safety and well-being, so long as they obeyed Commander Aman's orders. Then in no time, he mounted his horse and led his men down the way they came, to Nünveghett, where they expected the Palace invasion to be underway by the time they got there.

Aman was given specific orders to keep Will in his sight at all times, but as to what he would do should Will escape, Will never knew. Aman was at least gracious enough to let Will keep his horse, trusting him to fully cooperate. Jonoli was seated behind him as the women and their escorts started off down the mountain, heading for the desert where they would take the most direct route to the port town of Markereen. Will kept a sharp eye on the behavior of the men, and was quite pleased with their progress; they barely touched the women and conversed with them politely, and even gave them sandals to wear for their trek through the desert. It was good to know that he would leave them in good hands.

Soon after they had reached the desert, Jonoli suddenly went limp and fell from the horse, crashing to the sand below. Will quickly jumped off and went to her, lifting her head up from the ground and saying her name in a state of panic. A crowd soon formed around them; Aman made his way through them, dropped the scarf over his face, and asked what the matter was.

"Is there a doctor here?" Will asked. "Please, she's growing fevered."

Aman looked around him with concerned eyes. "I don't believe—" he started.

"Well, if there's no one here, we need to get her to Nünveghett, right away!"

Aman shook his head. "We can find a doctor in Markereen. Hensin, I'm leaving her up to you. Get her on your horse and—"

"No, I'm not leaving her!" Will cried. "I'm going, too."

Aman shook his head. "Will Fontaine, this is hardly the time to—"

Will lifted up Jonoli and slung her across his horse's back, then mounted himself. "If you must, then come along with me!"

Aman, still shaking his head, proceeded to mount his horse and headed off, chasing after Will who had gotten a head start.

They rode across the desert, the wind chill giving both men the shivers. Aman complained to himself that Will should not be the one giving any orders, but as long as he got him to Markereen and on that ship, at least his job would be done.

When the squadron was little more than a splotch on the horizon behind them, Will suddenly came to a stop and gently brought Jonoli off. Aman turned around and cried, "What are you doing!? We have no time to rest. Get back on your horse!"

"I need to check on her," Will said arrogantly, lying Jonoli down on the ground.

"Of all the stupidest things—" Aman grumbled. He dismounted himself and approached his two companions.

Will was kneeling over Jonoli, inspecting her for something—fleas perhaps. He then lifted his head and said, "Commander, I think you should take a look at this."

Aman frowned and grew closer. He kneeled down next to Jonoli, unmindful of Will beside him. He carefully checked for signs of irregularity, such as a poor complexion or an unsteady breathing rate. He was just thinking to himself that Jonoli wasn't making a sound when Will forced a rag over his nose and mouth. Aman grappled him, but due to the sharp breaths he took in the rag, he was already starting to weaken. The rag was soaked with the drug Jonoli had taken from the prison, and he had no way of escaping Will's grasp once the vapors filled his lungs.

He collapsed, and Will carefully let him down on the ground, throwing the rag away. "I hope I didn't overdo it," he said.

Jonoli, the picture of health, sat up and said, "I hope so, too, but what's done is done. You need to go to Nünveghett now. Hurry!"

CHAPTER 22
A TIME TO ACT

IT WAS A SIGHT THAT HADNT been seen since the days of Bansel the Terrible: The working men of Nünveghett–*Vaisyas* and *Sudras* alike–were leaving their homes and heading for the Emperor's Palace. Their faces were grim and determined, their hands holding all sorts of weapon–swords, bows, axes, and even pickaxes and garden hoes. They ordered their women and children to remain in their homes and to not leave under any circumstances–especially if martial law was declared.

The messengers of the resistance did their work with speed and accuracy, banging on doors and delivering their message with only a few words: "The time to move is now." Many of those messengers were caught by soldiers and interrogated. Some of them talked, revealing what they were doing–but even so, the damage was already done, judging by the crowded streets.

Nünveghett had a large and strict night patrol; at daybreak, the patrols lessened, figuring that the burglars and drunkards were done making mischief by that time. Even when news of the resistance's existence spread, the patrol schedule remained unchanged. That was why the resistance chose daybreak to get its forces moving; as the soldiers dutifully did their daily exercises, the commoners marched towards the Emperor's Palace, ready to give the Emperor pieces of their minds.

Not all men joined the parade; a good many decided to stay home and leave the resistance up to the rest of the city. Nevertheless, the resistance managed to rally a force of nearly two thousand men–about nine-tenths of the city's male citizens. Many women wanted to join the cause, too–most of them unmarried–but they were rebuked by the men on the streets, and most of them were forced to stay indoors.

It wasn't long before fighting erupted. The soldiers, peering out from their training facilities, saw the streets filled with men headed for the same place, and they took up arms and hurried down to the gathering forces. They started by demanding to know what was going on, and then either started attacking or started being attacked. The battles were fierce, the blood flowing in the streets by the gallons. Still, the fighting proved to be more of a benefit than a hindrance to the resistance, as dead soldiers supplied the citizens with fresh weapons, armor, and horses.

The division of eight thousand that had returned from Sancrat had been dispersed by that day, most of its members having returned to their homes throughout Carsiss; so the best that Nünveghett's military could come up with was a force of around seven hundred men, many of whom were still haunted by the devastation that Kojari had wrought. Shrewd commanders and generals realized that force was not enough to cripple the resistance movement, so they ordered their forces to hurry to the Palace, where they would make their stand by the outer defense wall.

Emperor Baku first learned of the insurrection when he was saying his morning prayers. He was in a shrine that was set deep in the Palace, so he couldn't hear the growing noise outside. Three soldiers, risking his wrath, banged on the door and demanded for him to come out. The Emperor threw the door open, looking ready to roll some heads for the disturbance. The three soldiers talked all at once; their words were mostly gibberish to the Emperor's ears, but he did catch something that made him start moving:

"The city's moving towards us!"

The Emperor stepped out on a balcony and was stunned to see the Palace catapults being used for the first time since their installment. They heaved large piles of rocks, which rained on the crowd that gathered on the other side of the Calkune River. The crowd was not very big or dense, but it was clearly growing in size, fed by the nearest street outlets. Their yelling and screaming filled the air, sounding like the white noise of a waterfall, only more colorful.

"What the hell is this?" the Emperor asked disdainfully, never being one for surprise.

"They are the citizens," a soldiers said beside him, clearly in awe of the spectacle.

The Emperor gave him a rather murderous look. "So get down there and order them to desist!" he yelled. He turned and looked at the small company around him, which consisted of both soldiers and Palace servants. "All of you, do something! Help with the catapults! Guard the entrances! Not a single one of them gets inside that wall, you hear me!?"

They did, and as much as they were hesitant to harm any of their fellow citizens, they acted well enough—because, of course, they were acting out of fear for their lives.

Fighting on the streets continued nonstop for much of the day, although most of it grew more concentrated outside the Palace defense wall. Palace forces continued to fight from above the wall, throwing arrows and spears at the crowd and slinging more rocks and other hard objects from the catapults; many soldiers were struck by return arrows and were quickly replaced. From within the courtyard, soldiers banged on large drums in perfect unison, sounding like the beating of the heart of war.

The resistance managed to swim across the river and use the *ghets* from further down to reach right up to the wall, where they futilely tried to throw grappling hooks and set up ladders. But the soldiers were ready for them, pouring hot, slick oil down the ladder rungs and slashing the ropes with freshly-sharpened blades. The crowd was soon forced to withdraw from the wall, seeing that too many men were being killed by Palace forces. The waters of the Calkune were stained red, as well as the *ghets* and the main bridge. Drawing back proved to be a problem, however, since the undisciplined men in the back did not understand why they were being pushed back and resisted the pushing.

Atop the roof of a bakery shop, Artiman Noonshun, one the resistance leaders, shook his head in dismay. He had expected the wall to be climbed over by midday, but by the way things were going, it might happen later than they thought. He hadn't wanted to do a siege, as it would be too time-consuming and would allow Palace reinforcements to arrive, but it appeared that was the only option left to him.

He looked to be tearing his hair out when he was approached by one of his nearest comrades—the former owner of the bakery shop named Madick Treyboia. "Good news?" he asked.

"Great news," Madick replied. "It seems we can go *under* the wall."

Madick related what Will had told him, and Artiman gave new orders to a group of his most loyal men. The men descended from the roof and sluggishly made their way through the crowd and to the Palace.

The sun was only three hours away from setting when the tides began to turn. General Taniko—the very same one who had led the dragon hunt—was standing just inside the museum in the Palace courtyard. He was well aware that the resistance indicated great changes in Nünveghett, that the attitude of the general population would never be the same throughout the rest of his years on earth—but he stood with the kind of glow that only good tactical news could give him: Several messengers had successfully penetrated enemy lines and were making their way to surrounding populaces, which would send reinforcements to bring the resistance movement to its knees. Inevitably, the citizens would be held captive in their homes, and the ones responsible for the movement would learn of pain centers they never even knew they had.

Still, we don't know what the hell they want, he thought. *We should probably call for a drawback and start peace talks. Of course, we won't give them anything they demand, but if we pretend to compromise at first, we can start stepping towards peace. I mean, those are our own people out there! They're not like the Mulvars with their petty caravans and flashy tricks—they're all Carsians. Different war strategies are a must, because we can't damn well kill them all!*

The war drums continued, sounding from the Emperor's garden, the smithy, and the library. The beaters were replaced hourly, for the drums had to keep going, never pausing, as was the Carsian tradition. The soldiers needed their blood boiling, especially in a confusing time when their own people were turning against them. When the general thought again of the ones responsible for the break in the peace, he vowed to attend their torture sessions himself.

He then received a hell of a surprise. He didn't notice anything wrong in the courtyard right away; it took the yelling of several men to shift his attention, even though it was happening right under his nose.

The shrine dedicated to Siva had four little booths, one on each side. Men were suddenly darting from within the nearest booth as if they had all been crammed into there. They were coming from the underground tunnel, of course—the secret escape route for the Emperor and his family should the Palace fall under siege. The Emperor had been asked to use the tunnel earlier, but in his pride he refused, citing that he should have no reason to run from his own people.

Half a year ago, if Lord Harrington had brought Will down the tunnel with a torch, they would have seen a manhole not far underneath the marble statue of Siva. The manhole led to a vertical passage with ladder rungs set into one side. It went down about nine meters, then turned a corner, heading straight for the mountainside temple to the east. It ended at another manhole inside the temple, just behind a wide altar and covered with a cheap rug. From there, the Emperor and his wife Annell could have climbed to the top floor and taken a secret route over the mountain leading to a small armory station, where they would be given horses to make their escape with.

The problem was (so the general thought with a sneer) that the route was supposed to have been kept in the strictest confidence. If the resistance was pouring out of the booths, then there must have been a leak somewhere—no that that mattered anymore.

"Take them out!" the general yelled. "Carsians or not, they are not allowed in the Palace!"

The soldiers drew their arms and charged at the mob. Although the soldiers were more disciplined and experienced, the civilians fought like savages, swinging their blades quickly in all directions and making bloodcurdling cries. The soldiers gained some ground, though, picking the resistance off like rats. General Taniko ordered them to push the resistance back into the tunnel, and they certainly tried, but there was only so much they could do against the force of hundreds of men pushing on each other's backs.

It wasn't long before the citizens found the exit inside the museum. The general sharply turned to them, his grim expression meeting their ominous ones. He was alone and out of earshot of most of the soldiers. In all respects, he should have run; it was the only sensible thing to do and it would not have been considered dishonorable.

Instead, he drew his scimitar and pointed it at the civilians. "If this is what Carsiss has come to," he said, "then have at me!"

Despite his superior armor and weapon, he had no chance.

The Emperor had been the height of confidence throughout the siege, looking on from his high perch. Annell was beside him, upset beyond consoling and losing her determination to stay beside her husband. She had been talking about retreating through the underground tunnel, but the Emperor assured her that reinforcements would arrive before the siege got any worse.

Then the resistance appeared in the courtyard, and both of them lost their nerve. The Emperor gripped the banister and gritted his teeth; Annell fell into despair, yelling that all hope for them was lost. With reinforcements still far away and the escape route no longer an option, Annell turned to her husband and demanded him to order a withdrawal—it was almost as if she had read the general's thoughts earlier.

"Annell, you don't understand," the Emperor said. "If they're coming here, it is for my head."

Annell shook her head, then cried out and started sobbing. She clutched her husband's vest, but he broke free and headed down the hall.

Moments later, trumpets sounded from the Palace windows. In most other countries, that would be the signal to charge; in Carsiss, it served as the signal for retreat. The soldiers posted at the catapults and furnaces stopped what they were doing and turned tail; those on ground level closest to the Palace did the same, even though civilians were right on their tails. Many of them were too thick in battle to retreat, and so they met their ends despite their orders and discipline.

The Emperor hoped the withdrawal order would be seen as a olive branch, but if the resistance made no return offer, then the men would inevitably take over the Palace and have their way with the inhabitants. The soldiers had been severely crippled, their numbers dwindled; there would be no stopping the resistance.

But to the Emperor's great relief, more trumpet blasts sounded from the streets. The resistance leaders had apparently spared no expense on the instruments, for there were enough of them to have their sound carry into the Palace courtyard. The civilians heard and obeyed quite willingly, knowing that their leaders weren't just fooling around. Some of them gained control of the gate; they took off the steel bar and threw the doors open. There were a few men who crossed the bridge heading for the Palace, but the men who retreated made sure to turn them around. Those in the temple waiting to enter the tunnel dispersed and went outside for further orders; those who freshly went out of the tunnel were quickly redirected outside by messengers.

Baku came through a door leading him to the top of the defense wall. He stopped to observe the retreat of the men in the courtyard; when the courtyard was empty and the gate closed again, he headed pasted the battlements until he reached the point above the main gate. He stared at the citizens across the river for some time, his jaw set and his eyes squinting both from the sun and from the animosity and disappointment that beat within his heart.

Artiman and Madick barely let him out of their sights, waiting anxiously for to say something. Neither man spoke except Artiman, and that was only to give the order for the crowd to fall silent.

The Emperor fanned out his arms and cried, "I applaud your effort. You have gotten the best of me, whoever you are. The time for hostility is over; let us now work out our differences. I will hear your terms for peace at the Palace. Bring yourself and your high commanders to the entrance."

The Emperor hastily retreated. Artiman turned to Madick and gave his biggest grin. "We've got him!" he cried with a laugh.

It was slow-going through the crowd, even when mounted on their horses, but Artiman and Madick reached the bridge and crossed it to the main gate. Two other horsemen accompanied them—two of their most trusted commanders. Artiman commanded for the gate to open; the soldiers atop the wall gave the okay, but warned the resistance leader not to pull anything funny. They darted through the gate and headed for the Palace. Artiman was a little concerned over how the gate quickly closed behind him, leaving them trapped inside the courtyard, but it was something he had to bear to get what he wanted.

The Emperor was found waiting from one of the balconies closest to the ground. Annell beside him was the first to speak:

"You monsters! How dare you turn our own people against us!? Don't you even know what you've done? The Heavens will surely turn against us!"

Artiman, who was pushing fifty, hadn't lost his so-called singing voice; his words reached the two of them as clear as a bell. "Frankly, My Lady Eminence, I'm surprised they haven't already. The Mulvars have been nearly wiped out; their blood is on each of our hands. It's true they are thieves and vagabonds, many of them, but there are many goods ones, too, earning their livings through honest trade. Seeing their numerous dead is a pity beyond words. When I set out on my campaign to win the hearts of the people, I had little idea what I would accomplish. If the people hadn't felt as strongly as I do about the 'war' on the Mulvars, I wouldn't be standing here right now."

"Very good," the Emperor said, though he was clearly unmoved. "And just who are you to do this to me?"

"I am Artiman Noonshun, son of Greiks Noonshun."

The Emperor raised an eyebrow. "Noonshun? Greiks Noonshun ... I've heard that name before."

"He met your father shortly before he passed away. He asked

for a favor that Emperor Orissu could not grant him."

The Emperor waved a dismissive hand. "Enough—what do you want?"

Artiman squirmed a bit in his saddle. "I want an end to the war on the Mulvars."

"I thought so. As much as it pains me, I shall have it done."

"Let me finish, Your Eminence. I want an end to the practice of blood feuds as well. The *Brahmans* have long been decrying this practice, and I think it's about time we listened to them."

The Emperor sneered. "Those *Brahmans* are rogues, heretics! I've already agreed to break the feud with the Mulvars, but this is ludicrous!"

"I know your father had been wronged by Marsoon Diachhe, but he begs forgiveness! He wants the war to end, while I believe it shouldn't have started in the first place! Blood feuds have made it possible—if you blame one, you might as well blame them all!"

The Emperor made no reply, only stood there staring, trying to antagonize Artiman.

"Also—" Artiman paused, not for effect but because his next request might prove to be too much, even in his own eyes. "Your promise to break the blood feud with the Mulvars must be enforced, and so I ask of you ... please raise me to the state of *Ksatriya.*"

The Emperor widened his eyes, then pounded a fist on the banister. "No—by the gods, no! You can make heresy all you like, but you will not force me to make heresy myself!"

Artiman sadly nodded. "My father asked the same of your father. He was a fool for that, but I see no other way—unless you can somehow make me an unofficial member of government, with only minimal power of command."

"Unofficial?" the Emperor asked in disbelief. "Now you are talking nonsense! The other *Ksatriyas* will not stand for it. They may end up killing you. That is not a threat; it is a foretelling well out of my hands."

"I am willing to risk it ... and if you wish to appease the hearts of your people, you should risk it, too!"

"I have risked enough already; do not tell *me* about taking chances! I remember Greik Noonshun now: My father first laughed at him, then was angry at him when he tried to force his hand. You have done much better, but that does not make you any less of a fool!"

The Emperor paused for thought. Artiman thought he saw his eyes glancing at the main gate and the mass of people on the other side, but he couldn't be sure from his vantage point. The Emperor then said, "We need to discuss more personally. I will meet you in my room. I am willing to compromise, but only if you order the citizens to retreat and go about their daily lives."

Artiman gave a suspicious eye. "This is a trick."

"No, this is no trick, Artiman Noonshun."

"You will not harm me at any time?"

"No."

"Nor any of your men?"

"Absolutely not."

"Do you swear by your honor?"

Besides a shocked Annell, the Emperor clicked his heels together and placed a fist over his heart. "By my honor, I swear."

Artiman nodded. "I will return," he said, then turned his horse and rode back to the gate.

The other men followed suit ... save one.

It was one whose head and face were covered by a long scarf wrapped together and worn like a turban. He ordered his steed to resist following the others and thus remained behind under the Emperor's immediate gaze. The others assumed he was Aman, for he wore Aman's red belt and a golden symbol of an ocean wave on his turban. When Artiman and his commanders were a fair distance away, the man pulled the scarf down from his face and removed it off his head. Although his dark skin was apparent even with the scarf on, at that point it was all too obvious.

Will looked up at the Emperor and cried, "Emperor Baku! You haven't forgotten me yet, have you?"

The Emperor bent a little over the banister, his expression the very description of shocked surprise. Annell looked horrified, on the other hand, having believed that the man she had seduced was dead, since her husband had assured her of it.

"Will Fontaine," the Emperor said at length once he regained his composure. "If I were you, I would turn and go back right now. You are in the middle of Carsian affairs—you have no place here!"

"You may be right," Will admitted, "but the affair between me and you can't be ignored. I won't let you!"

"What affair is that?" the Emperor asked wearily.

"Lord Harrington is dead by your order. I've come to avenge him."

"Your Lord Harrington was executed. He tried to assassinate me, didn't you hear?"

"That must mean the Prime Dieschsuch is a liar. He said my lord was a scapegoat you made to push your case for an invasion of Thayland!"

"Push my case? There is no case! You are a traitor as well, Will Fontaine, and I should not have to suffer you anymore!"

At that moment, Artiman returned with the other two. "Will Fontaine," he said loudly, "what in the great white heavens are you doing here?"

Will turned to him but had difficulty in looking him in the eye. He felt as if he had egg on his face after disregarding an order meant to safeguard him, and then virtually ruining Artiman's peace plan. But then he remembered his thoughts when Artiman asked to be raised to the level of *Ksatriya*—how it seemed that the whole resistance movement was only a pretense made to gain political power. Will found his voice again, the same one he'd been using on Baku: "I'm doing what I have to do here. I can't let Baku treat me like a dog and get away with it."

"There are more matters at stake here than just your pride," Artiman said harshly. "Don't you know the battle is over? Now we must make amends like rational men, do you hear me? Many men and soldiers have died, and we must think of reparations other than more blood spilt!"

Will started to say something—about how his conflict with Baku was more than just some petty blood feud—but he kept silent, curious instead to see where Artiman would take matters from that point.

"Follow me, Will Fontaine," Artiman said. "That is an order!"

Artiman was a little too arrogant in making an order, but Will did as asked. The soldiers opened the main gate without asking, and Artiman and company went and stopped in the middle of the bridge. Artiman unsheathed his scimitar and raised it in the air, shouting, "Victory!"

The crowd followed suit, making the largest unified cry of celebration heard that day. To Will's ears, their cheering sounded a little out of place after many hours of battle cries and shouts of pain and agony. He chalked it up to his inexperience—it was the first full-scale battle he'd ever been in other than that with Kojari, and it was nothing like the training sessions and knight tournaments in Thayland, where no one got killed, only hurt every now and then.

He was pretty sure, though, that once the people went back and witnessed the blood covering the streets, all thoughts of celebration would empty from their heads.

It was, perhaps, blood spilt for one man's ambitions.

No, *all the Mulvars will be spared,* Will thought. *And Ambri will be spared. I don't believe Artiman was bullshitting about that; he truly wanted the 'war' to end all along.*

And that meant that all of Will's participation in the resistance would be worth it. He breathed a sigh of relief beside Madick, whose smile faltered when he glanced at him. Will's softly grim face was enough to sober Madick back to reality.

Artiman addressed the crowd, telling them to disperse and go about gathering the dead, who were sure to receive honorable burials, every last one of them. It would then be time to repair and pay for damages as well as everyone saw fit. Artiman then encouraged them to continue on with their normal business, as hard as it would be, because the memories of the dead would be best honored by retaining the peace and not asking for unreasonable reparations.

"And most of all, be proud of this day," Artiman cried, "and work with your Mulvarian cousins, for it is for them and for your children that you fought so hard and gallantly!"

The crowd cheered again, at that point pumping their fists and shouting in unison, as if they were at a sports game.

Artiman said to Madick, "Take the young man here to the shop, and keep yourselves there until I return. I don't know how long I'll be, but I promise to return by the time the scorpion shows."

Madick nodded, as well as Will, who assumed "the scorpion" meant the constellation in the night sky. Artiman returned and passed through the main gate while Madick led Will to his bakery shop. There he offered him a meal of bread, cheese, and water, and opened his guest room upstairs.

"Aren't you angry with me?" Will asked.

"I was there when you questioned Halicut," Madick said. "Artiman wasn't, so he may not understand why you came here."

"I thought he was informed of Baku's plan to invade Thayland."

"He was. I don't think he's forgotten about it, it's just that he doesn't want to deal with it right away. He has to tread carefully, and that means dealing with one thing at a time."

"I'm not sure about that, Madick, but at least I made *sure* he didn't forget."

Will rested comfortably for the first time in weeks, lying in Madick's guest bed. He had trouble falling asleep, though, for he constantly thought of loose ends he had yet to tie up, such as his business with Commander Aman. He had left Jonoli high and dry with him, and he not only hoped they had made it to Markereen, but he prayed that Aman didn't get angry and lash out at Jonoli, especially over his missing belt and headpiece.

He told Madick about it, which was the least he could do. Madick laughed and said, "Don't worry, as soon as he learns of our victory here, he'll forgive you."

It did nothing to assuage Will's fears, for Madick hadn't consider Jonoli into the equation.

Will fell asleep eventually, and he dreamed of his recent fears coming to life, but he counted it a blessing that he remembered nothing upon awakening. It was Madick who woke him up, saying that Artiman had just arrived and wanted to see him.

They met outside among a small company of men holding lanterns for them to see by. The city seemed to be conducting its normal business, with couples walking the streets and drivers pulling rickshaws for patrons. But the gravity in the air was unmistakable—people didn't say much, and the women looked morose and downtrodden, whether they had lost loved ones or not. Blood stains in the sand marked where bodies had lied, and injured men were commonplace.

"Yes, Artiman?" Will asked sourly. His muscles were sore and he was sleep-deprived, so he was in no good mood.

"First, I must thank you for all you've done for us," Artiman said. "You've played a big part in the recruiting, and you've led the men here valiantly—it's too bad everyone thought you were Commander Aman. Where is he, by the way?"

Will explained, and Artiman said nearly the same thing Madick had.

"I've talked with Emperor Baku," Artiman continued. "First, the good news: He's had a change of heart about the 'war' on the Mulvars. He's admitted that he's heard pleas from commoners and ignored them, because his overlords wished for the 'war' to continue. Now, even if he enforces martial law, he can't have the 'war' continue—because I have friends in other town and cities who will still start trouble should the Emperor bring all his troops to

Nünveghett."

Will nodded, even if he was sure Artiman was merely bluffing. "And what's the bad news?"

Artiman sighed. "The Emperor ... I think I know what his game is but ..."

"What? What is it?"

Artiman shook his head. "He wants to duel you, in the Palace courtyard. I tried to reason with him, but he threatened to try me for harboring a traitor to Carsiss. We worked out a compromise: He'll let you go only if you sign some sort of confession."

"A confession of what?"

Artiman seemed evasive, wanting to dodge the subject. "The Emperor wants you to confess to certain acts of dishonor. He said there was a battle you never joined in but collected the spoils afterward, and other things."

"That was the massacre," Will said, more loudly than he had liked. He made a few breaths to steady his nerves. "That wasn't a battle, Artiman—that was the massacre in the canyon. And the only 'spoil' I collected was the Mulvar child."

"I know, Will Fontaine, but ... let's go inside." Artiman ordered his men to keep guard outside the door. He took a lantern from one of them and led Will inside the bakery. He laid the lantern on a table and invited Will to take a seat. He balled his hands together and rested them on the table; Will imagined he looked much the same way he did in Baku's war room. "Will, I know the Emperor wants to invade Thayland; I know that's what you're here for. I want you to leave everything to me. I can convince the Emperor that a war on Thayland is the worst thing he can do now. I'm sure he wants to do it to further his legacy, but if I show him the numbers, he'll see he would end up failing."

"No, you can't," Will said. "Baku is still trying to make a case to justify an invasion. He's doing this by challenging me to a duel, and if he can't get his duel then at least he'll have a signed confession. Either way, he wins: He'll have his evidence that paints me as a traitorous, dishonorable pig, the same as all Thayland citizens."

"I see what you mean—the Emperor is certainly being stubborn. But let's say you walk by signing the confession. Once I convince him his invasion will fail, he'll definitely agree to burn the confession, since it'll be useless to him, anyway."

Artiman gazed at Will, gauging his conviction. Will still didn't look persuaded, so Artiman took a deep breath and said, "Will

Fontaine, I'm trying to give you a chance to finally leave Carsiss alive. I meant it when I said I want no more bloodshed. I don't want you to face him and get yourself killed—that would just be a waste. So what do you say?"

Despite appearances, the offer *did* seem appealing to Will. He'd been wanting to escape Carsiss for a long time, and if he could do it with Ambri in his arms uncontested, then things would work out better than he had hoped. But there was something Artiman hadn't considered, and it had more to do than just warrior's pride.

"You know not what you ask of me," Will said. "When I get back home, I have to make a report to the King; I'll have to tell him everything that went on here. I'll have to include Baku's invasion plan, and I may even have to say that I could have done something to stop it, but instead you allowed Baku to live and keep the throne. I don't want to include you in it, but if my people pressure me ..."

"Can't you lie to them, or just bend the truth a little?" Artiman asked. "Or don't you have any faith in me?"

Will leaned over the table. "Baku killed Lord Harrington. His family and the King will want to know where he is. They'll have to know the truth, and there's no correcting it. Do you see now?"

Artiman looked like he did see; everything was becoming clear to him. Baku had just killed a Thayland nobleman, and once the King learned of it, he'd swear revenge on behalf of himself and the lord's family. It wouldn't even matter if Baku was persuaded to ditch his invasion plans; the only way to prevent the King from waging war himself was to have Baku go to the King's Palace and grovel at His Majesty's feet, and then perhaps agree to be executed in reparation. And everyone knew *that* wasn't going to happen.

"It's actually in your best interest to let me take his challenge," Will said. "If I kill him, you'll have little to worry about; if he kills me, you'll be left with a sorry mess on your hands—you and Baku both."

Artiman sat back in his seat, then banged a fist on the table. "Damn him! I just wanted to end the 'war' on the Mulvars, but he's had to complicate everything."

"You wanted more than just that," Will said accusingly. "You want to be a *Ksatriya*."

"Yes, like my father. It's only because my great, great grandfather was a *Ksatriya*. He was an overlord who killed another lord in a duel, and then went to kill his late enemy's entire family. Emperor Esmail was displeased, so he lowered him to the level of

Vaisya, which his descendants have been ever since. It was wrong for Emperor Esmail to do that—he's probably upset the heavens. So my father wanted to correct it with Emperor Orissu, giving my family back its original title."

Will thought his forefather was lucky that Emperor Esmail didn't have him executed, but he kept it to himself. Carsiss had plenty of unsettling differences with Thayland.

"But the resistance against the war was no ruse," Artiman continued gravely. "It was not just a tool to make people join me and battle the Palace. I've truly hated the 'war,' and I'll see to it that it ends right away, and permanently."

"For my sake and yours, I hope so," Will said with a wary eye. "Now, has the Emperor arranged a time and place for the duel?"

CHAPTER 23
THE EMPEROR AND HIS CHAMPION

BEFORE ANSWERING BAKU'S CALLING, Will had a cook make him a roasted pheasant as a late dinner. He figured he'd need all the energy he could get; plus it would make for a good last meal on his potential last day on earth.

Later on the street, Will drew out his longsword—the very one he had when he awoke in the well. It was of a simple design, nothing remarkable about it in the least. There was no sign that it came from an otherworldly source, forged perhaps by some higher power—yet Will believed it *was* not of the earth, nor forged by human hands. He had no idea if it possessed any exceptional strengths, nor did he get any strange feelings about it. It was just an ordinary sword, through and through, and any notions of it having significant powers were only from his imagination.

In other words, he'd have to defeat Baku through his skill, not through some heavenly influence.

Still, it was a nice sword, well balanced, polished to a mirror sheen and very well honed. He practiced some moves with it and grew more confident about the upcoming duel. Even if Baku should wield some large scimitar, he was sure he'd match it or better.

He was distracted in his practice, however, by some of the questions that plagued him in those days: *Why was I brought back to life? Why couldn't it happen to any other? Why was I in a well fully clothed and armed? Was it to fight Emperor Baku? Should I be content with this unstable peace and let the King handle everything on his own? Or am I meant to face Baku alone?*

"That's a nice blade," Madick said. "I never asked you where you got it. Is it from Thayland?"

Will suspended practice for the moment. "Yes, it is. I found it for sale by a merchant here in the city. I know I shouldn't have gotten it since there are a million others just like it in Thayland, but it reminded me of home, so I couldn't help myself. It was stupid of me. I mean, just look at it—not very impressive, is it?"

"What do you mean? I've seen you with it, and it suits you just fine. Or maybe you mean it isn't decorated? Pff! I know Thayland blacksmiths like to set jewels and inscribe patterns onto their swords, but it's all just for show. Those kinds of swords are for display only, not for combat."

"I was told by Sir Blackstone, my mentor, that smithies decorate only their best swords, tempering them to the best degree. That's because they want their artwork—their *signature*—to endure for a long time. Still, this *is* a good blade. It'll be ideal for putting a tyrant in his place."

According to Artiman, Baku had arranged for the duel in the Palace courtyard. He did it without waiting for a response from Will, which wasn't unusual; if Will didn't show up, Baku would brag about it to his immediate audience and declare himself the winner.

Will wouldn't give him the satisfaction. He only wished he could have arrived in style, mounted atop one of the decorated horses of the city's minimal cavalry; instead he had to arrive on foot and make his way through the gathered audience.

The Emperor had chosen a large plot of land west of Siva's shrine to hold the match; it was surrounded by men, all soldiers, dressed in full regalia and armed. Torches large and small were set up on stands in the dueling area, allowing ample lighting to see by under the stars and darkened moon.

As Will passed them by, the soldiers cheered and patted him on the back. He was apparently no enemy of theirs, and they were looking forward to a good fight. It lessened his nervousness and brought about a measure of hope, albeit a small one. Memories of sword practices with Baku unsettled him more than he allowed to show, and he thought there was enough cause for belief that he wasn't going to make it through the night alive. Baku was a masterful swordsman who knew both quickness and accuracy; he had encouraged Will by saying he was not half bad, but since he had later betrayed him, those words didn't mean much presently.

Instead of the upcoming fight, Will tried to focus on thoughts of home, of sparring lessons with Tony and Sir Blackstone, of all the lessons he had learned both from his successes and his failures. It occurred to him that Sir Blackstone was still expecting him home soon, having no idea what had taken place in Carsiss and what role Will had played in it.

He also thought of the ray of light, which had brought him back from the dead. Perhaps it had seen the duel coming, and it was counting on Will to win at all costs. Perhaps it had seen a Carsiss where every Mulvar was dead and Baku was sending ships across the ocean to wipe Thayland off the map and dub it "New Carsiss," and it had seen that only Will could prevent that from happening.

All thanks to him saving a baby.

Emperor Baku stood near the crowd closest to the Palace. All his armor was mostly below the belt, such as vambraces and leather padding; he wore nothing on the upper body except gauntlets on the forearms. It was in contrast to Will's attire—a soldier's uniform he got from Madick with a leather vest, a pair of gauntlets, and pads on the shins and forelegs worn underneath roomy trousers. He would have worn a helmet, but Madick claimed that they were against Carsian dueling rules, and he was glad to see that Baku wore none either.

Seeing Baku brought new memories to mind. He saw with terrible clarity the woman in the canyon, lying on her side, her hair swaying in the breeze, several arrows embedded in her stomach. He saw the Mulvarian man who ran out of a burning tent and was pursued by soldiers, his life cut short by a sword to the throat. And lastly, he saw Tanalac, his old commander, lifting up the child whose name would be Ambri, asking who her parents were and if they would like to join her in death.

Will took a place in the circle on the far side from Baku and stood in grim defiance.

He couldn't see Baku's features from so far away (the distance between them was at least twenty meters), but Baku sounded like he was smiling as he spoke: "Will Fontaine ... it is my regretful duty to face you, for I thought of you as a friend, an ally. But you have aggrieved me in many ways, and though I would like to forgive you, your crimes do not merit it. You are accused of many acts of dishonor, staining you and your country's reputation."

Will rolled his eyes, but then regretted it. If anyone saw him do that, they'd think he was not taking the duel seriously, which ironically would "stain" his reputation just as Baku said he had.

"You had refused to enter battle, only to collect the spoils when the fighting was over," Baku continued. "You had abused your ambassador's privilege by boarding in my Palace when it was not your place to do so. You had started a conflict with your superior officer which left him scarred and ashamed. And finally, you had not only disgraced me by lying with my harem, but you had committed the unforgivable offense of lying with my wife."

"No, you liar!" Will cried.

"I do not lie!" Baku screamed. "She has confessed it to me, to

everyone! To the Dieschsuchs and the city. I have forgiven her as everyone has ... but there can be no atonement for you. You can hold no excuse, so I will hold no regrets when I carry out your sentence!"

Baku pumped a fist into the air and let out a battle cry, prompting the audience to do the same. Will merely stood his ground and let the cheering fill his ears and his heart with its acidic quality ... but in his mind, he cursed Baku with a colorful vocabulary. It seemed that truth had no place in that battle circle, only the conviction in one's words.

Baku fell silent, and the soldiers followed suit nearly all at once. "Tonight, I have thought of facing you in combat ... but you are still so young, barely a babe. We would be a mismatch if we started right away. You must prove yourself to me, Will Fontaine—to all of us—that you are strong enough to face me. And so, I give you my champion—one who has proven so loyal to me that he has surpassed me in strength and size, all in order to protect the emperor and country he so loves. Come, Babi, and face your opponent!"

Will furrowed his brow, smelling a rat the size of all of Nünveghett ... but when Baku's champion stepped out from the crowd, his features smoothed out, his eyes wide and his lips parted in disbelief.

Babi was a monster of a man, so incredibly big that Will wouldn't have imagined it so if he wasn't seeing him for himself. Baku wasn't kidding about his strength and size: Babi had to be at least two and a half meters tall, almost the length of two cutlasses put together. He had no muscles—he had boulders tucked into his skin, finely shaped and bulky, wrapping around his skeletal structure like taffy on a stick. He had a decent amount of armor on, including a helmet with two crescent blades protruding from the top like rabbit ears. His features seemed vertically squished, as if they were on a sponge that had been stepped on. He had no sword; instead he wielded a club so wide it could have once been part of a ship's mast. He pounded the round end of it into one hand, then rose it into the air and gave a battle cry that put Baku's earlier effort to shame.

Will swallowed back the lump in his dry throat. He found it easy to label Baku as a coward, but he gave him credit for putting on a good show for his men.

"Babi," Baku called. His champion turned his head to him,

seeing his master's proud and resolute eyes. "Make him sorry ... make him meat."

Babi cried out again and started on his way towards Will, holding his club out in front of him.

Will cursed his unbelievable luck. Not only was Baku sending that gigantic and gruesome monstrosity to out to kill him, but he was surrounded by men who would not help him. Someone should have at least cried foul at the unfairness of it. Although he was a fit and competent fighter, he was only twenty-one years old and still had plenty of growing to do. To send a giant like Babi after him and call it a "test" was certainly one of the lowliest things Baku had done so far. If Baku's "champion" had turned out to be Tanalac, then things would have been different, because at least Will had a grudge with him, too ...

He put all thoughts aside. He realized that fear made his feet reluctant to step out of place, so he forced them to move, to take the first few steps towards Babi. Truth be told, he was terrified, even more so than at the thought of fighting Baku. It was probably just a case of mind over matter, but just looking at the size of Baku's champion and trying to rationalize how such a massive figure could come into being was like seeing a ghost for the first time—another experience had known firsthand.

At least he had an idea of how to win. Babi's outfit was common among some of Carsiss' most elite soldiers, especially the generals. It was a clever assortment of leather padding and steel-link chain mail that protected vital organs and offered few weak points. A noteworthy part of it was the steel plating shaped like the rim of a cup that bordered the neck, just high enough to make decapitation impossible. There *were* weak points, however, if one knew where to look. The area between the metal rim and the helmet, for example, was usually either left bare or covered with only flimsy cloth, for the chain mail was attached to the underside of the rim and ended there, and the breastbone was considered well protected by only the rim.

And there was one other weakness, too—one he had to see closer to see. He feared that Babi might have worn a more advanced model of the outfit where that weakness was corrected. But if it wasn't corrected ... that was where he would strike. But he couldn't be sloppy by assuming as much; he had to get closer and see ...

Will stepped up the pace, drawing his longsword and holding it at the ready by his side. Babi did the same with his club, eager to do a job similar to what Tanalac and his thugs had done to Will, only on a larger scale.

Will rose his sword, appearing to be on a suicide charge, but then stopped roughly two meters away, allowing Babi to take a swing at him only to hit air. A prouder warrior would have barged in and make a thrust, but Will veered around him, leaving a wide berth between them. Babi drew in closer and made a vertical swing that would have shattered his skull had Will not leapt to the side.

Babi grunted and didn't relent, swinging away at Will in hopes of making his lord emperor proud. But Will was sort of an expert at guessing an opponent's next move by looking at their initial stance. He avoided Babi's swings with relative ease, almost making it look easy. The only hard time he had was when he was forced to do a barrel roll to the side, where he had to make sure he didn't turn his blade on himself and had to quickly recover to look at Babi again. Babi made a low swing, which was only natural since Will had been low on the ground. Will jumped over the club in the nick of time, thanking his God that Babi was as slow as his biceps were huge.

And yet Will still didn't have his look. He needed to get behind Babi, and Babi didn't want to let him out of his sight. He needed some kind of distraction.

He tantalized Babi, calling him names like "Mighty Thor" and "Paul Bunyan" (a hero of a Thayland tall tale who chopped down trees with one swing of his huge axe). Babi predictably grew upset and charged him. Will led him near one of the torch stands, which was little more than an iron pole with a broad base covered with loose sand. He waited until Babi was right next to it, then threw his sword at it. It landed behind Babi, who groaned with anger and turned around to mark the fallen torch's location. That gave Will his look, and he was satisfied. He had to get his sword back, though.

Will led Babi away, remarking how fast Babi had become since the torch incident. It was either because Babi was more enraged or because Will was getting tired; either way, Babi often got too close for comfort. At one point, Babi landed his club near his foot; he lost his balance and fell on his back. Babi could have pounded him like a raw steak, but instead his club switched hands and he stooped down to grip his right foot. Will fortunately pulled that foot away and got back up, but he learned a lesson: As young and well fed as he was, he couldn't keep up the pace he was going much longer. The crowd was getting restless, too: The cheering was turning into catcalls, the men growing anxious to declare a victor.

Will ran, trying to keep a wide berth between him and Babi. Babi chased him for short time, but then stood his ground and gazed at him—a move that Will didn't think a mindless galoot was capable of. Apparently, Babi deduced that Will was returning to his sword, for he turned to the fallen torch stand and waited for Will to get there. When Will was mere paces away, Babi tossed his club like it was a twig for his dog to fetch. Will kept a close eye on the club, marking its trajectory. He was experienced with noting the normal trajectories of javelins and discuses, but a large club was a different matter. He had little idea of how much it weighed and how air resistance would play on it, so he couldn't anticipate where it would land. He was only certain he had to make a split-second decision to avoid being crushed.

When it got too close for comfort, it was clear that it was going to land where his legs were going to be near his sword. He jumped, and the club landed underneath him with a terrible impact. He jumped clear over it, landing safely beside the torch stand. He picked up his sword and ran away, for Babi was charging ahead to retrieve his own weapon.

Will halted near the crowd, taking a moment to observe their expressions. He recognized a few of them from his soldier days, and he wondered what they would think if the war on the Mulvars was truly ended. Would they feel cheated, wronged, defiled? Would they persecute Mulvars if those people should ever walk the streets? He hoped not, but hoping would not be enough to erase their deeply-ingrained prejudices.

He turned back to Babi, who stood and stared at him, taking his own breather. *Soon,* he thought, *I'll have to end this. I've been lucky, but I can't hold out forever.*

He lifted his sword and howled. Some of the soldiers behind him followed suit, and soon the entire crowd was letting out bloodcurdling cries of rage and excitement. Not Babi, though—he kept his cool, laying his focus on Will and waiting for his next move.

Will began to charge at him, still howling and giving the appearance of wild enragement. He wanted Babi to think he was desperate and had just lost control of his wits; that way, Babi's guard would be down when he made his decisive stroke.

Babi brushed the sand off his club's makeshift handle and made ready for the screaming fool who was running towards his death.

Will ran as fast as he could at first, but subtly decelerated as he neared Babi. He kept an eye on his club, wondering how Babi was going to swing it. It turned out to be a vertical arc, which Will easily avoided by veering to the right. As Babi landed his club on the ground, Will rushed past him, nearly close enough to touch him. As quickly as a deer and as accurately as an eagle, he swung his blade and slashed the exposed tendon above Babi's left heel, then took a few sidesteps and swung the other way, slashing the other tendon. He was lucky that most Carsians favored sandals over boots, even the soldiers in uniform.

Babi tried to turn and face Will but suddenly collapsed. It was then his turn to howl, his deep voice full of pain, surprise, and most of all, frustration. He tried to get back up on his feet, using his club to help him, but as soon as he bore his weight on one foot, he fell again and started howling anew. He tried again several times, not even attaining minimal success. Finally, he settled for standing on his knees, hanging onto his pride even in his humiliating defeat.

Babi *was* defeated, but Will wasn't satisfied because he knew Baku would not be. Babi had to go down, and he thought of only one way to do it without taking the giant's helmet off.

Will drew near him, as loathe as he was to do so since Babi could still grasp him, get him into a bear hug, and squeeze the life out of him. Without hesitation, Will jumped as high as he could, positioned the tip of his sword above the rim covering Babi's neck, and plunged it past his breastbone and down into his innards.

Babi didn't react much, for he didn't have the time to. Will stepped back and watched, hardly believing what he had done and unable to tear his eyes away from it. His sword was jutting out from near Babi's neck, over half of the blade stuck in the man's body. Babi was still trying to howl, but his efforts were minimal, pathetic. He was clearly trying to stay conscious, fighting for his life and all the leftover potential he had. But there was only so much one could do with a blade that brushed against the heart, and as soon as a few lines of blood ran from his lips, Babi fell face-first to the sandy earth and remained still.

Whispers and clinking armor were then the only sounds the soldiers emitted. Many of them looked at their feet and shuffled them, while others fingered their sheathed swords or leaned on their spears. A few of them even broke into tears, crying not only for their fallen comrade but at how a "dishonorable" foreigner could bring him down

Baku merely gave an expression of loathing and contempt.

"That was not an honorable fight," he cried out matter-of-factly.

"Yes, you're right," Will cried back, heading for Babi. "Ironman here could have lobbed my head off."

"If you think it is over, it is not."

Will replied only with a cynical smile and a shake of the head. He tried to pull his sword out while facing Baku, but the blade stubbornly stayed where it was. He ended up showing Baku his back and planted a foot on Babi's shoulder in order to pull it free. The blade was red with blood, as well as the sole of his left boot which stepped in the puddle of gore flowing from Babi's wound.

"You have killed my champion," Baku said, "so now we move onto the next stage."

Will turned to him and cried, "And what's that? What new condition have you made up now?"

Baku furrowed his brow, not missing the insult. "Only you and me."

"Fine," Will said, mostly to himself. The pain of his beating heart grew noticeably stronger, which he hoped wasn't only from his growing agitation.

Baku was given a scimitar, then he started off for Will with an unassuming pace. He looked like he had no intention of underestimating his opponent. Not only had Will killed his champion, but he had eluded his efforts to frame him and had returned alive after Tanalac had sworn he was dead.

Will again cursed his luck, unbelieving that he had to face Baku when already dog tired. But of course, he had gone through a number of things he had previous thought were unbelievable, returning from the dead being only one of them.

When Baku got near, he stopped and gave Will a strange look. Will couldn't guess what was the matter was with him, but it soon became apparent.

"Your eye," Baku said.

Will grinned. "Yes, what about it?"

Baku took a step closer, then decided he wasn't just seeing things. "You lost your eye! I *saw* that you lost it! But now you have it back. How!?"

"You really want to know why?" Will plunged the tip of his sword into the ground. "You made the gods very angry. *Very* angry. You've been killing their children, the Mulvars, and plotting to invade your ally. They've had enough of you for a while now; their vengeance is past due."

"How do you know this?"

Will shrugged. "Because they told me. After your man Tanalac did a number on me, the gods fixed my wounds and gave me my eye back. They then said it was up to me to bring you to them. Believe me, I wish there was some other way, but I can't have you kill every Mulvar and go to war against Thayland."

Baku became lost in thought for a time, then looked with at Will with a half-proud, half-pleading look. "I saw three things in the Sands, Will Fontaine. One was the image of the men in strange suits; the second one was Marsoon Diachhe's head on a pike. The last one was of me, descending to the throne of Thayland and sitting with Annell at my side. It is a destiny the gods cannot prevent—not if the Sands show it. And once I take your king's throne, I could leave Carsiss here ... for you."

Will furrowed his brow. He'd never thought Baku would try to bribe him out of their duel, but that was just what he'd done.

Baku raised his free hand, never taking his eyes off Will's face with its brand new eye. "Think of it, Will Fontaine, you could be the supreme ruler of all of Carsiss. We could have free trade, and tournaments, and slaves. All I ask is for your cooperation and for every damn Mulvar to be wiped out. And why stop at Thayland? We could conquer your old enemy, Thorain, and expand from there. There could be two empires, working together in peace. It could be something even the gods may envy."

Will thought of his own vision in the Sands of Carsiss, of him sitting on the Emperor's throne. He truly believed that the Sands showed possible moments in time. He really *could* be the Emperor; Baku really *could* be giving a sincere offer instead of resorting to more backstabbing. He had a taste of being a leader, talking to the citizens and ordering resistance troops. The Emperor's throne was a huge step from that, but he felt he could fit into it in time.

Carsiss could be all his, and more.

Will smiled and shook his head. "What did I just get done telling you? The gods sent me to deliver their vengeance, and I'll be damned if I'm going to be on their hit list as well. You've done things you cannot take back ..." Will pulled his sword out of the ground and pointed it at Baku. "And I haven't forgotten about the Mulvar child I saved. I'll not kowtow to a coward who sought to kill a baby. Did the Sands ever tell you *that?"*

Baku raised his own sword. "I don't know how you got your eye back, but I don't believe you spoke with the gods. It is impossible!

They do not care about the Mulvars!"

Will was jarred by the first statement—he thought Baku could read the lie in his eyes. But after the last statement, it was clear Baku was just being delusional, making up a reality that best suited him.

And with that, they fought. Will let Baku make the first move, and he didn't wait long. Baku started with a thrust, which Will countered by pushing the blade up. He right away circled around Will, hoping to back him into the crowd, leaving him vulnerable. But Will matched his line of movement, knowing when to fall back so he could stay close to the center of the field. The crowd was going wild, the men pumping their fists and cheering in delight. Some even opened bottles of rum and passed them around, like at a regular party.

Will was caught off guard when Baku started jumping attacks, leaping into the air and viciously swinging his scimitar down. In Baku's first one, Will lifted his blade at the last second, the impact nearly pushing it as far back as his forehead. Will fell back, clearly jarred. He needed time to gather his wits, a luxury Baku didn't allow him. He pursued him with standard slashing, but made a jumping swipe every now and again.

Will couldn't have time to recuperate, so he thought back to his exercises with Tanalac. Those memories brought on a sense of shame at first, for Will remembered how awkward he'd been on the first day; but he shortly regained his confidence, remembering that he had adapted to the exercises rather well. He knew Sir Blackstone would probably not approve, but he tried a few leaping attacks himself, always from a fair distance not only because of his inexperience, but also because Baku could cut him down in midair like a piñata.

His reflexes from those many days of exercises came back, and he soon made leaping strikes with relative ease, sometimes catching Baku off guard and forcing him to fall. He even thought he did them with more grace than Baku because of the lighter weight and smaller shape of his blade, but he didn't trust himself to do them very often. He realized that when Baku tried one himself, he could cut him down in midair, perhaps pinning him like a pig on a spit. The problem with that, though, is that he'd leave himself open for Baku to slice his head open or bury his scimitar into his shoulder.

Only once did they leap at the same time. Their blades connected with a terrible impact and they landed on the ground awkwardly. Will decided to leap again, which turned out to the best decision he made in the whole fight, for Baku swung low to the ground, hoping to injure Will similarly to how Will had injured Babi.

The rum bottles ran dry not long before Will landed a decisive stroke. He had a cut on the neck—not serious, just a flesh wound that did minimal bleeding—and his arms were getting sore. Baku had just done a leaping attack, and Will tried something new: As soon as Baku landed, Will pushed his blade away and rushed into him. Baku was only a little disoriented, but Will managed to get his blade near Baku's right hand and slice the webbing between thumb and forefinger.

Baku dropped his sword, dumbfounded. Will stepped back and landed a roundhouse kick on Baku's stomach, forcing him down. He kept a close eye on his fallen opponent, and on his sword, too, which Baku might try to retrieve right away.

Baku eyed him like a cornered fox, wondering how the hell his younger opponent could get the best of him. He crawled away a few steps at first, appearing to make the wiser choice of retrieving another sword and drawing Will closer to the crowd. But suddenly, when he thought Will's guard was down, he lunged for his sword. Will pounced on him immediately, slicing deeply into Baku's right forearm.

Baku cried out in pain and surprise and ran back. Blood flowed from his wound like water; he looked at it with wide eyes and squeezed the elbow with his other hand, hoping to cut the circulation. He then turned his gaze at Will, giving him a hateful look that could have cut him down if looks could kill.

Will kept his blade up, at the ready. As long as Baku still breathed, his work was not done. He wondered if Baku was going to plead or bargain again; even if he did, Will had decided he would not listen. Even if Baku had staked it on his honor that he would let Will live and never launch an invasion of Thayland, matters between them had gone past the point of no return, as far as Will was concerned. Baku had proven himself to be a liar of the most terrible degree, as well as a monster beyond redemption.

It was time to be out with the old and in with the new.

Baku grew closer, step by cautious step. He could no longer wield a scimitar, for he needed two hands to do so. Instead, he acted on desperation: He pulled out a knife from a sheath attached to a vambrace and dashed at him, his mouth open and his tongue fully extended. Will charged himself, intending to run past while slicing the arm that wielded the knife. Things didn't go as planned, for Baku made a split-second decision to switch his aim from Will's head to his left rib.

Both men ran curved paths that were supposed to meet, but Will managed to veer himself just far enough away from Baku to avoid his knife and yet strike him with the tip of his blade. He felt and heard the tip hit something, but he wasn't sure what, having missing Baku's good arm.

Will ran a good distance away from Baku and turned to face him. Baku did not do the same as expected, not even running at him in hopes of stabbing his back. He kept his back to him, appearing to nurse a new wound. It took Will a moment to notice that the crowd had fallen completely silent, indicating that their leader had been given a devastating blow. Still, it was not enough to keep him from losing his footing, so he wondered just how much damage he had done.

Baku stood his ground for the longest while, trembling violently. Will was just about to draw near when Baku finally turned and revealed what was wrong: His neck had been deeply sliced on the left side, with so much blood pouring from it that his chest was covered in it. He held his eyes wide open as if the eyelids had suddenly grown very heavy. His mouth looked like an O, as if his jaw had failed and could not be brought back up. He groaned like a diseased banshee, his voice muddled from his blood and the sliced windpipe. It was incredible for him to remain on his feet, although he surely wouldn't be for long; like Babi before him, he was gripped in a losing battle for his consciousness.

Will gave him a disgusted look. It was painful to see him thus, no matter how he detested him. He planned on letting him bleed to death, but the crowd suddenly started issuing a chant. He at first couldn't make out what they were saying, but as more voices joined the chorus, his choice became clear.

"Cut off his head! Cut off his head!"

It wasn't that they were eager to see Baku die; it was that they, like Will, were pained to see him in such a horrible state. Will raised an eyebrow and sneered. He had heard several stories of decapitation, most of them occurring in wartime, but he never thought he'd do the practice himself. But seeing Baku feebly clutching his neck and making pathetic groans, he knew it would obviously be a mercy killing.

He walked up to Baku, sword at the ready, always at the ready. Baku showed no sign of seeing him; Will wouldn't be surprised if Baku was incapable of seeing at all. Will stopped a few paces away from his opponent, his gorge starting to rise from hearing Baku's sickening groans up close. They were bubbly and desperate, the sounds of death and decay, hopelessness and tragedy.

Will drew in a deep breath, steeled himself, and quickly ran for Baku, swinging his sword at his neck.

He felt the blade go all the way through and shut his eyes immediately after. The sounds of a rolling object and a collapsing body were his only indications of vengeance served.

The crowd cheered. It didn't matter to them who won, either Will or Baku; it seemed they were prepared to accept whatever path the duel's result would put them on, which was a good sign of change for the better.

Will opened his eyes and gazed at the crowd. He breathed hard and revealed no emotion, save a feeling of relief. He carefully listened to the cheering, wondering if the soldiers were sincere about their acceptance of the victor, then remembered that it was Baku who had set up the duel, which made a world of difference in the soldiers' attitudes.

He thought the crowd would rush in to meet him and carry him on someone's shoulders. Instead only one man met him, which the soldiers probably anticipated. Will was caught off guard at the identity of the man: Prime Dieschsuch Halicut, who had been released and returned to the Palace by Artiman.

"Will Fontaine!" Halicut cried. "Well done, very well done at your excellent duel! You've defeated the Emperor, and according to the laws of succession, you are now the rightful ruler of Carsiss. Congratulations!"

Will shook his head. "You're joking. Well, actually it doesn't matter if you are or not. I'm nobody's emperor, but thanks anyway."

"That's no problem, no problem! An emperor always has the right to pass the Scepter to anyone of his choosing, though once he does he cannot contest him to get it back."

"Thank God," Will said with a grin. "Now that's a piece of politics that actually makes sense."

CHAPTER 24
JONOLI'S CHALLENGE

"YOU THINK IT'S OVER?" ARTIMAN asked. "Think again. Once the former Emperor's vassals hear about the resistance and his death, they'll drop whatever they're doing and rally up their troops. Many of them are probably on their way right now. What are you going to do about that?"

"Please, sir, address him as Your Eminence," Prime Dieschsuch Halicut said. "He is your emperor now."

"That's all right, Prime Dieschsuch," Will said. "Please go on, Artiman."

"Well, the only thing that could lessen their anger is how Emperor Baku had died in a duel of his own choosing, and *not* because of the resistance. That could make a big difference. I'm not a fool, *Your Eminence*—that's why I had the men retreat the Palace at the first sign of surrender. If we had killed him, the overlords would tear us apart, for we are all *Vaisyas,* unworthy of doing battle with him. But as it turned out, the Emperor fell to a lone man—a man in no caste, an outsider of our social structure. The overlords will have to acknowledge your divine right to the throne and forget all about the resistance."

Will yawned, although he tried to stop himself from doing it. He had just gotten up from a well earned rest in his old Palace room; when he learned that Artiman requested an audience, he invited him to the Palace war room right away. He had a bandage on his neck concealing the wound Baku gave him. It would make the first real scar since his resurrection, when all his previous scars (including those that Tanalac made with his short whip) were erased clean. "Actually, I don't think they could just forget about the resistance. They may blame you for forcing Baku to duel me."

"But that's not true," Artiman interjected.

"No, it's not, but they'll think of any excuse. We'll need a spokesman—someone the overlords already know and trust, someone who knows all the details of what really happened ..."

Will looked at Halicut, and then Artiman did the same. Halicut darted his sight from one man to the other. He was confused at first, but then realization rung like a bell. "What, me!?" he asked, already sounding on the edge of hysteria. "No, it's dangerous! You can't force me out there! What if I get attacked?"

"You won't be alone," Will said. "I'll send an escort guard with you, of course."

"But how large will this escort be? It can't protect me from the thousands of men the overlords will bring."

"You dare to defy your emperor?" Artiman asked. "You even forgot to call him 'Your Eminence.'"

Halicut would have turned pale if not for his olive skin. "Forgive me, Your Eminence, I've forgotten my place. It'll take some time before I—"

"Please, Halicut, will you do it or not?" Will asked irritably.

"Oh, yes, I suppose ... it's my duty to obey your orders, Your Eminence."

"Good. I wish I could be the one to do it, but I'm sure they'd gut me on the spot. But you already have command over them, so they'll listen to you. Just have faith and you'll do fine. With just a little luck, you can prevent any more fighting and save a lot of lives. It'll be your finest hour."

Halicut, who had been drooping his head, perked up at that. "My finest hour? Hmm ... you could be right, Your Eminence."

And so it was that on the following day, the Prime Dieschsuch, with a few of the other Dieschsuchs and a generous escort guard, rode through the many units of soldiers and minutemen directly towards Lord Hineson Bek, the overseer of Darmine province.

In the lord's tent, Halicut explained how there had been a resistance movement who had kidnapped him but treated him well, and once they had marched against the Palace and reached a sort of stalemate, he had been anxiously returned, unharmed though a little shaken. He claimed Emperor Baku had talked to the resistance leader (whose name he wisely left out) and had agreed to some of his terms—and he then promptly requested a duel with the rogue Thayland ambassador, Will Fontaine. He further explained that Will had been framed as a traitor by Baku, which explained Will's grudge with Baku. Their duel was an honorable one, even when considering the initial fight with Babi, who fought for his master with valor and deftness (a point that Will would have strongly countermanded).

He ended with Baku's glorious death—an end fit for an emperor, Halicut claimed, for he fought with every ounce of strength he had in him. "And so Will Fontaine is the rightful successor of Carsiss, and you owe him your respect. But if you still do not like the fact, let me assure you that Emperor Will Fontaine seems likely to pass his Scepter onto someone else very soon."

Lord Hineson picked his head up from his fist and hesitantly nodded. "Prime Dieschsuch," he said, "I see you're still the irritating little nit you've always been ... but you've always been fair and trustworthy, so I've no choice but to acknowledge this Emperor Will Fontaine. Although I don't like the idea of a son of Thayland sitting in the throne, what I don't like more is this news that Emperor Baku was a backstabber. He'd always been that way of course; when I heard he begot Lord Faisal's wife with child, I knew not to trust him overmuch. But this ... this is definitely the worst thing he's ever done. Gods rest his soul, maybe we're fortunate after all."

Lord Hineson was merely the first one. Soon the entire city was surrounded by overlords demanding that the Palace be released and swearing vengeance on the resistance leaders. Halicut's position grew more hairy and unenviable, but he kept at his work, going from one overlord to the next and explaining the situation to them. To his amazement, they all accepted the passing of the throne, though with varying degrees of enthusiasm. Lord Darric of Dekla province had been close to Baku, and the news of his death hit him hard; he vowed to never pledge loyalty to the throne as long as Will was in it. On the other hand, Lord Faisal, a lesser lord of Dekla whose five-year-old son looked nothing like him, was delighted to hear of Baku's demise.

Halicut regularly sent messengers to report his progress to Will, who was only a little relieved upon hearing them. He had been growing paranoid with the city besieged by Baku's former vassals, who incidentally became *his* vassals. Learning of their acceptance lessened his fearful state, but he was sure many of them held inner grudges and made plans for revenge. He couldn't pass the Imperial Scepter and leave Carsiss soon enough.

He was having dinner with all the Dieschsuchs still present in the Palace when he was approached by a servant. "Forgive the intrusion, Your Eminence, but will you be staying in the Emperor's quarters this evening?"

Will shook his head. He intended to sleep in his old bed again; if he went into Baku's old room, he'd feel like he was trespassing somehow. "No thanks. I won't be the Emperor for much longer, anyway."

The servant bowed and left the room.

"Does that mean you won't lie with your wife?" Dieschsuch Qadeem asked.

"What, my wife?" Will asked. "I'm not married."

"Well, of course you are, Your Eminence. Lady Annell is married to the Emperor, and since you are the Emperor, that means she is yours."

Will gave Qadeem a hard look, not because he didn't believe him, but because he thought it imprudent to be expected to lie with Annell—she who had been involved in Baku's invasion scheme.

After dinner, Will asked to be led to Annell. She had locked herself in the Emperor's quarters where she refused to leave. Will had a servant use a key and open the door, then stepped inside to confront Annell. She was sitting by her dresser drawer made of fine beech wood, looking at him through the vanity mirror.

"Annell."

"What do you want?" she muttered. "I'll never sleep with you, if that's it. I'd rather die than do that."

"Don't worry, the feeling's mutual," Will said monotonously. "I just came to see how you are."

"I'm fine." Annell held her head in her hands for a while, then rose from her seat and faced her new husband. "Baku was more of a man than you'll ever be. He knew what he wanted, and he wasn't afraid to take it."

"Yes, I'm sure, Annell ... but it was disturbing when he sought a baby's death. Surely, you and Carsiss deserve better."

"It was a Mulvar! The Mulvars run a slave trade with Rozimi and Bune. They kidnap Carsians and sell them to their noble houses."

"And the baby is entirely to blame? No, she's mine now, and she'll never grow up to be a slaver, if that's what she was meant to be."

"You're delusional, Will Fontaine. You are the ugliest, most undignified—"

"Why, thank you."

"—most foolish, brutish, rude—"

"I'm charmed."

"—and barbaric man I've ever met! You could die and I'd spit on your grave!"

Will wagged a finger at her. "Flattery will get you nowhere."

"Get out!"

Will didn't need to be told twice. While roaming the halls, he mulled over what she had said. The Mulvars were slave traders, even at present? He wondered how Lord Harrington never learned of it. He was ashamed though he had no real reason to be. He supposed there were heroes and villains on both sides of the conflict, neither having much excuse for the atrocities they committed. He could only hope that Baku's savage killing campaign would make the Mulvars change their ways in the future, though it was a harsh lesson that should never have been.

Early next morning, he learned what happened to Resistance Commander Aman, courtesy of a courier sent by Aman. After Jonoli had told him what happened once he came to in Markereen, he ran to the nearest stable, took a rental horse without paying, and took off for Nünveghett, where the fighting was already underway. He had little difficulty reaching the Palace, where he had seen the soldiers atop the wall in a state of panic, which he later learned was caused by the invasion from within the courtyard.

He ended the message with two statements. First, he claimed that while he was disappointed to have missed out on the movement, he was glad that everything turned well and that Will was still alive and faring quite well—even better than expected (Will shook his head at that part, wondering if he should expect more pathetic schmoozing from such people). Second, Jonoli was unharmed, and she and the rest of the harem were due to arrive at the Palace and ask for an audience with Will.

Not an hour later, the harem were found in the Palace's main hall, bearing gifts of gold, jewelry, precious stones, and vials of oil, water, and sesame. Jonoli acted as head of group, despite the new misgivings of the other women about her. Will must have posed as quite a figure in her eyes, for he had shirked his common clothes and gone through Baku's old wardrobe, favoring the silken dark-blue vests and trousers and tightly-wound turbans. He no longer looked like the rough commoner that she knew—he of the golden heart and large hands who had always held Ambri so gently. Currently, he appeared as little more than another bold *Ksatriya*.

Jonoli knelt before him along with the other women, holding out a small golden case. "Your Eminence," she said, her voice shaking slightly. "We offer you these gifts, which come not from our coffers but those of the lords of the city, who pledge their undying loyalty to you."

Will shook his head a little. He knew the local lords didn't approve of a son of Thayland being Emperor, which was why they didn't give their gifts in person.

"And we offer you our services—either the same as what we offered your predecessor, or other services as you see fit. Our lives are yours, our emperor."

"Nonsense," Will said and started towards her. "I release you of your bondage to the throne, all of you. Whether you stay or leave is up to you."

"But Your Eminence," Prime Dieschsuch Halicut said, stepping into place beside him, "please think of the next emperor. He may want to keep the harem."

"I'm sure he can make his own harem," Will said, amused. "And also, this is the least I can do for their mistreatment in *Qualini Durakur.*"

Halicut gasped, apparently unaware of the Soul Breaker's role in Baku's past schemes.

"Come on, get up," Will said, laying a hand on Jonoli's shoulder. Jonoli obeyed, still holding onto the gold case. The other women reluctantly followed suit, many of them daring to look at their two leaders. Jonoli, however, did not raise her eyes, preferring to stare at Will's vest. Will put a finger under her chin and rose her head, meeting her gaze. "Don't worry, everything will be all right, I'll see to it."

Jonoli glanced at Halicut nearby, who had a large smile plastered on his face. One more look at Will convinced her—Will was still the same as before, and she no longer had to fear her distant heritage with the Mulvars.

He kisser her, and the two embraced like they hadn't seen each other in years. Jonoli let the gold case fall from her grasp, which landed with a terrible impact that rang in the large hall. Halicut winced and quickly retrieved the case, then retreated as if the two lovers were on fire (which they were probably were, in a figurative sense).

The other women stood where they were and looked around, dumbfounded. They had little idea of what to do at that moment, having been sure they'd fall back into their old routine lives. As it turned out, all but two returned to their old quarters that day, and one that had left later came back and begged the current Emperor to be let into his harem. The other one of the two found work as a seamstress, and eventually married and bore eleven children. Such continuous childbearing took quite a toll on her figure, but, as she had put it, it was "a worthy sacrifice."

Later that day, Will performed one of the last great acts of his reign as Emperor: He gave a speech at the mass funeral of all those who had died in the resistance movement, both soldier and civilian alike. He offered his respects to both sides of the conflict, saying it was a deep pity that so many should die for one man's sins. He then went on to express his opinion of the "war" on the Mulvars, and to encourage the entire nation to seek peace and prosperity with their nomadic cousins:

"The time for bloodshed is past. It is time to strengthen Carsiss anew, not by clinging to feuds of ages past, but by embracing and respecting each other's heritage and ways of living. A country cannot survive by enduring inner turmoil, which many of you have come to believe. Please, I beg of you, seek those out who do not understand, those who believe that war and battle are the only ways to end bitter conflicts. Explain to them that the gods have made us all in their image, and that there has to be more to our creation than to initial chaos and sorrow."

The audience clapped politely but strongly, much to Will's relief. Afterward, he and Jonoli strolled in the grounds, offering words of sympathy to the mourners. Truth was, he wanted to leave and escape the processions by cooping up in the Palace—but that was something he'd never do. He knew the visit would be hard, but he felt he owed it to the people of the city, for he had helped rally the resistance forces with his underground speeches. Plus, he thought the burials would be a good time to get his ultimate message across.

He had meant every word in his speech, but he could have eaten them at the sight of Tanalac.

He spotted him only a few meters away; he was paying his respects by a burial mound with his wife and daughter. His back was to him and he couldn't identify his family, but his build and height within his military uniform was unmistakable. Madick had failed in capturing him, but Will didn't hold it against him—he had known it was a tall order in the first place.

Jonoli tried to stop him, but he marched right up to Tanalac and roughly tapped him on the shoulder. Tanalac turned around, angry at being interrupted. His look of malice was wiped clean when he recognized Will staring up at him. "Y-Your Eminence!" he said, and bowed with his hands held together in front of him.

"I was hoping I wouldn't see you again," Will said. "For your sake." He glanced at Tanalac's wife, who stared and trembled with fear, her daughter hugging her leg and looking no bolder.

Tanalac held his bow. "Your Eminence, I ... I pledge unto you my service."

"Why?"

Tanalac faltered in his bow, taken aback at the question. "Because you are my Emperor."

"Well, how convenient for you."

"Your Eminence ..." Tanalac sounded like he knew he'd have to say something that pleased Will, or else he'd spend the rest of his days with no more importance than a dog's. He stood and said, "Your speech was ... enlightening. It moved me beyond words."

Will smiled. It was a small smile, but it sufficed to lesson Tanalac's stress. "I'm glad to hear that. But Tanalac ... do you really live for honor? All that you did to me—was it somehow for honor?"

"I lived only to serve my emperor."

Will eyed the stars of rank on Tanalac's military vest. He grasped the pin they were on and removed it, then placed it into a pocket. "From now on—for the rest of your *life*—you are no longer a commander of the Carsian army. You'll be assimilated into the unit you will no longer lead." Will took a step closer, craning his neck up further to keep Tanalac's gaze (he was tall, but at least he was no Babi). "You may think it is honorable to serve your emperor, but there is no honor in betraying your subordinate. I trusted you, until that night you attacked me in my room. I was there to slay that accursed dragon, and then you sent a gang on me and left me for dead. No, there is no honor in that whatsoever."

Tanalac looked no different, except for his Adam's apple, which was raised to hold a lump in his throat.

Will stepped back. He gave Tanalac a momentary hard look, then glanced at his wife. "Ma'am," he said with a nod, then returned to Jonoli, who walked with him with a tighter grip on his arm. The people around them had grown solemn and quiet after the scene.

"I thought you were going to kill him," Jonoli said. "Just like Baku."

"I killed Baku because I felt I had to," Will said. "But that doesn't make me cold-blooded."

Once they left the cemetery, Will had Jonoli take him to where she had left Ambri for safekeeping. It was a large house where an extended family lived. They were friends of Jonoli from far back.

"Before I joined the harem," Jonoli said inside their rickshaw, "I was a servant for Lord Nevriel. The head mistress sent me to market on a regular basis, where I made a few friends and contacts. The Nahily family in particular often took advantage of me; they asked me for favors and business contacts within my lord's mansion. They've owed me ever since, and their place is the best one I could think of to bring Ambri to."

Soon after they parked in front of the house, they were swamped by children, who all recognized Jonoli despite her new luxurious silk *sari*. She introduced Will to the adults, never stating that he was the Emperor at his request.

An old women led Will to one of the children's rooms, where Ambri was. Will stepped in almost expecting to see Ambri lying in a crib; instead she was sitting on the floor p`aying with toys with two other infants. It had been longer than he thought since he'd last seen her, and he was amazed at how big she had gotten. She had a full head of hair and could grasp toys with relative ease. Her eyes still seemed large and her cheeks were plump—those were the only signs of the baby Will had rescued in the canyon months ago.

He hesitantly knelt beside her and said her name. If Ambri didn't recognize him, she at least recognized her name. She held her arms out to him, and he picked her up with a sigh and a laugh. He held her close for a moment, resting his hand on the back of her head, then eased his hold on her and gazed into her dark, beautiful eyes. He didn't expect her to know he was the one who had brought her through the desert with little shelter, for it really didn't matter. He would tell her the story one day, and no matter what she thought of it, it wouldn't make it any less true.

"Safety in numbers," as the saying went, and it was true with Ambri's hiding place. The seven adults and ten children of the household had made sure that Ambri's every need was looked after, and their many eyes made up a small spy network that warned the family when soldiers came to search the place. They told Will the house was raided two times during Emperor Baku's search campaign, during which time Ambri was kept hidden in a small underground storage space that was separate from the regular basement. The soldiers never thought to inspect the floor under a certain drawer, for they were happy enough to be sent to the regular basement.

Will couldn't thank the family enough for the bold favor they'd done, and he asked them what they would like in return. Their answers were numerous, as the children wanted toys and pets, while the adults wanted money and horses. One of the elderly women just wanted him to raise Ambri good and proper, which Will gladly agreed. He made his goodbye by saying he wished he could leave Ambri with them a little longer, for she had seemed happy there, but he was leaving Carsiss soon and wanted to bring her with him. He then promised to get them something nice and went away in the rickshaw.

The next day, he had a servant buy two horses and a box of sweet tarts in the market, and then sent them to the Nahilys, with no strings attached.

With Ambri safe and sound in the Palace, Will's next task was to choose his successor. He had a long list to choose from, but a decision would not come easy. Most of the neighboring overlords had been very loyal to Baku, and they were partially Will's enemies, for they would surely strike at him if their honor didn't hold them back. Giving any one of them the Imperial Scepter would be like opening a tiger's cage in an enclosed room.

Prime Dieschsuch Halicut was an easy choice, for he had the most experience in Palace affairs, but he didn't seem strong enough to hold the Emperor's throne. Madick and Artiman were out of the question, for while he owed them for their roles in Baku's downfall, they were not *Ksatriyas* and thus could not hold a government office.

He asked Halicut for his opinion. Halicut paced the war room, looking thoughtfully at the map of Carsiss, thinking of someone who could take the throne and not make an enemy of Will. "What kind of features are you looking for?" he asked.

"Someone who's strong of mind, has a firm opinion but is open to suggestions ... someone who would prefer to live in peace and seek diplomacy in initial conflicts, and who would go to war only if necessary. A good mind for finances and trade wouldn't be bad, either."

"You mean someone like you?"

Will paused. He hadn't thought of it that way. "Yes, like me, somewhat."

Halicut turned around with an inquisitive yet cautious eye. "I know of one lad, he used to come here to use our smithy and visit the museum."

"A lad, you say?"

Halicut looked apologetic. "Yes, I believe he is twenty-five, or turning twenty-five this year. He is Lord Namin of Termeric House. I know he is young, Your Eminence, but I swear he has a good disposition, and he's very intelligent. He is a scholar who is tutored in his home."

Will was skeptical about giving the Scepter to a young man. Of course, he himself had just turned twenty-one last January, and he knew how easily swayed a young mind could be. Emperor Baku had made quite a good impression on him—so much so that he could hardly believe he was responsible for the slaying of the Mulvars until Halicut convinced him otherwise. "Would he know what it is like to be Emperor?"

"Oh, yes. I've talked to him, and he was very curious about the Emperor's responsibilities. He showed a good understanding of what it took to run a nation, He is still immersed in his studies, but he can complete them while still in the throne."

"And what about Annell? Namin won't just be an emperor—he'll be a husband, too. I have a feeling Annell won't take too kindly to him, with him being a kid and all."

"You might be surprised, Your Eminence, but if that is the case, he can divorce her without any trouble. He could keep her around as a concubine, or marry her off to another lord, whatever he chooses."

Will nodded. "I'll have to arrange a meeting with him soon."

"It could be as early as tonight. He lives in Nünveghett, so he should know everything that went on here."

"Good, you do that. And Halicut ..."

"Yes, Your Eminence?"

"Is it true that the wandering Mulvars are involved in the slave trade with Rozimi and Bune?"

Halicut paused for thought. "I believe there is a slave trade run in Rozimi and Bune, but there is no evidence of the Mulvars' involvement. I believe Emperor Baku planned on accusing the Mulvars for that, justifying his 'war' on them. If I may ask, where did you hear that?"

"Annell told me," Will said, sounding serene and nonjudgmental—but inside, he was fuming. *Annell, I could kill you for saying that, and for thinking me so gullible. And I could kill myself for actually* being *so gullible. And Halicut, you're not blameless either, knowing so much yet not doing anything about it.*

His thoughts must have been reflected in his features somewhat, for Halicut was then eager to leave the room. "By your leave, I shall arrange the meeting, Your Eminence."

Will had dinner with Jonoli and Ambri—a simple feast that included spicy peppers, melons, avocados, goat's milk, and roasted crocodile (which Will first mistook for chicken). A servant interrupted them just when they had their fill, saying that Will's special guest had arrived.

Will met Namic in the front hall with Jonoli beside him holding Ambri. He was shorter than Will and with a lesser build that had room for potential. He appeared older than his true age and wise beyond his years. He had a golden feather embedded on his red turban—the sign of a firstborn who would inherit a large estate. He kneeled and joined his hands together in front of him. "Your Eminence," he said, "it is a supreme pleasure to make your acquaintance. I have heard of your great deeds, which will surely place your name among legends."

"Yes, well, I just do what I can," Will said.

"And is this the Lady Annell? She is more beautiful than they describe her, surely a fallen star roaming the earth, a living jewel all in herself."

Will broadly smiled, but then looked at Jonoli's face, which was one part concern and one part outrage, and coughed. "No, you should pay your respects where they are due. This is my consort, Jonoli."

"Oh, I apologize to the Lady Jonoli, I meant no offense." Namin was clearly embarrassed, but he wasn't shocked. If they were in Thayland, Will and Jonoli's relationship would have been an outrageous scandal. But in Carsiss, where nobles often had many wives and concubines under one roof, it was a nonissue.

Will took Namin to Baku's old study, where they could talk in private and in close quarters. Will found himself slightly distracted by the prophetic hourglass, but he tried not to show it. He and Namin discussed the young scholar's plans for the future (he was going to secure a government position, possibly one in development or internal affairs) and his aesthetics (he had opposed the "war" on the Mulvars and wished to see deeper and involved relations between Mulvars and Carsians). He seemed just as Halicut had said: An intelligent individual of a good disposition and a good understanding of how to run a nation.

"Okay, I'll be blunt with you," Will said. "I summoned you because I intend to pass the Scepter to someone very soon. The Prime Dieschsuch recommended you, so I thought I'd have a look at you and consider you for the throne."

"Me, Your Eminence?" Namin's eyes darted around the room as if it had suddenly filled with people. "If I may ask, why? You would make a great Emperor, and I am still too young."

"I would not make a good Emperor because I am a son of Thayland and not born into your caste system. I am not a *Ksatriya* and will not pretend to be. Everyone knows this and resents me for it. As for your age, let me tell you that I'm only twenty-one years old and even less suitable for the throne than you are. You at least have the right education, and you've been in Carsiss all your life. If you need any help, Prime Dieschsuch Halicut will be with you every step of the way."

"But, Your Eminence, I could not think of being Emperor so soon. I ... I do not think I could do it. And the Lady Annell ... what would she think?"

"What the Lady Annell thinks doesn't matter; her time is past. What matters is what *you* think. I'm not going to pressure you on this, because being Emperor is not going to be easy, especially since you'll be replacing an old dynasty. But it's your decision, and I'll leave the offer open for three days. In three days' time, if you haven't decided yet, I'll have to pass the Scepter to someone like Lord Hineson or Lord Darric. Please consider it—I want to leave Carsiss in good hands. You are dismissed."

Will saw Lord Namin leave in his horse-drawn carriage from atop a balcony. He then stepped inside, to a guest bedroom he shared with Jonoli and Ambri. He went to Ambri in her brand new crib, checking her breathing and skin temperature. He then turned to Jonoli, sitting at a desk and writing in a journal she had just started. The three of them had no blood relations, and yet Will thought of them as a close family who came together easily after all the trauma they had endured.

And yet it wouldn't last. Will was going back to Thayland with Ambri and had to leave Jonoli behind. He had asked her repeatedly to go with him, to make a new life in a more tolerant nation, but she refused, saying that Carsiss was her home and always would be;

and besides, she could speak only a few words of Altrin.

Jonoli would have to be left behind, though he hated to do it. It was why he had not been very intimate with her ever since their reunion, even though they slept together. He had thought about it and he knew she'd be willing, but he was working to cut all emotional ties with her, to make the time of their parting less painful.

And she must not have taken him because she was cutting ties from her end as well.

"Our time is growing short," Will said. "I promise you that Ambri will be well taken cared of. She'll be happy in my lord's household. She may be put to work as a seamstress or a stablehand; she could take up art and make paintings or frescos. Anything she wants to do, she can do it. I may even take her to the Palace and make acquaintances with the nobles there. I won't make her into a trophy, because I'm bringing her there for her sake more than for mine. I'll—"

Jonoli put down her quill pen. "I'm sorry, Will ..."

Will paused. "Sorry? For what?"

Jonoli rose and drew closer, but stopped some paces away. "I'm sorry, Will ... I'm so very sorry, but I am contesting you for Ambri's custody."

Will furrowed his brow, absolutely shocked. "But Jonoli, I—" He stopped there, rethinking his words. He was going to say that he was the one who brought Ambri through the desert, keeping her safe and well fed and hydrated; and he was the one who convinced Baku to allow her to stay in the harem's quarters. But Jonoli would say that she had seen after Ambri when he couldn't, that she had brought her to a safe place and kept her silence when under the whip in *Qualini Durakur*. She would say that she endured numerous lashings for Ambri's sake—a torment that Will had taken responsibility for. She would say she had as much right to claim Ambri's custody as he had, and she would be absolutely right.

He sighed. "Jonoli, you knew my intentions from the start; you knew I was keeping Ambri when you took her in. I'm sorry for all you went through, but I couldn't have foreseen it. I ... I want only the best for her, and I can't do that in Carsiss, you understand?"

Jonoli folded her hands together in front of her and kept her head down. "I know that, Will, and that's why I'm sorry for doing this. But I cannot let you do this to me—I *can't*. For many years, I have only *pretended* to love my lord and his guests; only now have I found people to love, both a man and a child. And now I must see both those people leave me for good, with no promise of return?"

Her voice had the same quality it did back in the tent on the mountain trail—saddened and very unlike her. It made the hairs on the back of Will's neck stand on end.

"Will, I love Ambri, and for you to take her away, it ... well, I don't think I could take it. I don't know where I'll go—maybe I'll stay in Nünveghett, just so long as I'm far away from the Palace—but wherever I am, I don't want to be there alone." Her eyes grew misty, blinking to fight back tears. "Will, I can't be left alone! You have Thayland and I have Carsiss, and if you take Ambri to Thayland, I'll have no one to give me reason to live! At least you have your lord and a solid future ahead of you; I'll have to start anew, and I'm not sure I'll want to if I have to forget all I went through. Please, you have to understand!"

Will breathed deeply through his nostrils and started pacing about. All along, he knew he was being selfish, but he had thought Jonoli was strong enough to go on without him and Ambri, and thought she had believed the same thing. But she was only human, with the same needs and desires as he. She shouldn't be left alone to face life's cruelties, without an anchor to ground her and shape her motives. But still ...

"No, Jonoli, I can't allow it. I offered you to come with me, but you always refused. If it's the language barrier you're concerned about, I can help through it, only ... only let me take us to Thayland, where we'll have a roof over our heads and a foundation to stand on."

Jonoli shook her head. "You pretend not to care, but you cannot lie to me. You know I can't leave with you, and I can see you don't want to leave me with only myself. I want Ambri with me—*need* her with me—and I don't want to force you, but ..."

She paused, unsure of how to put gently what she would say.

"What is it?" Will said threateningly. Jonoli didn't sound sad anymore; her fiery spirit had returned, so he didn't feel like going easy on her. "If you can't have Ambri, what would you be willing to do?"

Jonoli looked at him square in the eye. "There's always some way. I'll do whatever I need to do to have Ambri. It is unfair for you to take her away."

"What is it? What are you planning?" Will waited for an answer, but Jonoli kept silent, her eyes uncertain. "What, are you going to steal her away tonight? And what if *I* take her and hide her away? What would you do? Would you wait till the last second, board my ship and slit my throat?"

Jonoli gave him that look again—one part concern, one part outrage, only that time there was more outrage. Her eyes were wide, her brow wrinkled only a little, her jaw set with determination.

Will fell into an uncomfortable silence. He thought back on what he said, and it was like a slap to the face. He looked down in shame, then raised his hands palms-out as a sign of peace. "Okay, I'm sorry, I crossed the line there and I take it back." His tone was sincere, and he sighed in bitter defeat. "So what is it? How are we going to settle this? It's not going to be a fight, that's for sure."

Jonoli's thoughtful and serene look told him he was forgiven. She gazed at the carpet in front of the mantel, then looked up with a small, hopeful smile. "What about a horserace? You could take two horses from the cavalry, and we could race in the mountains."

The first thing that came to Will's mind was a memory of his horserace with Adam Berryworth, which ended in scandalous failure. Still, the more he thought about it, the more attractive the suggestion was. He had almost won that race with Berryworth; why couldn't he win against Jonoli?

But there was one thing wrong with the picture. "Well, I suppose we could," he said, "but can you ride a horse? Carsian women aren't allowed to."

"I was born and raised in Carsiss, but I spent five years in Bune as a servant in a nobleman's house. I was often sent to town to pick up supplies, which I did on horseback. In Bune, people frown on women on horseback, but it is not disallowed. It's been years since I was on a horse, but I'm sure it'll come back to me after a while. And since you're the Emperor, you can allow a small breach in Carsian law."

"Yes, I could ..." Will thought more about it, remembering the mountain path to *Qualini Durakur,* which could very well be the site of a horserace. He also tried thinking of alternatives to settle their dispute (including arm-wrestling, of all the craziest things), but nothing was as attractive as a good old-fashioned horserace. "Fine, we'll do it. Tomorrow, if we can. I'll let you practice, but the sooner we get it done, the better."

"Agreed. I'll have to leave the choice of horses up to you, since the soldiers wouldn't like to see a woman looking at them."

"Yes, of course I will."

"Please choose the best ones."

Will nodded, and the two of them extinguished the lanterns and candle flames and climbed into bed, as awkward as it was to do so. It took Will awhile to fall asleep, what with his new conflict in mind. At one point, he thought of the journal Jonoli had started. He wondered if she had been writing the things she planned on saying to him, trying to make her argument work on paper before it formed on her lips. He had thought her stronger than that, but again, she was only human, not the state of perfection.

CHAPTER 25
PARTINGS

FIRST THING AFTER BREAKFAST that morning, Will went out and found two horses he was told were picks of the litter. They seemed healthy and in good shape, with sturdy builds and shiny coats, so he ordered them to be put aside where they would wait for him.

At the Palace, Will found a pleasant surprise: A letter from Lord Namin, saying yes to Will's offer. It said little else, only that he was excited and would receive the Scepter in any manner of Will's choosing. Will told the Dieschsuchs the good news and ordered them to make plans for a ceremony to be carried out the very next day. "The sooner I leave the throne," he said, "the fewer chances my enemies have of seeing my ugly face."

He then led Jonoli to the Emperor's carriage, where she would ride to the head of the mountain trail they had chosen to race on. The two horses picked for the race ran alongside the carriage, one ridden by Will, the other by a horse trainer named Tamric, who would act as the flagman and judge.

They stopped at a safari office near the mountains which housed the rangers who oversaw the mountain trails. The rangers were pleased to accommodate a horserace involving their new emperor, but were surprised and uneasy upon learning that his opponent was a woman. They had assumed that Tamric would be the opponent, so when Jonoli mounted her horse they snapped at her, ordering her to dismount or else be charged with illegal activity. Will countermanded their authority, assuring them that Jonoli had the right to ride. Yet they remained adamant in their conviction that no Carsian woman should be on a horse.

"Damn it all, listen to your emperor!" Will cried. "If you don't step down right now, I'll have you hung by your thumbs for three whole days, not a minute less!"

They stepped down after that and kept their distance.

Jonoli rode her steed up the closest path, while Will and Tamric asked the rangers and safari bookers which mountain trail was best for them to take. "Well, you have your low-end trails which are pretty safe," said one burly ranger pointing at a map, "then you have your mid-level trails if you want more of a challenge, as well as a breathtaking view of the city. But if you want a race you'll never forget, you'll take what we call the 'nosebleeders,' where the elevation is so high, your blood boils from being so close to the sun and escapes through your nose."

"Does it really get hotter up there?" Will asked.

The ranger paused for thought. "No ... actually, it gets colder. But you're close to the sun, so your blood boils."

Will furrowed his brow. "Okay, that makes sense."

"I remember the race between Lord Hunnelac and Lord Nansu," said one ranger, who was as thin as a twig and had his clothes hang on him like laundry on a line. "They took a nose-bleeder trail, and Lord Nansu's horse got so excited it leapt off the cliff and dove headfirst all the way down. Now *that* was something."

Will shrugged. "I once saw a knight lose his arm from a jousting lance, and yet he lived. They say he hung his arm in his trophy room."

The rangers laughed.

"So what shall it be, Your Eminence? A nose-bleeder or a mid-level?"

Will considered. "I don't know—I mean, it's just a *horserace*. I couldn't care less about the view."

"But if you take a nose-bleeder, you'll go down in history, Your Eminence."

"Yeah ... Baku wanted to do that, and he did, just not in the way he expected. No, it's just a damned horserace; I'll go the coward's way and take the bunny trail."

None of the rangers said anything to that, though Will knew they'd have some wicked barbs for him once he wasn't around.

Jonoli returned from her ride sweating in the crisp air, grinning from the exhilaration of speed and power that she had almost forgotten (though willingly breaking a silly law without retribution may have played a part in it, too). Decked out in her leather riding gear and looking down at the men with her sharp eyes, she made quite the imposing rider, a possible addition for the proud army of Thayland. *Sadly,* Will thought, *that is not to be.*

"So how was it?" he asked.

"Wonderful! It's been so long, yet I feel I could take on the world!"

Will smiled and nodded, then mounted his own steed and paced around with him, getting a feel for the animal's posture and attitude. "Tamric? Anytime you're ready, we'll go."

Tamric first asked if they wanted to take a leisurely ride through the path Will had chosen; both parties agreed and headed off together, not pushing their mounts, only trotting alongside each other. Neither of them said much, only commented on the trail conditions and the weather, which had clear skies and mild winds, perfect for a race. Will noted two sharp turns in the middle of some deep gullies, which could make or break the race for either of them. It was around those turns that the trail turned especially rocky and hazardous, which could turn and twist a hoof and cause a horse to either stumble or fall altogether.

When they returned to the safari station, they saw two red flags mounted on either side of the trail, marking both sides of the combination starting and finish line. They brought their horses to the invisible line and waited for Tamric's instructions. The rangers watched from afar, clearly not pleased to see a woman in a saddle but not foolish to go against the Emperor's wishes again. *I'll bet if I win, they'll go on about how a woman cannot handle a horse,* Will thought. *Well, hell, I'm not going to lose just to prove them wrong.*

Tamric took his place beside a flag, holding a small banner. "The rules are simple: Whoever crossed the finish line wins. There is no cheating—no weapons or fighting from horseback is allowed, and no shortcuts are permitted. If you stray from the intended path, you will lose. If at the end of the race either of you are in dispute as to the fairness of the other, the race must be done again, only with an escort behind you riding one of the carriage horses. Hopefully, both of you will abide by the rules, as it is the honorable thing to do. Now, are you ready?"

Will glanced at Jonoli, who then glanced at him and quickly drew her eyes away. Anger rose up in him like a bubbling spring; it wasn't much, but it was there. He could hardly believe he had to further struggle for Ambri's possession, and yet he had agreed to the race because he honored Jonoli's reasons for her challenge. He thought back on his trek through the sweltering desert, anxious about Ambri's health yet proud that he had saved her from Tanalac's foolish pride. Taking Ambri from Jonoli wouldn't exactly be saving her, yet it felt right to do it, even if it was also selfish. "We're ready, Tamric."

"Very well, on the count of three. One ... two ... *three!*"

Tamric waved his banner and they were off, bounding down the trail, kicking their mounts like they were rusty machines. The familiar clopping of the hooves were rapid and desperate, like the sorrowful patter of raindrops reflecting the mourning of the Hindu gods.

Will managed a head start, but Jonoli quickly gained on him and passed. He wasn't very concerned, for the harder Jonoli drove her steed, the faster it would tire and burn out. Slow and steady didn't exactly win the race, either, but Will planned to push his horse in the last stretch, passing Jonoli when she was in no state to keep up.

They progressed through the valleys like ants on the march, kicking up a fine spray of bronze-colored dust in their wake. Will wondered if he was wise in choosing the low-end bunny trail, which grew high and scenic only at two points. Truth be told, his ego had been bruised at the prospect of racing on a guaranteed "safe" path, his pride injured by how the rangers didn't hold him in high esteem. But there were times when he and Jonoli rode beside each other and fought for space. They never rose a hand against each other, but they rode uncomfortably close, daring one another to drive their horse hard enough to pass; Will could imagine such doing struggles on a cliff, which might have been the late Lord Nansu's downfall, and he realized he had made the right choice.

Bushes proved to be a unique hazard on the trail; they usually weren't very large, but the horses made sure to keep clear of them lest they scratch up their legs and flanks. The danger the bushes posed became more apparent at one point when the two riders fought for space on the trail as one particularly tall bush loomed ahead on the right side. The race had become a miniature version of "chicken," with Will on the right and Jonoli on the left. Will had to either pass Jonoli just in time to clear the bush or fall back and get in behind her; in the end, he opted for the latter choice, partly in his decision not to drive his horse so hard early in the race.

Another hazard were the sharp turns Will had noted earlier. They were both right turns, formed by arrowhead-shaped walls that climbed perpendicular to the ground. The first turn was uneventful, with Jonoli in the lead and Will trailing behind her. The ground was rocky, but the horses deftly stepped on them with no incident.

It was the second turn that, in Will's mind, determined the outcome of the race. Will blamed himself, believing that he should have stuck to his original plan and not act out of desperation.

They were alongside each other again, Jonoli on the right and Will on the left. As they approached the turn, Will felt a lump in his throat, believing he should not let Jonoli keep the lead around the turn. The turn marked the beginning of the homestretch, and he badly wanted to be the first to step onto it.

Jonoli wrapped around the sharp tip of the arrowhead wall easily enough, while Will gave it a wide berth, pushing his steed harder than he ever had. He dug his stirrups into its ribs and roughly whipped the reins like a slavedriver, fully intending to rack up the speed and dart past Jonoli before she could gaze any speck of dirt on the other side of the arrowhead.

His horse slipped on the loose gravel, its legs splayed out nearly to their breaking points. Will realized his error and discontinued driving, instead hugging his horse so he wouldn't get thrown off and praying that the steed wouldn't keel over.

The horse kept its legs moving, struggling for balance and maintaining steady footing wherever it could find it. Soon it was trotting along with no problems—no broken hooves, limbs or spirits. Will, who was plenty shaken himself, allowed the horse to move a slow pace through the rest of the gully, taking no chances for a second incident.

He knew he had lost. The slipup had cost him the race, and there was no chance he could catch up to Jonoli. He made as if to strike his horse's neck, but he merely pumped his fist instead, pinning blame not on the horse but on himself. He had gotten reckless, desperate to gain a lead in a theatrical fashion. He paid his price for it, trotting until he reached the race's homestretch, kicking his horse into a run when the ground turned smooth again.

Jonoli didn't end up being the heroine of the day, for her crossing of the finish line was met by jeers from the rangers and bookkeepers, none of whom expected to see the female contender come out ahead. Once Will arrived, the men demanded some kind of answer as to how Jonoli could win. They asked if she had pulled a dirty trick or had some other unfair advantage. Will dismounted and shook his head, saying that the fault was his. Everyone groaned.

Jonoli dismounted after Will had, as if she had waited for him to do it first. It was hard for her to gaze upon him, as it was the other way around. She feared that he would commit an act of passion he'd regret later, perhaps lashing out at her like a cowardly guard in *Qualini Durakur*. The same fear resided in him as well, and thus he briskly mounted his horse again, and after a quick order for Tamric to escort Jonoli back to the Palace, made off for the Palace himself, pushing his steed more further than he had to.

He had lost Ambri. If he honored his agreement with Jonoli, he would never take her to Thayland, keep her under his wing, let her grow up not as a female *Vaisya* but as a member of a lower caste that had gained more prestige in his country over the years. Sure, she wouldn't be a noblewoman like Sir Blackstone or Lord Harrington, but she would be able to own property, arrange meetings, and marry whomever she liked.

But instead he'd have to leave her in Carsiss and trust Jonoli with her care. He owed it to Jonoli for all she did for him, and it was wholly unfair for him to just leave her with nothing to show for her deeds. Nonetheless, he hated the fact as deeply as the marrow in his bones, even though he would accede to it, if only because his bloomin' honor demanded it of him. It was the same honor that made him show mercy to his enemies after Baku's defeat, such as Tanalac and Annell, and to deny that honor would be to deny his dignity and moral standing.

Plus, his master, Sir Blackstone, wouldn't have it any other way. If he was there, he would stress about how chivalry demanded Will to keep his promises and to recognize when and how to deliver justice. He would surely say that Will did the right thing in leaving Ambri with the woman who had spent the most time caring for her, and Will would have little choice but to agree. He had a lot of respect for Sir Blackstone, and when he truthfully related his unbelievable stories to him (except for how he had died and came back to life—a detail he'd have to fudge), he hoped the master would not say he acted in a manner unbecoming of a knight and a Christian.

But still, the loss of Ambri pained him, and in apparently more ways than one. He was just out of sight of the safari office when his heart was suddenly in torment, greatly paining him with every beat. He clutched his chest, barely holding onto the reins with one hand. He brought his horse to a stop and dismounted, his knees soon meeting the street. He cried out and breathed in deep puffs. The world swam before his eyes, his senses dimly aware of his immediate surroundings. People went to him to see what the matter was, and he shooed them away, waving his arms more forcibly than necessary.

He had heard of people having heart attacks, and he was convinced he was having one himself. What else could it be? The only problem was that he was too young to be having one, and still healthy and strong. It would have surprised him more but for how his heart had been acting since his resurrection, sending a little bit of pain with every pump. The pain was currently amplified ten times, signaling some sort of failure or mismanagement.

And then suddenly it was gone, as if it had never been. The pain was still there, but it was of the bearable kind he had grown used to. He stood up and kept a hand on his forehead, still taking deep breaths until the world stopped turning in his eyes. He gave the people around him an apologetic look, then quickly mounted his horse and rode away.

He had feared death as he fought Baku and his champion, though he did not run from the risk of it. At that moment, riding back to the Palace, he feared death once again, and even more so. He admitted to himself that his death might come soon because of his struggling heart, and if so he had to pass the Scepter to Namin Termeric as soon as he could, before the Scepter suddenly became free game to any who wanted it.

At dawn of the next day, he met the three heads of Termeric House in a guest suite of the Palace: Namin and his father and mother, Palic and Kimli. They were dressed in their best clothes, which were mostly made of silk except for Palic's outfit, for he preferred simple cotton. Kimli was clearly delighted for her son's ascension to the throne; Palic, however, was too proud for that.

"Who's ever heard of a ruler reigning while his father is still alive? No one, it's impossible!"

"It *is* possible if I say so," Will countered.

"Everyone's going to laugh at him! They'll point and say, 'There goes Namin the Too-Young, who bested his father for the throne.' I tell you, they'll eat him alive. Here in Carsiss, no one is allowed to step at a higher station than their parents."

Will pointed an accusing finger. "You are exaggerating. I've never heard of this silly rule, and I'll hear no more of this." He turned to Namin. "Don't let your father control you, you hear me? It is you who will be Emperor, not him. After the ceremony, the best he can do is give advice. As long as he's here, he'll be under *your* roof, not his."

Palic tried to talk throughout Will's pep talk, even though Will and Namin made as if not to hear him. Namin continued not to hear him in his response: "Do not worry, Your Eminence, I will be my own master. I'm sure there is a reason why you chose me and not my father."

"Hello!?" Palic cried. "Do you hear me? This is outrageous! No one will stand for it! You're being completely mad!"

Will groaned and said, "Have you forgotten who I am? I am your emperor, and you must agree with any decision of mine! The gods didn't allow me to oust Baku for no good reason. You'll either trust my judgment or stew in the dungeon for a while."

Palic appeared utterly shocked, and Will rushed Namin out into the hallway while the effect lasted. "Lord Namin, are you sure you're up to this?" he asked with fists on hips.

"Yes, Your Eminence, I'm sure. Like you told me, I won't let my father control me."

"It's not just your father I'm worried about. There are overlords out there who are far more intimidating than he is. They'll try to bully you to get what they want, to put you into their line of thinking. They'll be after you soon after I leave."

"Are you losing faith in me?"

"I can't help but to. I know how these things work. You're still much younger than these overlords, and they won't just ignore that. Not only do I worry that they might poison your mind and values, but I worry they'll try to harm you, to intimidate you. If that happens, you may fault me for it, and I'll be kicking myself."

"So what should I do?"

"Be your own man, just like I said! Determine what's right and what's wrong, act on your own instincts, and be able to smell a rat when your advisors aren't around. I'm leaving the scepter to you not just because I want to maintain good relations between our countries, but because I want a capable leader who can lead Carsiss to peace and prosperity. Can you be that leader?"

Namin smiled and nodded.

Will nodded back, then drooped his head and shook it. "Good God, if my friends were to hear me say all that, they'll rib me for sure. But Lord, I still mean every word of it."

They took a walk in the halls and talked of future projects they had lined up for themselves. Namin, for instance, planned to petition King Fredrick for more water free of levies, while Will wanted to find a good woman before he left Sir Blackstone's tutelage.

Annell approached them, her eyes filled with worry. "Your Eminence ... Lord Termeric ..."

"Lady Annell," Will said. "Something bothering you?"

"I come to give you news." She paused, fiddling with her hands in front of her, then found the courage to look at the men squarely in their eyes. "I am with child."

Namin was stricken more so than Will, who made a subtle expression that could have been a grimace. "My lady," Will said, "that is excellent news. So, Lord Namin, what do you think of that?" He was afraid Namin would resent her for carrying Baku's child, and not his own.

Namin paused for thought, then said, "The child shall be a *Ksatriya,* sent here by the gods to do great things. I shall take it in my care and look after it like it was my own."

Will nodded. "Just how it should be." He smiled at Annell, who looked noticeably relieved. "My apologies for my rudeness the other night; it was inexcusable."

Annell nodded, but did so with cold disinterest. "My apologies as well, Your Eminence." Her eyes, though, said otherwise. She still did not forgive Will for slaying Baku, nor would she ever. She might have had plans for revenge, and the thought of it forced a cold shiver down his spine. He imagined that another corny speech would merely be wasted on her, for she had strongly made up her mind to dwell on hate and intolerance, to hold self-importance above the well-being of her nation.

"Anyway, my congratulations," Will said, wondering why it took Baku so long to get her pregnant in the first place. Perhaps the rumor of his particular "preferences" had actually held some water. "I'm sure Lord Namin will be an exceptional father."

"Yes, I will," Namin said, "but only if the Lady Annell chooses to stay in the Palace after I divorce her."

The ceremony was small, performed in a small prayer room. The attendants were four of the Dieschsuchs—Halicut included—Namin's parents and surviving grandparents, several local overlords—excluding those who had begun to lay siege on Nünveghett—and the guards posted around the room (notably absent was Lady Annell). The Dieschsuchs were disappointed at how small the gathering was, but they understood why Will wanted it so: A small ceremony meant little chance for an assassin to kill him and the future Emperor. His paranoia was still running rampant, for he never wanted to underestimate the malice of the overlords who had favored Baku.

Among the attendants was one whose very presence threw Will off guard. She was the woman in his second vision in the Sands of Carsiss. She had supposedly been his wife in the vision; in the prayer room, she was clearly the wife of one of the overlords. She wore a scarlet *sari* over a pink dress, wrapping it around her head so evenly that only her features were revealed. Her husband must have been jealous of her to make her dress as such; if she had been left to bare her head, Will was sure she would have made quite a presence in the room. Her beauty and knowing eyes would stand out in any crowd. He thought of asking her to introduce herself, but he didn't want to complicate matters; he decided to just get on with the ceremony and be quick about it. Still, she *was* intriguing, and it was hard to keep his eyes off of her.

A *Brahman* priest stood before the altar, who gave a homily and recited passages from the *Vedas*. He had Will repeat things that had him acknowledge his surrender of the throne, and then had Namin repeat vows he had to make before he could ascend to the throne—simple vows meant to ensure the esteem of the gods and the *Brahmans*, as well as to ensure that Namin would do nothing to displease the gods. The ceremony ended with Will simply handing the Imperial Scepter to Namin, who then held it above his head like a jousting champion with the silver cup. The gatherers vigorously clapped for a long while, clearly pleased to see a *Ksatriya* holding the Scepter.

It did Will a lot of good for his peace of mind to see Namin so confident. He held the Scepter like it was made for him, and he made his way about the people with confidence and assuredness. Of course, being a leader was natural to him due to his experience as a nobleman ... but his confidence also came from another source that was more superficial.

Just before the ceremony, Will took Namin into his study and showed him the Sands of Carsiss. "This is no ordinary hourglass, as you'll see," he said. "I believe this had helped to encourage Baku's bloody ambition—but trust me, I think he was misled. I think he didn't understand just how the hourglass works exactly."

Will had Namin turn the hourglass over and peer into the falling sands. Namin was shocked when he saw the image, and he wanted Will to see it to prove he wasn't going crazy. Will insisted he keep looking, then asked what it was he saw.

"I saw myself as Emperor," Namin said. I was dining with the King of Thayland; I recognized the crown he wore and the broach on his cape—the cross and the claw."

"And where were you two?"

"Here in the Palace. We were talking about something, but I

don't know what."

"Were you arguing?"

"No, but that's just the thing: I don't know much Altrin, which means either the King could speak Carsian or—"

"Or you could speak Altrin. You saw the future, Namin. Honestly, I thought you'd see something more momentous, but it *was* important. The Sands told us that you'll make a great emperor. You'll keep your alliances close and broaden your horizons."

Will then pointed a finger and used a rougher tone. "But remember this, Namin: The Sands showed Baku that he would be the new King of Thayland. Obviously, that didn't happen, so obviously you can't trust everything the Sands show you. In the Sands, you can behold greatness—but it is greatness that isn't inevitable. Keep that in mind, and you'll do fine."

Will didn't stick around for the festivities. He made rushed goodbyes to the Dieschsuchs and the harem ladies, said a final farewell and good luck to the newly enthroned Emperor Namin, then left the Palace and rushed to Markereen by horse.

About an hour later, he arrived at the docks. He left his horse at the stables and headed for a cargo ship in the middle of loading its shipment. He had a ticket with its shipping company for passage back to Thayland. At the foot of the pier was Jonoli and Ambri, waiting for him. He and Jonoli had barely spoken since the race; the only exception was when Jonoli asked for the time and location of his departure.

He had wondered if she would keep her promise to see him off; upon seeing her there, dressed in a red silken *sari* with warmer clothes underneath, her hair bound into a simple ponytail, he remarked how foolish he was to doubt her.

Jonoli was talking to two Carsian sailors (probably not about the finer ways to map ocean currents) while keeping an eye on Ambri crawling around the planks. She picked Ambri up when she spotted Will and went to meet him. The sailors behind her looked down and shifted their feet, anxious for her to get her goodbyes done so their joint courtship could continue.

They met with an awkward silence among the crashing of rolling waves and the clattering of busy dock workers. Ambri shrieked and fidgeted in Jonoli's arms, which was probably in protest at being denied her freedom to move around, plus the aggravation from the chilly spring air that stung her reddened cheeks. Summer was only a few months away, and the temperature was bound to sharply climb in a few weeks.

"Want to hold her?" Jonoli asked. She handed Ambri over to Will, who shushed her and held her hand with his free one. Will thought Jonoli might shed a few tears judging from her expression, but they never came. Some might mistake that for a sign of a cold heart, but Will knew better. There was something more to her—a roughed hide, a sharp survival instinct. He began to believe she would do just fine when left on her own, just her and Ambri.

Of course, doubt arose every then and again. *Jonoli seems to have a tendency to fall into indentured service. If she does again, it may hinder her in caring for Ambri. If God wills it, she won't find herself part of another harem ever again.*

"Goodbye, Ambri," he said in a low voice. "You keep Jonoli company, okay? Be a good girl for her ... though a little nagging goes a long way." He looked at Jonoli and winked.

Jonoli smiled. "I wish you would stay," she then said simply.

"Jonoli, I can't—"

"I know, you can't stay here; there are people waiting for you in Thayland. But I can dream. Just imagine, Will, if you stayed here, it would not matter if you were the Emperor or not—I would stay by you. We could go to the jungles of Rozimi and find work in building houses and bridges, or we could stay in the mountains and work as mercenaries protecting travelers from the bandits. You may not be a knight, but you could still do good things."

"Is that what you're going to do?"

Jonoli frowned as she thought of a reply. "No, perhaps not. I'll find something more tedious, like spinning yarn or shepherding sheep. I'll stay in Nünveghett and earn enough money to move east to the Naimiyan Mountains, where it's always cooler."

"Will you have people arrange a marriage for you?"

"Yes, but do not worry—I shall love no man who does not love Ambri as much as you have."

Will felt his throat lock up and lowered his gaze to the floorboards. He didn't know what to say to that, so he made no response, merely gave Ambri back to her.

"You've done so much here," Jonoli said, rocking herself with Ambri in her arms, who was fidgeting with anxiety. "You shouldn't be modest and keep it all to yourself. Go and tell everyone you see at home."

"I'm not sure anyone would believe me, but—"

"They'll *have* to," Jonoli said with a devious smile. "The sailors will all hear of how their shipping rights were revoked until Emperor Baku fell to a son of Thayland. If you tell your story to everyone before they hear it from the sailors, they'll believe you in time."

Will nodded, though he wasn't really listening. He grew somber and thought of how to say his latest concern in a way that would not make Jonoli upset. "Jonoli, don't be sorry for the race. I think it'll turn out for the best that way. You see ... I may not have been able to care for Ambri after all."

"What do you mean?"

"There's something that's been wrong with me since I came back from Sancrat—something that might not go away at all. It may be something I'll live with my whole life."

"What is the matter? Anything I can do?" Jonoli sounded deathly concerned.

Will sighed. "No, I don't think there is. I'm sorry to bring it up, it's just ... I want to let you know you did the right thing. I was probably foolish to plan on keeping Ambri."

Jonoli shook her head. "You don't trust me? Is that what it is?"

"No, it's not that. I trust that you'll take good care of Ambri."

"No, I mean if you do trust me, you'll tell me what's wrong."

Will paused, and in his thoughts he chided himself for bringing up the matter. "I'll look into it when I arrive in Thayland. Starting now, our lives are separate. We've chosen them to be, and I don't want you to regret your choice. Don't worry, I won't be entirely helpless."

Jonoli looked suspicious, but nodded. "Okay, if that's how it shall be."

Will glanced at the cargo ship. "I have to go now. Goodbye and good luck, Jonoli."

"Farewell, Will. Neither I or Carsiss will ever forget you."

They parted. Will went to the ship while Jonoli returned to the sailors. He kept an eye on her and the two suitors, looking for any signs of trouble. No doubt they would have questions about him, and if Jonoli was wise, she wouldn't brag about he had saved Ambri, killed Baku, and ruled as Emperor for three days. They never seemed shocked or appalled during their conversation, so Jonoli must have kept the details to herself.

Less than an hour later, the ship set sail. Will stood on the port bow, feeling the wind ran along his smooth scalp. He wondered at first if Jonoli was right about his story being told among the sailors; when he later heard some of the Thayland crew whisper about how Emperor Baku had died and been replaced with his killer, he smiled and admitted Jonoli knew what she was talking about.

He also thought of the dreams Jonoli had of them, doing mercenary and construction work. He had no doubt he could follow through on such dreams, but they were nonetheless a little daunting. He was not sickened by wanderlust; as much as he liked new sights, he also liked to have his feet firmly settled at times. Jonoli, on the other hand, had probably been bitten by the traveling bug and would soon leave Nünveghett, despite having a child to care for. He couldn't fault her for it, and he wished her the best of luck.

He had a lot of time to think on that two-week cruise, especially about his death and resurrection. They felt like they had happened ages ago, the memories not very fresh. It was probably because he had went through so much trauma since then, and the newer, more extreme memories pushed his resurrection the back of his mind.

Even so, he could still recall his feeling of carelessness while in the void, plus his sense of weightlessness and nonbeing. He couldn't help but to fret over those things, for if the afterlife was all about forgetting one's worries and deeds in life, then what was the meaning of life in the first place? Furthermore he had no sense of a god or gods in that void, which called his faith into question. He still believed in one universal and compassionate God, for he couldn't help but to, but it would have been nice for Him to speak to his weightless and careless soul, to acknowledge He was there with him. It would be like the poem where Jesus walked with a man on the beach in a dream, and Jesus said he had carried the man through the hardest parts of his life. Of course, God may have been the source of the ray of light that that brought him back to earth, but that wasn't a good way of communication since any message it conveyed was rather vague.

There were also the matters of his heart and his hair. He no longer had any hair on top of his head nor on his face, not since his resurrection. It was as if he was a newborn, which he actually was in a sense. And yet it made little sense. Since he had been reborn as a full-grown man, then why didn't he have his hair as he had before? It couldn't have been as if hair could not go through the resurrection process, because he still had his eyebrows.

Was it because he had been shaving his hair off anyway? It had become a preference of his in his recent years, though he had planned on growing it out when he reached middle age. Had God decided to send him back without hair as a sort of small favor, to give him the convenience of never having to shave again? It wasn't hard to believe, but it smelled fishy nonetheless.

And what of his heart? It hadn't gotten any better; it had in fact gotten worse, as his episode in the street had proven. He had had a heart attack, though he didn't have the terrible aftershock that an attack usually inflicted. He had survived and remained in good shape, but that didn't matter—he couldn't just ignore it and go on like everything was fine. His bad heart was bound to fail him someday soon, which was what he could not bring himself to say to Jonoli. How could it not? He could feel it in his chest every waking day, sending painful pulses like a miniature volcano. He tried not to complain of it and he had become good at ignoring it, but if it was the price to pay for being reborn as an adult, he might not have chosen to be reborn at all.

In the middle of his second week at sea, he had another heart attack. He had been lying in his bunker, waiting for sleep to claim him, when his heart suddenly started leaping like a frog and felt on the verge of exploding. He gasped and moaned, clutching his chest as if to keep his heart from jumping out. His roommates gathered around him, concerned but helpless to do anything but watch. It passed in under a minute, leaving him breathless and weak. Two people had run to get him some water, though they knew if it wouldn't help him any. He accepted it graciously and tried to assure everyone he was fine, not to much success. "Don't you worry about me," he said grumpily. "I'm a fighter, and I'll fight this like a thief in my house."

The attack wasn't as strong as the one in Nünveghett, but it made him worry all over again. His pride didn't want to acknowledge the fact that he might not have been able to care for Ambri, but reason had it otherwise, and he usually listened to reason. He worried he wouldn't live long enough to see thirty, a time when Ambri would be ten—old enough to know much of the world but not quite enough to look after herself. He would have had to leave her with Sir Blackstone and Tony—a prospect he would not have been comfortable with.

At least Jonoli's looking after her, he thought. *Even if I should return to dust, Ambri will be in good hands, and still in her homeland.*

Thoughts of his heart were making him slip into periods of depression. Before going to Carsiss, he had expected the ambassadorship would be a big step in securing a long and productive life; ironically, it seemed his resurrection would make it otherwise.

He indulged in self-pity but tried not to get carried away with it by training with his wooden practice sword. In concentrating on his form and movements, he could forget about his impending short life and merely focus on the present. Some of the sailors noticed him and asked for sword lessons. After an hour of practice, they thought of themselves as masters and wanted to start fighting for bets.

Will strongly discouraged them from any such foolishness and retreated into his cabin, where thoughts of Ambri and Jonoli drove him into depression again. He hoped that returning home and falling into his old life would make the pain of losing them more bearable.

CHAPTER 26
REPATRIATION

HE NEARLY BROKE IN TEARS at the sight of the expansive beach and the green hills beyond. He hadn't expected that but was only a little surprised by it. He had strong emotional ties to his homeland, which was why he had wanted to abandon a promising new life in Carsiss.

Upon docking at the port near Brussels, he somewhat expected to see Madick and Artiman there to greet him—or torment him. Artiman had asked Will to grant him the title of *Ksatriya;* Will refused, saying it was not in his place to make that grant since he was not a *Ksatriya* himself, even though he was Emperor. He had said, "The public outcry would be enormous."

They parted on ill terms, and then Artiman, Madick, and a few others (including some of the leaders of the resistance) retreated to Thayland under the guise of refugees. Artiman didn't trust any new Emperor to grant him the title, and since he couldn't protect him and his comrades under political protection, he had to make a new start on life in a place where the furious overlords were unlikely to sniff them out.

Artiman and Madick were nowhere to be seen, not even among the handful of Carsians present. The Carsians all shot him a look, and it was not because they were women attracted to him; they noticed his clothes, which were of the finest Carsian fabrics and design. He could have bought some Thayland-style clothing from a specialty shop in Nünveghett, but as a matter of status and accomplishment, he chose to arrive home looking like a Carsian.

He stopped for lunch at a short-order restaurant, then hired a horse-and-buggy to immediately leave for home. It was a three-day journey, during which time he mostly slept, ate, and read some of the boring books left behind in the buggy's glove compartment.

The wind was chilly and humid, the first array of spring blossoms blooming in the fields. Piles of dirty snow were left in many places, signs of a cold white winter that Will had graciously missed. He had never really noted the wide assortment of colors in the Thayland countryside, but after half a year in the deserts of Carsiss, the dark green of the grass and tree leaves and the rich brown of the soil had never seemed more sweet and appealing to the eye.

He made idle conversation with the driver, who expressed only a mild interest in his time in Carsiss. It felt very funny speaking again in Altrin after speaking Carsian for so many days and in many speeches. Yet it was a good feeling, letting his primary language roll off his tongue and feeling it naturally come back to him. It was tricky, though, for in Carsiss he had kept learning more Carsian words, and while speaking in Altrin with Franklin and Lord Harrington, he often popped in a few Carsian words here and there.

On his first night back, he made a quick stop at the St. Helena's Orphanage for Boys in Georgetown, where he impressed the nuns with some of his tales in Carsiss. Many of the elderly nuns admitted that they had thought well of him back when he was just a boy there, but they had never thought he'd be something as momentous as an ambassador of Thayland. Will smiled and said, "The work you do here, raising these children, is greater than anything I'll ever do, I'm sure."

Arriving at Augustine was a little like arriving at Nünveghett, what with the mountains in the background, the cluttering of small buildings, and the endless people.

And yet it was also different. Augustine was an innocent city that had seen no major bloodshed outside of the dueling parlors and the jousting tournaments; Nünveghett, on the other hand, had lost its innocence during the resistance movement. Will was the same way, leaving him a little bitter and frustrated. He wondered if Sir Blackstone had felt the same way after fighting in the last great war against Thorain, and he made it a point to ask him.

When he arrived at the front gate of the Blackstone estate, a guardsman asked Will who he was as he looked curiously at his clothes. "I'm Will Fontaine. Tell the master his esquire has arrived."

It took a while for the gate to open on the master's order, and the driver took the buggy up the hillside and in front of the mansion. Just when Will stepped off the buggy, Tony Beckins ran down the three front steps to met him.

"Will!" he said with a grin spreading from ear to ear. "I can't believe you're here! Just look at you—" He spread his hands, noting Will's exotic clothes.

"Tony," Will said, smiling yet slightly somber. His inside bitterness could have soured his homecoming if he wasn't careful. "Have you missed me? I wonder if you're still the lady killer I've left you as."

Tony kept a smile for a moment, but then turned even more somber than Will. "When we heard about what happened to Mr. Douglass, we feared the worse. He said he was framed by the cooks in the Carsian Palace, and Sir Blackstone hoped you wouldn't fall for the same thing."

"Well, I'm fine as you can see, but there's just a lot to tell. Does the master know I'm here, or is he out?"

Tony hesitated, pressing his lips tightly together and looking away. "The master is in jail."

"What?"

"It happened soon after you left. It had to do with your race."

"My race!? What about it?"

"Well, you remember Lord Mayweather, and the bet he had with Sir Blackstone? Mayweather said the race was fixed, so he took the matter to court and blamed the master for it."

"What? That's ridiculous! We didn't fix the race!"

"I know you didn't, but ... but Lord Mayweather said you did—and he had a witness. I can't recall his name; it was Mark or Michael or something like that. He was a guy about our age. He said he and two others had released those doves. Mayweather's negotiator said this Mark guy had been caught on the grounds in the center of the track just after you took off for Parkinson's Temple."

Will shrugged. "So what of it?"

Tony took a step closer and lowered his voice, not wanting the hired help to hear him. "This Mark guy said the master was the one who hired him."

"What?"

"It's true. Sir Blackstone denied ever knowing the guy, and his negotiator said Mark's word was suspect and that Mayweather needed more proof connecting Mark to Sir Blackstone. But Mayweather just cursed and screamed, looking right at the judges. I'd swear he was intimidating them. He must have known them somehow, since his estate is one of the biggest taxpayers in the capital, or so someone told me. Do you see what I mean?"

Will hesitantly nodded, better imagining the atmosphere of the courtroom. Some said that four pit bulls foaming at their mouths couldn't hold a candle next to the terror of a furious influential nobleman. Will didn't think so, but he did agree they were close.

"I wanted to speak in court," Tony continued, "but the master wouldn't let me. He said if things turned out bad, it was up to me to look after his wife and the estate. He didn't want Lord Mayweather to start pinning any blame on me and getting *me* imprisoned."

"How is the missus?"

"She took it hard; she wouldn't do anything for about a month. She's coping with it as best she can, but until the master returns, she won't be the same."

"Have you talked to Lord Mayweather since the trial?"

Tony took a deep breath through his nostrils. "No," he admitted, his tone reflecting his injured pride.

"How about this Mark guy?"

"Not him, either. I did talk to some of the court officials. I begged them to release Sir Blackstone, that it was all a misunderstanding, but they said the judges' decision is final and only the King can overturn their ruling. There's nothing I can do."

"Maybe there's something *I* can do. I'm an honored ambassador, and once I turn in my report, I'll petition for the master's release."

"No, you can't. Will ... they have a warrant for *your* arrest, too."

"Are you kidding me?"

"I only wish. That blamed Mark character accused you as an accomplice in fixing the race. If you go the Palace, they'll drag you to the dungeon."

"No, they won't. I must make a report; they can't stop me from doing that. They won't be so stupid to—"

Will cut himself short, catching himself.

"So stupid to what?" Tony asked.

"They wouldn't demand I write a report while I'm in jail, would they?"

After some thought, Tony said, "I think they would. These people are crazy, you know. They'll demand that you obey the law. They'll arrest you for fixing the race, and if you don't make that report, they'll do much worse than keep you in prison."

"Yeah, I think so, too," Will muttered helplessly. He started pacing around, thinking of what next to do.

"Will, I don't know what to do. I can let you stay here, but I don't think I can do that for long. They'll ask about you when you're expected back. Come to think of it, weren't you due back after summer? Why did you return so early?"

"I had to; the situation in Carsiss had become complicated." Will looked at his driver, who was waiting patiently to get paid. He may have been eavesdropping, though it wasn't likely since Will and Tony had been speaking softly some distance away. He then looked at the servants at the door, who were waiting to be ordered on where to take his luggage. "Tony ... I have an idea."

"What? You're still not thinking of going to the Palace, are you?"

"No. I'll pay the driver now, but I need more money for a trip back. And tell the servants to put my luggage back."

"Why? Where are you going?"

"I'm ... going to get help."

CHAPTER 27
A ROYAL WELCOME

JUST OVER TWO MONTHS AFTER Will left the Blackstone estate, the Royal Palace received some rather unexpected news: The Emperor of Carsiss was coming for a visit.

The message came two days in advance; in those two days, the Palace turned into a major work zone, with the servants doubling their efforts to clean the building and bringing in more supplies to make the Palace more hospitable. Rarely did they have such high-profile guests, and any bad impression they or their work made on the Emperor would reflect poorly on the King.

King Fredrick, meanwhile, thought the Emperor had given him and his subjects a short notice, and he had half a mind to scold him once he saw him. Still, he had to play it delicately, for Emperor Baku was a very proud man with a temperament as sensitive as a tadpole egg. He was also an excellent warrior who preferred the company of other well trained and well fit men who understood how it felt to lose their sense of civility on a battlefield.

King Fredrick, on the other hand, was something of a glutton, whose arrogance could be compared to his generous gut. He often fell into the bad habit of ranting, using many superfluous words to get to a point on an issue (many said that he must like the sound of his own voice, and they weren't too far from the truth). He was somewhat of an enigma, for while he insisted on only the finest clothes made of silk and furs, his long black hair was often unkempt and he bathed infrequently. (Before the arrival of the Emperor, he did bath, although he shooed away any servant who put a brush to his hair.)

Few people thought he'd live up to the high standards of his famous uncle and granduncle, for while he commanded a big presence, he was not as charming nor as enlightened. The two previous rulers had taken unprecedented great strides in bringing freedom to the kingdom, but King Fredrick did not seem interested in adding to their legacy, though he did admit a great respect for it.

He had met Emperor Baku only two times before, and he was confidant he could handle him with great flair. The Emperor never seemed impressed by him, which was to be expected, but at least the King was able to secure good relations between their countries. He was worried, however, over how one of his ambassadors had been extradited and how Lord Harrington, the noble ambassador, had not been heard from in months. They would be inescapable topics, and he'd have to tread on eggshells when discussing them.

Their meeting would have to be carefully planned and executed, but he was prepared to take up an iron fist, for if the Emperor had no satisfactory answers to his probing, it would all go downhill from there.

When the King of Thayland had an audience with his subjects, he met them in the throne room from atop his throne; when he met with his peers from other countries, he still received them in the throne room, only he stood at the bottom of the stairs leading to the throne. It was a simple and logical gesture: His subjects were reminded that they were beneath him, while the world's leaders were assured they were on the same level with him.

The red carpet had been shampooed until it was spotless, the marble floor tiles had been scrubbed so clean one could eat off them, and the ceiling sported numerous banners that heralded both Thayland and Carsiss. A few candles were lit even though the room was already well illuminated by the summer's daylight streaming through the tall windows.

The King kept his cool as he stood by an altar holding a few gifts of gold and perfume, his illustrious golden crown perched perfectly atop his head, his stringy hair coursing down over his fur-clad shoulders. He had heard that the Emperor was not bringing his wife, so King Fredrick's own wife was not in attendance, which was only proper.

When the massive double doors opened, the trumpeters on either side of the room brought their horns to their lips and blew a grand welcoming verse that lasted all of six notes played three times over. The Royal Messenger marched down and stopped halfway down the red carpet. "Your Majesty, allow me to introduce His Imperial Eminence, the Supreme Emperor of Carsiss."

The messenger made a low bow and stepped to one side. The King wrinkled his brow over how the Emperor's name wasn't mentioned, but that was an oversight he could look past.

As the trumpeters performed a snappy welcoming tune, a small delegation of Carsian soldiers and servants, all in their best clothes, marched down the carpet and took their places near the King on either side. One servant, he noted, carried a large box, which he gently placed on the floor beside him. It might have contained a gift, though something seemed a bit off. Under its red-and-gold paint job, it was clearly made of iron, which didn't make the most appropriate gift box.

The King was prepared to smile warmly at the sight of Baku coming to greet him, but instead he slightly frowned. The Emperor was dressed in a robe of red silk with gold trimmings that closely hugged his entire body, with a hood that concealed his features. He had fully expected to see Baku in his usual attire of a vest over billowy trousers and a velvet turban atop his head; instead he seemed like the kind of stranger you'd see in a pub in a questionable part of town.

When the Emperor stopped at speaking distance, the King bowed down slightly, trying to peek underneath his guest's hood. There was something very off about him, and yet he didn't want to presume too much. His entourage consisted of a few familiar faces, which helped to assure his guest's identity. He could have little doubt that the Emperor of Carsiss stood before him.

Then a thought occurred to him: Perhaps the hood was meant as an ill omen, a signal of a new Carsian policy that shunned all ties with Thayland.

It could have been a sign of an impending war.

King Fredrick swallowed and composed himself the best he could. "Emperor Baku, it is always a pleasure to invite you into my palace. Your room is ready, a banquet is being prepared, and a number of festivities is scheduled. Please, stay as long as you'd like! A week, a month, a year—as long as you need to whip my slothful staff into shape!" He laughed, a bit more harder than was prudent.

"Greetings, King Fredrick," the Emperor said, "but I'm afraid you've been misinformed. I am not Baku—he has been ousted from power. I am the new Emperor of Carsiss."

With that, the stranger threw his hood back. The King raised his upper lip and widened his eyes—a look that would have been comical under less dire circumstances. The stranger was not at all what he expected. Not only was he not Baku, he was not even Carsian. He was a dark-skinned fellow with narrow eyes and a shaven head (and there wasn't even a morning shadow atop his head, which was positively eerie). He spoke fluent Altrin with only a hint of an accent—the mark of a Thayland commoner.

The King was taken aback at first, but quickly gathered his wits. "What, you ... This is outrageous! You can't be the Emperor, it's impossible! Just what do you think you're trying to do, pull the wool over my eyes? You think you can just waltz in here with your Carsian friends and declare yourself the Emperor and get any damn thing I have to offer? I mean, just look at you, you're barely out of diapers! As I've said, outrageous! *Outrageous!*"

The Thayland soldiers who stood guard took a few steps towards the scene. The supposed Emperor and his delegation took notice and became wary. "Please, King Fredrick," the supposed Emperor said, "I want no trouble. I don't mean you harm, and I don't mean to fool you."

The King snickered, but he ordered his men to fall back. "You don't mean to fool me? Really? Well, of course you say that *now* after you took your damn hood off. I suppose you're now a tailor who can make me invisible clothes, is that it?"

The supposed Emperor signaled one of his men to step up. The man addressed the King with a bow, holding his fists together in front of him as was the Carsian way, and spoke to him in his native tongue. The King turned to an interpreter to his left, who was anxiously waiting for some work to do. "He said he is Doonkat Lavlin, the Dieschsuch of Development," the interpreter said, "and that Emperor Baku is indeed no more. This young man is the new Carsian Emperor."

"Do you recognize him as Dieschsuch Doonkat?" the King asked.

"Yes, I do, Your Highness."

"I don't believe it," the King muttered, then turned to a diplomat to his right. "Is he really Dieschsuch Doonkat?"

"He is, Your Highness."

The King turned back to the supposed Emperor with a foul look. "What's your name, son?"

The young man furrowed his brow for a second, probably at being called "son." "Will Fontaine, Your Majesty."

"Will Fontaine ... You mean 'Will' as in 'William?'" The King laughed heartily and glanced at his diplomat, meaning to share his joviality. "That's not even a Carsian name! Well, you've made me laugh, which is something I always appreciate, so I'll suffer you a little longer. Now, you understand why I think you're bogus, don't you?"

"I'm afraid I do."

"Yes, well why don't you amuse us further by informing us *why* you understand, hmm?"

"Emperor Baku was a fine ruler, which is why it's

understandable you don't wish to believe he is no longer Emperor."

"Well, I never—"

"Unfortunately," the young man strongly interjected, "Baku's better judgment had abandoned him. He made plans that would have poorly served both Carsiss and Thayland. I had no choice but to beat him in combat."

"'*Beat* him?' You don't mean '*kill* him,' do you?"

The young man slightly grimaced. "Yes, I do."

"And just what kind of plans was he making, hmm? No, wait, don't answer that! It won't even matter, for I don't believe Baku is actually dead. If you can prove to me he is dead, then maybe—just *maybe*—I'll accept your story and embrace you as a peer. Now, what proof have you?"

The supposed Emperor ordered in Carsian for one of his men present a token of proof—the Imperial Scepter, the Carsian Empire's mark of supreme earthbound authority. It had a huge ruby at its head with a golden handle clutching a shaft of beautifully finished cherry wood.

"Very impressive," the King said, feeling it in his hands. "But I've seen impressive duplicates of my own crown. Have anything else?"

He smiled a little at the look of dismay on the young man's face, but otherwise kept his composure. The young man then took a ring off his finger and presented it himself. It was made of gold with a large round ruby as the centerpiece, beautifully polished and crafted except for a flaw in the center, which seemed like a crack that never penetrated its perimeter. "This is Baku's family ring, the only kind in the world. Its ruby is unique and genuine and cannot be copied."

"Oh, yes it can," the King said, more out of stubbornness than reason. "I have an eye for jewelry, and I must say, either of those things can be faked if you have the money to do so. You'd better have something better than these."

The young man shook his head. The King thought he had won, but then the man said, "I didn't want to do this, but I suppose I have no choice. You wanted proof of Baku's death, here it is."

He motioned for the man with the box to approached the King. The man heaved the box up and did as ordered. The King took a step back, wondering if it was some kind of trick that would hurt him. The Thayland soldiers thought so, too, and stepped closer. Once another man lifted the box's lid, however, the King's curiosity got the best of him, and he drew near for a peek.

He saw the box's contents, and the smell it emanated caught him like a fishing hook on a carp's jawbone. "Oh, God, what is ... what's ..." He put a hand over his mouth and nose and started heaving, his considerable belly bouncing like a pogo stick. Without warning he turned and ran to the closest exit. His interpreter went after him, also covering his face and appearing ill and offended.

Will ordered the lid to be put back on the box and shook his head with a small smile. He couldn't blame the King for wanting some fresh air—he had also felt queasy when he checked on Baku's head shortly after arriving back in Brussels.

When Will had returned to Carsiss and requested an audience with Emperor Namin, he was given the runaround. First he was told he would see him shortly, then told he'd have longer to wait, then told he'd see him sometime soon, then had his appointment pushed back again. This cycle continued for five excruciating hours after Will had stepped into the Palace; he had often wondered if Namin had heard of his return at all. Although his patience ran close to its end, he told himself that he had waited two more weeks on board a ship for the meeting, so what was a couple more hours?

Emperor Namin, proving to be a gracious host, apologized for meeting him so late. He claimed that ever since he received the Imperial Scepter, he'd been very busy meeting the overlords and listening to their requests and demands. "You'd be pleased at my progress," he said. "I've given only fair judgment, for I look at a case from all sides before passing sentence."

"If only my own King did that," Will said, though he knew he was mistaken. King Fredrick probably wasn't involved in the messy affair between Lord Mayweather and Sir Blackstone.

Will asked the Emperor for a large favor: to cross the sea and ask the King to grant clemency to Will and his master. Not only would he pay off his debt to Will for granting him the Scepter, but he'd make his acquaintance with the King as well.

But the Emperor couldn't foresee himself capable of doing that anytime soon. He was scheduled to travel the kingdom and meet with more overlords, who were expecting him. If he shunned his meetings, the overlords would take it as an insult, which would never go well with a new emperor at the start of a new dynasty.

Will said he anticipated that, which led him to his next request: to bring several Carsian guardsmen, Dieschsuchs, and several trinkets back to Thayland so he could pose as the Emperor. It wouldn't be a total lie, merely a half-truth, since he had been Emperor for a time. Namin was reluctant, asking if Will would rather wait it out until he was available. "You could travel with me for the time being, live like a *Ksatriya* and see all of Carsiss. I would like that very much."

Will shook his head. "And while I'm having the time of my life, Sir Blackstone will be stewing in jail and the King will wonder where I am. No, Your Eminence, my time is growing short."

At that, Emperor Namin met Will's latter request, only instead of granting him the Scepter, he let him have the official facsimile, made to take place of the actual Scepter in case daring thieves should try to steal it.

Will thanked him and left for Thayland once again on a much more dangerous mission than posing as Commander Aman. Upon meeting King Fredrick, he was in truth unimpressed, believing as many did that he would not live up to the legacy that his uncle and granduncle had left him. His granduncle, King Henry, had freed the serfs, after which his uncle outlined women's rights and soldiers' privileges. It was hard to imagine the current king, who seemed arrogant and selfish and who was a better talker than a listener, would be able to grant more freedoms to the people.

After Baku's head was banished from the Palace at the King's demand, the King and Will the false Emperor met in a grand meeting hall. It had a long table with a glass-covered top, bordered by a total of twenty-six chairs made of the finest wood and velvet padding. Numerous paintings hung the walls, the most prominent of them being a large depiction of the crowning of Davis Hendricks the Light-Bearer, the first king of the Hendricks family line, whose royal dwelling was merely a large tent.

The King offered Will a seat and got right down to business. "I've just heard that you were one of my ambassadors to Carsiss. What in the hell happened that would make you Emperor? Baku didn't hit on you, did he? And then perhaps you killed him in his sleep? Because that's what I would do, if I was foolish enough."

Will told him his tale, fudging some details and leaving out the more extreme ones, such as his death and resurrection. He said that after the dragon had been slain, Commander Tanalac had tried to kill him, but he got away. He ended up joining a resistance group and learned a terrible secret from Dieschsuch Halicut: Emperor Baku was setting up the ambassadors to persuade his people to go to war against Thayland. After freeing the harem girls and besieging the Emperor's Palace, Will revealed himself to Baku and accepted his challenge. Leaving out his fight with Babi, he ended with his fight with Baku, whom he defeated and claimed the Scepter for his own.

"So you didn't seduce him," the King said. "I wonder if he really was like that or not. I guess we'll never know, not that it matters. But still ... was it possible?"

Will looked at him, bemused.

"Well, it's not like I ... well, I ... what am I saying? Never you mind, my overly young Emperor. So you stopped Baku from waging war with us, good for you. Now, where is the body of Lord Harrington, hmm? Did you bring it with you?"

"No, I didn't," Will said apologetically. "It's already buried in the capital's graveyard. I plan on asking the family if they'd like it exhumed for burial in Thayland. But right now there's a far more pressing matter I'd like to attend to."

"Hmm, yes? What is that?"

"I've only just arrived in Thayland to greet you, and I've learned that my master, Sir Timothy Blackstone, has been imprisoned for fixing a race to win a bet, and that there's a warrant for my arrest as well. Are you aware of this?"

"Well, no. There's so much going on, I can't keep up with every little thing."

"This is not a 'little thing' to me, Your Highness. I want to—"

"Oh, I see, you want your master out of jail. Well, let it be done, I don't really care one way or another. He didn't actually kill anyone, though, did he?"

"You mean ever since the war? No, he hasn't."

"Good, because *that* would then be a different story."

"I understand, but releasing him would not be good enough."

"Whatever do you mean, dear boy? Oh, I mean, Your *Imperial Eminence,* excuse me. Isn't that what you want, to free him from prison?"

"Yes, but Lord Mayweather won't stand quietly for that, even if it's on a royal order. I want to find proof that Sir Blackstone and I did *not* fix that race."

"You mean, you *didn't* fix the race?"

"No! There has to be proof of this, and me and my men are going to find it. Then we'll present it to court and show those judges they were wrong from the start."

"I see ... or better yet, *I'll* be the judge so I can rule in your favor."

Will opened his mouth to object to that, but something stopped him. He realized the King had just made an offer too good to refuse, and one he wouldn't put on the plate again. If he couldn't find irrefutable proof, he could rely on the King to at least preside over the trial. It would be as unethical as hell, but it was no less than what Lord Mayweather had done to his master. "Your offer is most generous, Your Highness," Will said, "but what can I do in return?"

The King suddenly grew grave and he leaned forward over the table. "Thorain is getting antsy. I hope to avoid war if possible, but if it comes to it, I'll ask you for reinforcements. That is all I want in return."

"I see ... I was hoping you hadn't forgotten about Baku's plan for invasion, and how I stopped it."

"Oh, yes, well there's that, but since we're allies anyway, you'd readily give us reinforcements. You should know that; you were an ambassador."

Will nodded, clearly humbled and a little worried. He was afraid he was in a little over his head, but he decided to continue his plan without fail. "Yes, Your Highness, of course."

"If I were you, I wouldn't care for another trial; I would just let the good knight go and not care one way what Lord Mayweather has to say about it. You're the Emperor of Carsiss now, you're above him."

"I want more than just Sir Blackstone free—I want justice."

"Justice, eh? Hmm, well, you *must* have been a knight's apprentice, then. Well, let's see if your little goody-two-shoes philosophy will do you any good. If nothing else, this will give me a good story to tell at my bridge parties. I can take only so many tales of someone's bad hair day or something cute their damn dog did. I tell you, if Lord Rumpelstein tells how a squirrel had made off with his wig again, I'll pull my *own* hair out!"

Will and his party were sent to the Kingdom Courthouse, where he met with Prison Chairman Geoffrey Hunter, whose job was to manage the nation's prison system. He was an scrawny, elderly man whose yellowing skin had seen better days. He looked up the paperwork regarding Sir Blackstone's sentencing in an old dusty filing drawer, one of many in his rundown office made of wood and steel. At one point, Will found a dandy-longlegs on his shoulder and brushed it off.

"Ah, here it is," Hunter said, pulling the file out. He laid it on his table, which had a long stack of books serving as a forth leg. "I remember this one; it wasn't too long ago. Timothy Blackstone, a knight of some good repute, got into a scrap with Lord Franklin Mayweather. Oh, how I hate him!" Hunter repeated himself in a singsong fashion: "I hate him, I hate him, I hate him ..."

"Why do you hate him?" Will asked.

"He's got some of those accursed judges in his pocket! He does favors for them, gives them inside information on the stock market, hands out some shares on his racetrack before big events. He lines their pockets with gold, and they pass sentences in his favor. There was the case where a stood pigeon told how Mayweather was dipping into the black market, so Mayweather set up some false witnesses and let his pathetic friends in the judges' box in on it, so they would know what was going on and vote in his favor."

Will smiled reflexively, thinking of how to find the proof he needed. "And what about Sir Blackstone's case? What did he do about that?"

"Oh, I don't know what he did about that, but I can tell you, if Blackstone is innocent, Mayweather must have done some twisted damn thing to get him into jail. Actually, I remember that Blackstone got off on the charge of petty larceny, but he was put into debtor's prison for the debt he owed Mayweather."

"What debt he owed Mayweather?"

"Why, the gambling debt, that's what."

"So the court said that he still owed Mayweather for the bet, even though he wasn't convicted of larceny?"

Hunter looked at the file for a moment, bemused. "Why, yes, that's it."

"Wait, let me get this straight: Sir Blackstone still owes Lord Mayweather money for the racing bet—a debt he wouldn't owe if the losing horse had actually won, which it didn't because the race was indeed fixed, which the court didn't prove was through the fault of Sir Blackstone, anyway. Am I right?"

Hunter looked down at the file again, trying to work all what Will said through his mind. "Well, I suppose that the court wanted to put Sir Blackstone in jail because Mayweather wanted them to, but since Blackstone is an honored knight, they thought it prudent to convict him on a lesser charge and thus slap him with a lesser sentence. Debtor's prison is more comfortable than real prison, and the jail time is considerably shorter—I should know. Does that make sense?"

Will thought for a moment, then nodded. "Yes ... yes it does. Doesn't make it any less idiotic, though." He briskly scanned the file, noting its basic details. He saw something he had nearly forgotten. "Mr. Hunter, who is this Marcus Thimble?"

CHAPTER 28
THE TRIAL

ONE WEEK LATER, ON A SATURDAY, Will saw his old master for the first time in a year. Sir Blackstone arrived at the Kingdom Court with an escort of prison guards, his wrists bound with chains and his face covered in unkempt hair. He eyed Will's Carsian guards with suspicion. "Will, is that you? What are you doing here ... and in such interesting fashion?"

Will glanced down at himself. Compared to Sir Blackstone's gray prison clothes, his baggy Carsian attire was luxurious. "So good to see you, sir," he said after the two of them shook hands. "As hard as it to believe, I am now the Emperor of Carsiss, and I'm using my clout to reopen your case. I'm going to make you walk free or may God strike me down."

"I'm inclined to believe you," Sir Blackstone said, still eyeing the Carsians. "But should you be doing this? I don't want you to risk yourself on my behalf. You have your own life to live, so—"

Will stopped him with a gesture. "What's done is done, and there's no going back, sir. Let's just go inside and prepare for the proceedings."

King Fredrick took his seat in court for the first time in three months. It was his duty to hear out certain cases of murder and grand larceny that occurred in the capital. Ordinarily a charge of petty larceny like that placed on Sir Blackstone was not worthy of the King's ear. On that day, however, there would be an exception.

The court hall was designed much like an ancient arena where gladiators used to fight wild animals and each other, where the seats were arranged in a circle to allow the audience to get an equal view of the entertaining carnage. The Kingdom Court, however, held negotiators instead of warriors and had a slick, marble checkerboard floor instead of well treaded sand. Overlooking the tables provided for the defense and prosecution teams were three box sections that held the judges and jury. The center box section was reserved for the King and his advisors, intentionally kept separate from the judge's seats so they couldn't whisper in his ear.

At the prosecution table was Lord Mayweather and his two highly-paid negotiators; at the defense table was Will, Sir Blackstone, and a negotiator provided by the state. Lord

Mayweather often glanced over at Will, unbelieving that the young man he had once greeted warmly in his house had become the Emperor of Carsiss. He appeared very uncomfortable in his seat, wondering if God had dropped him in his current situation to force him out of his heavy drinking habit.

Will, dressed in his elegant Carsian-style clothes turban and all, was a bit worried himself. He had only managed to find a few pieces of evidence that proved Sir Blackstone's innocence, and it was all merely circumstantial. Of course, he was sure the King would keep his word and free Sir Blackstone, but what he wanted was to use evidence, not his high position, to fulfill justice. He sighed, thinking he only had to work with what he got.

The King called the court into session, and being the impatient, brusque man that he was, called off the traditional recitation of the National Poem of Civility and Justice, which was over fifty verses long. "As you all may know, my very good friend, the Emperor of Carsiss, is with us here today," he announced. "So if you even think of doing the outbursts or mudslinging that usually goes on here, I'll have you arrested on the spot. We will all be on our very best behavior. Just think of this as Sunday school and you'll be all right."

The considerable audience in the room chuckled. The King sighed in displeasure, for he actually hadn't meant it as a joke. He looked down at a parchment in front of him. "This hearing was called for the reconsideration of evidence faulting Sir Timothy Blackstone for an incident that occurred on November eighth of last year, in which a horserace conducted on the Mayweather estate was obviously fixed in favor of Blackstone, who would have won a gambling bet. The prosecution may start the beginning argument."

The lead negotiator of Lord Mayweather, Brian Casov, rose from his seat and wandered to the center area, gazing at the judges and audience. He gave a briefing of the case the King had mentioned, briskly listing names and events like they were upcoming party plans. His quick tongue slowed down when he mentioned one Marcus Thimble, the star witness who claimed Sir Blackstone hired him to release the doves that distracted Will's horse. He also noted the names of the two riders—Will Fontaine and Adam Berryworth—though he didn't give the reason for their competition.

Will's negotiator was up next—a portly man by the name of Peter Worth. He stated that the star witness in the previous trial had given a false testimony, and that he had proof of it.

One Mr. Worth was seated, the King, who rested his head on one fist, asked the prosecution to present their first witness.

It was Marcus Thimble, fresh from his jail cell. He was a stringy lad with long black hair and deep-set eyes. Mr. Casov asked him what role he played in fixing the race between Will and Adam Berryworth. Marcus, sweating profusely as he looked at Will in his Carsian clothes and the Carsian guards around him, retold of how he hid in the bushes and released three doves just before Will's horse passed him, thus causing the horse to buck and allowing Adam to gain a wide lead.

Once the story was out, it was Mr. Worth's time for questioning. "Do you do odd jobs like this often?" he asked in a loud, clear voice.

"No, sir, not at all."

"Then why did Sir Blackstone come to you to fix the race? Do you and he go far back?"

"Why no, sir, we don't."

"Is it just because you were available? Your mother is a maid for the Mayweather estate, is she not?"

"Y-yes, sir."

"So when Sir Blackstone came looking for someone to fix the race, he choose you because you were just standing by, is that it?"

"I ... I suppose that's true, sir."

"And what did he offer you?"

"He offered me quite a bit of money, sir."

"How much?"

"Twenty thousand pounds, sir."

The audience let out a collective gasp.

"That's quite a lot, young man—enough to convince you to take a dangerous job with a risk of arrest. Did you ever see this money?"

"No, sir, it was to be delivered to me upon completion of the job."

"Is that so? Well, no further questions, Your Majesty."

Marcus was led away by soldiers back to his jail cell, looking unsure of himself, perhaps thinking he had said too much.

Mr. Casov went on to grill a number of witnesses who had seen the race nearly a year ago. They all said the same thing: Once Will's horse bucked at the sudden release of the doves, Will had decided enough was enough, and so he charged out of the racetrack, even jumping over a small gateway to avoid speaking with anyone. Mr. Worth had either few or no questions for each one, and the prosecution announced they had no more witnesses for the day.

The King gave a sarcastic little applause, then gave the floor to Mr. Worth.

Mr. Worth's first witness was Franklin Douglass, whose testimony revealed Will's reason for quickly leaving the racetrack: He had applied for an ambassadorship to Carsiss and needed to be at Parkinson's Temple on time for his assessment. "And might I say, I'm extremely surprised that he's the Emperor of Carsiss now!" Franklin cried. "Good thing, too; that stupid old Baku was absolutely no good!"

The King slammed his gavel down and called for order. "Mr. Douglass, no one wants to hear your rotten old opinion of the former Emperor Baku, so one more outburst like that and I'll have you held in the Fool's Square so someone can give you a crown of lettuce and tomatoes. Is that clear?"

Once the humbled Franklin vacated the floor, Mr. Worth called for his next witness: Mrs. Thimble, Marcus' mother. She was very nervous, so Mr. Worth decided to butter her up and assure her that no one in the courtroom was going to bite—not even His Majesty.

"Mrs. Thimble, on the night of November eighth, you had a visitor at your door, correct?"

Mrs. Thimble's reply was so quiet it was unintelligible.

"I'm sorry, but you need to speak up for the courtroom. Did you have a visitor on the night in question?"

"Yes, sir, I did."

"Who was he?"

"He ... he was a deliveryman."

"And what did he deliver to you?"

Slightly emboldened, Mrs. Thimble spoke loudly with a new conviction: "He gave me a large pile of money, all in five-hundred notes."

"How much money was there, Mrs. Thimble?"

"Well, I ... I didn't spend any of it, I swear ..."

"Please, don't be shy, Mrs. Thimble. Can you recall how much money was given to you?"

Mrs. Thimble nodded. "It ... it was around twenty thousand pounds."

Another collective gasp sounded upon mentioning the large number.

"Do you still have this money, Mrs. Thimble?"

"Y-yes, I do ... for a rainy day, you see. Please, I don't like talking about it; I know now it was for Marcus ... for what he did."

"Did the deliveryman happen to say who the money was from?"

Mrs. Thimble paused for thought. "No, he didn't mention it, only that the money was for Marcus."

"Thank you, Mrs. Thimble. I have no further questions for you."

Mr. Casov began his questioning by wondering if she still had the money. "Yes," Mrs. Thimble replied timidly. "I still have it, and I didn't spend any of it."

"Why didn't you report it to the authorities?"

"B-because ... I'm a poor old woman you see, and ... well, my son asked me to keep it."

"He asked you or told you?"

"He *told* me. He said he got the money for me, not for himself or for anyone else."

"So he had no plans to spend it?"

"Oh, I don't know, he never said anything like that. From the way he sounded, he probably didn't think he would be caught doing what he did, so he didn't do it for himself—only for me. So you see, I think you should go easy on him, because it was selfless, really ... he didn't mean any harm. He's not like those worse criminals out there who—"

"I'm sorry, Mrs. Thimble, but that will be all. No further questions, Your Majesty."

Mr. Worth's next witness was Daniel Shawl, a banker with Holyfield Bank, located in the district of Holyfield in Augustine. "I understand that your bank handles many of the finances of the Mayweather estate," Mr. Worth said, "and that you oversee those transactions, is that correct?"

"Yes, sir," Shawl replied.

"Just last Thursday, my client, William Fontaine, the Emperor of Carsiss, came to you and requested a file concerning Lord Mayweather's account." Mr. Worth went to a side table used to place evidence for trials and picked up a lone piece of paper from it. "And you gave him this, is that true?"

Shawl squinted his eyes as Mr. Worth brought the paper to him, then nodded. "Yes, that's it."

Mr. Casov got up from his seat. "Objection, Your Majesty. That is a confidential file of the Mayweather estate, and no authorization was given for its use as evidence."

The King thought it over, though he didn't take long. "Overruled," he said smugly. "As the Emperor of Carsiss, Mr. Fontaine is allowed access to any confidential documents as I see fit, and since the file came from him it is suitable for use as evidence."

Mr. Casov sat down in unexpected defeat; Lord Mayweather beside him almost looked as if he was trapped directly in the way of an eight-horse carriage.

Mr. Worth held the paper up as if in sacrifice to the gods. "This document explicitly describes the transactions made with Lord Mayweather's account in the week of November sixth through November twelfth of last year. On the morning of the eighth, an unusual transaction occurred. Mr. Shawl, could you please read for us what that transaction was?"

Shawl was handed the file and read it with squinted eyes. "Why yes, on that morning there was a withdrawal of twenty thousand pounds."

Yet another gasp came from the audience, one more loud and forceful than either of the previous. Contributing to it was Lord Mayweather, who was clearly as shocked as anyone, if not more so. Sir Blackstone smiled into the palm of his hand.

"Twenty thousand pounds in cash," Mr. Worth mused. "Would you happen to know exactly who made that withdrawal?"

"Unfortunately I did not work that day; an inexperienced assistant made the transaction, and when I questioned him about it, he said he couldn't remember who withdrew the cash."

"But in order to make such a large withdrawal, you need more than just the account number; you need an access code, known only by you and one other. Isn't that right?"

"Yes, sir, it is."

"So whoever made this transaction must have been from the Mayweather estate, wouldn't you say?"

"Well, I'm afraid I'm not responsible if Lord Mayweather were to let slip his access code to a friend or employee."

"But would you think Lord Mayweather would ever 'let slip' his access code to anyone he wouldn't readily trust?"

"Well, since you put it that way, no. Lord Mayweather is usually a very responsible businessman."

"Thank you, Mr. Shawl, I have no further questions."

Mr. Casov took the floor and observed the bank file himself, which he had known about and was dreading the moment when his opponent brought it up. "Mr. Shawl, once you discovered this unusual transaction the next day you came in to work, you questioned your assistant about it, true?"

"Yes, sir."

"Did he describe to you the person who made the withdrawal?"

"Well yes, sir."

"I thought you said your assistant couldn't remember who made the withdrawal."

"Well yes, sir, but after a time I jogged his memory for him. He said there were two people—a man and a lady."

"Did he describe them?"

"Yes, sir. The lady had long black hair and dark eyes; the man also had black hair and eyes ... and he was dark-skinned, too."

The audience started to murmur. The King was expected to slam his gavel down, but the noise wasn't disturbing enough to warrant it.

Will furrowed his brow. He smelled a rat, for he knew the audience had made a connection with him and the man who made the transaction.

"And your assistant didn't recognize either one of them?" Mr. Casov asked.

"No, sir."

"Thank you, no further questions."

Mr. Worth announced he had no more witnesses for the day, and the King adjourned the court.

Once the judges left for their chambers, Lord Mayweather approached the defense table. He shook Will's hand while avoiding eye contact with Sir Blackstone. "Well, you're just full of surprises," he said in an unsteady voice. "I knew there was something about you, though I never imagined you'd end up as the Emperor of Carsiss. How did you do it? What's your secret?"

"Well, Emperor Baku was up to something terrible, but I didn't know it until much later," Will said. "Fortunately by then it wasn't too late. Turned out he was trying to frame me for things I didn't do. By the way, you didn't do that to Sir Blackstone, did you?"

"No, I didn't ... Your *Eminence.*"

Will gave a mischievous smile. "Let's hope so; that was the very mistake that brought down the former Emperor."

The following Monday, with court back in session, Mr. Worth called for his first witness, Will Fontaine.

Will approached the stand well aware of the hundreds of staring eyes on him—including those of Sir Blackstone, the most curious of all. He was a complete mystery to them—a Carsian who spoke like a citizen of Thayland. He wondered if he would rouse their interest in their neighbor across the sea rather than garner more apathy.

Mr. Worth asked a line of predictable questions, such as if he knew Marcus Thimble before he left for Carsiss, if he had stepped inside the Holyfield Bank on the day of the race, and why he had hurried out of the racetrack after the doves were released. Will answered truthfully, which presented no major revelations.

Mr. Casov then asked if Lord Mayweather had known about his appointment at Parkinson's Temple. "No, I'm afraid not," Will replied.

"And why didn't you inform him of it?" Mr. Casov asked.

"Because Lord Mayweather was very excited about the race—so excited that he made that wager with Sir Blackstone. I didn't want him to think that my appointment at the Temple was more important to me than the race, since the race started only an hour before the appointment."

"So Lord Mayweather made a wager for you to win?"

"Yes, that's right."

"And did you and Sir Blackstone arrange the race to be fixed so that Sir Blackstone would win the bet?"

The question was the very heart of the trial, yet Will answered calmly and simply, with little passion. "No, sir."

"Are you sure? You never saw Sir Blackstone talking with Marcus Thimble or saw the two men together?"

"No, sir."

Mr. Casov asked a few more questions which didn't help his case. Once Will was freed from the stand, Mr. Worth called for his next witness, Antonio Fairway.

A man in his mid-twenties appeared in the back of the courtroom and marched across the checkerboard floor. He took the stand reluctantly and made his oath to tell the truth, clearly nervous about being there.

"You work at the Holyfield Bank, is that correct?" Mr. Worth asked.

"Y-yes, sir, I suppose I do."

"Please, don't 'suppose' anything. Do you or don't you?"

Fairway sighed. "Yes, I do."

"You were Mr. Daniel Shawl's assistant in November of last year, were you not?"

"Yes, sir."

Mr. Worth showed Fairway the file concerning the bank account of the Mayweather estate. "You handled this withdrawal of twenty thousand pounds on November eighth of last year, is that correct?"

"Yes, sir, that's right."

"Your boss, Mr. Shawl, said you described the two people who made this withdrawal—a young lady with long black hair and a man with dark skin. Can you still recall those features of the people in question?"

"Yes, sir, I can."

"Is either of those people here in this courtroom?"

Fairway made a sigh of despair and looked around the courtroom. "No, sir, I don't see any of them."

Mr. Worth gave him a shrewd look. "Is that true? Look at that man over there." He pointed at Will. "Would you say he was the man who made this withdrawal?"

Fairway looked carefully at Will. "No, sir, he wasn't the one."

"And what of the lady? She is not here?"

Fairway looked as if he were atop a hill amid flooding waters. "No, sir, she is not."

Mr. Worth pressed him for further descriptions, such as their clothes or anything peculiar. Fairway said that their clothing was simple with nothing extraordinary about them. When it was Mr. Casov's turn, he had only one question: Did the two strangers ever reveal their intentions with the money? Fairway said no.

In a surprise move, the defense rested their case. When the King asked the prosecution to call for witnesses, Mr. Casov also rested his case.

"Very well, we'll recess for thirty minutes," the King announced. "Prepare your closing arguments by then; after that, I and the judges will make our verdict."

The two negotiators talked to each other in the back hallway, but Lord Mayweather stayed away from the seated Sir Blackstone. Will congregated with his Carsian entourage, thanking them for their assistance and assuring them that their help would not be in vain.

Among the Carsians was Jonoli, who had mostly kept out of sight during Will's play as Emperor. She had happened upon him in her travels around the Imperial Palace, and though he was reluctant to lay his troubles down on her, she coaxed him into giving his whole story. She insisted on coming along since it was the least she could do in exchange for Ambri's custody.

Will was glad for it; they had grown closer than when they parted, though not too close for they knew their renewed companionship would not last much longer. She had stayed out of the King's Palace but was active in his investigation before the trial.

She especially proved to be a big help when they questioned Mrs. Thimble. Marcus' mother was uncomfortable in the presence of tough-looking Carsians, even if their leader was polite and spoke fluent Altrin. She didn't want to talk about her son for fear she would further incriminate him, but Jonoli, speaking in broken Altrin, clasped her hands and assured her that they had only her son's best interests in mind (even though she wasn't sure that was true). To Will, there was no doubt that Mrs. Thimble quickly relaxed and was able to speak thanks to the presence of another woman.

Jonoli had sometimes suggested that Will could stay in Carsiss if things turned out bad for him, but Will shielded those advances, especially after the King said that he would rule in his favor no matter what. Jonoli said no more of it during the trial, though she undoubtedly kept thinking of the possibility.

"To tell you the truth, I'm not sure we'll convince everyone Lord Mayweather was wrong," Will said. "I'm not even sure if he did it. I mean, what was his motive if he intended me to lose? ... Unless he wanted Adam Berryworth to lose and Marcus goofed up."

"Don't worry, everyone will see what a big fat loser he is," Jonoli said with Ambri resting in her arms. "Maybe everyone already knows that."

Will and the other men cracked smiles and laughed. Whenever Jonoli spoke of Lord Mayweather, she sounded as if she had a personal vendetta with him. It was purely out of concern for Will, of course, which made it sort of endearing.

"Of course everyone knows," Will said. "This was a long time in coming."

King Fredrick was an enigma: He normally tended to waste words, but sometimes he didn't like to. As soon as he sat down, he said, "Mr. Casov, please ... make your closing argument."

Mr. Casov, the very picture of dignity, made a speech claiming that the evidence brought forth by the defense was purely circumstantial and proved nothing beyond a shadow of a doubt. He reminded the court that Marcus Thimble, the man who fixed the race, had claimed from the start that Sir Blackstone had hired him, and there was little reason for him to lie.

Mr. Worth, in his closing argument, claimed that the sum of bribe money paid to Marcus Thimble's mother and the amount of the bank withdrawal made on the day of the race was no coincidence. The bank account belonged to the Mayweather estate, which could only mean that it was Lord Mayweather who paid off Marcus. Furthermore, Lord Mayweather must have ordered Marcus to be captured and claim that Sir Blackstone hired him; Marcus probably agreed to it as long as his mother was well off with the bribe money. Mayweather's motive may have been to frame Sir Blackstone because of some feud between them.

"And Lord Mayweather wanted to frame my client, Will Fontaine, for the set-up as well," Mr. Worth said, standing next to Will. "But never did he predict that Mr. Fontaine would become the Emperor of Carsiss, and thus avoid arrest. Fortunately for us—for Thayland and for Sir Blackstone, who is now milling about in a jail cell—Emperor Fontaine is not content with safely sitting on his throne and avoiding the manipulations of Lord Mayweather. He wants Sir Blackstone out of jail, for he knows that the good lord is innocent of fixing that race on November eighth of last year. Ladies and gentlemen, lords and mistresses, I thank you."

His speech was met with light applause, after which the King announced that he and the other nine judges would congregate in the judges' chambers. (Usually a jury of commoners decided on a verdict, even in a case involving nobles. But in Thayland, when the King himself presided over a case, the verdict rested on the King and the nine judges.)

The King was gone only ten minutes that seemed like an eternity. Will knew what verdict the King would go with, and yet he felt as trapped and uncertain as Sir Blackstone beside him. What the King's verdict would be was not as important as *how* he said it. Did the evidence convince him? Or was he left unimpressed?

He glanced over at Lord Mayweather, who looked positively ill. He had grown pale, and it was said he ate little that day and yesterday. He was more concerned with the verdict than Will was, though that did little to assuage Will's own fears.

The King returned with a rather chipper air about him, taking his plush seat and brushing his hands as if he sat at a great banquet. He waited for the other judges to be seated, then announced, "Ladies and gentlemen, due to the *overwhelming* evidence"—the emphasis on 'overwhelming' was ripe with sarcasm—"we have reached an easy verdict. This court has decided to dismiss all charges being held against Sir Timothy Blackstone, whereupon he shall be released as soon as possible. As for His Lordship Franklin Mayweather, the court has found him guilty of conspiring against a fellow nobleman, throwing a sportsman into unnecessary danger, illegal bribery, and illegal gambling. For these offenses, I hereby sentence Lord Mayweather to—"

"No, wait, stop!"

A collective murmur rose from the audience as one of their own suddenly got up and raced down the stairs onto the trial floor. Will and Lord Mayweather rose from their seats, both astonished at the identity of the disturber: Lady Moline Mayweather, nearly tripping on the skirt of her white formal dress. She rushed to her father but stopped paces away, facing the King high up in his stand with her arms raised as if asking for a hug. "Please, Your Majesty, you mustn't do this!"

"And who in the bloody blazes are you?" the King demanded.

Lady Mayweather started to speak, but her father interjected her. "This is my daughter, Moline. Please forgive her, Your Majesty; she knows not what she does. She is upset; she was unprepared for the grief that—"

"You can't arrest my father," Lady Mayweather insisted.

"And just why the hell not?" the King asked.

"Because I was the one who fixed the race."

The audience members could not contain their shock; the courtroom was filled with their cries of disbelief and outrage (one woman in the third seat in the fifth row up actually fainted, dropping her lunch of fish and crackers onto her husband's lap). Will sat himself back down with an unconscious effort. Whatever happened next, he planned not to get involved; he could merely watch and enjoy the show.

"*You* did it?" the King nearly shouted. "You!?"

"Yes, Your Majesty," Lady Mayweather said in an unsteady voice. "Marcus Thimble works in my father's stables, and I paid him to release those doves in front of Mr. Fontaine. I also withdrew the money accompanied with a servant of mine; I blackmailed him to pretend to be Mr. Fontaine."

"And what of the young banker? Did he know who you were and was what amiss?"

"He knew me but did not know what I was planning. I paid him off to keep silent."

"Your Majesty," Lord Mayweather uttered. "This ... this is too much all at once, and my daughter cannot take it. She is taking the blame for things I have done. Please, go on with your sentence and—"

"Oh, forget it, Mayweather!" the King cried out. "You're not going to buy *me* off, you bloody rat! Now, Lady Moline ... what did I tell you yesterday about outbursts?"

Lady Mayweather appeared flummoxed, unable to answer.

"I told you I would permit no outbursts in this courtroom while the Emperor of Carsiss is present. If you truly respect me *and* are truly concerned about your father, you would have explained this matter to me out of court. Now, if you would be so kind, explain to us the motive behind your actions. Why did you fix the race?"

Lady Mayweather turned her gaze to the floor, turning as red as an apple. "Well, Mr. Fontaine here, he ... he spurned me, you see, and ... and, well ... I wanted to get back at him."

There was a pause as the King waited for more. "That's it?" he asked incredulously. He slammed his hands down on his marble desktop. "My God, you mean it was for something that *mundane?"*

Lady Mayweather drooped her head and shifted her feet, her father staring at her in horror as if she was a ghost.

"I don't buy it!" the King cried. "There has to be more to it than that. What is it?"

Lady Mayweather looked up in confusion. "I ... I swear, Your Highness, that's all there was to it."

"I wasn't born yesterday," the King said at length, leaning over his desk. "No, wait a minute ... on second thought, forget it. It doesn't matter, anyway. Your motive at least makes *some* sense. But dearie, you did more than just *'get back at him.'* You've had a nobleman—a *war hero*—wrongfully imprisoned and stole money from your father ... *and* you had Mr. Marcus Thimble take the fall for you. No doubt the young lad fell for your charms; money can only do so much.

"Now, I'll have you know, dearie, that I was not going to send your father to prison; I was going to slap him with a heavy fine instead. That's because I couldn't figure out a proper motive. I mean, why in the world would he fix the race so he would lose? He had *no* previous vendetta with Sir Blackstone, I made sure of that. They weren't longtime enemies or anything of the sort."

The King slumped back in his chair and sighed. Lady Mayweather looked quite regretful, and fearful for what was to happen to her. Her father put a reassuring hand on her shoulder, implying he would stick with her for the long run. Will thought that was good of him, even though he would undoubtedly be furious with her later.

The King sat in thought for a moment, staring at his gavel as if it was speaking to him. He then sadly shook his head and said, "The court dismisses all charges held against Lord Franklin Mayweather and turns them all over to Lady Moline Mayweather. For these crimes–which are most heinous in light of the motive–I must sentence the Lady to no less than three years in prison with chance for parole after the first year. Case dismissed."

The King slammed his gavel down and proceeded to leave the room. Will turned to the Lady Mayweather, who looked shocked and miserable. He thought he should tell her that three years in prison was pretty damn lenient; a commoner would have gotten five to ten years. It was not in his place to agitate her, though, so he kept it to himself.

As he saw the King about to leave, an idea struck him. Strangely, it seemed like an idea he might regret later, but having acquired a taste for the theatrical, he thought it best to carry out the idea right then and there.

He stood up. "Your Majesty," he called out, "I beg your attention."

The King turned around, as did many of the other judges. "Yes, what is it?" he asked, not upset but merely curious.

"Your Majesty, in lieu of prison time, I'd like to suggest an alternate sentence. I call for you to pull out ... the Chastity Belt."

Much of the courtroom fell silent, the residents hardly believing their ears. Sir Blackstone looked at his apprentice as if he was crazy. All eyes turned onto the King, who furrowed his brow for a second then looked as if he had a brainstorm. He smiled and said, "Very well, the Chastity Belt it is, then. The Lady Mayweather must wear it for three years ... no, make that *four* years. And she'll do one year's public service for good measure. *Now* the case is dismissed." He slammed his gavel again and turned to leave in chipper spirits again.

Will sat to talk with his negotiator. But the Lady Mayweather turned to him and let out a piercing cry: "*No!* How could you do that to me!?"

Will looked at her with wide eyes, preparing to defend himself in any way.

"Bailiff, remove her from the court!" the King cried, though the bailiff was already on the move.

CHAPTER 29
A NEW LEASE

THE NEXT DAY, SIR BLACKSTONE let Lord and Lady Mayweather into his home, which had been well kept under the care of Mrs. Blackstone and Tony Beckins. The knight's hospitality was generous despite the grief his guests had caused him.

After his first sip of his earl grey tea, Lord Mayweather cleared his throat and said, "I have come to apologize for what I did. I only thought I was seeing justice being dealt, not imprisoning an innocent man. Moline here also has something to tell you."

He looked at his daughter expectantly. As she spoke, she couldn't tear her gaze from her hands in her lap. "My ... my apologies, my noble lord. I am at fault for your wrongful imprisonment; I can only beg your forgiveness."

Sir Blackstone sighed and raised a curious eyebrow when he gazed at her lap. A bulge rounded her waist from underneath her green dress—the Chastity Belt she was sentenced to wear for four years. It didn't serve as a punishment; rather, it was a deterrent against acts of promiscuousness. It was usually asked for from the courts by nobles who were afraid their daughters were getting out of hand. If a man about to engage in relations with the young lady saw the Chastity Belt on her, he knew two things were for certain: If he got his partner pregnant, the Chastity Belt would come off, of course ... and he, the father, would get no less than seven years in jail.

In other words, with her pedigree combined with the Chastity Belt, the Lady Mayweather was forbidden fruit twice over.

The courts had in their possession twenty Chastity Belts. Each one was made from an innovative design of chain mail and steel plating with a lock at the buckle. Each lock could be opened by the same key, and several keys were made and stored in the Kingdom Courthouse. Over the buckle was a plate bearing a cross, which said something of the motive behind the sentencing of the Belt.

"I accept your apologies," Sir Blackstone said wryly. "But you'll understand, Mayweather, if I refuse to do any more money matters with you."

"Yes ... yes, of course," Lord Mayweather said eagerly.

"You should remember I was going to waive any amount you owed me; in return you should have cancelled the bet, as any gentleman would."

"Yes, I see that now, sir."

Sir Blackstone pointed an accusatory finger. "And I don't buy that excuse that you just wanted to 'see justice being dealt'; any ordinary scoundrel could have come up with something better."

Lord Mayweather merely nodded, then anxiously turned to Will seated across from him. "Your Eminence, if I may ask: Why did you grant my daughter leniency?"

Will had been dwelling on that question himself, so he was prepared with an answer. "If this had happened a year ago, I might not have done that, even if I had the power to do so. I think my time in Carsiss changed me a little."

He turned to the Lady Mayweather, who gave him her utmost attention. "In Carsiss, there was a man who blamed me for things I didn't do, who tried to rob me of my dignity. It wasn't because I wronged him, but simply for being what I was—a citizen of Thayland."

Carefully, trying not to alarm anyone, he said, "I had to kill him, because there was no stopping him. I didn't believe anyone would willingly do it on my behalf. That's not to say I would want to kill *you*. I'm no monster. But you're still young, like me. I didn't mean to humiliate you; I wanted to give you time to think this over: Everyone in this world is not here just to give you what you want; they are not grazing cattle. You have to learn to take a little and give a lot."

Soon after the Mayweathers departed, Sir Blackstone turned to Will with a mischievous smile. "You didn't mean to humiliate her? But Will, you gave her the *Chastity Belt*."

Will shrugged. "Okay, so I lied a little."

* * *

That evening, Will traveled to the Palace with his Carsian entourage. Sir Blackstone had insisted on accompanying him, which led to an argument with raised voices. Will won out, however, even without using any pretenses over how *he* was the Emperor of Carsiss and thus outranked Sir Blackstone.

"Ah, there you are," the King said, receiving Will in a grand hallway filled with historical paintings. Two Ministers and royal servants stood behind him. "I must congratulate you on a job well done in that trial. I'll bet no one had any doubt that Sir Blackstone was innocent when you pointed out that bank withdrawal. Of course, I've seen better cases, but that was still quite clever of you.

Good show!"

Will raised an eyebrow. The King's tone was dripping with amusement, as if he was talking to a knight who had just creamed an opponent in a jousting tournament. "Thank you, sire, but I'm afraid this must come to an end."

"Oh, yes, you're going back to Carsiss. Of course, you must have lots to do back there, though I'll be damned if I know how a Thayland commoner can rule Carsiss. I wish you all the luck in the world—you're going to need it."

"That's just the thing, Your Highness—I don't know either, which is why I am dropping the Imperial Scepter."

The King furrowed his brow, suspecting that Will was up to some kind of trick.

Will nodded his head, indicating the Carsian entourage behind him. "My people here will take the Scepter back to an Emperor-in-waiting. With the Scepter goes my power ..." He knelt down on one knee. "I am your loyal subject once more, Your Highness."

The King raised his brow in disbelief. He glanced at the Carsians and noticed Dieschsuch Doonkat with the Scepter in hand, nodding as if in agreement with Will.

Will kept his eyes on the checkered floor, waiting for the King to say something. He was probably a fool for what he was doing, but if he had planned on freeing Sir Blackstone and returning to live in Thayland as he once did, there was no other way. Power of the highest order was not for him—he had no ambition for it and no divine right of God. If he could be a noble like Sir Blackstone, that was fine. But an emperor? Just the thought of it put a bad taste in his mouth.

Still, he was risking his freedom by incurring the King's anger. He was prepared for the worst-case scenario, and told the Carsians not to defend him if that scenario occurred.

One of the Ministers stepped beside the King. "You mean you betrayed the King's trust?" he asked. "You went around flaunting your power and played him like a puppet? We ought to hang you for that! No, hanging's too good for you; we ought to—"

"That's enough, Minister," the King said, pulling him back by the shoulder. "Young man, look at me."

Will did, trying not to betray his worry through his eyes.

The King took some time to think of what to say. At times, he uttered a few syllables to start a sentence, but then stopped to think longer. "I would not believe you were the Emperor if not for Baku's head," he started cautiously. "His ring and the Scepter were also helpful. I really think this is no trick."

"But Your Majesty," the Minister said, "he dragged you into court for a case that shouldn't have been of your concern. He is insolent beyond reproach."

"And what better things could I have been doing?" the King asked. "And besides, the young man did no harm. He freed an innocent man and drew out the real culprit ... and it was all very amusing."

The King gave Will a critical eye that revealed more delight than malice. "You could rule am empire, but yet you still want to be my subject. I won't pretend to understand, young man, but this is all for the better. You may go on home ... but first you must assure me that this 'Emperor-in-waiting' would happily give me troops should war break out here, since you can't do it yourself now."

"Yes, Your Highness. I'm on good terms with him, and I know he would honor your request."

"Good, excellent. But I still expect a full report of what happened in Carsiss. For the records, you know."

Will smiled and nodded.

"But be warned: I'll keep an eye on you. There's something more about you than what meets the eye. I can't place what it is, but ... I'll let you know when I need you. That is all; you're dismissed."

The King lead his servants and Ministers past Will and the Carsians. The quarreling Minister gave a respectful nod at Will as he passed by, either from seeing the King's wisdom or to incur favor from one who might be the King's new pet.

Will stood up and breathed a sigh of relief. The Carsians seemed pleased and began making their way to the Palace's entrance hall. Jonoli was there waiting for them. Will had believed she would start an outcry had the King taken him prisoner, so he ordered her to stay behind, much to her chagrin.

Will relayed the good news as Jonoli tried to keep Ambri from crawling away and making a fuss. "That's wonderful," she said, retrieving Ambri and sitting down with her. "I can see he is a wiser ruler than Baku had ever been. It's no wonder Thayland is so prosperous."

Will wondered if that was a hint that she was tempted to stay. He thought about further asking her to, but in her pride she would surely be angry. "Has Ambri said her first word yet?" he asked for the umpteenth time.

"No, but it should be any day now." She bounced Ambri in her lap and ran her fingers through her long hair. "So what now? I know the men are getting anxious to go back."

"I'll see if Sir Blackstone can let them stay the night—I don't trust the King to let them stay here any longer. And I was wondering if ... you and me can go stroll in the central garden. There's a band that plays there we could listen to—if you don't mind weepy ballads, that is."

Jonoli made a critical look, then gave a sly smile. "I won't mind if you won't."

CHAPTER 30
MAKING CONTACT

THE TWO MONTHS SINCE clearing Sir Blackstone's name proved to be thrilling yet bittersweet.

Shortly after giving up the Scepter of the Carsian Empire, Will worked on freeing Franklin Douglass from prison. He called for an appeal and managed to clear Franklin's name from charges of treason and conspiracy. Since no district negotiator contested the appeal, it was settled out of court. Will's testimony alone was enough for the judge panel.

Once Franklin was freed, he did an even harder thing: deliver the news of Lord Harrington's death to his family. Lord Harrington was survived by his son, daughter, and two brothers. Upon hearing Will's story, the daughter didn't understand why he didn't prevent her father's death. The brothers and son, however, understood there was little he could have done. The ambassadors were bound by duty, and Lord Harrington was not fully aware of the danger he was in.

Will then continued to serve under Sir Blackstone, which amounted to more battle training and hard labor. Yet the knight had grown too hesitant to push him so hard. After hearing his incredible story, he had seemed to revere Will as an equal if not a better.

Will insisted on not receiving special treatment, even though he had clearly grown in skill and experience after his stay in Carsiss. His reflexes were faster, he spoke with more conviction, and he saw things with more clarity. But he was haunted as well, having seen hundreds of deaths from the canyon massacre, the dragon fight, and the resistance movement. He needed more time to come to terms with those, which could best be filled with hard work.

He also missed Jonoli, who hadn't decided to stay after all. Their last night together in the garden had been nice and romantic, and it had eased some of his yearning—but the yearning was still there, still insisting on having Jonoli and Ambri by his side. He told himself he'd have to seek another partner, a fellow Thayland citizen who felt at home in Augustine.

As much as she praised his homeland, Jonoli had always been uncomfortable walking the streets of Augustine. She could hardly understand what anyone was saying, and some of the customs she saw—such as tossing buckets of dirty water into alleyways—seemed too strange and unnerving. He didn't like to see her so disturbed, and he promised himself he would never keep her that way even if it meant he had her where he wanted.

Ever since returning from Carsiss, freeing his master, and making his report to the King, there was nothing more he could do but wait for some kind of message from the King ... and one more thing. It was something he had been meaning to do even before he first left for Carsiss aboard the *Desert Lily*.

After two months of slipping back into his old life, he begged leave for a week. He rode Leaping Star to Georgetown, where he had a quick bite to eat and soon left for a plantation a few leagues to the west.

The plantation used to be owned by a wealthy old maid named Madame Zervas. It was later turned over to a wealthy family from Santa Mona. Every day of the week except Sundays, the citizens of Georgetown traveled to the plantation to work. The orphanage children also worked the plantation as part of an old agreement between the estate and the orphanages: The children worked while the plantation paid the orphanages' expenses. The townspeople worked there by choice; the children, though, worked there by force.

During his own orphanage days, Will had worked on the plantation as a farmhand; he mostly milked cows and made chickenfeed. Life was much simpler than it was currently, an endless cycle of work, football, games, and chats with his close circle of friends. It was good while it lasted ... but one day, it all came to an end.

One day when he was eleven, he had followed a runaway dog to the basement of a lakeside house that had been mostly torn down. In the basement was the ghost of a little girl named Marie, whose had died years previous and been buried in that basement. She had said there were people lying to King James, uncle of the current king, and that their actions would have terrible consequences on the future of the kingdom.

She had then sent him on a journey that both defined him as a person and defined the course of his future—and that was only the first time she had done so. The second time was shortly after the first, when she had told him it was in his best interest to seek an ambassadorship to Carsiss. From that point on, at the age of twelve, he had worked diligently to learn all about Carsiss and express his interest in going there as a diplomat.

He had good reason to trust her judgment. Marie claimed that as a ghost she could see into the future, and not only that, but several futures, different courses determined by the actions of others. She had claimed that Will's influence was necessary to stop those who were lying to King James, and thinking back on his involvement, he could easily admit she was right.

It was the same case with his ambassadorship to Carsiss; if not for his involvement, Emperor Baku would have gone through with his planned invasion of Thayland. Marie must have seen that, and if not for her gentle persuasion, the southern shores of Thayland would have seen a massive fleet of Carsian warships.

He had to see Marie to thank her; he could have been bitter about it, but in the end, the positives outweighed the negatives. But there was more than that: He had questions only she could answer—that is, if she wasn't so damn secretive, which she tended to be.

He rode Leaping Star to the old lakeside ruins. Some of the working townspeople saw him out there but knew him not to be an interloper. He had known some of them during his orphanage days, and he was known to go out there sometimes for reasons they could only guess at.

The place hadn't changed much since he'd last been there—all the old decaying furniture was still there and the holes in the wooden floor hadn't grown larger. Some of the local brats tossed stones into the place to upset things, so there were more stones than usual.

He went into what might have been a guest room and inspected the trapdoor leading into the basement. The iron lock and handle were very rusty but still sturdy. He opened the door, collected his riding cape about him, and carefully made his way down.

Rays of sunlight came in through the holes in the floor above; in them were seen lots of unclean air particles. He held one hand over his nose and mouth to avoid breathing them in, but as expected, the air grew as chilly as a winter's biting wind and the air particles disappeared. He could be no longer surprised at the phenomenon, though it never failed to amaze him. It was the unearthly work of Marie the ghost girl, of course, who held reign over the very atmosphere of the basement. As soon as the particles were gone, the air grew hellishly hot from the summer heat once again.

Marie appeared before him, a little girl robed in what looked like a potato sack—the only burial clothes her poor guardian parents could afford. She was as pale as the moon expect for some shades of light blue; an aura surrounded her body like the glow of a firefly, only less brilliantly. When he had first seen her, she appeared to be seven-years-old, even though she had died fifteen years previous; as he grew up, she kept that appearance on subsequent visits. It still seemed strange and unreal, though understandable: She had died at seven years old, so her ghost would remain at seven years old.

He knelt down to be at level with her. He gave her a small smile and held up a white tulip he had brought. "Hello, Marie. How are you?"

"I'm good," Marie said, though her tone suggested otherwise.

"Anything wrong?"

"No ... well, I know why you're here, and you're going to be mad at me."

"Is that what you see?"

"No, I didn't foresee it; I just know you will."

"And why is that?"

Marie just shook her head, her eyes downcast. If she had been flesh and blood, her hair might have swung into her face; instead it remained still, almost as if it was underwater.

"I went to Carsiss, just like you told me," Will said. "I stopped the Emperor from invading Thayland. That is what you wanted, right?"

"Well ... I did see you doing that, but that wasn't the real reason why I wanted you to go."

"I see ... is this the part I'll get mad at?"

"I don't know."

"Well, what's the reason?"

"To make contact ... with the Sands."

"The Sands of Carsiss? Why would that be important?"

"I can't tell you."

Will frowned. *There she is,* he thought, *being secretive again.*

"But believe me, it was really important," Marie hastily added. "Stopping the invasion was really important, too—not many others could have done it—but making contact with the Sands was just as important."

"But apparently not important enough to tell me."

"See, I knew you'd get mad."

"I'm not mad, just disappointed. I understand why you didn't tell me what was going to happen to me in Carsiss: If I had known, my involvement would have changed, and the future would have been rewritten for the worse. Am I right?"

"Yes, you're right," Marie said, a little excited and glad that Will understood where she was coming from.

"Do you know anything about the Sands of Carsiss?"

"Yes, a little."

"Do you know where it came from?"

"No."

"Well, do you know how it works?"

"Yeah, it shows you a future you can make, not a future you *will* make."

Will nodded, mostly to himself than to Marie. He had always suspected the Sands worked that way, though Baku was sure that the future it showed was inevitable; that made him so damn positive he'd win the fight and the ensuing invasion of Thayland.

Once he finally had that cleared up, there was only more concern to address. "Marie, I'm sure you know this, but I died once in Carsiss. Do you know about that dark place where you're weightless? Is that where you spend most of your time?"

Marie's excitement went down a notch. "Yeah ..."

"I saw a ray of light that sent me back to life. Was God behind that?"

"No ..."

The next question that came to Will's mind was, *Does God even exist?* But he had already asked that one a long time ago. It was, after all, a very natural thing to ask a ghost.

Marie claimed that she never heard God or any kind of voice from the 'other side'; she said she'd seen a tunnel of light that seemed inviting just by its very nature. But she strongly felt she had matters on Earth that needed tending to, so she didn't enter. It soon disappeared, never to be seen again.

"How do you know God wasn't behind it?" Will asked.

"Because, He doesn't work that way."

"He doesn't? So you're now admitting there *is* a God?"

"No, I'm saying He doesn't send people back like that."

"So who does?"

Marie didn't reply, only faded slightly, ready to disappear and slip back into the void. The air grew colder, portraying her mood.

"No, wait!" Will stepped in closer while hunched over. Marie stayed visible, only more transparent. "Marie, please tell me, who sent me back? Do you know?"

"I can't tell you," Marie said, her tone very flat and disturbed. If she was still alive, she might have been shaking.

"Why not?"

"Because I can't."

"Is something holding you back? Some other spirit or worse?"

Marie merely shook her head, then faded into nothingness. The temperature returned to normal.

Will called out for her again, but to no avail. He stood up, stepped near the thin mound of dirt that was her grave, and laid the tulip on it. Every time he visited there, he left a tulip because that was her favorite kind of flower in life.

He left the basement rather unceremoniously. Once remounted on Leaping Star, he made him go as fast as he allowed, anxious to leave the plantation and the ruins far behind him.

He had had his fair share of bad encounters with Marie, but that was undoubtedly the worst one yet. He had expected answers and got only the runaround. He was angry at her, true, but more than anything, he was concerned.

Marie was still keeping things from him. That meant he still had some part to play that would influence the future for the better. But he feared he would have to undergo further trials, perhaps ones more harsh than those in Carsiss.

He hated it. He felt like a puppet on strings and he hated it, suspecting that his life was no longer his to control.

God had granted His children free will, and should Will be stripped away of his own, he didn't think God was behind him anymore. Surely God wouldn't take away his free will—which meant that something else entirely was the one pulling his strings.

Marie had said with surety that God was not behind the ray of light. So who had it been? What other force could it be?

It couldn't have been the devil; Will didn't even want to consider it.

So what was it? What kind of being could be behind the Sands of Carsiss, and why the hell was it so important for him to touch the wonderfully strange hourglass?

Will rode on. He would be back in Augustine in roughly two days—back to working in his master's mansion, back to flirting with women and seeking the best of the bunch, and back to facing a growing rumor of how he had killed an emperor and fooled a king (he was becoming quite a celebrity, which he thought was more trouble than what it was worth).

Someday, he'd find out what it was. It didn't have to happen soon—he wanted more time to be prepared for it. But someday, it would eventually come to him. It was inevitable. Will firmly believed that one didn't just die and come back to life fully grown and fully clothed and not have the power responsible for it unwilling to get something back for it; it was the same dilemma with God granting him life in the first place.

He just needed more time to be ready ... or so he told himself. But deeper in his mind, he wondered: Just how could he get ready to meet his unexpected savior when he didn't even know who he was?

AFTERWORD

READERS IN THE KNOW WILL realize that India served as the model for the fictional Carsiss. However, it is not a perfect model. I've taken plenty of liberties to separate Carsiss from India, not the least of which is the practice of blood feuds.

There are two main similarities between India and Carsiss: Hinduism and the caste system.

Rather than feature some made-up religion, I've incorporated the real-life belief of Hinduism into Carsian culture. Hinduism is one the oldest and more tolerant beliefs on earth—and by "tolerant" I mean its followers do not easily dismiss other beliefs as false. Hindus believe in many gods, though they pay the most respect to the Hindu Trinity *(Trimurti)* of Vishnu, Siva, and Brahma.

Hinduism is not the only religion practiced in India; religions of all sorts have places there. By and far, though, Hinduism is the country's most widely held belief, with Islam being a distant second, practiced by an eighth or tenth of the population.

In this book, all the names and natures of mentioned gods are accurate to the best of my knowledge. If there are inaccuracies, please don't burn me at the stake, but I'll take the blame for them.

And now, the caste system—a social structure in India that's one of a kind in all the world. Indeed, the caste system is alive and well in India, all due to the belief in reincarnation.

There are four different social classes, or castes, in India, including the *Sudras*—the Untouchables. One can only be born into a caste, not incorporated, with no chance of rising or falling in rank (although there might be a way for one to become a *Brahman,* if he is dedicated enough for the priesthood).

As you can imagine, the caste system had come under scrutiny at times, especially concerning the lower class, the Untouchables. They live in squalor, living only to repent for their sins from a past lifetime. However, it is now illegal for anyone to persecute the Untouchables—just one result of the country addressing today's human rights concerns.

You might say that the caste system has India stuck in the Middle Ages, when people were serfs working under feudal lords. However, India is now a world nuclear power, producing electricity via nuclear power plants. People in the middle class live with modern conveniences, such as SUVs, cell phones, and miscellaneous junk like the Whip-O-Matic 5000™. I wouldn't even be surprised to see a widescreen LCD television or an MP3 player in an Indian pad. There is also a thriving movie industry called Bollywood making flicks every day starring the Indian counterparts of Julia Roberts and Tom Cruise.

All names and natures of the different castes in this book are accurate to the best of my knowledge. If you find something wrong, you know who to blame.

For further clarification on the differences between India and Carsiss, please refer to the following table.

INDIA AND CARSISS	CARSISS ONLY
The caste system	Blood feuds
Hinduism	Continuing genocide
Daily prayers and rituals	Imperial rule
Certain names like Orissu	The title of "dieschsuch" (dice-chek)
Extended families	Gang activity
Arranged marriages	Much of the Carsian language
Veneration of the cow	Most names like Ambri and Aman
Taking baths in a holy river	Dragons (wouldn't you think?)
Certain types of clothing, such as *saris*	Misperception of north and south
Certain types of architecture	
Yantras (symbolic diagrams or images)	
Story of the mother whose child neared a fireplace (based on an old Indian parable)	
Engravings depicting sexual intercourse	